## PRAISE FOR
### *DOWN SHIFT*

"K. Bromberg makes you believe in the power of true love. As she tells it, with a little hard work, a little trust, a lot of faith, anything is possible. *Down Shift* made me a believer."

—#1 *New York Times* bestselling author
Audrey Carlan

## PRAISE FOR THE NOVELS
## OF K. BROMBERG

"An irresistibly hot romance that stays with you long after you finish the book."

—#1 *New York Times* bestselling author
Jennifer L. Armentrout

"K. Bromberg is the master of making hearts race and pulses pound."

—*New York Times* bestselling author
Jay Crownover

"Supercharged heat and full of heart. Bromberg aces it from the first page to the last."

—*New York Times* bestselling author Kylie Scott

"Bromberg expertly captures the voice of a man torn between his tender heart and macho confidence . . . gripping."                                    —*Publishers Weekly*

*continued . . .*

"The more I read, the more I want. . . . Your emotions will be taken on one hell of an angst-filled, heartbreaking, gut-wrenching, mind-blowing, and wickedly sexy, beautiful journey."  —Book Crush

"There was a certain je ne sais quoi to the story that kept me reading till the very end."  —Smexy Books

"[A] highly emotional yet satisfying series, oh, and let me not leave out SEXY."  —Guilty Pleasures Book Reviews

"Well-written and with a great balance of dialogue and description."  —Love Between the Sheets

"An emotionally charged, adrenaline-filled, steamy, and passionate read. . . . K. Bromberg deliver[s]."  —TotallyBookedBlog

"This series is *everything* a true fan of romance would want or need."  —Sinfully Sexy Book Reviews

"An intense, emotional, riveting ride [that's] sexy, romantic, heartbreaking, and uplifting. This is the kind of book you don't want to put down."  —Aestas Book Blog

## Also by K. Bromberg

# DOWN SHIFT

## A DRIVEN NOVEL

# K. Bromberg

SIGNET SELECT
New York

SIGNET SELECT
Published by Berkley
An imprint of Penguin Random House LLC
375 Hudson Street, New York, New York 10014

ISBN 9781101991763

First Edition: October 2016

Printed in the United States of America
1   3   5   7   9   10   8   6   4   2

Cover photos: Woman walking toward ocean by Chad Riley/Getty Images; man by George
Coppock/Getty Images; seaside beach by Michael Melford/Getty Images

# Acknowledgments

I'd like to take a quick moment to say thank you to the people in my life who have encouraged me to *just jump* over the years. Whether you are family, friends, bloggers, readers, an editor, my agent, a teacher, a coach, or other fellow authors, you have all cheered me on and supported me at some point so that I felt confident enough *to try*. And sometimes taking that first step is half the battle.

So thank you. I promise to pay it forward.

And if you're remotely wondering whether I'm referring to you in the above acknowledgment, then I most likely am.

# Prologue

*B*lood.
　*There's so much blood. Coating my hands. Soaking into my Scooby-Doo pajama pants. The ones with the hole in the knee from that nice lady with the funny glasses at the Salvation Army.*

*It's easier to think about her. Focus on her. Instead of the blood.*

*It's everywhere. And it keeps coming out. Keeps spreading.*

*It won't stop.*

*I can't make it stop.*

Dust dances in the air. Little pieces float in the light showing through the crack of the blackout blinds of the hotel room. My eyesight is fuzzy. My mind exhausted.

And buzzed.

Because this alcohol-induced haze is much better than the dreams that won't stop. The ones that aren't really dreams anymore. The ones that started the minute I opened that box three weeks ago and pulled out the piece of paper that rocked my world.

I lift the bottle of Jameson to my lips. Take a swig. Except the burn's not there. The warmth is fleeting. But it's enough to numb my mind. To let the dreams fade.

To let the truth seem false.

*The Band-Aids. They're everywhere. The box is almost*

*empty. The white pieces I peel off stick to my arms—but they don't matter. The blood keeps coming. It doesn't stop.*

*I can't make it stop.*

Another sip. And then another.

I'm so tired. But I'm so sick of feeling this way. So sick of wondering if my adoptive parents knew. Of course they knew—so why'd they lie to me? Didn't I have a right to know what was on that paper? To accept? To deal with it?

Fuck no. Fuck yes. I just don't know.

Another sip. Then a gulp.

*The scissors. The shine of silver lying next to her. The dark red coming through my closed fingers as I try to fix her. Help her. Save her. Stop. The. Blood.*

*The taste of fear. My scared pleas. The helpless feeling.*

I can remember all that, so why can't I remember if I did or if I didn't . . . ? I must have. That's what the report said. Why would it lie?

*Wait.* There's sunlight. I can see the dust dancing. When did that happen?

A lift of the bottle. There's nothing left. An deep breath. Slumping back in the chair. Now I can't forget anymore. *Fuck.*

The pounding on the door startles me. I know I should have expected it. Know I'm fucking up again. But does it really matter in the grand scheme of things?

I know who it is before he even speaks. Somehow I knew he'd find me. Just like I know he's going to be pissed before I hear his voice.

Ask me if I care.

"Zander." Boom. Boom. Boom. His fist on the hotel room door sounds like thunder in my head. "Open up." Boom. Boom. Boom. *"Open the goddamn door!"*

And when I open it, there's the lightning: The bright light of the hall blinds me after so much darkness. I block the glare with my forearm. It's futile until he shifts his stance and blocks its blaze.

Colton.

My mentor. My boss. The person who knows me best. My dad. Well, adopted dad, but does it really matter? We stare at each other. His green eyes fill with concerned disgust as he gives me a once-over to take in my rumpled clothes—the same ones from last night—and makes a show of sniffing the air to let me know he can smell the stench of alcohol that's probably seeping out my pores.

Yes. *It does matter.*

Lies always matter. Especially when they're from people you thought loved you.

"You forget something?" There's a bite of anger to his question, and I'm buzzed enough that I don't think twice about my smart-ass response.

"Not that I can think of." My hand's on the door, swinging it shut in his face before I finish the sentence.

If I thought the sound of his fist knocking on the wood was loud, the sound when he slams it back against the interior wall is deafening. I deserve nothing less than his wrath, but it's proving really hard beneath this alcoholic haze to find any fucks to give.

He shoves past me, flicking the light switch on and bumping me in the chest with his shoulder as he passes by. It's all I have not to take everything out on him right now. Use my fists to relieve the anger and disbelief and hurt and every damn thing bottled up inside me.

Like all the shit that's definitely my fault but that I'd rather blame on him. On my adoptive mom, Rylee. On the whole fucking world.

The thoughts stagger me. I shake my head, try to figure out how I could want to raise my fists at the man who has helped to give me everything, and yet the images fill my head again: the blood, the Band-Aids, the scissors.

*My mom.*

The truth my mind has been hiding from me.

The one he has obviously been keeping from me too.

With my fists clenched and entire body vibrating, I force myself to remain where I stand and hold back the anger that's been running like a river through my veins the past few weeks.

"You know what I can't figure out?" he asks nonchalantly as he picks up the empty bottle of Jameson before tossing it on the perfectly made bed with a chuckle. And then a sigh. *"Why?"*

Such a loaded question. One I'm not quite positive I feel like pulling the trigger on answering. And yet my finger's itching to. I'm just not sure I can handle the blowback right now.

So I don't answer. The question hangs in the stale air of the hotel room, his silence weighing on me as he surveys the space. After a few seconds his eyes find mine and ask the question again. But I choose to be the asshole. It's just so much easier than having to admit out loud what I still don't want to believe myself.

"Why what?" I finally answer. Sarcasm tinges my tone. Along with a healthy dose of *It's none of your fucking business*.

"This isn't a joke, son." A lift of his eyebrows. Another shake of his head. His face a mask of disgust.

Just more shit I don't want to deal with. Questions bubble up inside me. Fester like infected wounds. Eat at me until I can't bite back the anger.

"Nope. It seems I'm the joke these days." The autopsy report flashes in my mind's eye. Fuels my fire.

He narrows his eyes. Tries to figure out where my hostility is coming from. "Damn straight, you are," he says, and for the first time I notice his lucky shirt and workout pants. His superstitious pre–fire suit getup.

Then it hits me that I've just royally fucked up. The thoughts flash through my mind. It's daylight. I'm supposed to be somewhere, do something other than get lost in this bottle.

"Ahhh . . . Did you forget about your scheduled track time this morning? Team testing for final adjustments? Or maybe you forgot about the race tomorrow altogether? After last night, I'd want to forget all about being here in Alabama too."

His last comment jogs a memory. Images flash: loud music; huge VIP bar tab; race bunnies sliding up, wanting a piece of me. *Everyone wanting a piece of me.*

Push. Push. Push. Everyone pushing.

*Snap.*

Smitty restraining me—biceps locked under my arms in a vise grip, pulling my shoulders back. But why? How?

What the hell happened? All I remember is him dropping me off back here. The hotel. My home for the week.

"Just having a good time," I say with a sneer. Covering up for the blank spots in my memory. "What the fuck do you care?"

He's on me in a flash. Forearm pressed into my chest, my shoulders backed up against the wall. He's quick. Guess I've never tested this side of him before.

Our eyes hold—father to son, mentor to protégé, boss to employee, man to man—and for one split second I see the hurt in his eyes that I want to ignore.

"Why do I care? *WHY* do I care?" he growls, voice escalating on each word and forearm pressing harder against my chest. "Let me count the ways. Showing up late to training at home is one thing, Zander. Thumbing your nose to your sponsors by standing them up at the dinner they throw in your honor as you sat in the bar next door and laughed so loud they know it's you? *Inexcusable.* The endless stream of questionable women. Sweet Jesus, Zander . . . I was all for getting laid when I was your age, but even I had some standards."

I roll my eyes. Snort in disbelief. *Does he think I'm buying his holier-than-thou bullshit right now when I've heard the old stories?* Like he didn't play the field in his day.

"You think this is funny?" he shouts with another hard shove to my chest. "My idea of funny isn't missing testing the day before a race when you're in the goddamn driver's seat to take another championship. Just blowing it off without a word. Letting your team down. *Your crew.* The hundred or so fans you had sitting in a VIP tent two hours ago waiting to meet their idol, and guess what? He didn't show because he was too goddamn busy getting shitfaced on cheap whiskey like a drunk. So you tell me, *Golden Boy* . . . how is that *funny*?"

"Get. Off. Me." I grit the words out even as I welcome the biting pressure of his forearm on my chest.

He steps back, but his hands take a little longer to let go from where they're fisted in my shirt. But I still don't move. His glare pins me motionless. There's disappointment there. Concern. And a shitload of anger.

I cling to the anger he's giving off, can relate to it, but for completely different reasons from the ones he has. *The irony.* He's pissed because he expects more from his son, and I'm furious because I expect more from my dad.

"You've been late, showed up to the track hungover, and have chewed out your crew and treated them like shit for no reason. You've blown off Rylee, been an asshole to me, and pulled away from your brothers. You've fucked up royally and *you're asking me* why I care? I think you need to ask yourself that question, son."

"It's none of your business."

"Bet your ass it's my business. Everything about you is my business and you're out of control." He talks right over me. The resentment I can hear in his tone causes my chest to constrict. "You've stepped way over the line."

"Like you are right now by getting in my business? Get the fuck out." I spit the words out, not caring that my anger is misplaced or that I can't take them back.

He takes a step toward me, head angled, jaw clenched, hands fisted. The proverbial gloves are off. "You hurting, son? Want to lash out at someone for something you don't want to talk about? Trying to throw all your hard work away with your bullshit stunts? It's best you remember who you're talking to," he says between gritted teeth, referring to the abusive childhood he survived before being saved and adopted. The implication being that he understands what's going on in my head. "I know rage like you feel, Zander. I know hate that burns in your gut and turns your heart black. But it fixes nothing. *Nothing.* I've tried to be patient. Tried to be here for you. Asked you to talk to me, let me be there for you in whatever you're going through, and you've refused. Now I'm watching you sabotage everything good you've got going for you, and you want me to stand by and let it happen? Are you out of your mind?" He takes a moment to catch his breath while I seethe over his words. Over my inability to get past this and just ask him the questions I need to ask.

Because hurt not only clouds your judgment, but can also blind you from the real reason you're mad.

"I've kept the press away. Held back Rylee from interfering. Given you enough rope to hang yourself and now . . . now I can't help you. Congrats, there's no more rope left. You've lost your sponsorship."

*What?* The silence in the room screams around me. It's so loud I let it drown out what he just said. Don't want to believe it.

*It's his fault.* That's all I can focus on. All I can rationalize. He didn't prevent it. He didn't fix this. He probably did it on purpose because he wants to control me. Control everything about me.

Including my past.

God, I need a drink. A whole goddamn bottle to make this just go away. To make sense of all the bullshit I'm selling myself when it sounds ridiculous just thinking it.

"You're lying!" My voice is completely opposite to his. Loud. Screaming. Enraged. And my head's so fucked-up that it hurts and craves the pain all at the same time.

"I'd never lie to you, Zander." Calm. Even. Dead serious.

And those words—the ones I know to be a lie—are like a match to the embers that have been smoldering over the past few weeks.

"That's bullshit and you know it!" I shout. Become unhinged, fists itching to punch something, and I'm sure ruining the drywall of this fancy hotel wouldn't win me any favors. My body shakes with the anger. The rage inside me takes over. "You lied—"

"And you don't think you're out of control?" Colton says, taking an aggressive step into me. Taunting me in my irrational state. "Since when is it okay to even think about taking a swing at your old man?"

*You're not my old man.* The words flicker and fade through my rage. Shock me. Plant thoughts in my head that I've never considered before. And even though they're bullshit, they still linger. Still taint my anger and jade my words.

"I'm perfectly in control," I grate out through gritted teeth. Anger. Spite. Frustration. All three spin on the merry-go-round in my head. Muck up the truths and feed off the confusion.

"Perfectly in control?" he asks with a disbelieving shake

of his head as he reaches into his pocket and grabs his cell phone. Confusion and dread run through me simultaneously. It's like deep down I know this can't be good and yet can't for the life of me figure out what he's going to show me on the screen once he's finished flicking through images. "Let's just say you owe Smitty big-time, because I'm done paying for your fuckups, Zee. This was the only picture taken last night. Lucky for you, the VIP room was empty by the time this happened. Smitty was worried enough about you to stick around to make sure you didn't get into trouble. The lone paparazzo who snuck through and snapped this had to forfeit his camera to the bouncer, because it was against house rules."

The look on Colton's face and his eyes trained on the image on his phone unnerve me. The anxiety breaks through the hold the anger has on me. Worries me. Makes me shift my feet in anticipation of something I know has to be bad to earn me this speech.

Thoughts ghost through my mind. A hot blonde. A dick-hardening kiss. A pissed-off boyfriend. Testosterone-laced tempers. My words, *"I'm Zander fucking Donavan."*

This can't be good.

"Cut the dramatics and just show me."

"Dramatics?" Colton thunders farther into the room as he holds the phone out so I can see it. I reject the image immediately. A moment of clarity amid the confused haze. Know it didn't happen the way the picture shows.

*Just the same way your dream about your mom was different than reality too.*

I stare at the image, my body tense, my jaw clenched, and try to fill in the missing holes between what's in my mind and what the picture shows. The worst part is I can't know for sure that I didn't do that.

"Is that dramatics, Zander? Looks pretty crystal fucking clear to me."

It's me all right. Fist clenched, arm cocked, a rage on my face like I've never seen before—but it's nothing like the look on the woman's face in front of me. Scared. Stunned. Fearful.

"That's not what . . ." I shake my head. Try to rationalize that her asshole of a boyfriend must have been next to her, out of camera range. The one my cocked fist was aiming toward. For a split second I see my dad in my face. My biological dad. The monster. The abuser. Everything I promised myself I'd never be.

I reject the thought immediately.

"It is you, Zander. Take a closer look. You think losing a sponsor is bad? Let this image get out—just how you think a lady should be treated—and you'll lose a shit ton more than that. You raised your fist to a woman." He shakes his head and chuckles in shocked disbelief. "And you don't think you're out of control?"

*Push*

"You need help."

*Push*

"To talk to someone."

*Push*

"This isn't the son I raised—"

*Snap.*

"I'm not your goddamn son, so quit acting like you're my father!" I shout at the top of my lungs with every ounce of rage and hurt and confusion that I've been fighting back down the past few weeks. Something, anything, to make this stop. To make the pain stop. The confusion end. Keep the past from tainting my future.

The lies from being true.

He stumbles back a few feet, eyes wide, mouth lax. For just a moment he stands there staring at me. Reining in his temper. Trying to comprehend what I just said.

The look on his face alone should knock the fight out of me—shock, hurt, disbelief—but the truths he just threw in my face, the ones I have to acknowledge but don't want to hear, are like kerosene to my anger. They create a back draft loaded with resentment that explodes instantly, wiping out all reason.

"Excuse me?" He straightens his spine. His voice comes out with a controlled calmness. And I should heed the warning. The loud, angry wrath of my dad is one thing, but the cool, even quiet manner is much scarier when you're on the receiving end of it.

*But I don't.*

"You heard me." Our gazes lock. Our mutual anger feels heavy in the room as I lash out the only way I know how to right now.

"Loud. And. Clear." The tone remains even, though his eyes reflect a wounded fury I refuse to acknowledge. He tucks the phone into his back pocket, nodding his head the whole time as I stand there wanting everything he means to me gone: salvation, hope, family, friendship, unconditional love. All I can feel is the crushing disappointment from everything I've done to purposely try to fuck this all up.

"You've left me no choice." When he looks back up, his expression is blank, shoulders squared, eyes hard. *"You're fired."*

"Come again?" *He wouldn't dare.* I'm leading the points. I'm the reigning champion. There's a reason they call me Indy's Golden Boy.

But as the silence stretches out and nothing about his posture changes, the lump in my throat gets bigger and it becomes harder to swallow.

"You heard me."

My laugh is loud enough to sound condescending. Part of me is in disbelief, but he wants to be a prick and go this route? Fine. I'll show him I don't need him or his lies. I don't need anything from him.

It's not like I've never been on my own before.

*Blood. Scissors. Band-Aids.*

But first, self-preservation. The hurt radiates through me. The stain on my soul darker than ever before.

"Fine. Got it." I shake my head, our eyes locked, with his saying, *Let me help you* and mine telling him, *I don't need your lies.* Confusion turns to anger. "I don't need you anyway."

"Good luck with that, son—Zander," he corrects himself quickly. The sting at the sound of my name on his lips is more than obvious. "And don't bother trying to approach any other teams. One, it's midseason and two, they won't hire you anyway."

"You can't do that." Anger turns to rage. He wouldn't threaten other teams to not hire me.

"Watch me." That cocky-bastard flash of a grin that unnerves his competitors is directed my way. He takes a step closer. "I've been around a lot longer than you have. No one would cross that line even for a *sure thing* like you. Oh, wait. . . . You're not exactly a sure thing anymore when you're losing sponsors, blowing off testing, and there's concern whether you'll even show for race day. It's not like you've been exactly discreet with your bullshit." He takes another step, a mocking laugh falling from his mouth. "Take it from a team owner. You've become a risk. A liability. And no one wants a loose cannon on their team regardless of how good of a driver you are."

Rage turns into a ball of disbelieving fury; I want to lash out at him with everything I have, regardless of the damage it causes. Self-preservation at its finest.

"Fuck you, *Colton*." His name is a sneer loaded with disrespect. I come out swinging with words I can't take back. Needing to save face when everything about me is being questioned. "It's always about the team with you, isn't it? The next victory. The next paycheck. Fuck the racers, right? Screw them and any shit they have going on—*lie to them if need be*—so long as they perform for you. Isn't that right, *boss*?"

*"Sticks and stones,"* he says with a lift of his eyebrows. The taunt of a smile. The ice in his voice. "You think that's going to get your job back? Think again."

"Fuck. You." I'm overheated, but my body breaks out in goose bumps, because the chilling look in his eyes tells me this isn't a joke at all. Not some psychobabble bullshit he's using to try to get me to talk like he has in the past.

He chuckles long and low again and the sound grates on my nerves as I try to wrap my head around everything that's happening: the dreams, the picture, Colton's no-bullshit punches.

"It's not just me you're hurting, but everyone else that depends on you. I'm leaving your car without a driver. Won't fill your spot. If I worried only about money, that wouldn't be the case, now, would it? What I'm worried about is you. You're out of control and pushing the limits, and I can't stand by to watch you crash and burn without stepping in. I'm sorry it has to come to this, but I don't mind being the asshole if it's going to save you. I've done it before and I'll do it again in a second."

We stand in silence, hearts torn apart, and so much of our connection shredded on the floor between us. For the first time since he's walked in here, I notice how tired he looks. Concern etches the lines of his face. And the need to say any more, damage us more, dies on my lips despite the discord still echoing within me.

With a nod of his head, he turns and walks toward the door. My eyes follow him despite the desperation for him to be gone so I don't have to see the defeat in his posture. He grabs the handle and hangs his head. "Take the time, Zee. Fix what you need to fix. Deal with whatever shit you need to deal with. Let someone in instead of shutting everyone out. It doesn't have to be me. Or Rylee. Or anyone we know, but let them in; you'll be a better man because of it. Sometimes it takes a new ear, a fresh voice, to put things in perspective for you. Shit, take a drive, a trip—I don't care—but use the time to make *you* right. Don't come back until you are. I don't know what's going on and I wish like hell you'd talk to me about it, but I understand better than most that sometimes you can't. My only advice is not to let the dark eat you whole. You deserve better than that." He clears his throat from the emotion clogging it, and I hate everything about this conversation more because of that disconcerting sound. "Regardless of what you think, you are my son and it doesn't matter how bad you fuck up—I'll always love you."

The door opens. Closes. The dust dances again. The silence suffocates me.

I fight the urge to go after him. I resist unleashing more of my anger and the need to yell and shout and trash the room to get it all out. None of it will fix a goddamn thing.

Grabbing the bottle of Jameson, I lift it to my lips until I remember it's empty. The crash of the glass shattering as it hits the wall across from me is deafening.

Shaking my head, I fall back on the bed. Try to make sense of what just happened. What I've let happen. What I didn't stop.

To my mom back then and to my family now.

The loudest thing I hear is the rejection from the man I've looked up to, idolized, who helped me heal. The man who just walked out of this room and hurt me more than he'll ever know.

*Can you blame him, Zander?*

I close my eyes and rub my hands over my face. My buzz is gone. The haze removed. Everything important taken away from me with the slam of the door: my family, my ride, my anchors. And the sting is real.

But so is the anger. The inability to rationalize. To accept. To ask the things I need to ask.

*To apologize.*

Fuck that. I'm not apologizing. I'm not the one who lied.

And I would never threaten to hit a woman, let alone actually follow through with it. The image on Colton's phone flashes through my mind. Another lie to throw in the pot.

The rage is instantly back. Misdirected but back. My body feels restless, but my mind is whipped to the point where I can't think about this any more. Don't want to. I just need another bottle to get lost in. Then I'll figure where to go from here, since it looks like I have some time off coming to me.

And yet I don't get up from the bed to walk down to the bar. I can't, because somewhere deep down that voice of doubt grabs hold of my heart and squeezes tight. Twists it. Letting me know there are two truths I have to accept before I can move forward.

I am Colton's son.

And I'm the one who killed my mom.

# Chapter 1

"You good, Getty?"

*Good?*

My mind flashes to a few hours ago. How jumpy both my heart and the rest of me felt when the man from table nine simply touched my forearm as he reached to get my attention for another round. The crash as the bottle of triple sec hit the hardwood floor. The immediate waves of panic. The rush of memories. *The fear.* From another place, another time, to rattle nerves already on constant edge.

And until now I was doing so well hiding my uneasiness behind my tough-girl facade.

But I saw the customers' stares. Heard my stammered excuses. Suffered the immediate regret of giving them a glimpse of the secrets I've kept hidden. Of the life I left behind.

So, *good*? Not by a long shot, but I'm not about to let Liam know. Besides, I'm making progress. It's been three months and I've already got a job, a place to live, and more freedom than I've felt in forever.

Baby steps.

Trudging uphill and through what feels like barbed wire.

But it's progress nonetheless.

I collect my distracted thoughts—exhale a sigh to cover up my preoccupation—before turning to look at the Lazy Dog's owner, walking beside me. A tight smile hits my lips when I nod. "It's debatable if I'm good," I finally say, trying to make light of the earlier incident. Add humor so that he doesn't ask more questions. It's something I've learned how to do way too well. "But I do know I deserved to be fired after dropping that bottle."

The laugh I force—the one that used to be my everyday normal— sounds hollow to my own ears. Funny how it seems so odd in this new life I've created for myself.

"Nah. Everyone makes mistakes." Liam's voice pulls me back from my thoughts. "It's no big deal. Really."

"I can add an extra hour on my shift or help cover during a game night if you get too busy. It's the least I can do." I slow down my footsteps as we approach the fork in our paths on the walk home from the bar.

"Not necessary. Besides, you should come in during a game. Be a customer. Most of us here are a little obsessed with the Mariners. It's a good time."

"Nah. Not my thing." Too many people crowded in one spot. At least when I'm working, I have the bar counter as my barrier. A space between me and any unwanted contact.

*Who am I kidding?* All contact is unwanted these days.

"Are you telling me you don't like my bar?" he laughs in mock offense as we stand on the corner beneath the streetlight.

"No. Not at all," I correct myself. "I mean—"

"Relax. I'm just teasing you." He reaches out to touch my arm and I freeze at his motion. Then curse myself. Shit. He obviously notices my reaction, because he pulls his hand back immediately, but his gaze remains locked on mine. Searching. Asking. Wanting more.

"I, um—thanks for walking with me. I'm beat and—"

"Getty?"

"Yeah?" My voice is cautious because I know what comes next and don't really want to venture there.

"If there was some kind of problem . . ." I'm not sure if the flash of hurt in my eyes stops his words, but they stop nonetheless. He nods in silent understanding. "Well, if you need any kind of help, I'm here, okay?"

"Thank you. I appreciate it," I murmur softly. "Good night."

I walk away, knowing he hasn't moved and is watching me make my way through the night toward my house. He's sweet and kind. So very different from what I'm used to, and so I need distance between us. It would be way too easy to lean on him, use his friendship to get through this, when I know better than anyone that the only person I can depend on is myself.

And yet the weight of his stare and the concern in his eyes are like magnets pulling me backward, begging me to find someone I can confide in, when all I really need to do is learn how to manage this new life on my own.

*Keep walking, Getty. You can let him in once you figure yourself out.*

I look out toward the moonlit ocean view beyond and take stock as to why I'm here. It seemed like the stars aligned when my mother's oldest friend offered to let me stay in the vacation house she and her husband were renovating before they could flip it. And because of that, I have a roof over my head. A place to reflect on what I want. A solitary space where I'll be able to come to terms with the mistakes from my past so I can have a better future.

You don't know they're mistakes until you make them. Or learn from them. Let's hope I've done both and can move forward.

I walk down the alleyway, past my car, parked in the narrow, shrub-lined driveway, to the front door of the old cottage. Skipping over the third step to avoid the broken wood slat, I remind myself that should be first on the very long list of repairs that I need to schedule for the house.

It's the least I can do, considering she's letting me stay here for free during the renovation.

Exhaustion hits me like a ton of bricks once I'm inside. I move through the darkened foyer quietly, in practiced precision, as if I'm still back in the Palo Alto house. I flick the light off in the kitchen, surprised I forgot to turn it off before I left, and ignore my grumbling stomach for the enticing hot water of the shower. Hopefully the muscles in my lower back will get used to my standing on my feet for eight-hour shifts soon, because this constant ache is annoying.

But it also means I'm doing this. Changes are really happening. *And the past is over.*

In a show of defiance no one will ever see and only I will understand, I make a trail of my discarded clothes as I walk down the hall toward the bathroom light I purposely left on at the end of the hallway: a beacon of imagined hot water calling my name.

Shoes. Shirt. Bra. Skirt. Panties. All come off one by one, throwing them to the floor in a messy trail as I go.

I'm exhausted, my mind still preoccupied with the mistake I made tonight dropping the bottle, so that when I clear the doorway, it takes me a second to come to my senses. The reaction is instantaneous—an earsplitting scream, a physical jump back, a shock to my heart, and hands immediately reaching to cover my pelvis and breasts—at the sight of the man standing in my bathroom.

And not just any man.

No.

But a buck-naked man. Dripping in water. I see a flash of ink on his back in the partially fogged-up mirror's reflection. One hand holds a towel up to his wet hair. The other is doing I don't know what, because I'm so fixated on his presence that thinking clearly isn't a priority.

"HELP!" I scream the moment I get my wits about me, body frozen in fear, mind reeling.

And even though his blue eyes look as shocked as mine probably do, his mouth spreads into a slow, disbelieving but definitely cocksure smile. "I've had women go to extremes before," he says with a chuckle, silencing my next shriek for help, "but this takes it to a whole new level."

In my confusion, my guard comes up instantly, although for some reason I don't actually feel threatened like a rational person would. I'm naked, hunched over trying to cover all my lady bits, caught between stepping back down the hallway and grabbing my last discarded item to cover myself up. But I know damn well my panties sure as hell aren't going to make a very good shield. Add to that there's no way in hell I'm giving him the wrong impression, that I'm retreating in fear.

"Who are you? What are you doing here?" I'm shaking with adrenaline as I hop around in the I'm-naked dance, every ripple and roll of imperfection on my body on display in the wash of bathroom light into the hall. My eyes flicker desperately to assess the situation I have absolutely zero control over. I want more lights on to flood the house and don't want them on at the same time.

"I believe I should ask you the same question," he says as he slowly lowers his hand, the towel now hanging at his side. Of course I look.

*And there it is. . . .*

I jump back like my eyes have been burned and yet first impressions are hard to erase: cut abs, that V of defined muscles, a trail of happy, and a more-than-impressive package. What the hell is wrong with me? There is a man in my house. He obviously just showered in my bathroom. *And I'm staring at his dick.*

"Put that thing away!" I command, with my hand reaching out to gesture at his waist before I realize that I've just removed my hand from my own breasts and offered a peep show of my own. Of course I replace it promptly but not before the man throws his head back and emits a deep laugh. It causes his Adam's apple to slide up, then down, chest to heave, and dick to bob.

I force myself to look away because . . . well, because he's a stranger. In my house. Naked. And oh my God, something is wrong with me, because I'm not running and calling 911 like I should.

When his chuckle subsides, he brings his head back down, so I can see the tears in his eyes from laughter. "That *thing* is my cock, and since this is *my* bathroom and you seem to be attempting to seduce me in *my* house, I don't think you have any right to tell me what to do." And with that, he leans a hip against the counter and folds his arms across his chest, eyes locked on mine and one eyebrow lifted. Everything else is left hanging out there in the wind.

"Your house? Seduce you?" At that point I realize I'm sputtering and shaking my head. "This is my house. You're in *my* house."

Confusion drifts across his face and his jaw falls lax. "Hold up." He lifts his hands in the *Hold on a minute* position, drawing my eyes back to where they don't want to be. If this whole situation weren't so unbelievable, it would be comical, and yet as true as that is, I don't seem to be laughing at all. "I think there seems to be some misunderstanding."

*"No shit."* Sarcasm is my fallback and it doesn't disappoint me now. A lot of good it does me, though, as I'm still doing the naked dance while trying to react to this surreal situation.

The look of disdain he gives me at my comment earns him no points in my book. "While I'm digging the socks with your outfit," he says with a smirk, eyes veering down and then back up to my strategically placed hands, "you should cover up." I catch the towel he tosses me and immediately wrap it around myself. I'm certain my mismatching knee-high socks make a statement about me, but I'm beyond caring, because I'm still alone in my house with a strange man and have no answers as to how this has happened.

With one hand clutching onto the towel at my collarbone, I use the other to motion to him. "You too."

A lightning flash of a grin glances across his lips. "Sorry, but you just took the only towel left."

Why is this funny to him? This is not funny. Not in the least. And neither is my procrastination over folding the load of towels currently sitting in the dryer. *Shit.*

I glance around quickly. Needing to keep an eye on him for safety's sake and not wanting to look too closely for obvious reasons. Instinct tells me he's not a threat and yet sensibility tells me he is. So I do the only thing I can, look slyly around for a weapon. Something. Anything.

But I'm in a hallway. Pickings are slim. When I take a step back, the ancient mini-blinds behind me rattle as my butt hits them. The sound clicks my mind into gear and I reach back and pick up the broken wand that opens the blinds sitting on the windowsill. Without thinking, I hold it up in front of me like a swashbuckling sword.

"How'd you get in here?" I demand in my deepest, growliest voice.

"With the key under the frog on the back deck." He doesn't even fight the smile on his face or make an attempt to cover himself up. Nope. He just stands there nonchalant as day, like he's used to women staring at his naked body.

Maybe he is. He said he thought I was here to seduce him. *Is he some kind of male escort or something? No. Wait. I have that all mixed up. He would be seducing me, then.*

*Focus, Getty.* Focus.

"What key?" How come I didn't know there was a key under the frog on the back deck? I jab the wand toward him to emphasize each word. "And the wood on the deck is broken. How'd you climb—"

"How'd you get in here?"

"I've been here and I'm the one asking questions."

That laugh again. Full-bodied. More than amused. Enough to make me wonder what it sounds like when he really means it. "Right. I forgot. You're one to give orders in a bath towel, socks, and holding that fierce sword of yours."

I fight back the urge to drop the wand regardless of how stupid I look, because I don't know this guy from Adam. "Answer. Me."

"Testy."

*"Now."* I jab the wand to show him that I mean it. The smile again, but this time he bites his bottom lip to prevent it from spreading all the way to dimple territory.

"Smitty gave me instructions on where to find the key. We made a deal. I get to stay here so long as I make some repairs for him."

*What?* "There's some kind of misunderstanding. Smitty messed up. I'm already living here."

"So I gather by your Custer's Last Stand demonstration," he says with an indifferent wave of his hand.

"How do you know him?" I already have a sinking feeling that something is seriously screwed up here and that I'm not going to like his answer.

"He's like an uncle to me." He shrugs. "You?"

"Darcy's like an aunt," I mimic him in reference to Smitty's wife.

We stare at each other as the knowledge that we've both been given access to this house settles into place between us.

"Well, Smitty must have forgotten that Darcy told me I could stay here, so you're going to have to find somewhere else to crash for the weekend." There. I said it. Take that.

"Good one." He seems unfazed by my comment as he waltzes past me in all his masculine glory and heads into the bedroom to the right of the bathroom. "But I'm not just here for the weekend. And I'm not going anywhere."

"Yes, you are!" I follow him the few steps into the bedroom and *whoa*, I'm greeted with a full male backside as he bends over to rifle through a duffel bag at the foot of the bed.

"Get your eyeful now, Socks," he says with a glance over his shoulder as he steps into a pair of boxer briefs and pulls them up. "Because after I call Smitty, I'm sure you're the one who'll find out you've overstayed the welcome."

He walks past me again, but this time I'm standing in the doorway. His body brushes ever so slightly against mine on the way out. I'm greeted with the scent of soap and masculinity fresh from the shower. I'm so busy admiring his ass, when I shouldn't be, as he moves down the hallway that it takes a moment for his comment to break through his enticing scent clouding my brain.

"Over my dead body!" I shout, rushing after him, clutching the towel tighter around me.

"That would be a helluva waste with that body," he murmurs from ahead of me. At least I think that's what he says, but I can't be certain and I sure as hell know he can't be speaking about me.

"What did you say?"

"I said you sure are messy."

"No, I'm not." He flicks on the hallway light just as the words leave my mouth. The path of my clothes is visible in all its cluttered glory. I cringe—not because of the destruction, but because he thinks he's right. When really he has no fricking clue of what's behind my messy trail. "Look, you don't get to come into my house—"

"It's Smitty's house," he corrects as he holds up one finger and the face of his cell phone out with the other hand.

"No, mine—"

"Zander." The phone crackles to life and a voice full of warmth comes through the speaker.

*So he has a name.*

"Hey, Smitty."

I open my mouth to speak but shut it instantly when Zander levels me with a look.

"Did you find the key all right? Get in okay?"

"Yeah. Right where you said it'd be. But man, that deck is a death trap waiting to happen." He laughs again. This time it's softer, flooded with the same warmth in Smitty's voice.

"I told you, you'd have to earn your keep."

"I will. I'm good for it."

A sudden heavy silence settles on the line. One I don't quite understand, but it's obvious at the same time.

"I know you are," Smitty finally says quietly. "Just as my word to you is good. I promised you I wouldn't tell them you were there—"

"There's a problem," Zander interrupts, unexpectedly changing the subject. And I can't quite put my finger on it, but whatever Smitty was talking about, Zander obviously doesn't want to. I can see it in the sudden darkening of his eyes and the tense set of his shoulders.

"What's up?"

"There's a woman here. At the house."

"Did you already forget what to do with one?" He laughs. "I thought you were long past the birds and the bees speech, Zee."

A genuine smile glances across Zander's lips, and his eyes flash up to meet mine. "I assure you I know what to do with one. But, uh . . . that's not what I'm talking about. There's a woman here. Her name's . . . ?" His eyes prompt me to respond.

All of a sudden I can't find my voice and when I do, I'm shy. Hating that giving him my name is almost an invitation for him to get to know me, when I want nothing more of this strange, obviously charismatic man than to see him walk out of the house and not come back.

I clear my throat. "Getty."

"Getty?" He gives me a curious glance as if he's questioning if I know my own name. I nod slowly to him because he's right—it still sounds a little foreign to me too.

New person. New name. New life.

"Smitty, her name's Getty. She says Darcy—"

"Oh shit." Smitty laughs into the line.

"Yeah. Oh shit." Zander's not amused.

"Hmm," he muses, "Darce went on a girls' trip up to the mountains. No service. She'll be home midweek. . . . I'll have to ask her about it then."

"Are you fucking kidding me?"

"Not in the least. There's two beds. One bath. You're a big boy. Figure it out," he says with another chuckle before the line goes dead.

"Goddammit. Smitty?" Zander swears again as he drops the phone onto the countertop with a thud. He braces both hands on the counter, head angled down looking at his phone while I look at him across the dimly lit room. Waiting. Wondering. Pushing aside the tickle of unease on the back of my neck as I hold tighter to the towel.

My gaze flickers around the room frantically. My instinct is to try to find the smallest corner to fade into. Figure out where the fallout of his temper will have the least impact.

After a moment, he lifts his head up and smirks. The tightness in my chest, the fear that crept in out of conditioning, slowly eases as I exhale.

"Well, shit. I guess we've been told," he says as he breezes past me down the hallway.

It takes me a moment to regain my bearings and realize I'm not back there and this stranger isn't Ethan, before I turn on my heel and rush once again down the hall after him.

"Whoa. Wait!"

"What for?" Zander turns back around like he has not a care in the world. Like he's not in his underwear with one foot currently trapped in the leg of my skirt, and I'm not in a towel with knee-high socks on.

"You're not staying here."

He chuckles. "Yes, actually, I am."

"No, you're not. There's a hotel down the road on the boardwalk. A bed-and-breakfast too."

"You heard the man. There are two beds. One bath. Pretty straightforward."

Oh my God. The man is infuriating. And pigheaded. "You're not hearing me."

"No, I'm hearing you all right. I'm just choosing not to listen." He works his tongue in his cheek and lifts his eyebrows in a nonverbal challenge. "Besides, I promised Smitty I'd fix the place up and as of recently, I'm a man of my word. So I'm going to do just that."

Something about the way he says the last statement tells me there is more behind it than he's letting on, but I'm tired from my shift and can't find the effort to care.

"You can do your repairs but stay at the hotel," I instruct in my sternest voice as he turns around and heads toward the back of the house. "A win-win for both of us." I attempt to infuse enthusiasm in my voice.

"Did you take the big bedroom?"

"What?" My head is spinning. Did he not hear a word I just said? He is *not* staying here. He can't. This is my space. Well, technically Darcy and Smitty's space, but it's been mine for almost three months. The first place I've had as my own, ever, and it's working—I have no other option but for it to work—so there is no way this is going to happen.

"I asked if this is your shit in the big bedroom in back?" he asks over his shoulder as he goes to turn the knob on the door.

"Did you touch it?" My defiance comes back immediately. My scattered thoughts are now focused. After being trivialized for so long, my privacy is so very important to me. Did he go in, rifle through my stuff? See my work, the bleed of my emotion onto canvas, and judge it?

"No." His answer is resolute. I'm right behind him, so when he turns around and sees what I can assume is the panic on my face, he angles his head and stares for a moment longer. "I opened the door, figured the stuff was Darcy's from the last time they were here. Didn't want to touch anything I wasn't supposed to, so I dropped my shit in there." He points to the only other bedroom in the house, right next to mine.

He's too close for comfort, so when he steps back to turn to face me, I retreat too. The space between us is clogged with his . . . his . . . everything about him, and I find it hard not to react.

"Wait. Stop." I hold my hands up, shake my head. "Just give me a minute here." *Give me space.*

"Take all the time you want in the world, Socks," he says, eyes full of a strange mix of humor and sincerity. And yet he doesn't step back, doesn't shift out of the way, so it's the wall behind me and him directly in front of me. *"Do you mind?"*

"Not at all." He doesn't move, just continues to look at me with a face that's the portrait of innocence, and yet a hunch tells me he's anything but.

"Personal space, here," I say sternly, motioning with my one free hand for him to back up some.

"Oh. Right. Sorry." He takes a small step back and fights the half-cocked grin on his lips. "But you're going to have to get used to us sharing it, since it looks like we're going to be shacking up together for the next couple of days until Darcy gets back and tells Smitty that your time's up."

That grin comes at me full force once he knows his comment has hit its mark with my sputtering lack of response.

"You're frustrating and irritating and . . ." *And handsome and too close and too many things I don't want to cloud my space when men are the last thing on my current agenda.*

"And you're still standing here naked in a towel. And socks. I've had a long few weeks. I'm tired. It's late." He looks at his watch and then back to me. "Why don't we go to bed and we can figure out the rest in the morning?"

"It's not that easy," I argue.

"Yeah, actually it is. You lie on your bed, close your eyes, and drift off to sleep. The only decision you need to make is back, stomach, or side. See? Easy."

I hate that he's turned on the boyish charm, because it's much more endearing for some reason than the naked-man-in-the-bathroom thing. "How do I know that you're not—"

"I assure you I'm a lot of things, but a creep or a murderer or a rapist isn't one of them," he states, stealing the thoughts from my head.

"Like you'd tell me if you were."

He laughs. "If I were one, I already had plenty of opportunities." He shrugs. "Besides, Smitty vouched for me. You heard him. Shut off your mind. Go get some sleep. We'll talk in the morning."

And with a flash of a smile and a nod of his head, he enters the bedroom next to mine and shuts the door with a resounding thud. I'm left staring at the faded wood door with unspoken words on my tongue and confusion cluttering my mind.

"Well then . . . there's that." It's all I can say as I slip into my own bedroom and stand there in the darkness, hunger forgotten, shower no longer a priority, and attempt to process the last twenty minutes.

I reach back and twist the handle on the door and test that it's actually locked, but as I sit back on the bed, I wonder if the lock is as shoddy as so many other things in this house. Besides, lock or not, if he wanted to open the door and get to me, one swift kick of his foot against the handle would grant him access.

The notion settles about the same time I hear his door open. I suck in my breath, my own thoughts and jaded reality melding a bit too much for my own liking, but when I hear his steps head down the hall toward the kitchen, I relax some.

Should I push the dresser in front of the door, just in

case? I've slept with enough fear in my lifetime; this is one place I don't want to have to do that.

Just as I'm about to move to the dresser and test its weight, there's a knock on my door. I jump out of my skin and feel stupid immediately. It's not like I didn't know he was here or anything.

"Just in case you're still scared of me and need some protection," he says with a chuckle through the door, which leaves me more confused until I see a glint off the moonlight as something slides beneath it. "Night, *Socks*."

I wait to hear his door shut again before I move toward mine and switch on the light. Fighting the laugh that falls from my mouth is futile when I look down to see the mini-blind wand on the floor.

*Smart-ass.*

Unsure what to do and feeling completely unsettled, I leave the wand where it is, throw on some pajamas, and slide into the bed.

But sleep doesn't come regardless of how tired I am. My mind goes a million miles an hour as I think about what just happened.

The bathroom standoff. The naked dance. The ludicrousness of having to defend myself with a mini-blind wand. All of it.

And yet none of it matters, because he's still here and I'm still left trying to figure out how I'm going to make him leave.

The funny thing is, I should have been petrified, especially on the heels of my freak-out tonight at the bar. And I was at first. My heart was pounding and adrenaline was racing, but not once did I run away and cower like I used to. There's something to be said for that.

Baby steps.

At least I just proved to myself that I'm making some.

# Chapter 2

GETTY

The sound of a hammer jars me awake.

The sky's just turning light, and I want to snuggle back under the covers and sleep a little longer. But when I rub my feet together, there are socks on them, and I *never* sleep with socks on my feet.

*Night, Socks.*

The words tumble through my sleep-drugged mind and last night rushes back in full comedic color.

I must be dreaming. I'll just go back to sleep, chase away the nightmare. Prove it didn't happen.

Just as I snuggle deeper into my covers, the damn hammer starts again. Shocks my mind awake. Tells me Zander really is in the bedroom beside me. And that my damn neighbor, Nick, must be working on his house and has absolutely zero sympathy for the fact that I worked the closing shift last night.

*Go away, Nick,* I yell at him in my mind. Groaning out loud. But what if Zander's not a morning person either? What if Nick keeps hammering and the noise drives him insane and pushes him toward the hotel in town?

Optimistic at the prospect, I slide out of bed, grab my fluffy purple robe, and wrap it tightly around myself. Already missing the warmth of the bed, I step over the wand

and open my bedroom door so I can check if Zander's door is still shut. It is.

*Keep hammering away, Nick.*

I tread lightly down the hall, brush my teeth as quietly as possible, and then head toward the front of the house just as the bang, bang, bang starts again. I know my intentions are bitchy and Zander's probably a nice guy, but I really need to keep this place all to myself. Need to continue figuring things out on my own. I have to heal my body, mind, and heart so I can figure out what's next for me.

Intending to sit on the front patio and let the steady pounding wake me fully, I pull open the door and am startled to see Zander with hammer in hand making the noise himself.

*Are you kidding me?*

Instantly discouraged, I know I should retreat. Go take advantage of the shower while he's out here and think of a new game plan.

Yet I don't move. *Can't.* Even though it's the last thing I want to be caught doing, I'm transfixed watching him: the sinews in his forearms as he swings the hammer, his hair falling over his brow as he leans forward, the drip of sweat that falls off the edge of his nose, and the bunch of his muscles beneath his T-shirt. The ones my mind can still picture bared like they were last night.

I'm pissed all over again. At him especially. About all those things inside me the sight of him hot and sweaty is stirring awake. At least last night there was humor and frustration. This morning is just a straight-up punch of—unwelcome—lust.

He definitely needs to go. To the hotel. To any of the other islands here off the coast of Washington State. Out to sea for all I care. Anywhere but here.

I take a step back into the house to provide some distance from his definitive virility and formulate a new plan to get him to leave. Hog all the hot water. Be a slob. Flush the toilet every time he's in the shower. Burn some awful-smelling incense. I don't know for certain, but the one thing I do know is that the longer I stand here and stare at him, the harder convincing myself to do something is going to be.

"Goddammit!" Zander swears, and drops the hammer with a clatter. The sudden noise has me stepping back into the doorway. He sucks on his thumb, swears again, and shakes his hand. "You just going to stand there and stare?"

The bite to his voice sounds very different from last night and for a moment I'm frozen in indecision. Then I swallow over the lump lodged in my throat, which used to be my norm, and tell myself that's the old me. Time to buck up and remember why I'm here and why I need him gone.

"Yep. Sure am." It's all I say, all I can think to say, but at least this time I have clothes on when I face him down.

Luckily he does too. What's unlucky for me is how perfectly they hug his biceps. And his pecs.

"You've lived here how long?"

I startle at the question. "Three months–ish."

"And you never bothered to fix this step here?" I stare at him. Big, blank doe eyes are my only answer, because I knew it was there and hadn't gotten around to it yet. Fixing myself is a big enough chore in itself. "Didn't think so," he responds when I don't answer. "And you still think you deserve to stay here over me?"

Everything within me bristles at his comment. My need to stand up for myself versus my need to not feel stupid are warring against each other, so instead of saying anything, I just shake my head and step back into the house without another word.

Ignoring Smitty's explanation last night, I immediately fire off a text to Darcy, which helps me to feel like I'm being proactive. I know he said she's not getting any service, but since I just walked away without a word from Zander when I should have stood up for myself, I figured I needed to do something to make me feel a little more in control of this out-of-control situation.

Needing time to think, I head to the one place in the house where I can block out the sound of the hammer and Zander's annoying presence: the shower. I take my time, purposely letting all the hot water run empty before I get out. The sweat ring on Zander's shirt says he went out for a run. A run means he'll want a shower. And oopsie, this house has such a small hot-water heater that maybe he should go to the hotel down the street, where they have a *massive* abundance of it.

But he's not waiting to take one when I leave the bathroom. In fact the hammer continues for a while, making it nearly impossible to ignore him. Or forget him. So in another attempt to shut him out, I close myself off in my room and take my time getting ready. I experiment with my makeup, as I find myself doing lately. It's a newfound freedom being able to choose different eye shadows or shades of lipstick or to wear none at all when for so very long I had to abide by what I'd deemed the Stepford Wife daily makeup application.

My easel calls to me over the top of the vanity. Sketches in charcoal sit there waiting for me to paint them with bright and beautiful colors . . . although for some reason, I think they'd prefer to stay in their black-and-white state with smeared fingerprints and tarnished edges.

Kind of like me. Kind of like my face.

I stare at myself long and hard in the mirror, take stock of the reflection looking back at me: wide-set jaw, full lips, rosy cheeks, peaches and cream complexion, a dusting of freckles I've never cared for across the bridge of my nose, longish light brown hair. But the one thing that holds my attention rapt is my eyes; their deep chocolate brown hue looks much less haunted than when I drove onto the ferry, unsure of what awaited me on the island.

I shake my head, pull myself back from thoughts about my old life. The designer clothes, five-star restaurants, and mandatory social-status outings—the finest of all things in life. But hand in hand with that went the complete and utter loss of control over my choices, the pretenses I had to keep, and the lack of truly living my life.

But here . . . here there is water and fresh air and space to create. There are genuine smiles and I'm just the new girl, Getty Caster, not Gertrude Caster-Adams of the renowned Caster family with expectations to fulfill and a husband with a reputation to uphold.

Zander's voice swearing loudly through the open windows (Mrs. Brown next door is not going to take too kindly to it) causes the ghosts to skitter back into hiding. With a sigh, I look down at my makeup towelette smeared with various browns and blues and reds and decide that my lip gloss and mascara will have to do just fine for today, because coffee is more important than cosmetics at this point in time.

Besides, I don't want Zander thinking I'm making any efforts for him. I won't hesitate to do my makeup for work or because I want to, but never again because I have to for a man.

Going through my morning routine, I pretend like the house is still mine, still void of the distinct scent of masculinity, and still drenched in the solitude I came here to find. And when I walk out into the family room, all three of the things I've tried to ignore slap me squarely in the face when I come upon Zander making himself at home. He's sitting on the couch, feet on the coffee table, and scowling at the television.

I notice it's a race of some sort. I intend not to give it or him more than two seconds of my attention. And of course that's impossible to do when I notice the huge gash on the side of Zander's leg, running from his ankle to about halfway to his knee. It's bruised and bloody and I immediately cringe at how bad that had to have hurt.

"What happened to your leg?" There's concern in my voice along with a healthy dose of curiosity.

"Someone has lived here for three months and has yet to fix the step or caution it off so that others might not put their full weight on it and fall straight through to the ground." He works his tongue in his cheek, but his eyes never wander from the television in front of him.

*Oh shit.*

"I'm sorry." The words are off my tongue immediately—instant reflex—before I shake my head and bite back the gushing apologies that automatically cue in my mind out of habit. "I didn't know. . . . I didn't expect you. Are you okay? Do you need a doctor to look at it?" I move into the room toward him, truly apologetic, but at the same time knowing I can't fix it now.

When he finally angles his gaze my way, the stare he gives me stops me dead in my tracks. "Don't." It's a warning, loud and clear, and one I don't need to hear twice.

We stare at each other, his oppressive mood filling the space between us in such contrast with the playful guy I met and actually kind of liked last night, regardless of how infuriating he was.

"It was an honest mistake. If I had known you were coming or going to get up that early, I would have . . ." My words fade off when his attention turns back to the television as clouds of smoke fill the upper right-hand turn of a track. Metal and tires fly as several cars connect with the concrete wall and one another.

He leans toward the television, jaw slack and eyes widening as if he were there, going through it himself, driving the car. "Unbelievable." He says it like a swearword before he picks up the remote and turns it off. "The man can do no fucking wrong."

*Guess he really likes racing.*

"Was that your driver?" I ask, hoping to break the tension.

His laugh fills the room. It's full and rich but with a tinge of contempt that has me taking a step back, leery of everything about his demeanor.

I feel stupid. Did I phrase it the wrong way? "I meant to say, is that the driver you usually follow?"

He coughs out an amused sound but says nothing further. There's something about his reaction that makes me feel like I'm being mocked. And then it clicks for me.

"Is that how you know Smitty? Doesn't he race or something?"

"Something like that," he murmurs, eyes back, fixated on the TV screen as if he's still watching the race unfold in his mind.

"Something like that?"

"Yeah. Something like that."

*Well, isn't he Mr. Talkative?* "What's his—"

"No, Getty. We're not going to do this right now." He carelessly tosses the remote on the table with a clatter as he removes his feet from it, face wincing in pain. "We're not going to do the get-to-know-you crap, because let's face it, you're going to be leaving in a few days. Then we're never going to see each other again, so why waste our breath bullshitting each other? Neither of us is going to say anything more than what we want the other to hear anyway. From what I gather, we're both here so we can't lie to ourselves anymore, so let's just save the pretenses. Deal?"

He rises to his feet, bringing our bodies near each other but everything else about us a million miles apart. I force a swallow down my throat because I hate so many things about the truth in his words. Despising that he's hammered the nail on the head about my reasons for being here when he's known me less than twenty-four hours. And hating that maybe I was secretly liking and loathing his company simultaneously. That maybe a part of me liked hearing another voice, enjoyed the laughter in his eyes last night, and the way he looked at me like I was more than just an object.

Does that even make sense? God, I'm so confusing. *You either do or you don't, Getty.* Kind of hard to desire both solitude and some company.

While I'm at it, I might as well hold a whole conversation in my head while he stares me down to make sure I understand where he's coming from. And I do. I definitely do.

I nod my head as I wait for the words to come. And with the words come the anger that he's an asshole and I shouldn't want to like him, because who is *that* honest when you've just met someone? I've had enough assholes for a lifetime—forgetting one more shouldn't be a problem for me.

"Deal." I purse my lips, shake my head, and turn on my heel without another word. Because he's right—I don't want to waste any more of my breath on him. I've already wasted enough that he's made my head spin.

# Chapter 3

Would it kill you to pick up your phone and
text me back to let me know you're okay? I get
you're pissed at the world. Believe me, I've
been there. Don't be a dick and try to deal with
whatever's going on all on your own. That's
what you have brothers like me for.

Staring at the text from Shane for the twentieth time in as
many minutes, I hate that I want to respond to it and at
the same time that I don't want to. I love my brother to
death, but I can't deal with him just yet.

He's the good guy. Checking up on me. Telling me he's
there for me. Being the good brother he's always been to me.

And I'm just the asshole. Needing to fly solo for now.

I delete the text.

I don't need another reminder of everything I don't
deserve.

# Chapter 4

GETTY

All day the bar has seen a steady flow of tourists, likely in a last mad rush to soak up island life and relax with a few drinks before the ferry leaves for the mainland for the last run of the day.

I've gotten to know its schedule, the ebb and flow of foot traffic, and then after the tourists load up and get on board, the locals emerge from their hiding places. They fill the Lazy Dog to capacity and bitch about the trash left behind by visitors, while thanking God for the money brought to the island's economy. It's the weekend routine here, something I've come to appreciate and depend on as part of my new normal.

"You good, Getty?" Liam asks from above the roar of the customers as someone hits a long fly ball in a close game playing on every television screen in the bar.

"Yep." I wipe down the bar top in front of me and take a few minutes to organize the clutter that amasses during a shift, thanks to the lull in orders with the bases-loaded situation in the game.

"Can you help me with service to table thirteen?"

"Sure." It's rare for Liam to ask me to step out from behind the bar. He knows I like it better behind the counter, but when it's super busy like it is tonight, I'll venture out into what I call the Wild West.

I hate it but know it's pushing the boundaries of my comfort zone, forcing me to engage and not be so skittish.

With a fortifying sigh, I pull up my socks, one zebra striped and the other polka-dotted today, the Lazy Dog uniform of logo T-shirt and mismatched knee-high socks as much of a landmark here in PineRidge as the ferry's horn that goes off every hour. I make my way across the crowded bar to the little alcove near the front. It's one of the bar's coveted spots, offering the table's occupant both a view of the ocean through the open windows and a clear sight line to the ball game. I get distracted by a few comments on the way, have a few laughs, stop to watch the next pitch, before I finally arrive at the table.

"What can I get for you tonight?" I ask the top of the ball cap before glancing back over my shoulder as the room collectively groans when the cleanup hitter strikes out.

I withhold a groan of my own when the customer lifts his head and I find Zander's vibrant blue eyes looking back at me. "Oops, we seem to be all out of alcohol," I say, sarcasm impossible to ignore as I start to walk away and leave him parched.

"Socks." His hand flashes out to grab onto my forearm the same time he says that stupid nickname he's given me. And the instant I feel his fingers tighten on my arm, alarm surges through me and has me yanking my arm from his grasp like I've been burned by fire.

"Let go!" The minute the words are out, I regret them. And not just the words but the audible sounds of fear and desperation woven in them.

Zander removes his hand instantly, but the look in his eyes is almost ten times more intrusive than the unwelcome panic his touch sparked. I wait for the questions to come, the look that indicates I have no right to react this way, and yet he says nothing. He just keeps his eyes locked on mine, making assumptions I'd rather he not make.

"Sorry . . . I, uh, sorry. Too much coffee today. What can I get you?" Heat warms my cheeks as I hold his stare and try to feign that everything is okay. That my heart's not racing and embarrassment isn't the reason I'm shifting my feet.

"Don't be," he finally says, breaking the tension between us and allowing the customers around us who've taken notice of my reaction to ease back in their seats. But beneath his hat, his brows narrow as his eyes tell me he's not buying the "too much coffee" line. "It was my bad. Whatever IPA you have on draft is fine. I'm not picky."

I move away from the table as quickly as possible, purposefully avoiding the stares from the regulars, since that's twice in two days they've seen me act like a skittish mouse. The last thing I need is to draw more attention to myself, so I'm thrilled that another server offers to take Zander his beer while I fill more orders behind the bar.

Once I get lost in the work, in the hustle and bustle of filling orders, I remind myself to ignore Zander's looming presence. I know he's watching me, can feel his eyes scrutinizing me from the other side of the room, even though every time I begrudgingly glance up, he's not looking my way. But in between delivering drinks and watching a few key moments of the game, I happen to notice people stopping at his table—men and women alike—chatting and laughing, almost as if they're enamored with him.

It's tempting to roll my eyes and snort in disgust. If they only knew what a grade A asshole he is. But then I'm left to try to figure out how, if he's new to the island, these people know him, because I'm sure it's not his charismatic personality drawing them in.

*Why do you care, Getty? He'll be gone shortly and you won't have to worry about it.*

A girl can hope.

"Good night." I shrug my sweatshirt on as I shut the door of the bar behind me and start walking down the streetlight-lined waterfront. My feet and back ache, but I made some great tips tonight, so I'm exhaustedly content.

"Getty?"

I nearly jump out of my shoes at the deep timbre of Zander's voice, and I'm sure I squeal like a little kid, but the jolt of fear overrides any sense of embarrassment. "Jesus!"

"Sorry. I didn't mean to scare you." Leaning with one

shoulder against the streetlight, he steps out of the shadows and into the light once I see him. He has a grocery bag in one hand and his other is shoved in the pocket of his pants. "You heading back to the house?"

"Yep." There's not an ounce of warmth in my voice. Not a trace of welcome. Not a hint that maybe I'd like his company walking me home because sometimes my overactive imagination turns the shadows into scary shit that doesn't exist. I keep my head down, keep moving, not wanting to question why he's standing outside the bar where I work at midnight when he left his table well over two hours ago.

It's not like I was paying attention or anything, though.

"Getty." Where mine lacked warmth, his tone is full of something else. Apology? Remorse? I can't place it, but it's enough to stop me in my tracks so I can turn to face him. I don't say a word, just wait for him to finish his thought. "I know it's late and you're probably tired, but do you want to go sit on the beach and have a beer?" He lifts his hand with the grocery bag, where I can make out the shape of a six-pack.

Bewilderment returns as a glimpse of the man I met last night resurfaces, not the one from this morning. I take stock of my fragile emotions and know I don't want to be the ball in his Ping-Pong match of mood swings. "No, thanks. You made yourself more than clear this morning. I'm happy with keeping my distance." I start to walk again, to gain space, because even though I know I need to keep moving, a small part of me wants to stay and try to figure him out.

"*Hmpf.* Now the socks make sense."

"Huh?" That comment stops me. He's got my attention now. "What are you talking about?"

A flash of a grin. A boyish shrug. "When I was lying in bed last night, I was trying to figure out what was up with your socks. It's not every day you meet a woman wearing nothing but knee-high socks, you know? I thought that style went out in grade school, but I'm a guy, what do I know?"

I crack a smile, kind of liking the fact that when he was

lying in bed last night, he was thinking of me. And then I stop myself. *"No."* Hands on my hips as his eyes narrow at the sternness in my voice. "You don't get to do this. You don't get to be nice like you were to me last night after what an ass you were with me this morning."

My own words throw me, since it sounds so foreign to be standing up for myself when normally I'd slink away without a word.

"An ass?" He makes it sound like I'm being unreasonable.

I twist my lips as I contemplate my terminology. "If you want nicer, we could use the term *grumpy*."

"I *was not* grumpy."

"Yes, you were. What? Do you have something against Sundays or something?"

"Now I do."

His cryptic answers make zero sense and are beginning to get on my last nerve. I'm tired, I'm hungry, and frankly I'd rather waste my energy on someone who deserves it. "You were grumpy. And you're starting to get there again."

"No, I'm not."

"Yes, *you are*." He wants to have a school-yard back-and-forth, I can too.

"No, I'm not. I'm just a moody guy."

"Grumpy, moody, same difference. And you weren't moody last night, so I don't believe you."

He reaches down and the crisp crack of a beer can opening fills the air. "Last night was . . . there were special circumstances."

*Huh?* "How's that?"

"You were *unexpected*." And the way he says it—so matter-of-fact—mixed with the intensity in his eyes causes something to flutter in my stomach. "It's not every night I come face-to-face with a sock-wearing, wand-wielding woman. I mean I'm so traumatized, I need to drink to cope with it."

"I assure you it won't happen again." I bite back the snicker but can't hide the ghost of a smile from my lips.

"Which part—the naked part, the sock part, or the holding-me-at-wand-point part?"

Images flash through my mind. Visuals of his physical perfection accompanied by the pangs of desire I refuse to acknowledge flickering to life. Ones I don't think I ever felt with Ethan. "How about none of them?"

"Good. That's good to know. Since they will no longer appear, then neither will my good mood." He holds a beer up, offering it to me, taunting smirk in place. I just shake my head to decline, but the widening smile on his face and the humor in his eyes slowly win me over.

"Liar," I say playfully, but something flashes across his face and is momentarily lost in the shadow cast by the bill of his hat. He looks out to the ocean and I sense that my comment unintentionally touched a nerve.

"If you want to talk about lying, let's just go there. Why did you come to the island?"

"Why did *you* come here?" It's an immediate knee-jerk reaction on my part: my wont to avoid talking about me. Hide the skeletons that need to remain buried in the closet.

"The Socratic method thing doesn't work for me, Socks."

"And your point is?"

"And yet another question to answer my question?" He lifts his eyebrows.

"I thought you didn't want to do the *wasted-breath bullshit thing.* Weren't those your words?"

"Yet another question?" he says, but when I just stare at him, he bobs his head up and down a little before relenting. "Well, yeah . . . But I was rude, and I waited out here to tell you so, because I owed you an apology."

"Oh." The sound falls from my mouth, my mind taken aback by this change of events. I know mood swings, am used to tempers being flipped on at the flick of a switch, but apologies are not something I'm familiar with. And I can tell that even though he means the words, they still make him uncomfortable. "Ah, and the good mood returns."

He laughs at my persistence. The sheepish look on his face is such a stark contrast to his dark hair shadowed in the streetlight, and I hate that a tiny part of my frozen heart thaws at the sight. Taking me by complete surprise, he grabs my hand and tugs slightly so that I stumble forward to wherever he is leading. And I do stumble. Not because he pulled with such force, but rather because the minute his hand touches mine, I swear it feels like my entire body has been shocked with an electric current.

Normally I'd roll my eyes at someone who made a comment like that, say she's overreacting and playing up the whole I-obsess-over-Regency-romances-so-much-I-have-a-wall-lined-with-bookshelves-to-store-them, but I can't this time. Because this is me. And *it* just happened. That unmistakable zap of chemistry. My neurons catching fire. The stilted hitch of breath in reaction.

And for a split second I think he feels it too. Because with our arms stretched between us, fingers linked, we stand motionless under the glow of the streetlight. Time stops and for that fraction of a second, we see each other in a completely different way. I avert my eyes. Want to shake it off. But when I glance back, there's something in the way he looks at me—interest, intrigue, desire—that tells me I need to sit down and have a beer with him on the beach.

"Maybe just a smidgen of a good mood," he teases; his words break through the sexual tension crackling in the air and bring me back to reality, where chemistry doesn't ignite and touches don't make you want. And yet I want. "C'mon, Getty, let's go sit on the beach, share a beer, and talk about crap that doesn't matter, since we're both intent on keeping our reasons for being here close to the vest."

"You mean you want to bullshit?" I feign shock, since that was the one thing he was insistent that we avoid.

"Mmm-hmm. Exactly that. Bullshit. Too bad it's so cold or I'd go make you jump in the water with me, the proper island welcome, or so I was told by the locals tonight. It could be our way of—"

"Breaking the ice?" I finish for him, and tuck my tongue in my cheek at my lame attempt at humor.

"Ahhh, look at that, the lady has some jokes."

"You better be careful," I say as I realize my feet have started moving without my consent and are following him the short distance toward the sand. "I see a glimpse of the nonmoody Zander again."

"Shit. I guess I need to summon Mander back up."

*"Mander?"*

"Moody Zander. Mander." He raises his eyebrows like he has absolutely no insecurities over his manhood in calling himself that ridiculous moniker.

And I don't know if it's the fact that I'm exhausted from work, that Zander is making me laugh with his silly humor, or that for the first time since I've arrived to Pine-Ridge Island, I don't want to head back to the heavy silence of an empty house, but his comment, his poking fun at himself, causes the guard I've been holding up so high to slip a little.

Laughter I haven't felt or heard in so very long bubbles out and over. Tears fill my eyes. The sound rings around us and melds with the soft crash of the waves on the shore. I hold my hands up as if I'm telling him to stop, but in reality I'm not sure what I'm doing other than making fun of his ludicrousness.

When I come back to myself, Zander is staring at me over the top of his can of beer. "You done yet?"

"Not hardly, *Mander.*"

A lopsided smirk tugs up the corner of his mouth. "You can't make fun of me and then not sit and have a beer with me. Mander rules." He holds a can out to me and after I stare at it and then back at him, I relent.

"I don't really drink—" I stop myself when he gives me puppy dog eyes. "Fine. Just one."

"That's what they all say." He chuckles as I take a seat beside him on a boardwalk bench.

"And then what? They're wooed into telling you all of their deep, dark secrets and fall madly in love with you?"

"Something like that." He nods his head and turns on the charm by flashing me a cocky grin.

"But I thought you were grumpy all the time. Do you get a lot of girls with your moody self?"

"And we're back to that again," he counters, pushing his knee over so that it knocks against mine.

I open my beer and take a timid sip of the bitter ale,

trying to hide my innate dislike of it. And I think I've done a pretty good job of masking the look of disgust on my face, but when I glance over, Zander's head is angled and his eyes are on me.

"You work in a bar but don't like beer? How's that working for you?"

*Ladies don't drink beer, Gertrude. It's classless and tacky.* My father's and Ethan's admonishments ghost through my mind unexpectedly. The chills that blanket my body have nothing to do with the spring storm moving in.

The memory, the constant refrain running through my mind, makes me want to chug this entire beer and wipe my mouth with the back of my hand in defiance. To reaffirm I'm no longer that woman.

"Fine. Good." I take another sip for good measure to try to prove I'm unfazed by the taste I never was allowed the chance to acquire.

"So I take it you were a bartender elsewhere? Before you came to the island?"

"Yes. Yeah." Old habits of grammar die hard, but I try to forget them as I focus on the fib at hand.

"And here come the bullshit lies I warned you about," he says with a chuckle.

"Seriously, I was—"

"No need to explain or lie, Socks. I watched you work for a few hours. You did a fine job. Filled orders quickly. Know how to pull a draft without foam. It's sad to say that I may have spent a bit of time in bars and can tell a greenhorn from a pro, but I can."

"Oh, so now you're a bartending expert?" It's a stupid comeback, but it's my only defense.

"I'm an expert at a lot of things, I assure you that. Most of which are ones I'm not proud of lately." There's a tinge of discord in his voice that makes me want to be the one asking questions, but before I can get them out, he shifts the topic of conversation. "What was so bad in your life that you ran here to escape from it?"

*Hello, curveball.* We went from bartending to invasion of my privacy. His question puts every part of me on edge. And it's not just his question but also the impenetrable stare through the darkness that unnerves me. The one that tells me he knows I am in fact hiding something.

My mind runs a million miles an hour. Did Smitty tell him the details? Did Zander search through my stuff in the house while I was at work and find something? Did my dad or Ethan send him to track me down and bring me back, even though there is nothing left to go back to?

"I'm not running from anything," I state with as much certainty as I can. His expression tells me he's not buying it, so I try to explain without going into detail. "I'm starting a new chapter in my life. It's so different here from where I used to live, and I needed that. A change of pace, I guess. But running, no." I nod my head to put the emphasis on my statement and yet he doesn't look away.

I'm the first to avert my eyes. I need to in order to prevent him from seeing things I don't want him to see. But even when I do, I can still feel the weight of his stare as I look out to the darkness beyond where we sit. To the ocean I can hear but not see.

The crack of a new beer can opening startles me, but I keep my gaze straight ahead, hope that by focusing there, the sting of tears on the backs of my eyelids will abate.

"I'll accept that answer for now, but I've gotta tell you something, Getty—I don't buy it. Sure, all of that might be true in a loose sense, but there's more there."

"You don't know anything about me."

"True. I don't. But I've seen a lot of shit in my life . . . more than you could probably imagine. So phrase it any way you want to, deny it every which way from Sunday, but until you face whatever it is, nothing's going to get fixed."

"You're overstepping boundaries for someone I've known only twenty-four hours." I try to play off the comment like I'm not irritated but can't quite pull it off.

"You're right. *I am.*" His admission is quiet, contrite, and so very unexpected after his dogged assumptions.

Silence descends on us as he lets it go, leaving me to dwell on the truth to his words that I'd like to pretend I didn't hear. Lightning flashes far off the coast, a subtle reminder that I'm actually on an island in the ocean, completely vulnerable.

Kind of like I was before I came here. No wonder when I first stepped foot on the wharf, I felt like I belonged instantly. And maybe, possibly hoped that the small-town atmosphere would mean that I'd be the outsider whom everyone left alone until I figured out if I wanted to stay or move on.

Of course, now that I know I want to stay, he's here. And while it seems he may have his moments of kindness, it doesn't mean I want a roommate. At all. I just want to be left alone in this place I've grown to call home. Where I can paint in private so that no one knows or can scrutinize my art and demean it. Where the last name Caster is like Smith or Jones and doesn't mean anything to anyone.

"What about you?" I ask, assuming the question isn't welcome but indulging my curiosity.

A heavy sigh in response. The sound of aluminum hitting against the edge of the trash bin near us rings out as he throws his empty can into it. Actions to buy him some time on an imaginary clock no one's watching.

"Everybody's running from something, Getty." His words startle me, unexpected honesty that hits home. A part of me wonders if he's telling me this to get me to talk or if he really means it. And as much as I want to ask more, get lost in his troubles instead of my own, I let it go, let us sink into the silence milling around us.

The cool ocean breeze. The warmth of a body next to me. The notion that someone understands when he really has no clue what I'm going through or have been through, but understands in his own way nonetheless. This is new to me. Welcome and unwelcome at the same time.

Because I'm supposed to be figuring myself out. Supposed to be dealing with this all on my own. Determined to prove to myself that I don't need anyone. That I can do this.

"There's a storm rolling in." Zander's quiet murmur beside me breaks the silence. How long have we been sitting here? I've lost track of time, absorbed in my own thoughts.

"I love sitting on the back patio and watching them move across the sea." Listening to the roar of thunder and the pelting sound of the rain. Then after the light show is over, I'll sit in my bedroom with the window cracked so I can smell the distinct scent of the rain.

"Please tell me you don't actually sit on that death trap of a deck?"

My wide eyes meet his raised eyebrows. "*Maybe*. Is it that bad?"

"*Rickety* is a compliment for that hazard."

"And so what, you're a carpenter? You're trading your skills for room and board?" Time to turn the tables on him. Put him in the hot seat for a bit, since I know he's still curious about why I'm here.

The laugh I get in response to my question is cynical at best. "No. Not a carpenter whatsoever. I'm the farthest thing from it."

My mind flashes back to earlier today and the constant pounding of the hammer. On how much time it took to replace the broken step.

"How do you plan on fixing the house up if you don't know what you're doing?"

"The same way you're being a bartender, I suppose," he says with a purse of his lips and a resolute nod of his head. "Figure it out as I go."

"Does Smitty know you're not a carpenter?" I wonder if I'm asking for fuel to add to my argument as to why I should stay and he should go, or because I just want him to keep talking. To help not make the silence seem so lonely tonight.

His laugh in response is genuine and rich and whole-hearted and brings a soft smile to my lips at the sound. "Yeah. I'm pretty positive he knows who and what I am."

"Then why . . . ?" There are so many ways I can end the sentence and yet I'm not sure which one I want an answer to the most: . . . *are you here? . . . are you sitting with me on a bench after apologizing when I never asked you to? . . . are you making me want to tell you things when I don't like to talk to anyone?*

"Because I owe him big-time. He, uh . . . helped me out with a few things. Kept me from getting in trouble in a sense when I didn't deserve his help." He shrugs, eyes trained to the darkness beyond as he absently reaches into the bag and pulls out another can of beer. "I needed a place off the beaten path to go to deal with some shit and he needed someone to repair this place, so we both agreed to help each other."

"A few weeks ago Darcy told me they'd finally decided on which carpenter to hire. I was going to help facilitate—"

"Yeah, they did. Then Smitty found out that he and every other carpenter who works here on the island is booked solid through the end of the year. He wanted to get the repairs going sooner than that so they can flip the house and get it back on the market before next tourist season starts. So . . ." He shrugs with a sheepish smile. "Me."

"And what if you're in over your head?"

He shrugs his shoulders at my comment, a forced smile on his face as if I've just touched a nerve somehow. "We're all in over our heads at some point, aren't we?" he says cryptically before lifting his hat, running his hand through his hair, and putting it back down. And for some reason I don't think he expects a response to his question, so I just remain quiet and study him out of the corner of my eye. "I'll figure it out. Can't be that hard. I promised him I'd get the job done, and I'll get the job done. Prove to him that my word is good again."

"Again? Did something happen that—"

"Boundaries, Getty." His voice is an even warning that I'm pushing him too hard when he backed off from asking me questions. And I know there is more hidden in his words, an underlying meaning I don't understand, and yet, I give him the same respect he did me.

I shift back to neutral ground: the repair issues. "So you just plan on wielding a hammer and winging it?"

"It's better I wield a hammer than a mini-blind wand," he deadpans, and then snickers.

"Touché," I laugh with a roll of my eyes, already knowing it was not one of my prouder moments. "But being a bartender and making a deck so it doesn't crash to the ground when you walk on it are slightly different skill sets. At least I can't kill someone if I mix a drink wrong."

"Oh, I've been killed plenty of times at the hands of a bartender," he says with a chuckle.

"I have a feeling that was your own fault."

"God yes, it was, but damn, the parts I remember were well worth it."

The suggestion in his tone is loud and clear. I hate the creative images that fill my mind of him in a bar: loud music, a slew of women surrounding him hanging on his every word in the hopes that they can get him to buy them a drink. Stake a claim. Even if just for the night.

Because he's that type of guy—by no fault of his own other than the good looks he was born with and that subtle charm that wiggles its way into your resolve not to like him. The type that a woman would gladly accept a one-night stand with, knowing ahead of time the hurt that would come when he'd walk out in the morning wanting nothing more.

Without knowing anything else about him, I already know he'd be *worth the hurt*.

I shake away the thought instantly, seeing as I'm not looking for that from him or from anyone. I've had enough pain to last a lifetime.

And yet images from earlier tonight in the bar flash back in my mind. How even though he had been here less than a day, he already had townspeople approaching him, talking to him, and not treating him like an outsider like they did me for a good few weeks.

"Did I lose you?" Zander's words pull me from my errant train of thought. A train that needs to derail and not fill my head with notions about what exactly he'd be like in any situation.

"No. Yes. Sorry." Why do I feel so rattled?

"Getty?" The way he says my name—part question, part concern—causes that panic to reemerge, because I don't want to turn this discussion back on me.

"It's nothing. What were we talking about?" He narrows his eyes and studies me for a moment. Asking without asking. *Can I help? Do you want to talk about it?* And I don't want to do any more talking right now. It's overrated. *"Don't."*

"Don't what?"

"Just don't, okay? I just want to sit here and drink this

beer that tastes like shit and feel the breeze start to pick up as the storm moves in, and enjoy the silence without being alone. Can you understand that?"

When I finally look over to him, his eyes meet mine with more understanding than I expected. He holds my gaze for a moment before acknowledging my request with a slow and steady nod.

"I can understand that more than you'll ever know."

# Chapter 5

GETTY

Thunder rattles the windows in the early morning. The clouds swirling and tumbling across the horizon block any sunlight.

The weather fits my mood and the mood is reflected on the canvas in front of me. Dark splashes of color rich in hue marble together to reflect a violent sky ready to erupt.

Music plays in my earbuds—a hard beat, a deep bass—and yet I couldn't tell you the lyrics if I tried, because I'm so focused on what's in front of me. I'm so engrossed because with each stroke of my brush, a part of my past leaves me with the movement.

Criticism. Control. Punishments. Expectations. Requirements. And the list goes on from my old life. My monochromatic one.

I dip my brush in a deep blue and slide it across the canvas.

*Your art isn't allowed in this house. It will amount to nothing. Good wives host parties. They have tea and join the Women's League and their job is to make their husbands look better. Not this ridiculous bullshit.*

My thumb smears the blue with the gray. A wash of two colors together. Blending into the background.

*Ethan doesn't mean it, Gertrude. He's a man focused on business and making it a success. He doesn't have time*

*for your female idiosyncrasies. You can't blame him that
you didn't do your job properly. God, how I wish your
mother was still around so she could show you how to be
a proper lady, because regardless of how much schooling
I've paid for, for you, you seem always to fail at it.*

Dark gray right on the center. Harsh strokes. Pressing
the paint into the canvas until it bleeds into its fibers.

*What do you think you were trying to pull tonight,
Gertrude? Do you think I don't know you wanted Fred?
I saw you talking to him. I saw you laugh differently. I
saw you flirt. Do you really think any man would find you
attractive? For Christ's sake, look at you. You're ten
pounds overweight. Your makeup is smeared like a damn
teenager. Do you think anyone else would ever want to
fuck you? It's a chore to make myself hard enough to do
it. You should thank your lucky stars you have me, because no one else would take you. Now get on your knees
and give me a proper apology.*

Tears on my cheeks. Salt on my lips. The storm on the
canvas and on the other side of the window feels nothing
like the one I rage against daily inside me. Dabs of white.
The froth of an angry ocean. The sign of churning turmoil. Of the ocean fighting against the shore.

*Don't walk out that door, Gertrude. That is an order.
I will cut off your trust. Your credit cards. Everything.
This is just a phase. You don't really want to divorce
Ethan. No Caster has EVER been divorced. You just
need to be more compliant and do what he says. If he's
happy, then the company will remain in good standing
and everything will be better. Gertrude. Get back here.
Gertrude!*

I fan black around the edges. Darkness. Sadness. Loss.
All mixed together in an endless cycle.

*The dark of night: my car packed with clothes and me-
mentos of the woman I don't really remember but have
the invisible scars to prove I used to be.*

*The bank manager: I'm sorry but all withdrawals need
to be signed for by both parties on the account. And it
seems to me that your debit card has been canceled as
well. Hmm. How very odd.*

*The pawnshop. My jewelry lining the countertop. Diamonds and emeralds and platinum and rubies. Trinkets of a life I was a part of but really didn't participate in now turned into a means to help me get something of my own.*

*The phone call to Darcy out of the blue. Biting back my pride. Asking for help from my mother's oldest friend, to whom I hadn't spoken in forever. Her offer to stay in a house they had just bought to fix up and resell. On an island off Washington. Was that far enough? The bickering over her refusing to take rent. Her promise of secrecy to keep my whereabouts from everyone. Her admission she'd always hated my father.*

*Driving off the ferry. Stepping foot onto the island. A breath of fresh air. Feeling hope for the first time in as long as I could remember.*

A deep breath. Yellow on the brush. A splash of color. A ray of light in this bleak storm. The sun trying to break through the darkness.

I set the brush down, unsure if the picture is done but knowing I am for now, worn out from the gamut of emotions that sitting with Zander on the bench last night unexpectedly stirred up. I've been here for months. Yes, I've had a few moments of sadness and some nights where the tears didn't stop, but at the same time I know I'm in a better place now. I can acknowledge that I'm slowly crawling out from under that veil of criticism that weighed so heavily I actually believed it.

How weak of a person could I have been to put up with it? Year after year. Criticism after criticism. Apology after apology. To not have walked away? To still believe his words hold some merit?

The tears slide silently down my cheeks. Fat odes to a past I'll never go back to. To a place I'll never allow my self-esteem to accept again. To a life of pretenses where people judge a book by its cover and believe a wife's continued apologies and excuses for things that were never her fault to begin with.

The music continues in my earbuds, a melancholy song about lost love, and a part of me wishes I could experience that grief. A deep sadness over leaving the person you know is your soul mate, the other half to make you whole. Because I had none of that, felt none of that. I was nothing to Ethan but a voodoo doll to manipulate as he saw fit. I was nothing to my father but a pawn in his business maneuvers—a means to keep his acquisitions in good standing.

Time has given me that clarity. Distance has allowed me to realize that the only love I lost was for myself.

And yet it's still a battle to move forward, to forget, and to find worth in myself.

A movement out of the corner of my eye scares the shit out of me. When I startle, my knee hits the tray in front of me and causes supplies to fall to the ground with a clatter.

"Jesus!" I bark out as I rip the earbuds from my ears. My pulse spikes erratically and my heart pounds as if it's been jump-started in my chest.

Zander holds his hands up in an *I'm sorry* motion as he moves into the room. "I knocked," he says, motioning to my earbuds and then back to the door, "but you didn't answer."

"And you invited yourself in?" I move out of the alcove and into the bedroom. My voice comes out less than friendly, which I won't apologize for, since he's the one invading my personal space. My gaze instantly flickers to the myriad of things around the room that are mine and private: the prescription for sleeping pills on the nightstand, my bra hanging haphazardly over the back of the chair, a mess of clothes still inside out near the vicinity of the hamper, the stack of designer clothes the local consignment shop has listed on eBay to sell for me to help make ends meet, the canvases stacked one upon another leaning against the wall.

*Oh God. My paintings.*

Before the thought even really computes, Zander is moving toward them with the strangest look on his face.

"No," I gasp. The thought of him seeing my work has paralyzed me. Caused panic to tickle the back of my neck and bring a tsunami of insecurities and fears of criticism.

Silence settles as he moves from painting to painting. Then the rumble of thunder from outside. My mind wills my feet to move, to protect my most intimate feelings that are splashed across a canvas, but I'm frozen. Ethan and my father may have criticized my scribbles in charcoal, chastised me for an occasional mention of how I'd like to paint too, but no one has ever seen what I've started in this new medium.

"Getty." His voice is soft, full of something I can't quite place, and all I know is the lump in my throat feels like it's the size of a baseball, because I'm having trouble swallowing over it. "These are . . ."

"No. Please . . . just . . . Zander . . ."

"Incredible."

*It's awe.* The sound in his voice is awe.

I watch him in my disbelief. The chance to sit back and let someone finally see my art proves stronger than my innate need for privacy.

He rifles through the paintings stacked five and six deep against the walls. His fingers skim over my feelings. Streaks of blue and gray and black and blends of shading and different textures. Anger. Insecurity. Sadness. Loneliness. Longing. It's as if his fingertips touching each one are acknowledging the validity of the emotions I've expressed on canvas. Telling me they are okay to feel when for so long I've been told I was being dramatic, that I needed to bite my tongue and do what a good little wife does.

He goes one by one through the artwork. Head down, concentration etched in the lines of his face, eyes focused. And then he moves to today's painting still on the easel; the one I'm still not sure is completed.

The emotions are still fresh in my mind, still tacky to the touch on the canvas. I feel exposed although I'm the only one who knows what has gone into the picture, the meaning behind it, the years of distress leading up to it. The hope created when I escaped from it. Zander stares at it for a moment, the pelt of rain on the window the only backdrop noise.

When he lifts his head and meets my eyes, the breath I didn't realize I was holding burns in my lungs. "I don't know shit about art, Getty, but these paintings, those sketches . . ." He shakes his head as if he's seeing me in a whole new light and for a split second I worry he sees my weakness. My inadequacies. Everything I hide and everything I wish I was. "They're unbelievable. It sounds lame, but it's almost like you can *feel* them."

I don't know what I expected to hear, but his description pulls at every part of me that still needed an ounce of validity. "Thank you." My voice is soft, uneven, and now that he's seen them, I don't know what to do. I feel ten times more naked than I did the other night. Vulnerable. Like I want to kick him out of my inner sanctum and keep him here to hear him tell me more at the same time.

"Where's your next showing at?"

My brow furrows and eyes narrow as I try to compute what he's asking me. "What do you mean?"

"Like I said, I don't know much about this kind of thing, but it looks like you're gearing up for an art show." He motions to the canvases lining the walls of the alcove. "So I was asking when it is. I mean, it all makes sense now."

"You lost me." I'm still recovering from someone seeing my paintings and the unexpected praise, let alone trying to follow him. "What makes sense?"

"You renting the house. Getting ready for the show here and then moving to the next place, for the next one."

My laugh is long and rich with a tinge of nerves lacing its edges. "There is no show. I'm not moving on." He angles his head and stares at me. "They're not for sale, Zander."

It's his turn to look at me funny, like he doesn't understand. "Why not?"

I'm not going to lie and say the confusion in his voice over my answer—like I'm crazy—doesn't give a boost to my ego.

"Because I paint for me." Silence fills the room as my words settle on him. The storm outside even seems like it stops to emphasize my statement.

"And your point is?"

The intensity in his eyes—dark blue sparks of color searching out mine across the room—and the demand in his tone knock me off-kilter. Transport me back to that person I left behind and never want to be again. On the spot. Body flushed with heat. An apology quick on my tongue even though I have nothing to apologize for. God-damn triggers.

Old habits die hard.

*C'mon, Getty. Get your shit together. He's not Ethan. He's just asking a valid question.*

Working a swallow down my throat, I shift my feet and look out to the stormy sea—my happy place—to calm my nerves jittering out of control. I try to explain. "Is there anything you have in your life that you're passionate about? A thing you do or place you go where you can get lost in yourself or . . . never mind." I shake my head. Suddenly embarrassed that I sound as stupid as I feel.

"No, I want to hear what you have to say," he says, which causes me to turn and look back to him. He takes a few steps toward me, genuine interest on his face, not the smarmy smirk I'm used to so that I can be mocked when I finish explaining.

"It's stupid really. Probably makes sense only to me."

"No." He takes another step closer.

I can smell his cologne, or maybe it's the scent of soap—it's clean—and I open my mouth to argue, but nothing comes out more than a meek, "No?"

Another slow, intentional step. If I put my arm out, my hand would be in the middle of his chest. Close. Too close—in so many ways.

"No," he answers resolutely. "I get it. More than you know. It's your escape. Your way to deal with shit."

Nothing like a guy to put it in plain speak and have it make perfect sense. "Yeah. Something like that."

"If you sell them, it doesn't make them any less yours . . . doesn't stop the feeling you get when you paint. It just means you get to do something you love and make money from it."

His points are valid and yet I still see my heart and soul cut open and on display for anyone to scrutinize, so while the thought is a good one, it's not going to happen. "Hmm." That and a shrug are all I give him in response, because it's food for thought but probably not something I'm ever going to take a bite out of.

"You just need to—"

*"Boundaries,"* I warn, needing him to know he's treading on shaky ground that I don't want to be treading on. The emotions of the morning have abraded my psyche and I don't want to be pushed any further. I've already shown him too much of myself as it is.

He nods his head, a silent acknowledgment that he's heard me. All I can do is hope he's going to keep on his side of the line.

"You're talented, Getty. There's no doubt about that."

I look away from him, the room suddenly in shadow as the clouds shift outside, and his next step toward me blocks the glow of light from the lamp. The room feels way too small, way too intimate without the harshness of the desk light.

"It's too personal," I whisper, giving him the only explanation I will give. Not expecting him to understand . . . but almost needing him to.

"That's obvious," he says, eyebrows drawing together, head angling to the side to study me. "But no one is going to see the same thing you see. Everyone's churning ocean is fueled by a different type of storm."

He shifts his feet, his body now closer; our eyes don't waver from each other's. "What's your storm?" The question is out before I can stop it, my own curiosity piqued.

Our proximity allows me to see the pang of hurt flash through his eyes, the sudden halt in his movements. The recovery comes quickly but not fast enough to hide that whatever he's running from affects him deeply.

"My storm?" he chuckles, self-deprecation in his tone and a look in his eyes he doesn't give me a chance to read. "I don't think it's ever really stopped churning, but there's definitely been a few surprise white squalls thrown in."

"Is that why you've come here? To escape it?" I push for answers, no longer wanting to feel like I'm the only one exposed, and curious to know more about this man before me.

"A white squall," he murmurs. And it's all there sitting in the depth of his eyes—the hurt, the indecision, the regret over whatever has happened to cause him to be here right now—and yet it's also so very well protected that I'm not sure what else to say. "You've been crying."

I blanch, hating that he has noticed, and at the same time, I pick up on the sudden change of topic. I'm immediately wiping my fingers under my eyes and trying to hide the evidence, although I'm not sure how much good it will do.

"I'm fine," I say, my voice infused with much more certainty than I feel. "It was just the song I was listening to. It was sad."

*Jesus, Getty, couldn't you think of a better lie?*

"Uh-huh." He takes another step forward. The simple sound almost an unspoken warning not to lie to him again. "Just the song," he murmurs with a nod as he reaches out, hand to the side of my jaw, thumb brushing over the line of my cheek.

That jolt I felt last night? That was nothing compared with the start and stop of my heart at the feel of his hand on my face. Skin to skin.

My lips fall lax. The sharp intake of my breath is audible in the silence. And I hate that I suddenly feel like I don't have a single clear thought in my mind, let alone an intelligent one.

"You've got paint," he says, mint on his breath, as he leans in to get a better view through the dimly lit room, "right here." And yet after his thumb rubs at the smudge, he doesn't remove his hand. He just keeps it there, our faces close, our eyes questioning so many things. Time slows.

"Thanks," I finally whisper, tongue darting out to wet my lips as I try to draw in a steady breath.

"And I'm smart enough to know it was more than just *the song.*" His words hit my ears, the deep timbre of his tone a soothing rebuke in a sense, because he is actually listening to me, really hearing me when I'm so unaccustomed to any man in my life caring above and beyond the surface.

Words. Thoughts. Confessions. The look in his eyes and the comfort of his touch cause my head to whirl, make me want to let him in, and use his shoulder for comfort when this isn't even really an option I'll afford myself.

Compassion from a man isn't something I'm used to, especially when it's directed at me.

Thunder rumbles. We both jump at the sound, the moment instantly broken. The gasp from my lips gets drowned out. Zander steps back with a startled shake of his head before turning his back to me as he walks toward the window, shoving his hand through his hair, a sigh filling the space.

"Fucking squalls," he murmurs as he hangs his head for a moment, the words weighing heavy in the room as I stand there trying to figure out what just happened. He turns and looks at me for a moment, eyes sincere, but the words don't make any sense. "I'm sorry . . . I just can't."

And with that, he strides from the room, leaving me with nothing more to look at than an empty doorway.

*What the hell just happened?*

I move to the edge of my bed, sit down, and try to sift through the myriad of emotions I didn't expect to feel around him: hurt, rejection, confusion, dejection. And I hate that I feel any of these from a moment that never should have happened with a man that shouldn't even be here in the first place.

He *just can't* what? Talk to me? Be in the same room as me? Be in the same house?

Kiss me?

*Oh my God, Getty, can you be any more ridiculous?* The thought flickers and fades away instantly, my stupidity at an all-time high. I really have lost my mind, the emotions of the morning running rampant and killing my brain cells. Whom am I kidding thinking stuff like this? A guy who looks like he does would most definitely not be into a woman who looks like me. Never.

Ethan's words come back to me now. *Disgusting. Overweight. Pathetic. Useless. Ugly.* They flicker through my mind and poke holes in the confidence I've slowly built from nothing.

And to think I had a moment when I wanted to let Zander in. A break in my resolve when I thought perhaps it might be a little easier to share a part of me with someone, because if we're both running from something, then that means maybe he just might be a little more understanding.

Jesus. Did I really think that was going to happen? Making myself vulnerable to someone else before I've even figured myself out was a stupid move. Shows I haven't come very far yet in this mile I'm traveling one inch at a time.

*Don't trust anyone. Trust is a false pretense. Something that's never really real.*

Well, luckily he came to his senses before I made that colossal mistake. Bolted before I unfolded my complex past like an origami bird and asked him to help me try to fold the same piece of paper back into a different shape.

I cover my face with my forearm and just listen to the storm rage on outside and take stock, try to disregard the hurt over the fact that obviously I did something wrong, that he saw my most intimate of emotions splashed over the canvas, and even though he praised me, he still rejected me.

*Stop it, Getty. Stop blaming yourself. Maybe it was him. You did nothing wrong but be you—well, the new you—so maybe it was his own issues that caused him to abruptly leave.*

I suck in a deep breath and fight through my doubt. Shed the pathetic part of me that wants to blame myself for whatever reason is behind why he walked out. Acknowledge that this is why I need to steer clear of anything and anyone until I've had enough time to deal with my past, forget the old me, heal from her scars, and fully embrace the now.

Realize that I need no one and nobody. That I can exist, live, thrive, all on my own.

They say loneliness adds beauty to life.

I guess I'm getting a whole new makeover.

# Chapter 6

"One of these days, Getty, you're going to realize that you're a local now and you're going to have to step on the other side of the counter, grab a drink of your own, and watch the game with the rest of us."

I lift the rag in my hand to acknowledge Liam's comment, which comes at least once a shift. I know he's just being sweet and that I'm not really a local yet. Besides, any free time I have, I like to explore the island or lock myself away with my paints so I can learn more.

But the idea of having a beer and relaxing with the game and a crowd of people sounds more than welcome right now. I definitely need it after my conversation today, the bad news it brought, and the pang of loneliness I feel from it.

A cheer goes up across the tables, causing me to look up. The bar hums with the buzz of an excited crowd—there's a tense game plus the sun is shining for the first time all week. Add to that an influx of tourists fresh off the ferry and the Lazy Dog is crowded, loud, and keeping me on my toes this afternoon with orders.

"An Arrogant Bastard, please."

I know who it is the minute I hear the request; somehow my body is attuned to him even when I don't want it to be. I don't look up, don't acknowledge him. Rage and irritation and everything within that range fire anew as I think about the phone call I had earlier with Darcy where I found out the bullshit he's pulled.

No wonder he's been MIA since the other morning when he left my bedroom.

"Well, that's a self-diagnosing order if I've ever heard one," I say under my breath, but even with my eyes focused on keeping the foam minimal on the pour, I can see his body jolt. *Good.* He heard me.

"Did I do something wrong?" he asks pensively, his body leaning over the bar some, so that I get that quick whiff of soap and cologne that now haunts the halls of the house after he takes a shower.

My laugh is long and low, the sound of sarcasm poured over ice. "Take your pick." I slide his glass across the varnished bar top and finally meet his gaze. My eyebrows are arched and my lips are twisted as I'm sure my defiant derision is reflected in my eyes.

The noise of the bar fades into the background—a groan over a bad call, a good-natured shout for a waitress—and yet his eyes hold mine in a war of wills: his asking what I'm pissed at and mine telling him he should already know. I find myself leaning in closer at the same time he does, waiting for him to fess up to his lies, but I'm greeted with a slow, lazy smirk that spreads across his mouth until it turns into a full-blown arrogant grin.

"You're speaking female, Socks. Can you please—"

"*Darcy.* There's a word for you." I lean my hips against the counter behind me.

"Technically, that's a name, but . . ." He chuckles over the rim of his glass.

"Don't act like you don't know what I'm talking about."

"I'm assuming you've spoken to her, then."

"What the fuck, Zander?" His eyes widen at my use of the word. I can hear my father's reprimand in my head. "I never agreed to staying in the house with you. To being roommates."

*Especially after the other morning in my room when you did whatever you did.*

"If you're worried about me seeing you naked, we've

already done that part, so it's not a big deal." He tips his glass to me, his smile unwavering.

Every word he speaks makes me angrier. "That's not the point!" I raise my voice in exasperation.

"Then what is?"

"I don't like you." *There. I said it.* But it's a huge fat lie and I'm afraid he can see right through it.

"Yes, you do, Getty. You don't drink beer on the beach with someone you don't like."

I glare at him, hating his reasoning. "Well, I don't like beer either, so . . ."

"You lost me. You don't like beer; therefore you don't like me?" The amusement in his voice for calling my rationality on the carpet makes me frustrated. Irritable. Bitter.

"Why would you tell Darcy that I agreed to—"

"Excuse me?" The voice to his left catches me off guard and prevents the verbal barb of rebuke from firing off my tongue. "Are you Zander Donavan? You are, aren't you?" The questions are followed by a nervous chuckle and a flush of cheeks and both have definitely caught my attention.

The orders waiting to be filled are forgotten as this gentleman piques my curiosity. *Who the hell is Zander Donavan?*

Zander's eyes stay locked on mine momentarily; a flicker of irritation at being interrupted fleets through them, telling me this conversation is far from over, before he turns toward the middle-aged man beside him.

The smile that was an arrogant taunt to me slowly transforms into a self-assured one, slow and steady, as he nods his head and reaches his hand out to the man. "Yes, I am," he says quietly. "Nice to meet you. And you are?"

"Oh man, this is so cool," the guy says, eyes wide and movements jerky as he shifts his stance and sticks his hand out. "Glen. Glen's my name."

"Nice to meet you, Glen," Zander says with a nod, eyes remaining on the man and smile still on his face, but there is a different feel here. Almost like he has a front up, on display, and I can't take my eyes off him or stop trying to figure out what I'm in the dark on.

"I didn't mean to interrupt, but I told my wife it was you, and she bet me I wouldn't come over here and find out. . . . Man, this is so exciting!" He rubs his hands together. When I look back to Zander, I can tell he's completely comfortable with strangers approaching him.

"Getty." Liam's deep baritone calls through the loud chaos of the bar and as much as I don't want to care about this mystery man who has waltzed into my life and seems to be here to stay for a while, I do want to know.

Struggling between curiosity and duty, I take a fortifying breath and nod my head to my boss, let him know I'm on the orders stacking up. Reluctantly I step away from my position that was perfect for eavesdropping, but not before I hear Glen say, "I'm sorry about losing your ride."

Those words repeat in my head during the rest of my shift. The bar only gets busier, so any spare moment I have is spent stretching my back or running to the bathroom, although I'd like to be asking Zander for an explanation.

I watch him, though. Sitting on the other side of the bar, surrounded by fellow patrons and to my dismay a few females. And it's not like it's because I care or anything, because I don't. Definitely not. It's just because I want answers I can't get while he's busy flirting aimlessly with women he'll probably never even see again.

His laugh floats across the bar and it's like the breeze fanning the fire of my irritation with him. I have no right to be annoyed except for what he told Darcy, and yet with each passing minute he's over there laughing and having fun, it increases.

I finish the next set of orders, realize that the end of that hour Liam mentioned to me is coming up. My eyes flicker back to Zander. To his dark hair curling up at the neck of his shirt and to how his fingers trail up and down the lines of condensation on his glass. Or that easygoing smile that says he doesn't have a care in the world although obviously he does or he wouldn't be here running from turbulent storms and white squalls.

"Why don't you pull yourself a pint and get off your

feet for a bit? Sit with the locals and watch the last few innings."

I look over to Liam, who's wiping his hands on a rag with that look in his eye that says there is no arguing with him. "Tell me something. You ever heard of the name Zander Donavan before?"

He gives me a slow and steady nod as his eyes narrow in thought. "A race car driver. Indy, I think. Pretty damn good from what I recall. Popular too. I seem to remember overhearing something on *SportsCenter*," he says, motioning to the televisions that blanket the bar, "that he left midseason with some controversy—"

"Liam!" His name is shouted from the other end of the counter and he holds up a finger to tell one of the regulars it will be just a minute.

"Is that . . . ?" Liam says, all of a sudden the dots connecting for him as he looks across the bar to where Zander is seated. He stares, lips parted, as recognition makes it hard for him to find the words to speak. "Holy shit, it is him. Well, what do you know? In my bar of all places too."

"Lucky us," I mutter under my breath with a hint of sarcasm that apparently only I can hear, because by the look on Liam's face he is more than thrilled to have Zander here.

*Great.* Now the man is invading this space of mine too.

"That definitely can't be bad for business. Him coming in here when you're on shift."

*"What?"* How is he even aware we know each other?

"Small-town life," he answers for me. "Everyone knows the two of you are living together up in the place on Canary. I knew he looked familiar, but couldn't place him. Just figured he looked like someone I knew." He shakes his head and looks over to where Zander is speaking to four guys who have stopped at his table to talk. I thought they were just patrons being friendly, but now the constant revolving door at his table makes so much more sense; they are fans who recognize Zander.

Beside me, Liam clucks his tongue and draws my attention back to him. The concentration on his face tells me he's trying to figure a way to market Zander's presence, and I hate the idea instantly. There's no need for him to be more in my space than he already is. "Lucky for me you're the one working here, since he seems only to have eyes for you. Hot damn!"

I roll my eyes, the rebuff on my tongue when his words really hit my ears. *Only has eyes for me?* Is he joking? When I glance over to my boss, he's dead serious. And now I'm the one having trouble forming words.

"Oh no. We're not together. I mean it was a mistake—"

"Your shift's over, Getty," he says with a knowing smile, saving me from my flustered response. "Go grab a glass of the poison of your choice. Enjoy the full house while I sort your tips out."

"Thanks." He retreats to the other end of the bar while I'm left trying to figure out what just happened.

It's the hum of the bar that I love, just not the people who make the sound. But I'm not caring whatsoever, because the Tom Collins in my hand is empty and my head is slightly fuzzy. Definitely one good thing about never being allowed to drink: You get buzzed off your first one.

And luckily tucked in the corner on the side of the bar like a hermit, I get to keep mostly to myself and enjoy the atmosphere but not really be a part of it.

"We never got to finish our conversation." I don't know why Zander's voice is akin to nails over chalkboard to me—possibly because I've been sitting here stewing about him and how much I don't want to be—but the minute he slides into the booth beside me, I jump. Without a single word, I rise from my seat, walk behind the bar and through the door to the back room that serves as a quasi break room and a storage area.

"What's your problem?" His voice is too close behind me—obviously he's following me when he's not allowed back here.

For some reason I don't take him as one who follows rules.

"I just want to get away from you." I turn around to face

him, realizing all of a sudden how small this room feels with him occupying it. "I told you, I don't like you."

*And why is that, Getty? Because he makes that fluttery feeling happen in your stomach? He only has eyes for you. Because you don't want to think about him or care about his white squalls and yet you do?*

I shake the thoughts from my head, my own little devil and angel warring within me. It's the last thing I need when I have a fight right in front of me that needs my attention.

"You're obviously angry at me for something. An argument goes a little smoother when both people know what the fight's about. . . ." He lifts his eyebrows and all I see is a taunt instead of a question.

"Shall we start with the word again? *Darcy.*"

"You mean *name.*"

"This is exactly why I don't like you. You're frustrating and arrogant and you think you can waltz back here, tell me what is going to happen, how to fight, what to do, after you don't even have the courtesy of telling me who you are." My words fall out in a tirade that makes no sense even to me. Why am I hurt, though? Is it because he didn't trust me enough to tell me?

And neither did Darcy, her nonresponse flickering through my mind: "That's for him to tell you. Just as your story is for you to tell him, if you want."

*It's not like you've told him anything either.*

"Does it matter who I am?" His shoulders square as he takes a step closer, hands at his side, eyes searching mine for the truths behind my words.

"No. Yes. Damn." *Brilliant.*

"That's a great answer. Very decisive." The smirk is back. So is the seductive scent of his cologne.

"Quit mocking me." I fight against the urge to walk out and leave this argument behind, uncomplicate things that are already so damn complicated.

"Does it matter who I am? What my job is?" I can sense he cares about my answer for some reason.

"No. Of course not. But you could have at least told me."

"It doesn't change anything, Getty, other than now

you can go search on the Internet about me, about my past, and read shit that may or may not be true. Is that what you want? Because I have a feeling there is a helluva lot more you want to say, so have at me."

"Oh." It's my only response, and our eyes lock. The prospect of looking him up never really even crossed my mind. But now of course that he's mentioned it . . . the idea will nag at me. And in that instant I think of myself, how upset I'd be if someone told him who I really was and how vulnerable and betrayed I'd feel. And then I wonder if that's his whole game plan here: make me feel bad so that I walk away from this argument feeling sorry for him. I don't think he has any clue that I've spent so many years being the wallflower in the corner, taking the blame, not fighting back, and I just can't do that right now.

Silence fills the space between us. Part of me wants to ask more and the other half that doesn't want to give more becomes a conundrum all in itself. The quid pro quo that I won't let happen. So instead I focus on him being in my space, in my house, in my life, when he shouldn't be. When I don't want him to be.

And yet he's still here, still waiting for my answer, still taunting me by his mere presence. A constant reminder of everything I don't want, can't have in my life, don't have the luxury to even consider.

"So can you tell me what my driving a race car for a living and Darcy have in common?" His voice pulls me from my thoughts, brings me back to him standing a few feet in front of me. "Are those what caused that huge chip on your shoulder to weigh you down so much you're being irrational and picking a fight with me for no apparent reason?"

"No reason? Are you crazy?" The smirk he gives me in return goads my temper and at the same time tells me I am giving him just what he wants: a fight. And yet I can't stop myself. I welcome it. "You called Darcy and told her that I agreed to be roommates with you."

"And?" He says it like he doesn't have a care in the world.

"And?" I screech. "I didn't say that. I didn't even think

that. How dare you tell her that I was willing to live with you when that's the farthest thing from my mind?"

"You'll come around."

"I'll what?" Each time I respond, the pitch of my voice rises. Each time he responds, I want to strangle him.

"You heard me," he says with a shrug as he takes a step forward, prompting me to take one back because right now I despise him with every part of my being.

"You're an *asshole*."

A lightning-quick grin flashes over his lips. "If you want to insult me, Socks, you better think of something better than that, because that's not an insult when it's a well-known fact."

All I can do is shake my head and tell myself this isn't worth it. There's no use trying to reason with someone who's being unreasonable, and he's taking the cake in that category. Drawing in a fortifying breath, I close my eyes for a moment; it's probably best for the both of us if I leave right now before things are said that shouldn't be said.

"Forget I said anything."

His hand is on my arm the moment I try to step around him. I should have expected it, should have prepped myself for it, but I didn't. I was too wrapped up in my emotions and my temper to steel my reaction. Biting back the startled yelp I want to emit, I yank my arm back as memories flicker and fade in my mind.

*Breathe, Getty. This isn't home. He isn't Ethan. It's okay.*

He looks at me, head to the side, eyes narrowed, as he releases my arm, but the question over my reaction is in his eyes. I do the only thing I can, lift my chin up in defiance and show him and myself that I'm not intimidated by him.

"Spill it, Getty. Let's finish this here and now. Get it over with. Why else are you mad? You want to throw the whole kitchen sink in? There's one right over there—I can try to yank it out for you, and add it in if you want." Sarcasm is thick in his voice and yet there is an underlying strain there as well that I can't quite figure out.

Let's face it, I can't figure anything out about him other than one minute he's nice and the next minute he's annoying. And that damn cologne of his. It's just frustrating that it's everywhere.

"Talk. Get it out," he taunts as he steps in to me.

I don't want to go here, don't want to sound like a whiny woman, like I'm the emotional wreck that I really am, so I reach deep down and make sure my voice is strong and steady when I speak. "The other morning, in my room . . . what was that all about?"

*You hurt my feelings.* My eyes say it, but my mouth remains silent.

"Ahhh. *That,*" he says with a purse of his lips and a stoic expression.

"Yeah, *that.* See? *Asshole.*"

"That was on me, Getty. Not on you." He blows out a sigh as he breaks eye contact and moves around the small space. And even though he's spoken the words, I'm not sure I truly believe them, because in the few seconds since he's answered me, his posture has changed, just like it did the other day. Defensive. Pensive.

"Look, I've lived with one man who had a temper and moods that flicked on and off." His movement falters from my words and he turns to look at me again. I swear the atmosphere of the room shifts instantly—tension and curiosity thick in the air around us. I know I'm telling him more than I want to, but he has to understand. "I can't live in that unpredictability again and you just forced me to with that phone call to Darcy."

"And the other morning I was unpredictable, and that, what . . . ?"

"It pissed me off. Made me feel like I did something wrong when I know I didn't. So do you mind explaining to me what the hell happened? Why you went from nice to asshole in a split second?"

"I warned you I was moody." It's the only explanation he gives, but I don't buy it.

"And I told you I've seen nice. That was a huge glimpse of it. What made you turn into a jerk? Why'd you walk out of the room, Zander?"

"Jesus Christ," he says as he moves across the room again, hands running through his hair, and teeth chewing his bottom lip. "I walked out because I promised myself I'd come here, straighten out the shit I've made a mess of lately until I could right all the wrongs. It's complicated and all I want is for life to be simple again. Black-and-white."

"But what does that have to do with *me*?"

He laughs softly, lines suddenly etched in the set of his mouth as he contemplates his response. "Because you complicate my plan."

"I do?"

"Yes." He shoves his hand through his hair again and steps up to where I stand. "Fuck yes, you do."

"You're making absolutely no sense. You don't even know me. What am I to you?" I throw my hands up, exasperated at the language gap between male and female.

"Absolutely nothing."

"Screw you." Hurt rifles through me. He's perfectly accurate and just made the point I was making myself, and yet hearing him say it with disassociation in his tone and indifference in his body language stings. My own insecurities rear their ugly head again as everything becomes crystal clear to me.

"Exactly." He chuckles a low and self-deprecating laugh and I'm so lost in my own confusion that I don't really hear it, comprehend what he's saying, because I'm already trying to piece together my next words.

"You've lost me, Zander. You can't have it both ways. You can't tell Darcy I'm roommate material because obviously you have zero interest in me—shit, just by watching you tonight with all of the women hanging on your every word, I know I'm definitely not your type—and then at the same time be mad I'm here because I complicate things. So sorry my presence makes it harder for you to bring your just-for-the-nights back to the house when I'm there and the walls are paper-thin and you know you can't have sex on the kitchen counter because I might walk in on you. You poor, deprived baby."

I'm out of breath, and anger and rejection are roaring

through my blood as he stares at me, eyes wide, lips lax, head shaking slowly back and forth as he digests what I've just said. As he realizes I'm an intelligent woman who has his entire game figured out.

"You're certifiable, you know that?" He takes a step toward me, a smile slowly spreading across his lips. And I hate that he's mocking me, despise that he's secretly laughing at me. "That's a great scenario you've conjured up in that female mind of yours, but I hate to tell you, you're way off base."

"Really? I'm off base? Why'd you tell Darcy you want to live with me?" My hands are on my hips; my tone demands a no-bullshit answer.

"Because I want to."

It's my turn to laugh and roll my eyes. I don't know what kind of game he's playing, but I'm over it. Over him and his back-and-forth and making no sense. "You *want* to and yet *I* complicate things."

"Yep." He nods slowly.

"That's all you're going to give me?"

That chuckle again. The one that tells me there is so much more behind it than humor and yet I wish I understood why.

"No. Yes. *Fuck*." He scrubs a hand over his face and for once I notice he seems uncomfortable and unsure of himself.

"That's very decisive," I mock.

"*You* complicate things, Getty," he murmurs as he steps into my personal space so that I can clearly see the look in his eyes even in the dimly lit room. And this time when our eyes meet, the amusement has been replaced with an intensity that I didn't expect. "Because there is something about you that continually reminds me why I came here. I don't know why you're here and you don't know why I'm here . . . and yet for some reason every time I look at you, I know I need to stay when all I want to do is run again."

His explanation blindsides me. The intensity in his eyes now makes perfect sense. I expected some smart-ass answer, some flippant response to skirt the issue and make the situation go away, and yet he did the exact opposite. And now I don't know how to respond.

"The other morning," he continues before I can speak, the tension back in his shoulders, "it wasn't you or your pictures or, *fuck* . . . Never mind." He lifts a hand to the back of his neck and pulls down on it as he tilts his head to the ceiling. His audible exhalation fills the room.

"No. Don't *never mind* me. Make me understand."

He slowly brings his chin back down as he takes a step closer to me. "You really want to know why I walked out the other morning?"

His close proximity and the look in his eyes make it difficult for me to think clearly. "Yes." I can barely hear my own voice.

"This," he says as he reaches out and puts a hand on the back of my neck. Alarm bells sound in my head and all I can think about is how I want to be running into the fire it's warning of right now, instead of racing to safety. I can feel his breath on my lips, feel the intention in his touch. "I. Wanted. To. Do. This."

Within a breath, Zander's lips are on mine. My head reels as the rush hits me. Heat and warmth and hunger and desire drown me in its libidinous haze as my startled gasp parts my lips, allowing him to slip his tongue between them to dance with mine. He tastes like beer and mint and lust all in one and my head is swimming and heart is pumping and *holy shit*, he's kissing me. Tempting me. Awakening me.

It takes me a second to clear the shock from my mind, because I'm stunned motionless, understandably, but when one of his hands moves to hold my jaw still and the other to cup the back of my head, reality hits. His groan fills my ears, low and throaty, and the sound spurs me on. Tells me this is real. My fingers are timid against his chest. My lips move with his, tongue teasing and skin burning for more of his touch. My body switching gears from angered frustration to unexpected desire.

And you'd think that after being with Ethan for so many years, I'd have to remind myself that Zander isn't him, but there's no need for that. No way. Because in the few seconds since Zander's lips have slanted over mine, there's been more heat, more want, than Ethan ever made me feel.

It's possibly due to the fact that he's forbidden. That I know having a man in my life is out of the picture right now. A *complication* I don't need. But hell if forbidden doesn't taste so damn good.

And just as I start to sink into the kiss, a moan on my lips, he abruptly pushes away from me with a measured mixture of aggression and regret.

"Goddammit!" he swears as he scrunches his eyes tight while I'm left with my lips swollen and all the parts of my body still tingling from his kiss. "I was fucking right," he mutters more to himself than to me as he starts to move again, pace the small confines of the room, an uncharacteristic nervous energy about him.

And I don't know what to do. Whether I should go, slip out while he does whatever he's doing, or stay here and silently attempt to recover from what just happened. I choose to stay put because my knees are too wobbly to walk just yet.

"This is all your fault, you know," he growls, pointing a finger at me.

"Mine?" I laugh, nerves tingeing the edges.

"Yes." Definitely no indecision in that answer. "I wanted to kiss you that morning. Stood there staring at your lips and wanted to know what you tasted like. Suspected that once I did, I'd only want more. But I'm an asshole, Getty. Moody. Selfish. Have screwed up a lot of things lately and the last thing I want to do is fuck you up, because *you* . . . there's something about you that in the short time I've known you gets under my skin when I don't want it to. Makes me wonder why you're here and what you're running from, when usually the only person I give a flying fuck about is myself. So yeah . . . I wanted to kiss you but also wanted to stay true to my word and why I came here. I can't do both. And so . . . *fuck*."

I jump when his foot connects with the trash can and it slams against the metal cabinet behind it. But the sound does nothing to my pulse, because it's already racing out of control from his startling admission. Luckily there is a shelf behind me, because I sag against it for support, my senses completely overwhelmed.

His words run in a loop in my mind as I watch him pace in frustration, anger emanating off him and slamming into me. I should be upset, feel rejected like I did the other day when he waltzed out, but it's kind of hard to feel that way when someone has just told you what he told me with his taste still on my tongue.

"Complicated," he murmurs along with something else I can't hear over a cheer in the bar that seeps through the door at his back.

"Zander." So many things I want to tell him. So much meaning in my single utterance of his name. *It's okay—I don't want to want you either. I get everything you're saying about why you came here. I can't have any complications right now.* Yet not a single one comes out of my mouth. Because while they are all true, right now, in this moment, I'd be lying.

He finally stops pacing and looks over to me with his hands fisted at his side and shakes his head. "I'm sorry. I shouldn't have done that. Kissed you. Shouldn't have laid my shit on your doorstep and made you feel like it's your fault. . . . This wasn't part of the plan when I came here. I was steering clear of women and then, fuck, there you were and now you're just *everywhere.*" When he takes a step toward me, I hold my breath, a part of me unsure what I want more: him to kiss me again or to walk away. "I think it's best if I stay on the boat for a few days, work there on those repairs, clear my head, get back on track. . . ."

*Boat? What boat?*

"Zander, I—"

"Save yourself, Getty. Let me go. You'll thank me in the end for it."

# Chapter 7

ZANDER

*I* wake with a jolt. *My heart racing and face sweaty from the nightmare. From the monsters and bad men who were chasing me. And the screams. They were so loud, so scary—they seemed so real. The last one begging for help was the worst.*

*I blink my eyes. Over and over. And the nightmare slowly goes away.*

*The bed creaks when I sit up. My throat is dry and this room is hot. Water. It's all I want and it's against my dad's rules to keep any in my room because of the cockroaches. I think about sneaking to the kitchen to get some from the tap, but I'm not allowed to leave my room after I've been put to bed.*

*Never. My dad's hand reaching for his looped belt. The sting when it hits my bare bottom. The threat of it keeps me from breaking the rules.*

*But maybe they're asleep. Maybe Dad's put enough of that* heaven *in his arm that he's on the couch in that kind of sleep where his eyes are partway open but he's really not awake. If that's the case, then Mom will be asleep in her room, because then that will mean the other men who come over will be gone too. The ones who sit with Dad and his lighters and crooked spoons and icky needles, because she'll only go to sleep after they leave.*

*Because then she'll know I'll be safe.*

*I cough, try to swallow to wet my throat, but it doesn't work. And now all of this thinking about water is making me have to go pee.*

*Like go pee really bad.*

*With my stuffed doggy tight to my chest, fingers pressing on the lumps in its stuffing, I get out of bed and tiptoe to the door. Right when my hand twists the knob, a scream fills the hallway. It's loud and horrible and sounds just like my dream did and scares me. I freeze, but it goes on and on and on.*

*Mommy.*

*Instantly, she's all I can think about, the only one I worry about. Tears blur my eyes as I rush down the hall. It's the smell that hits me first. That strange scent like when I get a nosebleed, but this time it's not just in my nose—it's everywhere.*

*When I enter the family room, my dad is standing near the front door. He looks funny, like something is wrong. His hair is in his face and his shirt is dirty with big, dark splotches all over it. He looks up and his face is scary mean, and he's out of breath like when he gets some of the "bad heaven" that makes him go kind of crazy.*

*I shrink back. I don't want to get in trouble for breaking his rules. Especially when he has this look on his face.*

*"Zander." My name is a whisper. There's a gurgle of sound. A whimper in pain.*

*The fear of my dad is forgotten the minute I notice my mom on the floor at the end of the couch. All I can see is her arm stretched out above her head and her face from the nose up.*

*"Mom." I say it once, but her name repeats in my head over and over as I run to her and drop to my knees. There's blood everywhere. It's all I can see, all I can think of as I grab her hand and tell her I'm here. My tears fall on her cheek. They wash away a spot of the blood there.*

*And holes. There are holes everywhere on her. Little holes marked in red. Big holes with even bigger red. On her chest and her tummy and her arms and her throat.*

*She moves her head to look at me. Her hair falls off her*

*face and I see it. The handle of the scissors looks funny standing up out of the side of her neck.*

*Her previous warnings not to run with scissors flicker through my mind. Did she run with them? She couldn't have. She's lying down.*

*Something's not right. Can't be. My brain isn't working, my body frozen in fear.*

*"Dad!" I remember he's in the room. Look up to get help. But he's right there. Looming above me. Like the monster in my dream. And I see the spots on his shirt are dark red. Just like the dots of it over the skin of his arms. His hands.*

*Just like blood all over my mom.*

*She gasps. I think she says "No," but I don't know because it sounds like she's underwater.*

*My whole body shakes. My eyes blink over and over, but I can't make this nightmare go away.*

*Get up. Call the police. Get help. Save her. Save me. Mom. Oh my God, Mom. I need Band-Aids. Fix her cuts. Stop the bleeding. It will help.*

*Band-Aids. Go get them to help her.*

*But I don't move. Can't.*

*"If you tell anyone you saw me, I'll do the same thing to you." His words shock me. But I know that tone. Know when he uses it, he means business. The sting of his belt on my bare bottom is a constant reminder to listen to him.*

*The door shuts with a slam.*

*I need to help her. Have to. My hand on the scissors. The blood like a river. The silver stained red.*

*A gasp of breath. Blank eyes staring up at me. Her hand limp in mine.*

*If you tell anyone you saw me, I'll do the same thing to you.*

*It doesn't matter.*

*I won't tell anyone.*

*I don't think I could speak if I wanted to.*

"Where the fuck am I?" Something startles me awake as the dream ends, disorients me, confuses me. I take quick stock of things: It's dark outside now and the towel from my shower earlier is still wrapped around my waist.

I shove up out of the bed, swing my legs over the edge, and scrub my hands over my face to give myself a second to deal. And to give me time for a running start to escape if this is the dream and that was my reality.

My pulse pounds. My head is so fucked by the nightmare it's not even funny. The breath I blow out doesn't help. The repeated *fuck*s I say out loud to the empty room don't either.

I've dreamed that nightmare so many times I know it by heart. Because it's not a dream. It's my memory. My childhood reality. So perfectly clear. Like I'm back there. The smell. The fear. The sound of my mom's voice. So damn bittersweet. My mom's last words, my last memory of her . . . is my worst memory of her. Time hasn't faded any of it. Time hasn't healed old wounds.

Fuck no.

But why now? Why did the nightmare come back after so many years without it?

And then I remember the one part of the dream that's new. *The scissors.* The hilt in her neck. The slippery feel of it beneath my fingers. Her whimper in pain as I pulled on it. The gush of blood. How I tried to save her.

*And ended up killing her.*

I roll my shoulders. Take in a deep breath. Rationalize in my adult mind that the little boy trying to save her didn't really kill her. The autopsy may have said that the cause of death was her bleeding out when the scissors lodged in her jugular vein were removed, but I know deep down she was dead before that.

But knowing it and accepting it are two entirely different things. And accepting it and not letting it fuck you up is even harder.

I nod my head and take a deep breath, knowing that's why I'm here: to deal with the past at last so I can make things right with those who gave me a future.

And it's all because of the goddamn box.

The one delivered to my house out of the blue weeks ago that stole the peace I'd found years ago. The one I made the mistake of opening. The words on the first packet of paper I picked up knocked me flat on my ass.

Causing me to question everything I've ever known. About myself. My memories. And the fact that others in my life knew the truth when I didn't.

That fucking packet of paper: a copy of my mom's autopsy report. The truths it held shocked the shit out of me. Brought memories and images that I'd repressed as a child to come back with a vengeance and fuck me up. Those truths had been much too harsh for a seven-year-old boy to accept. I'd moved forward never knowing there were blank spots in my memory that needed to be filled: my hands on the scissors and the final sound she made when I pulled on them.

*Does it really matter all this time later?* Yes, because if I couldn't remember something so goddamn significant, what else am I not remembering? What else has been kept from me?

Fucking ghosts I thought were dead and buried are now back with a vengeance.

That's why I shoved the autopsy report in the box, taped the flaps of cardboard back up—to try to pretend like the life I've been living isn't built on a lie.

Like the memories aren't bullshit.

And now that box sits in the corner over there and taunts me. Makes me wonder if the rest of the stuff in there is just as jarring as the first thing I saw.

Curiosity—it's more dangerous than fear.

*It's the reason why I'm here.*

And while I'd like to be angry at Colton for firing me and forcing me away from the track, this isn't on him. Not in the least. I'm man enough to admit that.

To myself anyway.

Distance has allowed me to see that. The step back Colton forced me to take, the time to reflect with a clear head without the distractions I was drowning myself in— alcohol, women, adrenaline—allowed me to realize the truth.

And now I'm left not only to deal with the ticking time bomb of a box in the corner, but to figure out how to right the wrong choices I made.

Hell yes, I could take the easy way out—torch the box

in a bonfire and choke on my pride and call Colton to apologize. Stifle the curiosity and take back the brutal words I said when I was pissed at the fucking world and just needed an out. Anger is the one emotion that makes your mouth work faster than your mind, and you better bet your ass my mouth was running.

But that wouldn't solve shit. I'd still be fucked in the head and apologies are just a Band-Aid placed on an open wound when you cut someone as deeply as I cut Colton.

I know from experience—they don't always stop the bleeding.

"And that's why you're here, Donavan," I mutter to myself as I flop back on the bed, the sight of the ceiling much better for my psyche than the taunting cardboard box. The one I need to man up and open. Prove that without the distractions, I can deal with it. That its contents won't fuck me up any more than I already am.

Besides, I can't chase the ghosts away for good if I don't face them head-on.

And yet my first week in PineRidge is over and it still sits there. Unopened. Untouched. The question is, what else is in there? My curiosity calls for me to open it. My mental stability tells me to waste a whole roll of duct tape on it and seal it off forever.

Fucking Christ. I've dealt with this shit already. Dealt with it as a kid by crawling inside my own mind and not speaking for months. Dealt with it through endless hours of therapy and countless nights curled up in a ball, afraid to go to the bathroom for fear of what I might find again. Leading to a wet bed and a fucked-up head.

And then when my dad did come back for me, I had to deal with the chaos he brought with him again. The gun he held. Rylee, my counselor back then, protecting me at all costs. The taste of fear in my mouth. The tiny bit of desire for him to win so maybe I would die and could see my mom again. Then the gunshot. More blood again. A policeman standing over his body.

And then the freedom in knowing he could never come for me again. The fear that ended.

So yeah, I dealt with it all right. Kind of don't have a choice when you're eight and all alone in this big, bad world.

*Who am I kidding?* I'm still dealing with it every day. And if the first thing I pulled from the box messed me up so much I was willing to throw everything important to me away, what happens when I open it again and discover more things I can't cope with?

*But that's the point, dumbass.* To come here, deal with my shit, and prove to myself I'm the man I know I am—the man that Colton helped make me. Only then can I go back home and redeem myself. To my adoptive parents, to my crew, to the fans.

"Fuck, this is fucked," I groan as I bring a forearm to cover my eyes when I hear the front door slam. Followed by the pad of footsteps. A giggle that throws me. Then the squeak of that damn bathroom door. And the whole reason I went and slept on Smitty's boat—the sleepless nights with a beer in hand watching the phosphorus light up the water and the tinkering with mechanical shit I have no business tinkering with—to get some space and perspective on why I'm here in the first place—just flew out the damn window.

*Getty.*

The old pipes in the house creak. The telltale sound that she's taking a shower. And a shower means she's naked. Goddamn, if the image of her standing in the hallway naked except for those mismatching socks that first night we met doesn't come to mind. Not like it's gone very far from my thoughts to begin with.

And yet I told Darcy we were cool with rooming together. How did I think that was a good idea? My hair-of-the-dog-that-bit-you theory—room with a woman and then maybe I could avoid the temptation of all the others—isn't working too well for me now.

Daily reminders of her naked curves definitely don't help.

Not to mention I went and kissed her. Kissed her when I had no business kissing her, because I thought maybe if I got it out of my system, I'd be done and over thinking about it. Yeah. Like that had a chance of happening the minute she made that little sound in the back of her throat that made every part of me want to lay her down and get to know what other sounds she makes.

But more than that, I shouldn't have kissed her after the way she jumped when I grabbed her arm to stop her from walking past me. That in itself tells me she's here to deal with her own shit, and kissing an asshole like me isn't going to help in the least.

I've seen flinches like that before. I lived the first seven years of life watching my mom do the same exact thing. Jump over nothing. Shrink into a corner to be out of the way.

Getty's not my mom, though. She doesn't need to be saved. She obviously saved herself.

*Get that through your head, Zander, and leave her the fuck alone in* all *aspects.*

*You're roommates. You're both dealing with shit. Sleeping together—because let's face it, that would definitely not be a hardship if the way she kisses is any indication—isn't going to fix either of you. It would just complicate matters when they're complicated enough as it is.*

But fuck, is it tempting.

Lost in thoughts of her, I jump when my door suddenly flings open. Getty is standing in the doorway, hands on her hips, cheeks flushed. And fully clothed. So obviously my thoughts of her being in the shower were purely for my own sexually frustrated benefit.

She flicks on the switch just inside the door. Light floods the room.

"And the wonder boy has come back from his stint as Popeye!" she says with dramatic flair as she waltzes in, catching me off guard.

"What can I do for you, Getty?"

"Do for me?" She laughs, her eyes moving wildly around the room before she beelines straight for my dresser. "You know what you can do for me, *Mander*?" she says over her shoulder and with a bit of contempt. She picks up some racing magazines I have stacked on the desk, lifts them a few inches, and then drops them back down with a thud. The top one slides to the side; the bottom one is askew. "You can stop making everything so damn *perfect*. You can stop lining up your shit on the bathroom counter so it's all *perfectly* straight. When you empty the damn dishwasher, you can stop making the forks in the drawer sit *perfectly* on top of each other. Lined up. You can—"

"Getty?" She's going postal on me. While I've been with enough emotional women that her display doesn't completely rattle me, something about her acting like this registers on my radar.

"Hmm?" She says it like she has not a care in the world. Maybe she's not frantic after all. Maybe she knows exactly what she's doing—and that's even scarier. Also intriguing.

"What are you doing?" My curiosity is definitely piqued. I don't mind her touching my things. I invaded her privacy first. Her paintings were ten times more personal than my cologne and magazines, and yet I ask because I'm fascinated over what has caused her to storm into my bedroom like hell on wheels and start ranting.

"Perfection is overrated," she states as she picks up a folded shirt from the top of the dresser and tosses it carelessly onto the chair beside it. While I know she's referring to my stuff and how I prefer everything to be in its place, the sound in her voice makes me think she's talking about a lot more than just organization.

"Good thing I'm far from fucking perfect, then."

"That makes two of us," she says with a bit of a giggle, mood changing now that she's done whatever she set out to do. Turning around, and for the first time since coming into my room, she locks eyes with me. There's something off about her, something I can't place, but I know the minute she notices what I'm wearing.

Or rather, *not* wearing.

Her eyes widen, then roll as she throws her head back and laughs in disbelief. "Seriously? This *again*? I mean I may not know much, but I know *that's* more than above average in size." Her giggle fills the room as she motions her hand out in front of her and gestures to my dick, bobbing her head for emphasis. When she lifts her gaze back up from the overtly long stare at my package, it's then that

I notice her eyes are a bit glassy. Realize her last words were a tad slurred.

*Well, shit.* Seems Getty has had a few to drink.

I fight the grin on my lips, her compliment boosting my ego, but the sight of her tipsy is even better.

"Don't think I can't see you laughing at me, wonder boy. Do you really think I'm going to fall for your bullshit again? *Beautiful paintings, Socks,*" she says, mimicking my voice. I can't help but laugh. ". . . then run away. *I don't want to kiss you, Socks.* Kiss me and run away to a boat. A boat? What are you, Captain Jack Sparrow? And now? Now you probably planned this so the towel conveniently slips off so I fall at your feet. And then what? We're gonna sleep together and then you'll run away again?" She steps forward and right into my space, finger poking my bare chest. "Dream on, Mander."

And while her acting bit is pretty damn comical, it's got nothing on the image she's put in my head of her on her knees and the towel at my feet and her lips around my . . . *Fuck. Stop thinking about it.* This towel won't hide shit if I'm flying half-mast from the thought.

"First Popeye and then Captain Jack? Every woman's fantasy." I laugh. "You been drinking tonight, Getty?" She sways a little when she shakes her head, and I hold on to her shoulders before she falls full-court press into me. She shrugs out of my grip immediately, but not in the startled way she did the other day. More bothered because she doesn't want any help.

"Maybe." Her grin tells me *definitely*, but I let it slide. "Just a little. Liam wanted me to settle in on the other side of the bar, watch the game, be a local. So I did. And it was fun. So *screw Ethan.* Screw him and his *A lady would never be caught drinking* bullshit. I did. So what would he think about that?"

*Ethan?* The name throws me. My quick reply fades as I focus on the name and how it reveals a tiny piece of her past that she guards so closely. A part of me wants to ask more, question her when she's more apt to talk . . . and while I may have no problem skirting the line of morality, this is one line I won't cross.

"Nothing's wrong with a few drinks and watching the game." I play it safe. Prefer to let her business stay her own. No fair taking advantage of someone in any capacity when she's drunk. "You should have told me. I could've used a beer or two and would've liked to catch the game."

"I thought you were busy sailing the seven seas or something." She snorts when she laughs and it's fucking adorable.

"Not hardly. You should've asked." *What are you doing, Zander? Thought you were going to try to steer clear of her.*

She looks at me for a second, eyes narrowed, as thoughts visibly war across her face before she walks to the window. She looks out to the lights in the bay for a few moments before turning back around. "Sorry, but that might have *complicated* things."

She shifts her eyes to mine when she says the words, a lift of one eyebrow and a purse of her lips to reinforce her sarcasm. We stand in silence, letting her taunt ricochet in the space between us, building tension with each passing second.

"Define *complicated*." I can't resist. Know I shouldn't push the buttons I don't want pushed, but fuck if I don't like tipsy Getty a whole helluva lot.

Her smile is fast and devious as she steps toward me, and I fucking love it. "*Complicated*," she says as she walks right up to me again without hesitation and lifts onto her tiptoes so that her mouth is right at my ear when I lean down, "would be if I kissed you right now."

Fucking Christ. I'm standing in a towel, can feel the heat of her breath on my ear and her tits brush against my chest when she breathes in, and she goes and says that? I must be off my game, because there's that split second where we both freeze, both know we want it to happen, but I don't think I could stop at just a kiss.

Hell no. Not right now. Not with the bed behind me and that playful dare off her lips. Not with her drinking. Not with my promise to myself.

But hell if she's not making things painfully hard. In *all* areas.

She retreats a few steps, eyes still locked on mine, like a slightly different woman stands before me from the one I'm used to. The mismatched knee-high socks may be the same, but the defiant smirk on her lips, the flushed cheeks, and the eyes full of life are all different. There's a new-found confidence about her right now. A lack of inhibition. Her constant guard has relaxed. A hint of the real her that she hides beneath whatever bullshit she's dealing with is peeking through.

"You didn't answer," she says, and she's right. There's no way I can, because hell if she's not making *complicated* look welcome.

"Is that what you want?" I'll play her game, answer her question with a question. With her eyes trained on me, I lean back and grab a pair of gym shorts from the bed. Her gaze flickers down to watch as I slide them on under my towel before letting it fall. Now I can get that earlier image out of my head. At least we're on a bit more of an even playing field. But the one I really want to be on is the horizontal one behind me.

"I want a lot of things. . . ." Damn. The way she says that—throaty, full of invitation—causes a chill at the base of my spine.

"You and me both, Socks."

"I don't want to like you, you know." She tries to stifle the yawn but fails miserably.

"I don't like me either lately, so no worries." The admission is out of my mouth without thought. Her head jogs back and forth at it, eyes narrowing in a way that causes a little crease in her forehead.

"What do you—whoa!" That carefree laugh of hers fills the room again—breaking the moment—as she holds her hand to her head. "Did you feel that? The room just moved." Her hushed whisper makes me laugh too, thankful for the interruption.

"It didn't move at all, but you're probably going to want to go lie down."

"Oh, is that what I'm supposed to do?" She's looking at me with eyes widened in question, lips pursed in an O shape, and surprise written all over her face.

Innocent. Trusting. Beautiful. Time to step back. Regain that distance.

"Let's get you to bed."

"Don't tell me what to do, Zander. No one gets to tell me what to do ever again." She crosses her arms and gives me a death glare that's so damn cute I want to laugh at her. And then she sways. "I think I'm going to go to bed."

"Good idea." I follow her out of my bedroom door and watch her open hers. "I'll go get you some Advil."

I grab two pills and when I shut the medicine cabinet, my eyes veer to the bathroom countertop. To my deodorant and lotion and hair gel all lined up in a perfect little row against the wall.

Her words come back to me. Bug me. Make me wonder if they're another hint at the life she lived before this cottage. I walk halfway down the hall before stopping, shaking my head, and going back to the bathroom. Not certain why I'm doing it other than that I know what it's like to have a trigger—a thing to remind you of something you'd rather forget—I knock over my deodorant onto its side and slide my gel out of line.

I stare at them for a beat. Question why I'm even bothering. *For the same reason you're bringing her Advil. Because you care.*

Fuck.

When I knock on her door, it swings inward and she's dead center on her bed, sound asleep. There's something so peaceful about her. Something that makes me want to just sit here and stare at her, because it's kind of calming.

*Jesus, Zander. You're really doing well on the distance thing, aren't you?*

# Chapter 8

**Repair List**
~~Replace Front Step—third one~~
Replace Missing Roof Shingles
Back Deck = Death Trap
Fix Lock on Patio Door—Sorry, Mr. Ax Murderer
Fix Bathroom Mirror
Rain Gutters
Repair Shutters
Add Handrail to Front Steps & Paint
Add Light in GS
Connect Internet for God's Sake
Bulldoze House and Rebuild ☺

The last line makes me laugh out loud into the empty kitchen, the whole thing amusing. I drop the pad with Zander's scrawled penmanship and pick up my coffee.

"What's so funny?"

I cringe inwardly at the sound of his voice floating down the hall, flashbacks from last night coming back to me in bits and pieces. While I may not remember it all, I sure as hell remember sliding my hands up his bare chest and whispering in his ear. Attempting to be sexy. Trying to play him like he did me. And of course with a few drinks under my belt I may have felt like I pulled it off, but I have a feeling I looked more like an idiot. I keep my eyes angled out of the window when Zander enters the kitchen.

"The last thing on your repair list," I murmur.

He makes a noncommittal sound in agreement. "How's your head this morning?"

"Okay. Not bad. Just a little headache. Thanks for leaving the Advil on the nightstand. That was nice of you."

"No biggie."

God. We're doing the as-few-words-as-possible thing here. I must have really been an ass last night. Or pissed him off. With a sigh I turn to face him and damn if I wish I hadn't stayed facing the window. He has bedhead and his eyes are a bit swollen from sleep with a pillow crease on his cheek. His shorts are slung a tad too low on his hips, so that damn happy trail of his is highlighted in all of its glory, drawing my attention to what's below it when I shouldn't be looking there.

*I may not know much, but I know that's more than above average in size.*

My comment from last night flickers through my mind. The sight of him all rumpled from sleep looking like something you want to crawl next to and cozy up with pushing it to the forefront.

*Can I die now, please?* If I said that, what else came out of my mouth?

"About last night . . ." I fumble for what to say as the intensity in his blue eyes holds me hostage. "I'm sorry if I said or did anything that was . . . I don't normally drink. So—"

"No need to apologize. You were cute. Funny. Carefree. I liked it."

Carefree? *Me?* I'm practically stuttering as I try to respond with a rush of heat to my cheeks as I blush. "Do you really know how to do all of that?" I ask, motioning to the fix-it list to try to change the subject.

"Nope." He answers the question, but his eyes are still locked on mine, still asking unspoken questions about the last topic, when I don't want him to.

"Then how are you going to fix it all? Hire someone?"

"Nope."

"You're awfully talkative this morning," I huff, and somehow the exasperation helps me find a little more footing in this back-and-forth that has become our norm.

"I'll look on my laptop. Google it if I have to. I'm not worried about it—I'm pretty good with my hands."

"Oh . . ." I scrunch my nose up, trying to keep my mind on track and not the skill of his hands. "There is no Internet in the house." Why do I feel so stupid saying that? Admitting that I'd rather be closed off from the world for a bit than have it at my fingertips with a search engine.

"I noticed. I'm going to get that set up while I'm here too. In the meantime if I need it, I'll just do what you do."

*Huh?* "What I do?"

"Yeah." He shrugs like I should know. "Use your hot spot on your cell."

"I don't have Internet on my cell."

He whips his head up and stares at me like I have three heads, mouth open, surprise he can't quite figure out how to verbalize fleeting through his eyes. "What do you mean you don't have Internet?" His voice sounds like his face looks: astounded.

"No biggie." I repeat his words back to him as I try to scramble to explain and sound credible. I can't just come out and tell him my cell's a burner phone so just in case my dad or Ethan tried to track or trace me somehow, they wouldn't be able to. I've already been there and done that with them, learned my lesson.

Besides, it's not in my budget right now.

"So what happens when you're driving and you get lost?"

"Who said I wanted to be found?" The quip is off my tongue without thought. Suddenly a wave of memories hits me hard and fast. *How do you think I knew where you were today, Gertrude? One little click and the app installed on your phone just like that without you ever knowing. I know everything you do. Everywhere you go. Every move you make. You are mine. Don't ever forget that.*

I push the memory away. Shove the panic down. And am met with Zander's unforgiving eyes, which reveal that he's making assumptions I'd rather him not make about my remark. I attempt to save face, change the direction of the questions I know are coming. "That question is ridiculous, really. If I were lost, I'd just pull over and ask for directions." I force a laugh, but I don't think he's buying it.

"No. Let's go back to the first comment." He braces his hands on the counter and leans across it so I'm unable to hide from his stare.

"Let's not." *End of topic, Zander. Let it go.*

"Who'd be looking for you, Getty?" His tone—the *don't hide this from me* part—makes me want to scream and yell and stomp my feet and tell him he's crossing those boundaries I don't want crossed.

Instead, I make sure my voice is implacable when I answer him. "No one."

"Is that what *Ethan* would say?"

Everything about me freezes—my mind, my heart, my lungs—at the sound of the name. My past, my fears, the place I never want to see again, rush through my mind like I never left.

"Did he send you here?" My voice is quiet steel when I speak, although my insides are a twisted mess of anxiety.

"Who is he, Getty?" His voice softens, but the determination in his eyes never wavers.

"No one you want to know and none of your business." I force myself to stop fidgeting with the pad on the counter, my unease clear as day.

"Except for the fact that he's the reason you're running."

"Butt out, Zander." I begin to round the L-shaped counter so I can exit the tiny kitchen, but he just steps in front of me to block my path.

But unlike with Ethan, I feel no fear of him. I don't have to scramble to see where I can disappear to. Rather there is the need to protect my secrets, keep my place and identity here limited to only what I want people to know about me.

"If you're in trouble, Getty . . . please, I can try to help you. All you have to do is ask."

His words tug on every part of me that's tired of fighting this alone, tired of being lonely. And yet I know more than anyone that all it takes is one person to know, for that person to comment offhand to someone else, and somehow, someway, Ethan would find out.

"Boundaries." It takes everything I have to utter that single word. Body tense. Pulse racing.

"You don't want me to step on your boundaries, then don't come in my room a little tipsy and act all hell on wheels and compare me to your ex. Because he is your ex, right, Getty?"

"I said it's none of your business." I grit the word out between my clenched teeth. Hating myself and worrying over whatever else I said last night and at the same time needing to stop this conversation before he pushes too hard.

"Like hell it is. Don't you think it's important for me to know if some man is going to waltz in here to try to take you back or whatever the fuck is going on here, so that I know how best to protect you?"

*Put the wall up, Getty. You need no one. That's how you're going to survive this—heal from this—by depending solely on yourself. Push him away. Protect yourself.*

"First off, Ethan is no one to me. Secondly, no one is going to be waltzing in here, and more importantly, I'm not yours to protect." I hold his stare, meet it with a resolve I definitely don't feel. His words start to sink in and break a chip off the walls I have up around me. I can't think about it now, about how a man I just met is offering to protect me when the ones that should have done it never did.

"You keep thinking that, Socks. Keep thinking that just because you're not mine . . . whatever the fuck that means to you . . . that I shouldn't defend you, and I'll keep pretending you're not running from anything, and we'll see how far that gets us." There's a bite to his voice telling me I've offended him, and I welcome the sound. If I've pissed him off, then maybe he'll keep his distance.

"Can I go now?" I'm a bitch in how I say it, put out, annoyed, but I can't be any other way. There's a flicker of something in his eyes—hurt, distrust, disbelief. I can't put my finger on it, but I really can't care, because I need to escape this situation.

This time when I try to move past him, he lets me. And thank God for that, because a few seconds longer and he'd see the tears welling in my eyes and my hands shaking and I don't want him to.

I don't want him to know how much hearing that simple name has affected me. How in a split second it's like Ethan is here, his voice angry in my ear, and all the progress, all the strength I've gained, disappears.

With my bedroom door closed at my back, I slide down it until I'm sitting on the floor.

The mental chastising begins immediately. The disbelief of how stupid I could have been to drink enough to say something about Ethan. What else did I say that I don't remember? What other information did I give Zander to be curious about?

Then comes the worry. The fear. The doubt. Zander mentioned Ethan one time and I go into shutdown mode: lash out, be a bitch, protect myself, push away. I thought I'd gotten further than this emotionally.

Just proves the invisible scars are the ones that cut the deepest and stay with you the longest.

A part of me wants to go back, talk to Zander, apologize, thank him for his concern. But I know I can't. I know my biggest asset right now is my isolation. My aloofness. The knowledge that I need absolutely no one.

So I hold on to my anger and fear. Hold on to the memories of the mansion in the hills where everything from the outside looked perfect, but on the inside life was as cold and controlled as a prison.

*Stay strong, Getty. Stay strong and smart and alone and he'll never be able to hurt you again.*

The sky rumbles angrily as I look out the front door. Hues of gray and charcoal mar the horizon—there's another storm about to hit PineRidge. Grateful to have heard Zander leave earlier to get his run in before the storm hits, I know I have no chance of bumping into him before I leave for work. No opportunity for him to ask more questions.

I head back into the kitchen and grab my keys out of the basket there, resigned to having to drive my car to work so that I'm not stuck walking in a downpour tonight when I get off shift. Besides, it's probably best to run it, considering I've barely used it since I've come here.

When I put the key in the ignition, the engine turns over a few times but never starts. Panic tickles the nape of my neck. It's just that I haven't used it in a few weeks. That's all.

But after the third or fourth time, still nothing.

No. No. No. The word repeats over and over in my head as I fight back the tears that sting and the emotion welling up like a dam, which I fear I'm not going to be able to stop once it starts.

Can this day get any worse? First Zander pushing boundaries with his mention of Ethan. The confrontation with him buckled my resolve, like a slap in my face, showing me how quickly I can be pulled back into that dark place I'd emerged from—the fear and the lack of control—making me realize that I'm nowhere near as strong as I thought I was. And now there is something wrong with my car when I don't have the money to pay someone to repair it.

And I *need* my car. It's my only way to run should they find me. The symbol of my freedom and a reminder of that first step I took to make my life my own.

Ethan and my father would turn their noses down at this old car and maybe that's part of the reason I love it so very much. The symbolism. The defiance.

*The fuck-you to them.*

"One more time," I murmur as I turn the key again. Once again there is nothing but the sound of my choked sob when the first tear falls. And being in emotional-overload mode, I'm mad at myself for crying. Pissed at the car. Unfairly furious with Zander because he started my day like this and the ball just kept on rolling downhill.

I get out of the car, slam the door shut, and just stare at it for a minute while I work myself up to walk to the Lazy Dog.

"Sounds like something's wrong with your car?"

Zander's voice has me gritting my teeth and wishing him to go away. I don't answer, just wipe the tears from under my eyes with as much dignity as I can, and start toward the house to get my umbrella.

"Getty?" I ignore his call and walk right past him, hating that he keeps seeing me in moments when I'm frazzled and a wreck. Footsteps on the wood floor tell me he's following. "If there's something wrong with the engine, it's not a big deal. There's a shop on the other side—"

"I need my car." Knowing his eyes are on me, I'm flustered and for the life of me, I can't remember where I left my umbrella. Like a madwoman, I start rifling through things, the clock ticking away and my urgency growing as the start of my shift looms closer.

"We live on an island. The bar is only a couple blocks away. Your car not starting isn't the end of the world."

"Leave me alone, Zander." He wouldn't understand.

My closet. The alcove in the hall. The family room. And I still can't find the damn thing. All with him right behind me. Breathing down my neck. His presence adding pressure to his silent scrutiny.

"Why here, Getty? An island's not exactly the best place to go if you're running from something. That car of yours is only going to get you so far until the ferry comes."

His taunting words knock the wind from my sails. Try to coerce an answer out of me. And I falter for a moment, eyes searching and mind questioning myself for the millionth time on why I picked this location. The answer was simple back then when my only thought was to get as far away as possible. The combination of the island's seclusion mixed with a place to stay for free was more than enough for me.

But I don't owe an explanation to anyone, least of all him.

"I need to get my car fixed." I say it again, mentally calculating how much tip money I've stowed away in my secret hiding place while also estimating how fast I can get the consignment shop to sell my clothes to earn more.

"I can fix—"

"I don't need your help." I bite the words out. Mad and upset and overwhelmed.

"I'll call a tow truck for you, then."

My eyes well with tears. My stubborn anger turns to embarrassment. "No."

"No?"

"I can't afford it." My voice is barely a whisper.

"Come again?" I hate the condescending tone in his voice. The disbelief.

"Leave me alone, please." He's still behind me when I speak, but a rush of heat floods my cheeks in a mortification like I've never known before.

"You can't be that broke living on your trust fund."

I swear my neck almost breaks from the whiplash his words cause. They're completely out of the blue and so far off base that I don't know how to respond or why he'd make such an assumption. I try to regain my footing, but my anger at his shitty comment overrides all reason.

My glare meets his and the smirk on his lips is so chock-full of arrogance I say the only thing I can. "Fuck. You."

"Why not just call Mommy or Daddy up? I'm sure they'd overnight the money."

*Poke. Poke. Prod.*

Angry tears burn in my eyes. Disbelief that he's saying this shocks me momentarily as I try to figure out how I was so wrong about him. How, after his offer this morning, I thought he was a good guy. Nice. Caring.

And now all I can see is the truth. To say it stings is an understatement. To admit I was wrong, even more so.

I look at him as I shake my head in astonishment that I'd actually thought I had a friend in this solitude. And yet I was so very mistaken.

"Just a phone call away."

*Poke and poke and prod.*

"You don't know shit about me, asshole."

"I know designer clothes when I see them. Seen enough to know that robe you wear costs a pretty penny. You can dress them down, shrug me off, but there's no hiding how expensive your threads are."

*Poke and poke and poke and prod.*

Fury still burns through me, but my need to gain back some ground turns out to be even stronger. The conversation from the bar with his fan the other night flickers in my head, gives me the ammo I need.

*Poke and poke and prod and poke back.*

"You want to get in my business—how 'bout we start digging into yours, huh? Why'd you lose your ride, Zander? What are you running from? You've got to screw up pretty bad to lose your ride and all of the sponsorships I'm assuming go with it, right?"

"Fuck. You." He mimics me, but I can see that my barb has made its point. That my I'm-gonna-hurt-you-because-you're-trying-to-hurt-me got the reaction I wanted. "Fuck this. Figure out how to fix your car on your own, then."

He throws his empty water bottle into the sink, knocking some silverware with it. The clatter fills the empty space around us before he strides down the hall.

"No worries," I shout after him. "Pretty ironic I have the revered race car driver Zander Donavan living with me, but he's such a goddamn pretty boy, I bet he couldn't find his way underneath the hood to fix an engine if he tried."

The door to his room slams, windows shaking with the force as I'm left standing in an empty room, frazzled, hurt, and very late for work.

# Chapter 9

"If anyone cancels or calls in, I'll make sure to get you the extra shift."

"Thanks, Liam," I tell him on my way to the door of the Lazy Dog, fingers crossed in the hopes for extra tips.

"You okay getting home? It's blowing like a bitch out there." Liam steps around the back of the counter he's wiping up, concern etched in his kind eyes.

"I'm good," I lie, not wanting any company. "Zander's going to pick me up."

"I knew he was a good guy like that." I force a tight smile. "Next time have him come in before closing. He's the talk of the town, albeit it doesn't take much round here. He's good for business," he says with a wink. "I still can't believe *the* Zander Donavan is here on our little island."

"Night," I say just as the door closes so he doesn't see me roll my eyes.

The wind hits me the moment I step outside, whipping the strands of my ponytail at my cheeks and stinging my skin with pinpricks. Instantly I regret not having my umbrella, but honestly, I didn't want to stay in the house another second with Zander, so thoughts of finding it went by the wayside.

And now of course as the sheets of rain pour down beyond the overhang where I'm standing, I regret it.

A perfect ending to a shitty day.

With a sigh, I slink along the overhangs of the waterfront stores, my body tired and my mind emotionally exhausted. Worry over how to fix my car still looms front and center, but now there's the added dread that I have to go back to the house with Zander there and figure out how to coexist with him with minimal interaction.

Because I definitely don't want to talk to him.

The overhead protection from the storefront ends and rather than venture out into the rain, I perch on the edge of a bench. The whitecaps froth on the water, their color a stark contrast to the churn and twist of the dark sea. I get lost in the night, in watching the waves, my thoughts veering to earlier. To the fight with Zander. To the sudden about-face in his actions. To the slow night in the bar that allowed me too much time to think. To the ghosts and doubts Zander stirred up with his accusations.

"Don't waste any more time on him," I mutter to myself with a shake of my head. When I'm sure there's no lightning, I start the walk home. Within a matter of minutes, my hair is plastered to my face and my clothes are sopping wet. My fury at Zander intensifies with each squish of my sodden shoes. Plus these are my one good pair I use for work to minimize my achy back and now they're completely waterlogged.

And if they don't dry right, if they shrink, if they get mildewed from this damn walk home in the pouring rain, I don't have the budget to buy new ones. Especially not with the unexpected outflow of cash to get my car fixed.

With each whip of wind, each squish of a step, the closer I get to the house, my temper is more primed to finish addressing the bullshit that Zander started. To get answers as to why it's okay for him to ask and demand and yet when I push at him in turn, he storms out and slams the door.

My teeth are chattering and I'm so damn cold I'd rather risk the rickety deck than take the extra time going around to the front of the house. I climb the crooked stairs with caution, making the frame creak with each step, but it's quicker and brings a hot shower that much closer.

Luckily when I enter the house, even though the kitchen light is on, Zander's nowhere to be found and his bedroom door is closed. Good. He can stay there for all I care.

The shower feels like heaven—the hot water stings my face and turns my skin bright pink from the extremes in temperature. My irritation, my anger—everything builds as I know Zander's in his room nice and cozy warm while I was walking home in the freezing cold rain. I know it's not his fault my car didn't start, but he was the asshole who got me so flustered I didn't get my umbrella.

Definitely his fault.

Dressed in warm jammies and hair wrapped up in a towel, I leave the bathroom to find the house absolutely freezing. Wind rushes down the hallway and I hate that tickle of dread in the pit of my stomach. Why is the front door open? The inherent fear creeps up my spine over the possibility that my influential father and his puppet Ethan have found me and come to take me back home.

No, not home. *This is my home now.*

I glance back to Zander's door—still shut—and debate whether I should knock and ask him to go check it out, my own overactive imagination taking over.

*No, Getty. You don't need any man, let alone an asshole like Zander, to help you.* And the notion that I immediately wanted to get his help makes me dislike him even more. If he didn't barge into this house, lie about us wanting to be roommates to Darcy, then I wouldn't have a choice in the matter. I wouldn't be able to hesitate. I'd have to act. And that's the whole point, right? I came here to prove I don't need anybody or anyone and yet the first time I get a little scared, I become a chicken.

*Quit being such a wimp and go shut the door.* The wood's swollen from the rain. It probably didn't click shut all the way the last time Zander used it.

With a nervous laugh and a quick glance at the mini-blind wand, I head down the hall to find the front door slightly ajar. *See.* Just the wind and rain.

"Goddammit!" The sound of Zander's frustrated shout

scares the shit out of me when I'm already on edge. I jump at the sound coming from outside, my nerves rattled but my temper lit from the combination of his comments earlier and his carelessness at leaving the door open.

I'm not sure what I expect to see, but what I do stops me dead in my tracks.

The hood of my car is up, a mechanic work light hanging from a hook on its underside, and Zander is bent over the engine. It takes me a good second or two to believe what I'm seeing, but when I do, I can't seem to look away.

I'm a little shocked. Somewhat unsure. And have a bit of a bruised ego after my strong opinions about him being an asshole. But more than anything, I know that there's something about him that captivates me.

And it's not because he's doing whatever he's doing under the hood of my car to obviously help me out. No. It's so much more than that . . . and at the same time, nothing at all.

*It's the way he looks.* Hands braced on the front of the car, head hung down in concentration, water dripping off the bill of his baseball cap. And of course his shirt is plastered to his body, so that even through the rain, I can see the cords of muscles flexing as he reaches forward with the wrench and adjusts something. He seems to be a bit of bad boy, wounded soul, and life of the party all mixed into one package—effectively the anti-Ethan—and maybe the realization right now when I'm still semimad at him kind of knocks me back some. Makes me look a little closer when I should be looking the other way.

Despite what he said today—the quick barbs and the unapologetic push for more information—he obviously has a good heart and is trying to help me even though I was a bitch to him. I pushed his buttons on purpose to keep him at far enough of a distance to stop pushing mine. And yet despite everything, he's out in the pouring rain working on my car.

And more than anything, *it's the way he makes me feel* watching him. That warm feeling down deep in my belly. The goose bumps racing over my skin that have nothing to do with the temperature outside. How I want to go out and talk to him even though I still want to be mad at him. It seems so odd that I can't remember what it feels like to have someone take care of me—not since my mother died—and yet now that I feel it, I can't believe how much I've missed it.

Thoughts race through my mind. The kind that make you want and need, and I'm not in a position to want or need anything; I shove them away. Try to convince myself he's fiddling with my car because he feels guilty about the things he said to me earlier.

*But what guy does that, Getty?*

I can't like him. I just can't. It's not in the cards. Hell, it's not even in the damn deck. And yet there he is. Soaking wet. Doing something to help me because I told him I couldn't afford it.

Not only that, I insulted him, lashed out. I'd like to think maybe I did it to see what he'd do—whether he'd help me—so I could see the true nature of his character, but I was so angry there was no forethought in my off-the-cuff words.

Now I stand here at one o'clock in the morning having traded places with him—me warm and dry and him wet and cold—and the need to talk to him overwhelms me. And not just because he's helping me, but because as messed up as it is, in a sense, he's the only friend I have.

I venture into the kitchen to find a peace offering. Maybe I can round up some cookies or a beer or something, but the offerings are meek considering my appetite lately has been nil and money's been tight. So when I open the refrigerator and find it stocked to the gills with fresh produce and beer and everything else I could imagine, I'm a tad taken aback. I open the cupboards and find them just as full of cereal boxes and cookies and pasta.

My vision blurs in the face of the humility that washes over me. I bite back the urge to storm out there and confront him. I'm embarrassed that he actually heard me when I said I couldn't afford to repair my car; that he realized that was why the house was so light on groceries and took it upon himself to run to the store and buy food.

In the pouring rain.

My pride wars with the attraction I feel toward him. I don't want a handout of any kind. Don't want the pity of a man—let alone any other of the islanders here—in any way, shape, or form. Because it was my choice to flee and leave my old life behind. All the privilege. The control that ruled my every waking moment.

The punishments.

I knew it was going to be tough. I knew it was going to be lonely. And so I hold back the tears of frustration, my own self-pity, and wonder how to thank Zander for all of this and at the same time to tell him to never do it again without sounding ungrateful.

I close the cupboards, bottom lip between my teeth, and reach into the fridge for a cold bottle of beer. But it's when I open the drawer of silverware to get a bottle opener that I get an even bigger surprise than the food. I know it's silly and stupid, but when I look down to the tray, the silverware is sitting every which way. Gone is the perfect alignment from yesterday with everything in its proper place. The slot for forks has the big ones mixed with the little ones—some tines facing up, some tines facing down. The spoons too. The knives are a mishmash of butter and steak thrown in several slots.

In disbelief and filled with gratitude, I stare at the disarray. Such a mess wasn't allowed in Ethan's house. And there's a small part of me that sags in relief at knowing I wasn't wrong about Zander or his kind heart. That he has gone through all this trouble—even messing the silverware drawer up—to give me whatever he thought I needed based on my rant the other night, even though he didn't understand why.

I've been shown a lot of kindness in the last few months. By Darcy with this place to live and Liam with a job when I have zero experience, but this by far has been the sweetest thing because of the history behind it.

Grabbing the beer and a beach towel, I head to the front door, but just as I'm going out, Zander is coming in. Water drips off every inch of him and pools on the rug inside the front door.

Our eyes meet, blue to brown, and in that instant there

is so much I want to say to him but there are no words to express it. I hold the beer and the towel out to him despite feeling even more ridiculous considering I'm offering him a cold beer when he's probably freezing to death.

He looks down at the beer and the towel and then back up to me with a scornful expression, but under the hardness, I see a softness in his eyes. Part of him feels like a schmuck and is completely uncomfortable being a good guy when he's the self-proclaimed asshole.

Tension builds in the silence. Just as I'm about to speak, he reaches down to the hem of his T-shirt and pulls the sopping fabric over his head. His hat falls off with it as he goes. Yes, I've seen him naked before, but with the veil of shock removed and his kind heart revealed, I'm seeing him in an all-new light. I take in the defined muscles of his torso—not too big but not too slight—the V that disappears beneath his waistband of his worn jeans, and the strength of his hands when he reaches out to take the towel and the beer without a single word.

He brings the bottle up to his lips and takes a long, lazy drink, face tipped up to the ceiling, while I unabashedly admire the obvious work he puts into his physique.

"Thank you." I may say only two words, but they're filled with meaning.

He pauses and slowly lowers the bottle, taking his time to meet my gaze. With a nod of his head, he works his tongue in his cheek. "Your alternator is bad. I pulled it out but have to wait for the new one to come in. I had the garage in town order one for me."

"Thank you. I'll pay you for the parts and your time and—"

"It's on me." He shrugs nonchalantly.

"I won't take your charity or your pity. I'll pay you back."

"That's not needed. Besides, I didn't do much."

"You're fixing my car. You went grocery—"

"We were running low on food. It was my turn to buy."

"It was more than that. It was—"

"Drop it, Getty." His warning is loud and clear and while I hear it, I feel it needs to be said.

"You didn't have to—"

"Getty." The look in his eyes and the tone in his voice stops the rest of the comment on my tongue. "Quit being so goddamn stubborn and we'll be fine." His eyebrows lift up, a challenge thrown down.

"Quit being such an asshole."

He fights the smirk on his lips and I can tell he's a tad surprised by my quid pro quo. But this banter between us is where we seem most comfortable, what we always come back to, so the fact that we fell into it so quickly means that our fight just might be over.

And while I'd prefer to get some answers on why he said the things he said and pushed so hard, I can also let sleeping dogs lie so that there's a bit of peace too.

"Let's get one thing straight, Socks," he says after running the towel through his hair, biceps flexing with the action, before hanging it over his shoulders. "I have eight brothers, so if you want to fight, I assure you, I'll win every time. *Hands down.* And for your information, I didn't run away. Not like you. I was out of control. Hurt some people and needed to deal with some of my own shit before I can return home to make it right." He steps closer, face angled down so I can see the truth in his eyes. "I came here to get some clarity, some time to myself away from the chaos in my life, and fix up the house for Smitty because I owe him. *Big-time.* I'm not here to take your house away. I wasn't sent by anyone to find you and bring you back to wherever you're from. And while most days I'm a grade A asshole, that doesn't mean I don't have manners, and manners mean I wouldn't hesitate to protect you if need be. That's how I was raised and that's not going to change."

I think of the groceries, the repairs to my car, the damn silverware drawer, and know without a doubt he wouldn't hesitate to defend me at all. "Thank you."

"And another thing—this is how I am. I'm loud and brash and in-your-face if I need to be, but that doesn't mean you need to shrink inside yourself, because I'm not a threat. I'm not going to hurt you." He takes a step closer as my mind whirls wondering if it's that obvious how skittish I am when his temper makes an appearance. "You want to know why I pressed you earlier? Why I stepped into the role of pushy asshole? Because this is a small town, Getty. People talk. People gossip. And they're going to want to know more about the new girl in town who keeps to herself and is rattled after a glass bottle breaks on the floor while she's at work. So you better start knowing the answers to the questions before they're asked. You need to be prepared for assumptions, pressure for answers, whispers around town. You need to be able to give it to them with a straight face and off the cuff, or your cover story isn't going to hold."

I swear to God I feel like this is a Ping-Pong match. One minute I like him and the next not so much. But the problem is right now I don't like him because he's telling me truths I don't want to hear. He's making me realize that as prepared as I was to do this, create a new life for myself—it's still hard as hell to pull off and I haven't been doing as good of a job as I thought.

Worrying my bottom lip with my teeth, I take in what he's saying, try to hear the advice for what it's worth, but still have a hard time not stiffening my spine at the reprimand.

"You don't know anything about me." My voice is slight but strong, my need to assert myself front and center despite his calling me on the carpet.

"That's where you're wrong, Socks. I might not know where you're from or why I ruffled your feathers today, but I know you're stronger than you give yourself credit for. Whatever it is that you ran from back home, you did it. You got out and are making it on your own. That takes guts and you deserve mad props for that. I know you like things messy and are goddamn cute when you're tipsy. I know you're stubborn as hell and gorgeous as fuck. And that your kiss tastes like an aged whiskey: something I want to sip slowly, feel on my lips, savor on my tongue, and take my time with before I get drunk on it." With a lift of his eyebrows and a nod of his head, he walks past me, leaving me with my mouth agape and eyes wide.

I can't move. Just stand staring at the door in front of me as I try to process what he just said, what he meant by it, and yet there's no use because we just had a whole one-sided conversation and that need to banter with him is gone. Lost to the tingling in my lower belly and the wild spinning of my thoughts.

"Oh, and, Getty?" Zander calls out to me from the kitchen, refusing to continue until I turn to face him, standing there unabashedly shirtless. "If you ever call me *pretty* again, we're gonna have a real problem. I guarantee you there is nothing *pretty* about me."

I almost smile at the fact that out of all of the crappy things I said to him, that is the one that bugged him the most.

"You *are* kind of pretty, though," I murmur, unable to resist goading him further, needing to try to get us back on an even playing field. Because hell if right now I don't feel like I'm on the low end of the teeter-totter.

His immediate response? A snort to signify that his chiseled abs and the tall, dark, and handsome thing he's got going on are nothing more than average.

"Last warning, Socks." His eyes flash with mirth. And what looks like desire.

An unexpected part of me—the one who usually hides and doesn't ever take a chance—wants to say it again. Just to see what he'd do if I did.

*"So damn pretty."* I don't know who's more shocked at my comment, him or me, but we stand there for a moment, gazes locked, unspoken words warring across the distance between us.

He walks toward me with a predatory gleam in his eyes and a salacious smirk on his lips that catches me off guard. "I know I said you were brave, Getty, but now you're just playing with matches."

I draw in a long inhalation as he steps right in front of me. I can't look at him. My nerve is suddenly gone. Outside, rain pelts the roof. The constant drip into the bucket in the hallway serves as a metronome to this anticipatory silence we are dancing in. The goose bumps on his chest are the only thing I can focus on.

When his thumb and forefinger direct my chin up so I'm forced to meet his eyes, every part of me hums from his touch. From the want of something I don't quite understand myself and couldn't ever put into words. Our eyes meet—his intense, mine searching for answers that aren't his to give—before his gaze flicks down to my mouth and then back up again.

"Not yet, Getty." He closes his eyes for a beat, and I see what I think is restraint reflected in his grimace, before a ghost of a smile spreads on his lips. "I don't think you're ready to light this fire just yet."

And once again, he nods his head, tongue licking out to wet his bottom lip, before turning his back and walking down the hallway without saying another word. I watch him move, turn into the bathroom, shut the door. Hear the shower turn on, the pipes creak. But I don't move a muscle. His words—all of them—repeat in my mind and stoke the sweet ache they created that my body can't deny.

With a loud sigh, I shake my head and walk to my bedroom.

I think we're going to need a damn hose in the house to keep this fire out he's already lit in me.

# Chapter 10

ZANDER

Shane said you're not answering his texts. So now you get me, the best brother. Hope you're figuring everything out. We're all worried. Just want the best for you. Dude, you keep standing me up for our weekly round of golf, so I'm taking lessons while I wait for you to get your ass back home. It's up to you how many I take . . . so please, take your time. I'll be at scratch before you know it. Besides, lessons are being charged to your membership anyway. Miss ya, bro. Oh, and be prepared, if you don't answer, we'll just keep moving through the ranks until you do.

The smile comes easily. Thoughts of my second to littlest shit of a brother, Scooter, who's getting too damn decent at golf for his own good and way too big for his damn britches, by the words in his text. Scratch golfer, my ass. There's no way he's even close to par.

He can't be. I haven't been gone *that* long.

And with the smile comes the anger. The guilt. The *how can he care about me when I was such an asshole to him?*

I glance up from the sawhorse to the beach for a moment.

Rein in my temper. And let myself miss home for a split second. The constant ribbing between all of us brothers and the relentless bitching to mind your own business from at least one of them.

Shit, I got what I wanted. To be left alone. To not be nagged and coddled and asked for the hundredth time what my problem was. To not have to see the hurt and disappointment in their eyes when I fucked up *again*.

But all these goddamn texts—the ones I get every few days or so from one of my brothers like they're on a schedule—make it all that much worse. I don't deserve their concern after the way I treated them.

They should kick my ass is what they should do. For the birthday party I missed. The phone calls I didn't return. For showing up at Ricky's house plastered and picking a fight. I've done so damn much I hardly recognize the man I was to them.

And yet today, another text. Another reminder of the family I don't deserve. And of the weight I carry until I can make this right again.

I look back down to the message on my phone, my thumb hovering over the keyboard. *Fuck*. What do you write when you don't know the right words to say what you need to say? I set my cell down. Pick it back up. Exhale a breath. Shake my head. Type Thanks. Delete it because it's lame, and yet while I don't know what to say, I still need to say something. Anything. To let him know I'm trying to sort myself out. And not ignoring him. To thank him for sticking with me when I don't deserve it.

Thanks for giving me time.

# Chapter 11

With my hands covered in streaks of pinks and peaches and oranges that match the sky at sunset on the canvas, I'm shocked at the time when I glance over at the clock. But my art always allows me to get lost in it, so I shouldn't be surprised that four hours have passed when it felt like only forty minutes.

A Sunday off from work and away from the bar meant the urge to paint has been overwhelming. But I'm not sure if it was the creative outlet or my desire to avoid Zander that really fueled my need to be locked away in my room.

Because *I am* avoiding Zander—and his matches and fire and swoony words and defined chest and bashful kindness. In fact I have been for the past week; the few extra shifts at the bar I picked up have made it that much easier for me to do so.

I'm not used to this kind of thing. What am I supposed to say to him? Ethan courted me with bouquets of roses, dates for dinner or the movies, pecks on the lips I mistakenly thought were romantic at the time, and abstinence before marriage.

Proper at all times. Every date was a well-synchronized dance to win over my affection, make me believe I was desirable, so that he and my father could secretly join family empires. And then after marriage . . . the real Ethan showed his true colors. Hurt me enough until I ran away.

So this—Zander—I don't know how to handle his close proximity. His bruising kisses and intense eyes and unexpected admissions and kind heart beneath his brash exterior. The cocky smile and strong hands and brutal honesty. How do I deal with all these weird tingly sensations he keeps making me feel? I just don't know. So I've been avoiding him. Sneaking down the hallway after he goes for his run in the morning or heading straight for my room when I get off work. No time to chat or make an idiot out of myself when I'm not face-to-face with him.

But now that I realize how long I've been sitting here lost in my painting, I suddenly feel the ache of my back and the strain on my eyes from the constant concentration. And recognize that I'm starving. When I enter the kitchen, the television is on low, and Zander's on the couch with his back to me, feet up on the table. He doesn't turn or acknowledge me, although I'm pretty sure he heard the creak of the wood floor as I walked in. I'm okay with that, since at least I have a few more minutes to prepare myself to face him.

But as I walk into the family room with a bowl of cereal in hand, I realize there is no amount of preparation that could stifle the way he makes me feel: lust and irritation and want and frustration all rolled into one. So I do the only thing I can and sit on the opposite end of the couch from him and settle in to eat my cereal, hating that I feel awkward in my own home.

"Hey," I finally say softly, not wanting to interrupt but letting manners get the best of me.

"Hey." That's it. No glance my way.

Determined not to let him have the run of our house while I slink away in avoidance, I settle into my seat and turn my focus from him to the television.

He's watching a race. The drone of the cars going around and around the track is constant, while the screen switches between the lead car and then the action farther back on the track where cars pass one another and change positions. I've never really watched a race before—too lowbrow for Ethan to care for—but there is a definite draw to it, something thrilling, that I think I can understand.

In my peripheral vision, though, Zander is much more interesting to observe. His body language seems tense, hands fisted as if he's behind the wheel. He grimaces every few seconds like there's been a mistake made that I'm sure the layman fan would never notice.

But he doesn't speak, doesn't move, just scrutinizes the racing world he's been removed from. And that in itself has to make it brutal to watch.

So we sit on the same couch, both viewing the race but for different reasons. The only sounds come from the clink of the spoon against the glass bowl. Or a mutter under his breath. The announcers droning on. The creak of the couch as I shift positions.

"Let's see if Colton Donavan can clinch this, Al, or if the absence of his teammate affects his ability to help block Grayson Dane from slingshotting past him on the final turn. He's been running smooth and fast all day. Both have new tires and are good on fuel. But Dane has two more teammates on the track. Let's see how much help they'll be able to give him."

The race unfolds lap by lap, turn by turn, pass by pass, and as each second ticks by, Zander leans forward farther and farther: elbows on his knees, hands clasped together, and his features etched in intense concentration. The events on-screen own his attention so much that I don't even think he remembers I'm there sitting beside him.

"Goddammit!" he swears angrily as he shoves up off the couch and watches a blue car pass a red one. The announcers are going wild, but I'm too busy watching the emotion play over Zander's face to hear what they are saying.

When I can tear my eyes off him, the camera is following the winning car on its victory lap before panning back to the second-place car turning into the pits. Zander squints his eyes as if he's waiting to catch a glimpse of something. The shot moves back to the victor before he sees it, because he angrily mutters something under his breath before throwing the remote down.

The back door slams. The pounding of a hammer starts.

And I'm left looking at a closed door with my empty cereal bowl in my hands and a lot of unanswered questions.

That is, until the field reporter begins to interview the second-place racer. His name is splashed along the bottom of the screen in big, bold letters—COLTON DONAVAN—and seeing it in print causes puzzle pieces to fall into place.

The matching last name. The missing racer from the team. The lack of help on the track.

*All of it.*

Even though I've never followed racing, Colton Donavan is definitely a name I've heard before—synonymous with his prolific successes and his renowned family—and obviously somehow related to Zander.

Of course—how could I have been so stupid to not make the connection? That was Zander's team, his ride, and the reason he now hates Sundays. It's everything he left behind.

Did his team lose today because he wasn't on the track? Now the grumbling and the storming out make sense to me. When the hammer pounds harder and harder outside, it's a clear indication that my assumption is correct.

I try to ignore him, busy myself with picking up the house, cleaning the kitchen, folding the towels in the dryer, but the continued sound of the hammer keeps dragging my thoughts back to Zander. Curiosity nags at me. What did he do? How bad was it?

Bored and yet too preoccupied to go back to painting, I stand in the kitchen and fight my own bad idea. Wanting to go sit in the sun for a bit before the incoming storm moves in. Close my eyes and soak up the rays while I relax.

Except whom am I fooling? I'm not going out to sit in the sun so much as I'm going outside to sit with Zander—the man I've been avoiding.

So I grab a bag of chips and head out in the direction of the incessant pounding noise and the occasional muttered curse word. When I step into the frame of the open sliding glass doors that lead to the deck, I'm surprised to see that Zander has ripped almost the entire thing down in the past few days—he's starting to reinforce the remaining pieces.

He's in a white T-shirt and blue jeans, hammer in hand, bent over in concentration with a level and a box of nails at his side while he lines up the next piece of wood. And I hate that I catch myself admiring his body. Taking note of the patch between his shoulder blades where a trail of sweat has darkened the cotton fabric of his shirt. The flex of his biceps as he works. The light flecks of sawdust in his dark hair. The small trace of blood on his forearm where he must have scratched it on something.

"It's therapeutic. Grab a hammer if you want to give it a try."

His voice jars me from what I thought was my private admiration of him. Heat fills my cheeks at the realization he knew I was there staring.

"I—I don't know how to . . . ," I respond, suddenly flustered under the scrutiny of his stare behind the tinted lenses of his sunglasses.

"There's no skill needed, Socks." He bends over the toolbox and, after grabbing a hammer, holds it out handle first. "It's not flowery or girly, but it does the job. Just don't hit your thumb."

My eyes flicker from the tool to his face before I cross the few feet between us and take it from him. And now that I have it, I have absolutely no clue what to do. Luckily he senses I need direction, because he summons me over to where he was working.

Taking the pencil from behind his ear, he proceeds to measure and mark small circles in the middle of the two-by-four he lined up on a section of handrail, while I stand there feeling stupid with the unfamiliar weight of the hammer in my hand. Plus now that we're so close, my instinct to avoid him has returned with a vengeance.

"I want you to hammer nails into each of those marks, okay?"

While a big part of me is surprised and even excited to do something constructive with my hands, I'm also afraid I'll make a mistake and mess something up. I must look like a deer in the headlights, because he belts out a laugh before taking a step closer to me.

"C'mere. I promise it's as easy as it looks. You take

this nail here and then you tap the top of it until it bites into the wood." He steps behind me, body ghosting mine, before taking hold of my hands and directing them into proper positioning. And hell if he didn't just make hammering a simple nail on its head a lot more complicated.

Because I'm sure I could have figured it out—it's not rocket science after all—and yet once our bodies are touching, the scent of his cologne in my nose, the feel of his warm breath hitting the side of my face as he leans his head forward to demonstrate with our paired hands, the attraction hijacks my concentration. His comments from the other night return to front and center in my mind, when they weren't buried very far to begin with.

He holds my hand over the handle, and his fingers help me grip the nail as we tap the head of it into the first marked location on the wood. "See? Simple."

*No, complicated is more like it.*

But I bite my tongue, nod, and concentrate through the distraction of his presence when I take control of the hammer and tap the nail in farther. He steps back after a few more taps and I feel like I can finally breathe again, think again without him clouding my thoughts.

The work is slow going. For every one nail I tap in, I swear he taps in four or five, but there is some truth to his comment about it being therapeutic. There's a sense of stress release in the repeated activity of pounding the hell out of a little metal nail: the clink of the hammer, how it starts to disappear into the wood, then one final hard hit to make sure it's completely seated.

"Eight brothers, huh?" I ask, trying to stick to a safe topic.

"Yep." The thump of his hammer interrupts his sentence. "Before I was adopted, I lived in a boys' home called the House. There were eight of us over the time I was there. We all kind of grew up together. Consider each other as brothers." *Thump. Thump. Thump.* "I was adopted eventually. The lady who ran the House, she and her husband ended up adopting me after a bunch of shit happened that's complicated. But it didn't matter to us. I mean, yeah, we don't have the same last names and it's not official by any law, but that doesn't matter to us. We're brothers."

"That's seven, right?"

"Yeah. My adoptive parents had a son. So eight." He shrugs and, without warning, turns on the table saw and effectively ends the conversation.

We work in silence after that. The ferry's horn sounds out occasionally. Zander mutters a harsh swear every once in a while, but other than that, it's just the steady (him) and unsteady (me) thump of hammers. When I run out of spots on my marked board, he sets up the next board for me with minimal words exchanged.

"Maybe someday, you'll trust me enough to talk about it." His quiet comment spoken over his shoulder as if he's talking about the weather throws me momentarily. Causes that little flicker of panic to come to life.

"How do you know this is going to hold up? The deck?"

*Smooth, Getty. That redirection was really subtle.* I mentally put the heel of my hand to my forehead as he belts out a long laugh that tells me it sounded as ridiculous to him as it did to me.

"Very casual," he says with a nod. "But I appreciate the attempt."

The smile is slow but on my lips nonetheless, and I love that he can do that to me—make me laugh at my idiosyncrasies. It's not something I'm used to by a long stretch.

"Okay." I work my tongue in my cheek as I try to figure out how to answer him. "How about I'll talk to you as soon as you talk to me?"

His snort comes loud and clear. "The difference, though, is you can look me up. Know who I am. Where I came from. I'm not hiding any of the truths, just trying to figure out how much I want to listen to them." He hits the nail with enough force that the sound echoes off the clapboard of the house before he looks over to me and lifts his sunglasses up so I can see the blue of his eyes.

I avert my gaze instantly, afraid he'll be able to tell from the flush on my cheeks that I did give in to temptation. Ventured to the library yesterday to use the Internet to see whom I'm living with. And of course, after taking all the time to build up the courage to go in there and overcoming the worry that he'd somehow find out—small town and all that—the damn computer was broken. Shipped out to the mainland for repairs.

"You, on the other hand," he continues, pulling me from my thoughts, "are a goddamn mystery in all aspects, so your offer isn't exactly fair."

Our eyes hold each other in the waning sunlight; the challenge to give him a better answer is communicated without words.

"Let's just say I have Daddy issues. Is that a good enough answer?"

His sharp, self-deprecating laugh is the last thing I expect. "You and me both, Socks. So no good. That cancels each other out. Next confession . . ."

I direct daggers his way. My emotions are warring over what to tell him, even though I know I can't just yet. There's too much at risk for me—emotional and otherwise. "I don't really want to like you, but you make it damn hard not to. There. That's a confession."

That's all I'm giving him with his quick grin and baby blues and coaxing questions.

"It's a start. I'll take it."

# Chapter 12

"I can't believe I let you talk me into this," I groan, but inwardly I revel in it. The red and white checkered tablecloth, the half-eaten pizza sitting on a metal stand, and what he called the wimpy starter wine shared in glasses between us. How after we came in from working on the deck, he told me to get dressed because he was taking me to dinner to thank me for helping.

Of course I refused.

But I'm so glad he persisted, because getting out, seeing the town through his eyes, showed me that I needed to have a little fun. Everyone he greets knows who he is because of his job, and really being a local instead of fading into the background has been liberating. In fact I can't remember the last time I enjoyed myself like this.

"We forgot to make a toast," he says as he lifts his glass up. I roll my eyes but can't help smiling.

"To friends," I offer up, unsure what we should be toasting, but I figure this is as good an option as any given our situation.

"No. Not to friends." My eyes flash to Zander's at the sound of his forceful reply; I'm a little surprised and a lot curious. "Because friends between the opposite sexes leads to friends with benefits and that *always* ends in disaster. And you know what, Getty? I don't want that with you . . . so let's just say 'to *us*'"—he pauses, tapping his glass to mine—"whatever *us* may be."

"To us," I murmur as his eyes search mine. All the while I'm trying to figure out what part he doesn't want with me: the friends with benefits or the ending in disaster.

The rest of the meal passes how the whole evening has, with us fabricating sordid backstories about the people sitting across the restaurant from us: townspeople we don't know but will remember from here on out from our silly game. How the quiet mom with three rowdy boys in the corner really is a dominatrix for hire at night, or the gregarious busboy hoards Barbra Streisand memorabilia in his basement.

The speculation and laughs are endless, but they don't stop Zander's toast from repeating in my mind as we walk back home to the cottage together.

"Your toast? I don't want that with you either." Maybe it's the few glasses of Moscato that have gone to my head or just that I've thought about his comment enough, but there's no denying the tinge of hurt to my tone.

Maybe he didn't hear the hurt part.

But I have to give it to Zander—while he falters mid-stride, he doesn't ask what I mean. Rather he nods his head and keeps walking the rest of the way home without saying much more. He opens the door, turns on the light, and heads into the kitchen to put the leftover pizza in the refrigerator all without a word as I stare at his silhouette and wonder what he's thinking. What I did to piss him off other than agree with him.

Because I'm used to things—whatever they are—always being my fault. Every mood swing. Every bad day at work. The change in the weather for God's sake, if I were to believe Ethan.

So I stare at the broad lines of Zander's shoulders, his hair disheveled from the wind on the walk home, his eyes focusing on where he's pushing the house key around on the counter, and I wonder what I've done wrong this time.

"Tell me something, Getty." He lifts his head finally

and meets my eyes. "If you were in the restaurant tonight and saw the two of us, what story would you have made up to explain us being there?"

His question throws me momentarily. His eyes hold fast to mine as he rounds the front of the counter and leans his hips against it. There's something so distinctly masculine about the stance that I stop and stare for a moment before answering him.

"Why?"

"Just humor me." He flashes me a heart-stopping grin, and between that and the intensity in his eyes, it's impossible to refuse when he pats the counter beside him for me to sit.

Suddenly leery of being close to him when I've been just that all day, I move slowly and take my time hopping my butt up on the countertop, scooting back so that my legs are dangling over the edge.

"If I was making up a story about us, I'd say that we were friends who met for dinner after working all day."

*"Friends."* He makes a noncommittal sound and then shifts so that he can meet my gaze. I squirm under his quiet scrutiny: eyes narrowing, tongue tucked in his cheek, hand placed way too close to the side of my thigh. "That's all you've got, Socks?" He shifts so that his pelvis is against the counter, hip hitting my knee. "That's not very creative coming from an artist."

I start to scoff, immediately reject his label, but the warning look in his eye stops it on my tongue. "Sorry."

Annoyance flickers over his face, but it's gone just as quickly as it comes. "Don't apologize."

I begin to say *I'm sorry* again and stop myself, heeding the cautionary tone in his voice. "What's your story, then?" He doesn't like mine—then he needs to give me his. But the minute I make the comment, I feel like I've just played right into his hands even if I can't figure out what the end-game is.

"I'm glad you asked." A shift of his feet. His hips slide farther into mine. That flutter of something deep in my belly. "I would have seen a famously successful painter—world renowned in fact," he says with a lift of his eyebrows, "going to dinner with the inspiration for her next painting. He's a championship-winning race car driver. Ruggedly handsome. Not *pretty* at all."

I scrunch up my nose. "A little pretty."

He places his hand on my knee and squeezes gently, a playful warning. But his hand remains there and even as he continues speaking, all I can think about is the sudden warmth and weight of his touch. "They are there discussing their next project."

"What if she doesn't paint people?"

"Oh, she does."

"She does?"

"Yes. She's branching out. Challenging herself. A nude of him is next on her list."

I throw my head back, the laughter bubbling up and over, and the sound of his laughter mixed with mine is comforting. "No. Not a nude. He's not *pretty* enough for a nude."

"Touché," he says with a shake of his head, and his grin widens.

"Tell me more about them."

"She's trying to ply him with cheap wine, get him drunk, maybe take advantage of him a little later." I raise my eyebrows. "She thinks she can teach him a few things in *all* aspects."

"Oh." The sound falls from my lips. *Is he implying what I think he's implying?*

"*Oh?*"

"So they're more than just friends, then?" My mind runs wild. About as wild as my heartbeat when Zander moves between my parted knees so that he's face-to-face with me. And the dim light in the room that he just blocked with his change in position only adds to what suddenly feels like the intimacy of the moment. The shadow that falls over his face and the quick dart of his tongue to wet his lips draws out all kinds of feelings within me, that slow, sweet ache in the delta of my thighs included.

"Do you want them to be more than friends, Getty?" The way he says my name, the intention laced in that single word, calls to every single part of me.

And I know we're definitely not talking about a made-up scenario right now. We're talking about the frustrated kiss he gave me at work the other day and the fire he says I'm not ready to light that has kept me up thinking late at night.

"I don't know." I try to steady my breathing as he places his hands on the counter beside my thighs and leans his body into me.

*"You don't?"*

"No. I need to know more about them." I try to buy some time. Attempt to gain some clarity in the face of his powerful physical presence so I can decide which side I want to win: my need for things to remain simple with him or my want to feel more than just his kiss.

By the look on his face, I can tell my request throws him, but he recovers quickly. "More about them? Hmm. Let's see. She's had a troubled past. He wishes she'd talk more about it—trust him—because he's a much better listener than her canvas and paints are, but he understands that these things take time." Even with the sudden serious turn of the conversation, his last comment pulls the corners of my mouth up in a smile.

"And him? What about him?"

"You tell me." It's not a request, not a demand, but it's clear that he wants to know what I think of him.

"I think—"

*"She,"* he corrects.

"*She thinks* that he has this big persona he feels he must live by—the grandiose asshole." I get a lift of his eyebrows with the term. "He's stubborn and infuriating . . . but underneath all of that, he has a kind heart. He's confident and sure of himself in a way she only wishes she could be. And despite that, she knows he's been hurt somehow or has seen hurt, because most men aren't patient enough to stand back and let her go through what she's going through without pushing. And he isn't pushing, so she knows that he gets it, even though he doesn't know what 'it' really is."

He nods his head and runs his hands up and down my thighs. And I swear to God he does it out of a comforting reflex, because I can tell the minute he realizes he is doing it—his hands falter in motion, eyes widen momentarily—and yet he keeps them where they are and doesn't remove them.

"What about him? Why does she think he's here on the island?"

I twist my lips, so many theories coming to mind, and yet I'm not sure how to go about saying them. "Because he hates Sundays." Better start with some humor and see how he plays it.

That earns a soft chuckle from him. "Really?"

"Yeah. And probably any day that ends in *y*, since he's away from his passion, but she gets a feeling there's more there. She'd listen if he wanted to talk about it, but won't ask."

"Questions always get you in trouble," he murmurs.

"Not always," I muse.

"Does she want to be more than friends with him, Getty?"

*Hello, trouble.* Guess he's trying to prove his point.

An even intake of breath. The pounding of my heart. The scent of his cologne. The hope of possibility. "She's afraid." My voice is barely audible.

"Of him?"

All I can do is nod my head. His lips are right there. The memory of how they felt on mine front and center. "Of everything about him."

My chest hurts to draw in air. My body aches in a way I've never felt before. Anticipation. Fear. Uncertainty. All three surge through me. Deplete me. Revive me.

"Why would she be afraid of him, Getty?"

My name again. It's his way of bringing me back to the moment and out of my head, where the ghosts swim. His way of reminding me of my new name, of my fresh start, of new beginnings.

"Because she's the *disaster*. The one who can't do anything right. The one who can't teach him anything and so he's going to be disappointed when he finds out she's nothing like who he thinks she is."

He angles his head and stares at me, eyes searching and

so intense that I break our connection and look down to where his hands are on my thighs. "Not hardly a disaster. A little timid maybe. A lot gun-shy. But time will help that."

With a rebuttal held on my tongue, I visually trace the lines of his hands on my legs to distract myself. The broad fingers with a few cuts and scrapes from working on the deck. This whole conversation has pushed my thoughts out of my comfort zone. And I wonder what they'd feel like running over my body.

The thought makes me want to hyperventilate. The idea of him seeing me naked. Ethan's criticisms trying to force their way in my head.

*You're the worst lay I've ever had, Gertrude. So bad I may need to take up with the housekeeper just to be satisfied. Your body's too soft; your tits aren't big enough. And for fuck's sake, it's not my job to make you come. It's not my problem you can't get off. And if I ever see you try to do it on your own, we're going to have a big problem.*

"Uh-uh. Look at me. What's going on in that mind of yours?"

I can't. I don't want to lift my head so he can see every single thing about me—my inadequacies, my fear of experiencing more, my hope for more—in my eyes. Because I can't hide it. I can fight it, but I definitely can't hide it.

Since I'm focused on his hands, I follow the movement as they lift off my thighs and come up to cup the sides of my cheeks, forcing my eyes to meet his.

"I thought we were talking about *her*," I assert, needing to get this back in the make-believe realm, because his eyes are too honest, his touch too tangible, and I am starting to imagine the possibility of there being something more between us when I know he can't really mean it.

He nods in response, angling his head to the side as he studies me. "We are," he murmurs as if it's real, his eyes narrowing as he leans closer into me. "He wants to ask her so many questions but now knows she's afraid and he doesn't want to spook her."

"Maybe he should just ask. Maybe she'll answer him. Maybe she won't. They've had quite a few glasses of wine after all."

"Ah, yes. Liquid courage. It does wonders for the nerves, or so I've heard." I've never been this close to another man for this amount of time besides Ethan. It's unnerving and exhilarating all at once to know that this is my choosing. "Maybe he's afraid of her too."

I snort in jest. "You're kidding, right? Look at him and look at her. There's no need for him to be afraid of her. She's average and he looks like he just walked off the pages of a magazine ad."

"I think she's not seeing herself clearly."

"Well, I think he's full of shit. Tell me why he's afraid of her, then." I sound defensive, bothered, and maybe I am. All that's missing is a huff and crossing my arms across my chest in denial. But perhaps I'm so conditioned to the Ethan setup where he built me up just to tear me down that I'm afraid of believing any compliment.

"Because he's afraid he'll get too close to her. He realizes that regardless of how strong she is, she's still fragile emotionally and that they have some kind of connection despite their constant bickering. He worries about what it will do to her when the fix-it list is done and he has to go back to his real life."

His explanation captivates me. Pulls on my heartstrings. Causes an unexpected mini-flutter of panic at the idea of him leaving. So I decide to voice some of my thoughts out loud. "So he's afraid for her?" I need clarification so my mind doesn't run wild with this and make anything I want out of it.

"No."

"*No?*"

"No, he's afraid for *him*. What if she paints him with an incredible set of abs? A perfect eight-pack that he can't seem to get in the gym regardless of how hard he works at it? I mean that's a valid reason for him to be afraid. To have to leave her when she makes him feel better about himself than anyone else has in a long time."

My inhalation is shaky. And while he's trying to add levity to the unexpectedly deep conversation, his comments still hit home with a sincerity I never expected from me. I can't help the small smile on my lips when what I really should be doing is figuring out whether he's serious about being afraid of getting closer to me, or if he is just saying it to lighten the sudden insecurity I have after admitting I'm afraid of him.

Or rather *she's afraid of him*.

I struggle to find a balance, because all of a sudden I feel outmaneuvered and a bit vulnerable, and my mind latches onto something he said.

"I would think if she's going to be painting him nude, he's going to be more concerned about the size she paints another area than just his abs."

He throws his head back and laughs while I sit with eyes narrowed wondering if I just in fact flirted with him. And while to other women, that may sound like the stupidest observation ever, for me, it's something I can't remember having done in the longest time. In fact I'm so used to downplaying every conversation with a male—sparse eye contact, proper distance between us, an air of disdain—for fear of possible repercussions that it takes a minute to compute that this really is me sitting on a counter with a very hot man standing between my legs.

Cue the nerves.

But it's hard to be too anxious when Zander is laughing the way he is and I'm the one who caused it.

"You've got a point there," he chuckles, and runs one hand through his hair, leaving it adorably tousled before returning his hand to the top of my thigh in the most natural of actions. "She has a very good sense of humor."

"Hmm." I'm busy watching him. Studying him. The little crinkles around his eyes when he smiles. The slightest dent in his chin that's noticeable only from up close. The five-o'clock shadow shading his jawline. "She does?"

"Yes, she does."

Silence falls around us as his thumb subtly rubs back and forth on my thigh. Tension fills the room as expectation builds over what's going to happen next.

My nerves reappear. The panic button suddenly pushed, so I try to escape the uncertainty of what to do or say next.

"I thought you said he had questions for her," I finally stammer when the unknown becomes way too much.

"He does."

"And . . . ?" I prompt when he takes a long pause, my mind struggling to stay alert when my hormones are all focused elsewhere.

He slides his hands up and down the tops of my thighs, his lips twisting as he thinks about what questions he wants to ask the most.

"He wants to know why she thinks she's a disaster. He wants to know what he can do besides be patient to help her." His voice becomes softer with each word, more serious, more intent. "He can't figure out why even though he's sworn to himself he needs to stay away from her, he can't seem to follow through."

"I don't think she can answer that last question for him." I feel the need to shift, fidget, under the intensity of his blue eyes and yet I do neither.

"True." He arches one eyebrow up, a shy smile ghosting his lips as he lifts his hands to my cheeks again. "Maybe she can answer this one for him."

"Hmm?"

"Do you think she wants him to kiss her?"

My breath stops. Heart pounds. Body stills. "Does *he want* to kiss her?"

"There you go answering a question with a question again, Socks."

"You didn't answer." Classic avoidance.

"Neither did you." That shy smile again. The brush of his thumb over my bottom lip, which takes everything I have to not close my eyes and sink into.

"Yes." *Oh shit.* Did I really just say that?

*"Yes?"* he confirms, voice soft but certain.

I nod my head. Swallow over the nerves that just seized up my throat. But all thought is lost as he moves ever so slowly into me.

"Good, because I don't think he was going to take no for an answer."

Processing his comment is impossible because his lips

are on mine and my faculties are temporarily and willingly drugged.

His lips meet mine with soft brushes asking for acceptance. I part my lips and grant him access to take more from me. Our tongues touch, intertwine, in a soft dance of greeting. His fingers frame my face, angling it, and my skin warms beneath his touch. The desirous groan from the back of his throat spurs me on, gives me a sense of confidence that whatever I'm doing is enough for him.

And God yes, it's doing it for me. His kiss is gentle yet demanding. So soft it feels like a dream, but I definitely know it's not with the heat of him standing between my legs and the taste of wine still on his tongue.

His hands move. Slide down my rib cage and cup my ass before pulling me closer toward the edge and into him.

My head is light. My heart is full. My nerves are slowly being taken over by the haze of everything about him: his cologne, the quiet murmur he makes, the pressure of his hands on my lower back, the softness of his lips, the finesse of his kiss.

My hands begin to move as our lips continue to taste and tantalize. Taunt and satisfy. I slide the palms of my hands over his back, where his muscles tense as his hands mirror mine. Both in unison. Me more hesitantly, him more sure in his touch.

I push away all thoughts of my life before: of Ethan and how after we were married, kissing was never allowed other than soft pecks outside the house for people to see how much he loved his doting wife. Of his crass comments about how mouths were good for only one thing and those apologies were not to be spoken but to be given.

I lose myself to the moment. To the here and now. To all of it. Lost in not thinking. To the feeling. To being wanted. To the simple sensuality of being kissed senseless.

My core burns with desire like I've never felt before. Molten liquid spreading from my center outward. The ache so intense it borders on painful. My lips tingle; my nipples tighten; my skin gets goose bumps.

Zander's hands inch their way beneath the hem of my

shirt. Roughened fingertips scrape ever so gently along that sensitive flesh just about the waistband of my pants. Shocks of sensation spiral up my spine and only add pressure to the need tingeing my reactions.

He gently slides them up my bare back at the same time he shifts his stance so that our bodies are perfectly pressed together with my body perched on the edge of the counter. And I'm not sure if it's the flash of a thought in my mind that he might want to take my shirt off or the sudden sensation of the hardened bulge of his denim-clad dick pressing between the apex of my thighs, but I must hesitate somehow.

Because he reacts.

Zander breaks from the kiss instantly, a startled gasp falling from my mouth as his hands come to my face so I can't look away. And before he can even say a thing, I'm instantly nervous: hands shaking, apology at the ready, rejection accepted, inadequacy verified.

His eyes search mine and I feel like such an idiot. What woman gets kissed senseless by a man and then hesitates when she can feel the evidence of her turning him on? It's not like he was grinding against me or rushing the moment. He's not guilty of anything other than being a virile man.

"Getty?" My name on his lips again. Concern etched in the lines of his face. My eyes desperately try to focus on anything other than his.

The fear takes over: of disappointing him, of my body turning him off, of not being enough, of scaring him away because of my lack of skill—take your pick.

"I'm sorry." It's a reflex. On my tongue and out of my mouth without thought.

And I get the reaction from him I wonder if I was subconsciously hoping for. "Sweet hell, Getty," he says in frustration as he pushes away from me, one hand shoving through his hair, the other raking down the back of his neck as he turns and takes a couple of steps away from me. "Will you *stop* apologizing? You did absolutely nothing wrong."

He turns back around, eyes begging and asking and

searching, and I don't know how to respond, since apologizing, being the one to blame, is all I've ever known for so long.

"I'm sor . . ." My voice fades off, the word—*once again*—dying on my tongue as his jaw sets in frustration.

How was it that seconds ago my blood was on fire from his touch and now it's heating my cheeks in embarrassment? I can't even be kissed without messing it up.

"I told you. *She's* a disaster." I can barely say it. I have to look away from him, focus on my clasped hands with my thumbs fiddling together. Can't bring myself to watch his reaction to my shame. But the condescending laugh I'm so conditioned to expect doesn't come.

Not in the least.

He comes into my field of vision, his hips, his chest, his chin, his eyes, as his hands tenderly guide my face up so that I can meet his eyes. "He doesn't think she's a disaster. In fact, she's quite the opposite. She's beautifully scarred, gorgeously flawed, irresistibly captivating."

Tears well in my eyes—his words are probably the nicest ones anyone has said to me in so long. He's not telling me it never happened. He's not telling me I made it all up in my head. Rather he's telling me that despite it all, there is still something redeemable in me.

The first tear slips down my cheek and yet he keeps his eyes unwavering on mine.

"I don't know what he did to you, Getty. Don't have a fucking clue. But I know he didn't treat you right. He took every part of you that you gave him and mistreated it somehow and so badly that you fear the things that should make you feel good. Laughter. Yourself. Your art. Your confidence. *A kiss.* And who knows what else?"

His words hit too close to home. Make me struggle for air under the weight of their presence in this moment. Their implications making me feel so very stupid for letting Ethan steal all those things from me.

"Please, Zander. Don't ruin tonight. I'm sor—didn't mean to . . . Tonight was one of the best times I've had in as long as I can remember. Can we just leave it at that? Please?" My voice wavers. The tears I'm holding back burn in my throat. His thumbs brush back and forth on my cheeks, reminding me of how much I've let him in.

"Oh, Getty," he sighs with clear affection as he rests his forehead against mine. We are nose to nose, his hands still on my face, the warmth of his breath feathering over my lips. There's something so comforting in the action, in the fact that, rather than run away, he stepped into me. I close my eyes and feel his concern, accept his compassion.

"One of these days you're going to find a man who treats you right," he murmurs softly. "Sweeps you off your feet. Treats you like you walk on water. Inspires you to paint sunny skies and calm oceans."

"Not nudes?" I can't help it. It just felt right to say. And as I reel that he noticed the correlation between my emotions and my pictures, he steps back from me, eyes alight with humor and a quiet laugh on his lips.

"No. Not nudes." He runs his hands down to my shoulders and squeezes them gently. "You deserve nothing less than the best, Getty."

"Thank you," I whisper, wondering how he figures into all of this, considering he was the one kissing me moments ago.

He breathes deeply, whatever it is I can see on the tip of his tongue weighing down the atmosphere around us. Is he thankful for my hesitancy because now that he's stepped back, he regrets getting involved with the head case that I obviously am?

I wouldn't blame him if he did. And I hate that I've already lost a little piece of my healing heart to this man standing in front of me with conflicted eyes. He's kind and patient and stubborn and my God, the man can kiss me so senseless I forgot my old *and* my new name. Is it stupid to say that? Yes. But when you've never known kindness like this, it's easy to give a part of yourself to the person who shows it, because when all you have are broken pieces to begin with, who's going to miss one more little piece?

*Seriously?* Why am I having ridiculous thoughts like this when three weeks ago I was ready to poke his eye out with a mini-blind wand? I look at him—blue eyes, dark hair, hard body—and wonder how he went from annoying to attractive. Am I that messed up—that emotionally wrought—that being nice to me is all it takes?

I hate that I don't know the answer to the question.

"I need you to hear this when I say it and really listen, okay?" he says, pulling me from my self-deprecating thoughts.

Here it comes. I was right. He regrets this.

I nod my head.

"Right now every damn part of me wants to kiss you again. Kiss you till we can't breathe, then lay you down on my bed and show you what it's like to feel that kind of worship. But God, Getty, I can't do it knowing that I might hurt you in the end when you've obviously been so hurt already. I can't make the promises you deserve. I have my life back home. My racing. My family. I need to sort my shit out, make my amends, and then in a few months I'll head back to it. That's not fair to you. I want more than anything to be the selfish prick I've been over the past few months and think only of myself. Sleep with you, feed that crazy need you've created in me, and then walk away when the time comes without a care . . ." He blows out breath and shakes his head like he can't believe he's not going to, before meeting my eyes again. "But I can't do that to you. I can't knowingly walk you into my storm without showing you where the lighthouse is so you have a way out before you even begin."

My eyes go wide and chest constricts as I attempt to process everything he's saying. The civil war happening inside him over being who he needs to be versus who he wants to be. Over what I know is best for me and what could break me again.

And of course all coherent thoughts vanish when he steps into me again, hands back on my cheeks, eyes locked onto mine. He leans forward and brushes his lips to mine in the most tender of kisses. The kind that makes you want to simultaneously sag inwardly and fist your hand in his shirt to demand more.

His unsteady draw of breath is audible—restraint held by a thread—before his blue eyes find mine. "I'm showing you where the lighthouse is, Getty. Giving you a way out.

It's up to you to decide if you want to step into my storm before it passes through or head for safety. I can't decide for you."

I begin to speak, my heart in my throat and my pulse racing, but he shakes his head to stop me. "Not now. You need to think about it. Sleep on it. Get a clear head and figure out your answer. I'll wait." When he reaches out to put one hand on the side of my face, I close my eyes and turn into the touch. My lips kiss the palm of his hand; his compassion has undone me in so many ways I can't think straight. "Good night."

"Zander," I call after him as he turns to walk down the hall.

He stops momentarily, head hanging down, broad shoulders set proudly. "Good night, Socks."

There's so much I want to say. *Stop. Wait. Yes. No. I don't know. I'm sorry.* But none of them come out, because I'm not sure which one I want to say the most.

I want to tell him that I don't care. That we should just live in the moment. Not worry about tomorrow or a few weeks from now when the to-do list is complete. Ask him to help me get over the hurdle of Ethan's lies by showing me how sex should be. Be the spontaneous person I aspire to someday be.

Desperation fuels my thoughts, makes me already miss how he made me feel tonight. But I can't tell him, because he's right. I already like him too much as it is. What's going to happen if I fall for him and he leaves and doesn't look back? Is it presumptuous? Yes. But at the same time, he's given me something that no one else has in a long time: *hope.*

*Oh my God, Getty. Get a grip.* Go back to painting angry thunderstorms instead of thinking of beautiful sunsets, because you're not going to ride away into one of them with him. You're naive if you think you will. While he may be a good guy, there's no place in his life for a wannabe painter/bartender in any capacity let alone as more than friends.

And he already said he definitely doesn't want friends with benefits.

*To us.* His toast echoes in my head as I hear the door to his bedroom close quietly, and I grip the edge of the counter to keep from acting on that want for spontaneity.

Now I'm left in the darkened kitchen with his kiss on my lips and his words in my head, wondering what exactly I want us to be.

The problem is the difference between want and need is a thin line called self-control.

And I've already been controlled enough in my life.

# Chapter 13

GETTY

Something jolts me awake with a start. The shadowed figure standing over my bed startles every part of me—breath, heart, imagination. And for that split second before he says my name, fear takes hold that Ethan has come for me.

"Getty."

"Zander?" My voice is drugged with sleep, mind racing with what he's doing in here as he lowers down to sit on the edge of the bed. I'd started to relax at the sound of his voice, but now every intangible part of me stands at attention.

And before I can comprehend much more—why he's here, why my stomach is somersaulting into my chest, why chills are racing over my body—he leans forward without another word and kisses me.

Soft at first. A brush of lips. A tug on my bottom lip. A hand brushing my hair off my face as he leans back to look at me through the moonlit room. And I know before he speaks what he's going to say.

"I want you, Getty."

"Yes." It's the only answer I can give. The only consent needed, because his mouth is back on mine before I can inhale my next breath. And while this next kiss is still tender, there's a tinge of hunger to it that's new and surprising to me.

I relax into the mattress, too many things happening at once to process them all. His hand running down the side of my rib cage. His other hand on the side of my neck, thumb hooked under my ear. The increasing demand in his kiss. The groan of desperation from his throat. His hand on my waist sliding under the hem of my T-shirt. A chilled hand on warm skin slowly sliding up. My soft gasp as he finds my breast. The arch of my neck. His fingers caressing. Tongue possessing. My sensations overwhelmed.

*The match being lit.*

I'm inundated. Lost to his touch and the skill of his mouth and the incredible way he makes me feel.

The stubble of the day's growth scrapes down the column of my neck, his lips lacing open-mouth kisses to soothe its sting. But I like the sting. Like knowing I'm alive and this is really happening. Then he cups my breasts with both hands, his mouth taking over their seduction in a kind of finesse I've never experienced. His warm lips and heated tongue suck and tease the tight bud of my nipple while his strong hands hold them in place.

The combination of sensations causes a blistering ache in the delta of my thighs. One that hurts so good.

"Fuck, Getty," he murmurs against my breast as one hand runs down to my hip, fingers kneading the flesh there as I thread mine in his hair and moan in response to the bliss he's creating.

Fingers feathering over the tops of my thighs. They tug my waistband. Skim across the top of my sex. Fingertips tickling right at the top of my seam, a subtle request for access. And I'm so lost to experiencing this with him—the hushed murmurs of desire and the touches laced with intent—that all I can think about is how much more I want of the way he's making me feel.

His fingers dance over my most intimate of flesh as his mouth finds mine again. This time his kiss feels more demanding, hungrier, and it's my only focus until his fingertips slowly part me and brush gently over my clit. My gasp of pleasure is swallowed by his kiss, the sudden tensing of my leg muscles his gauge of my definite responsiveness.

And my God . . . going from having no one touch me but my own hand to being treated with such reverence—soft and desirous and attentive—is like creating a spark in a room full of propane. Explosive. Fiery. Unrelenting.

His touch rocks me. It doesn't take much. Between the generosity in how he caresses me and the greed in his kiss, seconds tumble into one another as every part of my body burns bright and fast toward climax.

My hands on his shoulders. Fingernails into steeled flesh. Breath robbed. Head digging back in the pillow. Back arched. Hips bucking. Zander catapults me into the oblivious free fall of my orgasm.

"Zander." I cry out his name in a plea for him to keep going. A plea for him to stop for a second. And I can't decide which I want more as his fingers softly milk the last of the vibrations for me.

"Getty."

"Not yet."

"Getty!" More insistent. Hands suddenly on my shoulders, shaking me. My mind shocked to the present.

To the dark room around me. Zander standing over me, my fingers slick between my thighs. I freeze, trying to grasp dream from reality.

"You were having a nightmare. Called out my name. Were thrashing around," he says as he sits down beside me.

And if there were any way he could see my eyes and the mask of mortification that must be blanketing my face, he'd know the truth. That my dream was the furthest thing from a nightmare. But thank goodness for the moonless sky and darkened room. Or else he'd know that I'd just gotten off dreaming about him. That there was a damp patch in my panties from fantasy sex with him.

"I'm okay," I stutter breathlessly as I slowly withdraw my hand out from beneath the drawstring of my pants so he doesn't notice the movement. I push myself up, my body coated in a light mist of sweat, my muscles still contracting from the remnants of my orgasm.

My self-indulged one, it seems.

Could this get any worse? Having the man you're fantasizing is giving you an orgasm be the one to catch you in the act, so to speak?

"You sure?" He reaches a hand out and runs the back of it down my cheek. "You were moaning and moving— then you called out my name for help. It scared the shit out of me. Must have been a bad nightmare."

It takes a second to find my voice. The right words to say get lost in the embarrassment and the postclimax fog of endorphins. "Yeah. I'm sorry." I run a hand through my hair, pull the covers a little tighter around me. "I—I— uh, don't even remember what it was about. But thank you. I appreciate you checking on me."

"Was this because of me?" he asks, concern in his tone. The blood drains from my face momentarily as I wonder if he's caught on to what was really happening. "Was it because of the things I said to you tonight that stirred up bad memories—"

"No." I'm quick to cut him off, feeling like an ass that he's sitting here worried his honesty caused me to have a nightmare when in fact it was quite the opposite. But it's not like I can tell him that. "I watched a scary movie the other night. I'm sure it had to do with that."

*Smooth, Getty. Real smooth.*

"Are you sure you're okay?"

"Yes. I will be. Thanks. I'm sorry I woke you up."

*Please go back to bed and put me out of my misery.*

"I'll let you get back to sleep, then," he says as he stands from the bed, a handsome shadow in the night. "I'm glad you're all right."

"Good night, Zander."

"Good night, Getty."

We can't see each other's eyes, but we are sure as hell holding each other's gaze through the darkness, because I can feel it. After a moment of suspended silence, he nods his head and walks to the doorway as emotions war within me over wanting him to go and asking him to stay.

"I'm going to leave your door open, just in case you

need me," he says before his shadow leaves the doorway toward his room.

I hold back the immediate urge to go shut it should my nocturnal need arise again to have fake sex with him.

Sinking deeper into the mattress, I scrub my hands over my face and can feel the smile on my lips. I go back over the dream in my mind, because unlike what I told him, I remember every single part of it. Each kiss. Every touch. The sound of his voice thick with desire.

With a deep breath, I shake my head and feel like such a fool. How did I not know it was a dream? My lack of modesty and constant insecurity over my ability to orgasm should have been a dead giveaway. Even asleep, I should have caught that.

How am I going to face him in the morning? How am I going to look him in the eye and ask him if he wants a cup of coffee with his roommate who was getting off while fantasizing about him?

I close my eyes but can't sleep. There's no way in hell with the buzz of my orgasm still echoing through both my head and body.

Because if I thought a little piece of my heart was lost to Zander for his kindness, then a huge part of my awakening libido just pledged allegiance to him too.

# Chapter 14

There's a bite to the air. A chill that burns in my lungs and stings my cheeks. It may be the start of the summer season, but shit, mornings are cold here. Hopefully I'll be heading back home to Los Angeles before I get a chance to acclimate.

And I hate that my feet falter at the idea. Hate that the next fucking thought in my head is, *What is Getty going to do when I leave?*

This isn't a *thing.*

She isn't supposed to become a *thing.*

But fuck me, she is.

Then of course there's the voice mail from Rylee today, my adoptive mom. The one who saved me from my silence and deafening fear after my mother died and my dad came back to finish me off. The one who had to have known the truth all along from day one. I don't even have to replay the message because I can still hear it plain as day.

*Zander. It's me.* Her laugh. Nerves I'm not used to hearing in it vibrate through the connection. *Of course it's me— who else would it be, right? I just wanted to hear your voice, let you know I was thinking about you. A lot. I miss you. Of course I'm worried about you and want to call and text you to make sure you're okay, but I also know you'll call when you're ready. Oh . . . and thank you for texting Scooter and then Ace back. He's taking this hard . . . all of it . . . so thank you for responding and letting him—us—know you're okay. I'm sorry I'm rambling, but there's so much I want to say to you . . . so much I want to ask, but I know you'll come home once you figure whatever it is you need to work through.* Silence for a few seconds. A shaky sigh. Her not wanting to let go just yet. *He won't admit it, but Colton misses you too. He's moody and a bear to be around and won't talk about what happened that day between the two of you. . . .* Another sigh. A few words started and then stopped. Her concern is palpable in the silence and I know she's struggling to not give me her two cents on the matter. To keep the disappointment out of her voice and not rail into me that I'm the one who needs to man up and apologize for all of this. *It doesn't matter. I hope you find whatever you're hoping to find while you're gone. And I can't help but feel like there's something you're not telling us. All we want . . . all we've ever wanted is the best for you Zander. I love you.*

I've listened to the message several times this morning. It's become a type of fuel to feed my guilt over what I did, how I acted, and reinforcement that I need to really get my shit together. Open the box, face the facts. Deal. Cope. Yell. Rage.

Move on. Live life with a new norm I can't shove away but can start to put behind me.

*Quit being such a pussy.* Accept that whatever else is in that box doesn't affect who I am or what I've made of my life. It is what it is.

Easier said than done.

God, how I wanted to pick up the phone and call her back. Ask her the questions I need to ask: Did she know? Why didn't she tell me? What was her reasoning for keeping the truth from me all this time? Then I could get angry with her answers. Shout and rage and get all this pent-up emotion out. Then apologize ten times over for the ways I've hurt them . . . but pride is a hard thing to swallow when you feel like it's all you have left.

Right now my own need to cope is more important

than the urge to call her. But fuck if I don't feel guilty at the sadness in her voice.

*Push it away, Donavan. You've got to face the facts first and then you can face Rylee and Colton. Fix you, then them. You'll know what to say then. How to say it. Accept who you really are.*

When I reach the porch steps, I brace my hands on my knees and gulp in the bitter air. My chest hurts from pushing myself too hard. But after Getty last night and my less-than-satisfying jerk-off in the shower this morning while thinking of her, I needed to work off some of my frustration.

When I grab a Gatorade from the refrigerator, thoughts about our unexpected kitchen interlude litter my head. And isn't this why I went on a run? To clear my head? But the minute I'm back here, with the scent of her perfume and a pair of her discarded socks sitting on the family room floor, she crawls right back into my damn head.

Everything about her gets to me.

The look on her face when I was close to her. Her ball-tightening kiss. That little jolt of fear that I felt go through her muscles and sweep across her face. Her fear over something. How I had to step back and take stock. Remember she's not some road groupie wanting to get it on with points champion Zander Donavan. *The Golden Boy.* No, she's clearly a woman on the mend from something. One running from a past that was obviously shitty.

That in itself is enough reason for me to pause and step back, because when she gets that look in her eyes, like she has to look over her shoulder and make sure no one's there, she reminds me of my mom. The way I remember her to be: skittish, always apologizing, withdrawn. And that's a huge problem. It's a bright fucking beacon warning me away and yet I keep walking right into its light wanting to help, to be there for her, to get to know her better, when I shouldn't. Hell, I'm the furthest thing from qualified to help her.

What I should be thinking about is sex, sex, and more sex. With her preferably and not my own hand and a bottle of lube.

I can't get involved more than that. I have enough to do with my own issues that I need to figure out. And yet even though I warned her, I can't figure out why she keeps occupying my thoughts.

Living day in and day out with her is like tempting an alcoholic with a bottle of gin. You want to taste, want to sample, but know it's just going to bring you back to being selfish. Wanting only what you want without regard for anyone else or the damage it's going to do. While gin's not my thing, it sure as shit doesn't mean I wouldn't take a sip if I'm thirsty.

And last night, *damn was I thirsty*. What I wouldn't have given to take advantage of the situation—a gorgeous woman whose kiss tastes as good as her laugh sounds— but I couldn't willingly let her spread her legs without being up-front with her.

Well, I could have. I could've been a prick, enjoyed the coming weeks with her moaning beneath me without a scratch on my conscience about how my time here will come to an end. Have some fun, some great sex, and then part ways with nothing more than a *thanks for the good time* and an empty promise to call every once in a while.

*But I can't treat her like that.* There's something about Getty that has gotten under my skin.

At first I thought it was the want-what-you-can't-have type of thing. The temptation after promising myself to cut out the complications of adding a woman to the mix. I'm supposed to be here for me. But it's not that. Then I thought it was the innocent-woman thing. Her big doe eyes and blushing cheeks and obvious unease with men tell me she's not used to attention from the opposite sex. Fuck yes, it's attractive, gives me visions of being the one to teach her a few things, but I'm not the kind of guy who racks up points for deflowering the virginal type. There's nothing sexy in that. It's not a game, not something you do knowing you're going to walk away.

Maybe it's just because I actually like her. Think she's smart and naturally beautiful without trying to be, and when I can pry her out from behind the protective wall I know all too well, her personality is killer. And it's the mad respect I have for her for doing what my mom never did: getting out of an abusive relationship. Because while she may have never said it out loud, the signs are there. The ones someone who has lived in an abusive household can spot like a road sign even all these years later. And a woman that does that deserves the happily-ever-after she never got the first go-round.

So I'm fucked. I want her but can't give that to her, and hell if I'm going to be the one to add on to the hurt that already lingers in her eyes. I'm not that much of an asshole.

But I'm also not going to deny how much I wanted to slide between her thighs last night, clear the counter behind her with a swipe of my arm, and take and taste and satisfy until the sun came up. Instead I showed restraint like I've never had to before. I stepped back. Told her I wouldn't be staying long term. Gave her an out if she wanted one. And hopefully earned my conscience the A-OK to be free of guilt when we do sleep together, because it's her choice now.

A clear conscience, a conflicted heart, and a frustrated dick. Quite the trio. I have to hope that when she says yes, she still doesn't get hurt in the end.

Because she *will* say yes. I saw the answer in her eyes and heard it in the way she called my name. But I still walked away, albeit with an ache in my balls, before shutting the door so I wouldn't be tempted to go back.

Now I glance in her room before I enter mine. Recall how goddamn bad I wanted to slide into her bed last night, pull her against me, and comfort her after her nightmare. But that's being selfish, because I'm lying to myself. I wouldn't have been able to stop at just feeling her body against mine. Not hardly. Let's be real here.

*Go fix her car, Donavan.* Do something useful other than waiting with your dick in your hand for her answer. No time like the present. Besides, I'm already sweaty and dirty.

Maybe even earn me some brownie points too.

When I walk into my room to grab a clean shirt, the box in the corner catches my eye. Especially the chicken-scratch writing on the envelope taped to the outside and the Los Angeles postal origin. The letter in said envelope, from the person who is technically my aunt, explained that my uncle, my only living relative, died of an overdose.

Is it bad that I couldn't care less? Is it heartless that after a failed attempt to foster me when I was twelve for the monthly stipend to fund their habit, the both of them ceased to exist to me? That I'm grateful for their fuckups because it led to Rylee and Colton adopting me?

Why all this time later would she think I want to look at stuff she came across while cleaning out my uncle's things? Maybe she's just being decent, returning the contents because it's all I have left of my childhood. Then again, an autopsy report? Placing it as the first thing in the box so I'd be sure not to miss it. Maybe it was her final fuck-you.

So it's no wonder I'm hesitant to see the rest of the contents.

Besides, it won't be the first time I'll say good-bye to Mom. Or my dad. But that's just it. Will delving further into the box bring back more? Will it make me remember things my mind tried to protect me from?

*"Fuck,"* I mutter while my mind keeps running. *Fuck you and your doubt that makes me fear the worst, and fuck you and your hope that makes me want something more.*

Thoughts of burning the box rise up as I stare at it—I long to watch it go up in flames so I can hold tight to the memories I have. Of thinking my mother walked on water.

Bodies are buried for a reason—shouldn't their secrets be too?

Torching the box would make it easier all around. Rid myself of the source of anxiety that caused me to lash out and risk every single thing I've been given and worked for.

But since when has anything in regard to my childhood been that easy to get rid of?

Is it too much to want to connect to some good thing in the box? The kind of thing every kid deserves to have from his past? Would it be too much for there to be pictures? Something with smiling faces and my mom's arms wrapped around me with love? Something I can utilize to will back a positive memory to help smother the bad ones?

*But what if there aren't any good memories there?*

My fingers toy with the flaps of the box. The internal war continues to rage. *Fuck it. Just open the damn box. Shit or get off the pot. Look at one thing per day until you can handle more. That's why you came here in the first place, right?*

The sound of cardboard scraping against itself fills the room. Curiosity and dread rifle through me simultaneously. The stapled packet of paper is on top right where I left it.

My fingertips fidget with edges while I chew the inside of my lip, and I don't need to see the outlined diagram of a body with marks indicating stab wounds or read the words describing what I can still see in my mind.

I feel stupid for the nerves that have me hesitating—upset with myself for having them—but know men are creatures of avoidance by nature. We want to dominate, be in control, and yet the slightest crack in our foundations can rock our world.

And I've survived too many earthquakes already in my lifetime.

I set the report down and shuffle through the contents, purposely not looking at them closely. I need a good memory today, something to help ease the power this box holds over me. So I dig through the unorganized mess intent on finding the smooth, distinct texture of a photograph.

When I touch one, I know it instantly. My fingers make out what feels like a rubber band on the thin stack and I sigh in relief. I might retrieve another memory. A piece of normalcy from those first seven years of my life. My hands shake as I step back and sit down on the bed, nervous over the glimpse of my past I'm going to get.

*She's beautiful.* It's my only conscious thought when I see my mom for the first time in almost twenty years. Dark hair, light eyes, and a genuine smile. Sure, her clothes are worn and the car she's sitting in front of is a patchwork of Bondo and mismatched colors, but she's even prettier than I remembered. Time must have dulled the memories.

And sitting in her lap is a little brown-haired boy with skinned knees, a baseball cap crooked on his head, and a mitt on the grass to the right of them. *It's me.* The picture of a carefree little boy I don't ever remember being but who seems perfectly content in his mom's lap. I stare down at it until my eyes blur, try to commit it to memory as if the picture is going to vanish.

I'm so lost in the photo I forget there are more behind it. Once I remember, I continue the process with each one, studying it, trying to pull a memory from the image, thankful for the chance to reconnect with a lighter side of my childhood.

*I look like her.* That's what I see as I flip through them. The same eyes, the same-shaped mouth, a similar nose. It's weird to actually be looking at the pictures and be able to draw a comparison of myself with someone.

Then I come to a picture of my dad. He seems less scary then I remember. Faded jeans torn at the knees. Thumbs hanging in his pockets. A cigarette dangling from his mouth. His hair long and unkempt. His body scraggly. Bruises visible on the inside of one of his arms.

I stare at his face for the longest time, not to remember him, but rather to make sure I'm nothing like him. I take in everything about the picture, pick it apart, study it. And no matter how hard I try, all I see is the monster standing in the darkened doorway, covered in my mom's blood. And the vacant look in his eyes as he held a gun on Rylee when he tried to kidnap me so I couldn't testify after I'd regained my voice.

When I'm convinced we're nothing alike, I flip to the last picture in the batch. My mom's lying next to a sleeping me, my back to her front, her arm wrapped around my abdomen holding me close, and a soft smile on her lips.

Without thinking, I run my fingertip over her face and all of a sudden I can hear her voice humming "Are You Sleeping?" in my head. It's weird and I don't know what to make of it other than I vaguely recall how she used to curl up beside me on my bed, her lips to the top of my head, and the heat of her breath warming my hair as she sang the song to put me to sleep.

My heart pounds from the memory I never knew I had. A disbelieving smile spreads on my lips as I close my eyes and try to recall more, flipping through the pictures over and over, hoping to jog something else loose.

Excited about the prospect of having more memories from my first seven years to block out all the pain, I move back to the box to see what else it holds. I grab a stack of papers, then notice the cover sheet on the first packet I pull is the rap sheet for one Lola Sullivan. I glance over petty misdemeanors and then toss it back in the box immediately. I have zero desire to taint the image I've just gotten back of her in my head. There are newspaper cuttings that mention the murder and the search for my dad. Tiny one-by-one squares with no compassion for the woman who at the time was my everything. The next packet of paper is thicker. It's a case file from the Los Angeles Child Protective Services.

With my name on it.

By the width of the file, I have a feeling its contents won't surprise the man I am but might derail the little boy in me still looking for closure. It might blow the only memory I have of my mother when she's not covered in blood—the one I just got back—to smithereens and I don't think I'm ready for that just yet.

So I take the pictures, the reports, everything I don't want to face, and put them back in the box, tuck in the flaps so they stay closed, and walk out of the room without looking back.

But I have a new memory to hold on to when there used to be none.

I'll face the rest another day.

# Chapter 15

GETTY

The bar is packed. The warm weather and the cloudless sky in this unusual summer full of storms has caused a massive influx of tourists to flood the island.

The bar's abuzz as I take orders left and right from the other servers, so much so that I haven't had much time to think about last night.

Well, that's a lie. It's all I've thought about. A few botched orders more than normal prove the point. But the bar's so busy they've gone mostly unnoticed.

My mind drifts to Zander as I work. To our laughter at the restaurant. To the toast. To make-believe revelations about what outsiders would assume about us. To kisses that curled my toes and melted my insides. To honest confessions about what he can and can't give me. And then to the question he asked me to consider, if I could handle knowing there wasn't going to be more than the one thing he said was a disaster in the first place: friends with benefits.

A rum and Coke. A margarita with extra salt. A draft Guinness.

My knee-jerk reaction is yes. He was honest, up-front, and kisses me like the world is ending tomorrow—with every ounce of his being.

A Macallan neat. A gin and tonic. A round of IPAs.

*Is that really smart, though, Getty? Wouldn't you become*

*too attached?* No. Yes. *No.* I'd use the sex to help me get over my issues. Prove to myself that not all men are like Ethan. I hope. But isn't that kind of whorish?

Definitely not something a Caster would do . . . which pushes me to want to do it even more.

A vodka cranberry. A Jack and Coke. A dry martini.

But am I really capable of such a thing ? I don't know how to have casual sex. I actually don't know how to have sex at all according to Ethan.

What am I doing even thinking about this? It's a stupid idea. Such a tempting one, though. My doubt is ugly.

*And Zander is so pretty.*

I snicker under my breath at the thought, knowing he'd reject the description immediately.

Oops. Jack and *Diet* Coke. Not regular Coke. Messed that one up. Two seltzer waters. One glass of merlot.

Then the dream comes back to me. *And damn.* All doubts go out the window. Yes, it was a dream. My rational brain reiterates the fact I know all too well, but at the same time, a man doesn't kiss like he does and not know how to make love.

*Not make love, Getty.*

*Sex.*

Just sex. No love involved. The L-word is never to be mentioned. Just nitty-gritty, scream-out-as-you-come, render-your-legs-boneless, romance-novel-type sex like I've never experienced before. That's all he alluded to.

That ache he caused between my thighs comes back with a vengeance. I shift some, spill the overfull drink onto my hands as I move it to the server's tray.

A Coors Light—in a bottle. Another rum and Coke for table six—this time with a lime. A strawberry daiquiri.

*Just go for it, Getty. You want to be spontaneous? Be spontaneous. He rearranged the silverware drawer for you for God's sake.*

Justification at its finest.

But it is a good point. If I'm going to sleep with someone, at least I'd know he's a good guy. And probably has some experience under his belt. By the way the bar suddenly fills up with the local women busily texting one another when he comes in to watch a game or have a drink, I can assume he's had no shortage of women or experience in the sack.

An old-fashioned. Two Sculpins on draft. One Red Bull and Absolut.

Oh. But a lot of women means he's most likely used to experienced partners . . . and I'm far from that. I stop and stare off into space for a moment. Twist my lips. Remember how he kisses. His hands framing my face. The scrape of his unshaven chin against the skin of my neck. His cologne in my nose and taste on my tongue.

Done. I'm gonna go for it.

Really going to do it.

*Screw the nerves and the doubts and my insecurities.* Easier said than done, but I'm not living, not proving the old Gertrude Caster-Adams is gone, if I don't take a chance.

So I'm taking the chance. Decision made. No backing out now.

Four microbrews on draft.

"Gertrude."

That voice. The unrelenting condescension. The one that controlled my life for so very long. The one who believes I'm in the wrong.

I'm startled—my mind races, pulse thunders, nerves start to hum, body becomes flushed. But I don't move, don't waver. I keep one hand on the pull, the other holding the glass at an angle, and my eyes fixed on it.

I don't look up, just keep pretending I didn't hear what I thought I just heard.

There's no way. Can't be.

"Can you go grab me some more limes?" It's Liam's voice that pulls me from my panicked fog.

"Sure." My voice is barely audible, because I'm afraid if I speak normally, my father will recognize my voice.

I all but run from the counter, a half-filled glass of beer left sitting on the catch grate, and my body trembles with that flustered shock. I never look up. Never acknowledge him.

My only course of action is to hope that if I stay in the storage room long enough, he won't be there when I come back. Hearing his voice say my name would have been a figment of my imagination.

After I grab the limes, I sag back against the refrigerator, exhausted from all the emotions running through me: defiance, anger, fear, worry, homesickness when I shouldn't feel it. I close my eyes, lean my head back, and fight the urge to run out the back door and not come back. To not have to face him.

Because I knew my father would find me. He's Damon Caster after all. The man with no boundaries, no morals. Well, unless you are one of the lucky few he deems worthy of esteem according to his ridiculous standards. As for me? He rules his family like his real estate empire—with an unrelenting iron fist. I'm just surprised Ethan wasn't standing beside him.

Or maybe he was. It's not like I looked up.

The thought has bile rising in my throat. *Ethan.* The man my father had chosen to walk on water beside him. The one who broke every single part of me with his harsh demands and constant criticism.

"It's unacceptable for you to walk away from me." Disdain drips from his aristocratic voice. I shouldn't be surprised he followed me in here.

I set my shoulders and straighten my posture before I lift my chin and open my eyes to meet the ones that mirror mine in color.

He looks older. The immediate thought surprises me. And I reject it instantly. Because that means my leaving has been hard on him, and it should be. He should have picked his daughter's well-being over satisfying his protégé and upholding his public image.

But that will never happen.

Hasn't been the case since my mom died what feels like forever ago.

*"Father."* My teeth are clenched and hands are squeezing the bag of limes so hard I wouldn't be surprised if the peels ruptured under the pressure. "How did you find me?"

The flare of his nostrils tells me I'm insulting his long-reaching fingers. "Easily enough. The diamond in your wedding ring was laser engraved with a serial number.

The pawnshop registered it. We went down to speak to them and followed the trail you left. The contact phone number was that bitch of a woman I refused to allow your mother to see. A quick search into Darcy's life revealed a new mortgage she'd taken out, and I'm sure you can figure the rest out."

My resolve falters. I thought I had done everything right. "If I went to that much trouble to disappear, did you think for once, I didn't want you to find me?"

"Now, now. Let's stop your melodrama and focus on getting you home and away from the disgrace of this job behind a bar like some two-bit floozy hard up for money." His disgust radiates off him like a venom, poisoning the small room around us.

No *It's great to see you, Gertrude*. No *You look good with a little sun on your face and your hair not slicked back to perfection*. No *I missed you, sweetheart*. The small part of me that hoped maybe my leaving might have changed him dies a quick death at his comments.

"A job's a job, Father. My bank accounts seemed to have been suspended somehow," I say after clearing my throat to shake away the nerves vibrating in my voice. "Would you rather me have taken my clothes off to make money?"

The shock that passes over his face is priceless. Gertrude would never have spoken back to her father six months ago. "Remember who you're speaking to and that—"

"You deserve respect at all times," I repeat the mantra of my youth to him but this time with a tinge of sarcasm. The years of conditioning have me wanting to cower from the glare in his eyes, but I do my best to hold my own.

I can fall apart when I'm alone. I can let go of my emotions. But not right now. Right now I have to be the same strong woman who left and walked out of the life she was told to live.

"Your insolence is—"

"Getty?" Liam narrows his brow when he notices my father—a stranger dressed in slacks and a dress shirt—standing just inside the door. "Everything okay?"

"Sorry." I nod my head with dread in my heart that my

father is going to unleash his pompous self on my boss. "I was just coming with the limes." I hold them up to show him the proof.

"Okay. You sure?"

I know he can feel the tension in the air, see the contempt on both of our faces. But I try to reassure him by meeting his gaze, and the look I'm giving him to convey *just leave it* prompts him to nod his head and return to the bar without another word.

"I have to get to work."

"Actually you don't. You have obligations to fulfill and a husband to tend to and—"

"*Ex*-husband."

"Casters *don't* get divorced, Gertrude."

I shift my feet. Sigh audibly. Sweat mists down my back and my body vibrates in anger as we start the same argument we had days before I left. I try to head it off at the pass. "Why are you here?"

He startles his head like the answer's so obvious and I'm an idiot for asking—clearly I should be thanking him for coming to my rescue from this low-class life—and when I don't, his annoyance presents itself in the lift of one eyebrow. "To have you collect your things and bring you back home. Where you belong. Beside Ethan. As a part of the community."

*Walk back into the lion's den? No thanks.*

"No." Mentally I cringe and wait for the wrath of Damon Caster to come at me full-fledged. No one stands up to him, let alone his only child.

"You're being ridiculous and immature." His voice is low and even, but his jaw ticks in irritation. "I'll make reservations for dinner tomorrow night. My car will pick you up at five and we will come to some sort of agreement on how to end this ridiculous charade of yours. Figure out a good explanation for your extended absence and I'll bring you home with minimal exposure."

Always worried about what people think. I sigh. "And if I don't go?"

"You will be there or life might become difficult for you here on this island." Our eyes meet and hold, his threat loud and clear, his thumb pressing back down on me after less than ten minutes in his presence. Gritting my teeth is the only reaction I give him before skirting past him and out of the storage room.

But I don't head to the bar. Instead I make a right turn and head straight into the ladies' bathroom and shut the door behind me, make sure it's locked, and lean my back against it. Nerves and anger give way to the adrenaline-laced anxiety. My legs turn to rubber, and my frantic breaths make me dizzy before it all crashes down around me. I don't recognize the ragged sob that slips from my mouth as I slowly slide my shoulders down until I'm sitting on the tiled floor.

And that says a lot—that I'm sitting on this germ-ridden floor—but the complete onslaught of emotion over-whelms me.

Am I surprised he found me? No. But I'd expected to have more time before he did. And it's silly really, be-cause more time wouldn't do anything to fix this situa-tion. The letter I left for him, never mind the way that I left, should have been enough in itself to prove to him that I'm done living that life. Done being demeaned and ridiculed and thought of as a twisted dowry to keep the business intact.

I left to create a life with passion and creativity or so I could try something new without fear of mistakes. To live day to day without caring about social status or if I'll dis-grace the family name by his outdated standards.

I hate that the minute I saw him my knees began to buckle and I wanted to run the other way. But I am re-lieved that I didn't. I showed that I'm not the same "yes, Father" woman I used to be, so fearful of the consequences of disobedience. Yet I'm furious with myself because I wasn't yet one hundred percent the woman I want to be: saying no, asserting my will, walking away without worry-ing I hurt his feelings because he's still my dad.

And deep down some part of me wishes—hope against hope—that he might wake up from his self-appointed power trip and accept me for me. Love me for me.

I swipe my tears away knowing there's no chance in

hell of that happening. He is who he is and is not going to change. Accepting that is the hard part.

At least he came by himself. Left Ethan—his puppet—home to run his empire.

Aware I need this job desperately, I shove up off the ground and square my shoulders. *It's a start, Getty. Tomorrow night you won't be blindsided and will handle him better.*

The little voice in the back of my head says I don't have to go to dinner with him at all if I don't want to.

Maybe I'll just listen to her.

# Chapter 16

The music thumps out a bruising rhythm in my earbuds. A hard beat pairs with a screaming guitar and angry lyrics. Energized, I welcome the weight of the wrench in my hand and the distraction of fixing Getty's car to quiet the noise in my head.

But at least this noise differs from the racket that's been filling my head as of late. Giving me a reprieve of sorts.

My mind is in constant overdrive. The photos play on repeat through it like negatives on a reel—a ghost of a memory I can almost see but not clearly.

I prefer the almost-there ones to the in-living-color nightmares any day.

With my head under the hood and grease on my hands, I feel a little more connected to my old life. Feel a bit like my old self as I work on the engine.

Something to my right catches my attention and I startle when I look up to find a woman standing a few feet away. Her hands are clasped in front of her, an envelope somewhere in their mix, a nervous smile on her lips as she stares at me.

Stepping out from beneath the hood, I take my earbuds out and wipe my hands on a red rag and wait for her to say something. Anything. But she just stands there, feet fidgeting, and smile widening while her cheeks slowly turn red.

Fangirl down. It's the term my brothers use when they come to a race and witness the tongue-tied, finger-twisting, feet-shifting phenomenon that happens occasionally when I come face-to-face with female racing fans. The pang of regret is there instantly. Over how I've shut my brothers out. But I needed to. And I know they'll forgive me. This is nothing compared with what we've all been through before.

"Can I help you?" I ask as I take a step forward.

"Yes. I'm—hi—hello," she says, and then rolls her eyes with a chuckle as she smooths down the skirt over her hips. "I'm Mable from Mable's Closet in town."

The storefront comes to mind. Resale clothes on mannequins. Lacy curtains that look like they belong in a funeral home. A local townsperson or two always going in or out. Quaint. Classy. Completely feminine. And definitely a place I've steered clear of.

"Oh yes. Hi. Zander," I say as I hold out my hand and then lift my eyebrows in apology for its greased-up state. She reaches out anyway—a nervous chuckle, cheeks turning redder—and shakes it. "Can't say that I've been in there, but I know the store. What can I do for you?"

"Everyone here on the island is so excited that you're here. I haven't seen this much chatter since . . . since I can't remember when. Maybe when Dolly Parton came through a few years back."

My ego dies a slow, silent death. A few months off the gas pedal and I've become irrelevant enough that I'm being compared to Dolly Parton? But my reaction goes unnoticed as Mable continues on without a care in the world and without any need for me to be an active participant in our conversation.

"I mean you should see the phone calls and texts that buzz around Main Street when you go on your morning run. Or to the hardware store. I mean the thought right there—of you in a tool belt and no shirt—is enough to make the women around here suddenly need to nail something. I mean hammer something. Or . . . you know what I mean."

I can't help it. I throw my head back and laugh at this frumpy woman with round cheeks and a kind smile who means no harm with her ramblings that are making me blush. In an instant I realize just how small of a town this really is and how oblivious I was to everything going on.

She looks at me, lips in a perfect-shaped O and eyes narrowing as I shake my head back and forth. "You are exactly what I needed right now." My smile widens with each passing second.

"Well, I am a married woman, but I always wanted to try the cougar thing." She offers me a wink. "I've never been town gossip before . . . just the one spreading it, but you're easy on the eyes . . . and I could probably teach you a thing or two. . . ."

"I like you, Mable from Mable's Closet," I laugh, and think about how much I already love this new friend I've made.

"I like you too, *hottie*, as the ladies are calling you in town." She chuckles and shakes her head. "How was the food at Mario's last night? That new cook they hired sure can whip up some *mangia bene*."

And once again I'm reminded of the size of this town and how everyone knows everyone else's business. It's definitely annoying and yet a part of me likes the predictability.

"Yes, ma'am." I nod. "Now, I know you didn't come here to talk about pizza, so what can I do for you?"

"Oh, sorry. I'm sure you have plenty of stuff to do and I'm here blathering away taking up your time. I came to see Getty. Is she home?"

"I'm sorry, Mable, but she's at work right now. Took an extra shift. Is there anything I can help you with?" I ask out of courtesy, surprised the town gossipers didn't already know Getty's whereabouts.

"No. Yes." I can sense her hesitancy. "She normally stops by once a week to pick up her check and so I wanted to make sure she was okay but feel stupid now because obviously she has you here to occupy her time now and—"

"Check?" My interest is piqued. "She works at the store?"

"Oh no, honey. That's silly. I sell all of those designer clothes she has on eBay for her. I'd do it for free for her, but she gets upset if I don't take ten percent for my time. And so this here is a check for that pile she brought me last week to try to get the money to fix that heap over there you're working on."

Her words take a moment to sink in. And before I can fully process everything, Mable continues on. "What I'd give to have her eye. To be able to go to an estate sale and find these beauties . . . except I'd have a much harder time parting with them."

"She sure does have a good eye, doesn't she?" I murmur in agreement even though I already know she hasn't gone to any estate sales.

The piles of clothes around her room. My assumption that she was a spoiled trust fund kid with so many designer threads she didn't need to take care of them. The obvious burner cell phone. The lack of interest in having Internet access.

*She's not just starting over after a messy divorce. She's running from someone.*

I'm such an asshole. Like a royal prick of an asshole.

It's the thought that's on repeat in my mind as I try to wrap up the conversation with Mable, who keeps chatting away.

*Getty's not a spoiled brat in the least.* Her only use for the clothes from her past is to sell them to help secure her new future.

Like selling clothes to get her car repaired. Talk about feeling like a jerk after my "call Daddy and ask for money" comment the other night.

Yes. That's me. Asshole with a capital *A*.

"I can give her the check, Mable. I'll just set it inside on the counter for her." It's the least I can do. Her eyes narrow, and I kind of like that she cares enough about Getty that she's worrying over whether to trust me. If she only knew the purse I win in a single victory on the track. "I assure you I'm not going to take it."

"You sure?"

I should feel insulted, but I don't. "I promise."

She looks down at the sealed envelope in her hand and then extends it out to me. "Okay, well, you make sure she gets it. She's a sweet girl and deserves for good things to happen for her."

"Agreed. I'm glad she has you looking out for her, Mable."

I let out a whoop as Getty's car sputters to life. It may have taken longer than I figured it would between Mable's pit stop and a quick run over to the auto parts store for some oil to service her car while I was at it, but mission accomplished.

And I'll take anything to make me feel useful, considering my carpentry skills are definitely still being called into question and I feel like a fish out of water away from my everyday life. That damn deck is going to be the death of me.

When I rev the engine a few times, the sound reaffirms that I'm a bit less of a dick since Getty can save that money Mable brought her today for something more important, like treating herself.

After I let the car idle for a few minutes to make sure she's running okay, I turn her off in order to get cleaned up in time to pick Getty up from her shift. I owe her an apology but don't know how to go about bringing it up without the walls around her going up too.

When I slide out of the car and out from behind the raised hood, I do a double take at the black luxury town car parked across the street with dark tinted windows. I stare at it momentarily, thinking how out of place it seems in this quaint little town, before shutting the hood and heading for the shower.

*Time to eat some crow, Donavan.*

Maybe I need a beer first to make it go down a little smoother.

Or maybe I just want to watch the woman who's pouring it for me.

My bet's on the one that wears the sexy socks.

# Chapter 17

"I've got a surprise for you." I grow still at the sound of Zander's voice at my back and have to close my eyes momentarily. Tears of frustration over the encounter with my father have been burning the back of my throat for hours, and yet the immediate relief at knowing Zander's here tells me how much I've grown to depend on him in a sense.

And with the relief comes a reminder of last night's dream in full 3-D color. *Oh God help me.* There's no way I can look him in the eyes and not blush. Or think about the imaginary warmth of his mouth on my breasts. Hands on my thighs. Tongue on my—

"Getty?"

When I turn around from straightening bottles behind the bar, the first thing I see is that boyish grin of his. It distracts me momentarily as it tugs on my heart in ways I never expected. I look up to meet his eyes and blush like a kid with her hand caught in the cookie jar, guilt presumably written all over my face.

Our eyes hold for a moment, his searching, mine feigning normalcy, and in that flash of a second, I realize the anxiety I've felt all day over my father's arrival is gone. While it may be a momentary respite, it's pretty powerful that Zander can do that for me.

Then reality returns when he lifts an eyebrow and waits for a response.

"A surprise, huh? I could use one after today." I try to sound unaffected and yet I know he'll catch the tinge of resignation in my voice. "Super busy here."

"That so?" Impenetrable blue eyes search mine. Gauge if I'm telling the truth. And I'm not sure if he believes me.

With the regulars sitting at the opposite end of the bar, the longer our gazes hold, the harder it is to bite back all the secrets I'm holding from tumbling out. Because right now I need someone more than ever. Sure, it was tough in the beginning when I left my old life, but for some reason it's easier to run when there's no one in front of you bringing you back to that person you used to be.

And so right now I just need someone. A friend. *Him*.

"Lotta tourists today." I break our gaze and focus on wiping down the rest of the bar top. Doing my best to keep it together.

"Looks empty now."

"Mm-hmm."

"Something happen today, Socks?"

"Nope," I say, tight smile back in place. But when I look back up, it softens at the concern in his voice. "Does this surprise have anything to do with chocolate?"

His smile deepens. "Even better."

I untie my apron and throw it into the bin for laundering, which completes my cleanup duties, since I'm not closing tonight. "Better than chocolate? How about a foot massage?" My aching feet guide my thoughts.

His laugh mixes into the noise around us as I wave bye to Liam and come around the bar. "Definitely better, but I can make both of those happen if you really want them to."

"Really?" While I'm referring to the surprise being better than what sounds like nirvana to me, the fact that he even offered puts a genuine smile on my lips.

"Really," he affirms as he places his hands on my shoulders and directs me to the side exit of the bar. The heat of his hands, the sudden public display of whatever-this-is-between-us, and the quick little squeeze he gives them leave me knowing I needed this comfort from him at the end of my day.

But when I push open the door and see my car sitting in the parking spot across from me, the emotion I've been holding back comes crashing down on me. I gasp his name; then my hands automatically go to my cheeks where the tears I've fought all day finally win the battle.

The means to escape sits right in front of me. Zander has given me a working car to pack my shit in and drive away from the sight of my father and the impending dinner date tomorrow night. Forgo the fear and just move to another town, another place, create another life until I'm strong enough to not give in to the conditioning I've spent a lifetime living under.

"Getty?" Concern. Worry. "I hope that means you're happy."

I wipe away the tears coursing down my cheeks so that I can look at him with a smile. Zander. The man who represents new beginnings and the ability to make a choice when I never even realized I wanted this choice to make.

*Run or stay.*

And this right here, his selfless act, somehow triggers my confidence. Tells me to throw my doubt aside and choose to stay. Keep this new life I've created on my own. To straighten my spine in opposition to my father, show up for dinner instead of be a coward and run again, and prove to him I'm much more than he ever thought of me.

*I choose to stay.*

Emotion washes over me. The kind that chills your skin and warms your soul all the while stirring that slow, sweet ache in your lower belly because every part of you has just awakened to things you were sleeping through.

Without preamble, I step into him, bring my hands to his cheeks, lift onto my tiptoes, and press a chaste kiss to his lips in silent thank-you. My reaction seems to stun him and a part of me likes being able to do that. Smiling through the tears, I step back, top teeth worrying my bottom lip, eyes locked on his.

"Thank you." My voice comes out a whisper and I feel

like I've said this to him so many times since I held him at mini-blind wand point, but this time it means so much more than he can even fathom.

Something glances through his eyes and his lips transform with a shy smile when he reaches out to wipe the tears off my cheeks. With a simple nod he accepts my gratitude. "Wanna take a ride?"

My back is aching and feet are sore and all I'd thought about was heading home to soak in a hot bath, but nothing has ever sounded better. "Only if you take the wheel."

"Deal."

With the sun slowly dropping toward the horizon, the coastline stretches for miles ahead of us. The ocean is all I can see out the passenger window besides interrupted snippets of the pine trees standing tall in the rocky terrain. The windows are down and the chilled air whips through my hair, but I welcome it after the scent of alcohol all day long in the bar. And the blast of air is so loud in our ears that it's too hard to talk, so we drive in a comfortable silence, both contemplating our own thoughts.

And thoughts are something I have a lot of right now, when I wish I had none. I replay the scene with my father in my head just like I did a hundred other times during work today. No, my resolve hasn't wavered, but at the same time I wonder what he's going to say, how he's going to try to force my hand into returning to my duties and the marriage he refuses to accept is over.

The emotions rush through my mind like the wind through the window, constant and powerful. *Shut it down, Getty. Let it go.* So I try to do just that. I glance over to Zander and smile before closing my eyes, resting my head back on the seat, and allowing myself to enjoy letting someone take control of the wheel for a bit so I can just be a passenger.

I'm not sure how long we drive, but the deceleration of the car and a sudden bump of the shocks have me opening my eyes. Zander has pulled off the main road that meanders along the entire coastline of the island onto a rutted asphalt road. I look around in curiosity, but all I see are dense trees and a dirt road sloping downward in front of us. And just as I'm about to ask what's going on, the trees open up into an isolated clearing.

The waves churning in the ocean beyond us provide a breathtaking view. It's a clear day and whitecaps dance on the water and the wind rustles the trees. It's an astoundingly beautiful scene.

"Wow." One word. That's the only possible way to describe it.

"Yeah. Wow." But when I glance over at him, he's looking at me, and for a brief moment the thought ghosts through my mind that he's not talking about the view. I maintain our connection for a beat before shifting my gaze back to the water, a surge of sudden attraction causing my nerves to hum when they shouldn't.

"Mable dropped a check by the house today while you were at work. It's on the kitchen counter."

The subject change comes quickly enough to give me whiplash. And while I try to remain outwardly calm, my insides are vibrating with anxiety. So I sit there and wait for the questions to come, the barrage over what she's paying me for. Why I'm so broke. "Thanks." Time to change the subject. "How'd you know about this place? It's incredible."

"Liam told me about it."

*Oh.* "When were you talking to him?" I feign disinterest as warning bells sound. Worrying that maybe Liam said something to Zander about walking in on me in the stockroom today when I was with my father. Or maybe he asked Zander who it was, since I made sure to suddenly become busy any time he asked about the unfamiliar man.

"You were in the back, I think. He came over and asked me a few things, said it was a cool place to watch the storms move in."

I chew the inside of my lip as I stare out at the tranquillity of the sea. "But there's no storm moving in."

"Isn't there, though?"

*Oh. Shit.* The question and the searching tone in his voice catch me off guard and I'm instantly leery of stepping into this conversation. At the same time I long to talk to him about it. I keep my eyes focused anywhere but on him, draw strength from the beauty around me with the trees rustling high above us making the only sound.

"Who came to the bar today, Getty?"

Panic flutters. My mouth goes dry. My fingers twist together in my lap. My thoughts collide with fear. I want to tell Zander but am afraid what he will think of me once he knows how weak and stupid I was in the past. How I allowed myself to be treated.

No self-respecting woman puts up with what I did. So what does that say about me as a person?

"I told you I was adopted." Zander's unexpected comment startles me enough that I shift and turn to look at him, wondering where he's going with this. "If you were half as nosy as most people these days, you'd already have pulled all of this up, but I respect you more because you haven't. I appreciate you letting me tell you on my own terms. Especially because the reason I came to Pine-Ridge won't be in any of those articles. I'm the only person who knows why."

I nod slowly, curiosity piqued. "I'd rather you tell me . . . when you want to."

He's leaned back in the seat, one elbow propped on the window frame with his hand on his forehead, while the thumb on his other hand is tapping on the bottom part of the steering wheel. When he turns his head slightly and looks at me, there's a far-off look in his eyes and his Adam's apple bobs as he swallows. "I grew up on the wrong side of town. Drugs, alcohol, violence, you name it—they were always in my house for as long as I can remember, but that's not to say I remember much. When I was almost eight, I woke up in the middle of the night. My mom was screaming for help. She'd been stabbed. Many times. My dad was covered in her blood. He threatened to come after me if I ever told anyone."

"Oh, Zander." My comment is reflexive. So is the movement of my hand that reaches out to squeeze his thigh in sympathetic and silent support. I can't even attempt to wrap my head around what his eyes have seen or the pain he's lived with. Both as a little boy and as a grown man.

"I'm not . . . it was . . . *shit*," he says as he blows out a sigh and shakes his head. "I don't mean to sound so matter-of-fact about it, but that's the only way I can not let it get to me . . . because it does that enough already."

I keep hoping he'll look my way so that I can tell him somehow with my eyes how sorry I am. . . . I know my words won't amount to much. But he doesn't look my way. In fact he seems to focus everywhere else but on me as he works through the memories in his mind.

"I didn't talk for months. Couldn't. I was seriously messed up when I was placed in that home for boys I mentioned. All of their stories were equally as horrible as mine and with no other suitable family members to adopt us, we kind of adopted each other. *And we had Rylee.*" A smile ghosts his lips and softens his features momentarily. The love he has for her is blatantly obvious. "She ran the House and was a mother to all of us in a sense. Her patience and compassion were—are—the reason we all made it. How we survived." The smile grows wider. "One day this man came to the house to see her. When he walked in, I knew who he was immediately. It was Colton Donavan. You see, the one thing that my dad did with me was watch racing, and so the minute I saw Colton, for a second, I forgot about everything my dad had done. I was sad and scared and lonely and heartbroken and there was this larger-than-life person in this new place. And I know it makes zero sense, but seeing him made me feel close somehow to the little bit of good in my old life. He knelt down . . . and there was something about him—a connection, a moment, a something that somehow made a little boy want to speak for the first time in months. . . . It wasn't much, but it was a start."

Now it's my turn to smile as the comfortable silence settles around us. To imagine what Zander looked like as a scared little boy looking up to this giant persona and having a connection. And there are so many questions I want to ask him, so many things I want to say, and yet I do neither because I'm utterly fascinated how that broken boy could be the kindhearted man sitting beside me. The one who would mess up a silverware drawer just because it affected my own triggers somehow.

"Thank you."

"For what?"

"For telling me."

He looks my way for a split second and then shifts in his seat so his back is against his door, gaze focused to his thigh where his fingers intertwine with mine. I can sense he's uncomfortable by his lack of response, that he hates discussing his past, and yet for some reason he's doing it, so I sit patiently and wait.

"At some point Rylee and Colton started dating and they seamlessly included us in their relationship. All of us boys felt like we were a part of it with them. It was so cool as a kid to come from this broken life and then be a part of something we all knew was special. Fairy tales weren't a popular topic in a house full of boys, but we knew theirs was one." His smile flashes again, good memories leading the way. "Once I'd found my voice again, I was able to give a statement to the police about what happened. Formally identify my dad as the killer. And true to his words, he came back for me."

*Jesus. How much can one little kid take?* "Zander—"

"No. Just let me finish," he says with a shake of his head and a squeeze of my fingers. "I'm giving you the short version, but even that's pretty fucked-up."

"I'd say. . . ."

"I know it sounds like a soap opera, so bear with me. He tried to take me from the House. Kidnap me, in a sense. He held a gun on Rylee when she refused to let him take me. There was a police standoff and they ended up killing him before he killed her." He pauses, his voice stoic, disassociated from the traumatic events. And while I hear it, I also attempt to fathom the selflessness of this Rylee woman who risked her life to save his. "Rylee and Colton married. And right when they were about to have a baby of their own, my long-lost uncle sought me out."

He blows out a breath while my mind reels, trying to comprehend how he's as normal as he is with his violent family history.

"He wanted to foster me, when all he'd ever wanted before was to chase his next high. I was petrified of going back to my old life. And luckily Colton and Rylee feared what would happen if he was successful in getting custody and so with the support of my brothers, they adopted me to save me. And then we all lived happily ever after . . . until a few months ago."

He finally looks back up to me, face serious, eyes intense, and after being hit with all of that, I can't even begin to imagine what he could say now to shock me. But I know whatever it is, it's the reason he's come here to the island and into my life.

"A package arrived at my house from that uncle's wife. The letter attached said he'd died and enclosed were some things he'd kept that I might want to have." He shakes his head, and I immediately want to know what was in the box. "I have nothing of that life . . . my childhood . . . or anything of my mother's at all. No pictures, no trinkets, no proof that I even existed until I arrived at the House besides her state-written obituary. Obviously I was anxious to see what was in it."

"You don't have to continue." I need him to know that this is enough. That I get why he's doing this now. He's crossing that boundary we set on night two. The one we don't cross and we don't ask about. The one he's obliterating right now in the hopes that maybe I'll be comfortable enough to tell him who the man was at the bar today.

*I showed you mine—now you show me yours* type of thing. But he continues anyway.

"The first thing I pulled out of the box kind of rocked my world. Fucked with my head to the point that I shut the carton, taped it closed, and promised myself I'd never look at it again. Didn't need to know more. Didn't need to open the skeletons in my closet regardless of how much I wanted one little piece to prove I existed." He falls silent, runs a hand through his hair. His internal struggle feels palpable in the small space between us.

"I told myself what I saw didn't matter. It wasn't the truth. And then I started realizing that Rylee and Colton had to have known about it and they'd kept it from me all this time. They'd lied to me. And the combination of the two made me kind of spiral out of control." His self-deprecating laugh fills the car, while his cryptic comments leave me wanting to ask about what he saw in the box. About what was so devastating it would derail him to the point he'd hurt the family that he'd been given a second chance to have. As much as I want to, I tell myself that he's being an open book and I can't just flip to the epilogue to see how his story ends up before he wants me to.

"I fucked up every way possible, Getty. Had no regard for my job because Colton was technically my boss. I kept my brothers at arm's length, pushed Rylee away, was late to meetings, blew off sponsors. . . . It was bad," he admits with a resigned sigh. "And then one day Colton stepped in and told me I'd lost my sponsor because of it. God, I was such a selfish prick to him. So fucking angry at the world, and I took it out on him. So he fired me. Told me I needed some time to sort through whatever it was that was messing me up. And once I dealt with it, then I could come back and we'd talk about what's left of my career. If there was one left to talk about."

"And so that's why you're here," I finish for him. Shocked and hurting for him all at the same time.

"That's why I'm here." He nods. "I hurt a lot of people. Fucked up so many things. I was way off base in blaming Colton and Rylee for not telling me about what I learned on that damn sheet of paper. And as much as I want to make things right with my family, I can't yet. Not until I deal with going through the contents of that box and the fallout I fear, so that I've proven to myself I've got a handle on it. Then maybe I can prove to them I'm the man they believed me to be."

He blows out a loud breath and leans his head back on the seat. "God, you probably think I'm such a pussy that I let this one stupid thing . . . filled with who the hell knows what . . . fuck me up that much." He keeps his eyes closed and I debate whether he wants me to answer. A man's ego is a mysterious, fragile thing and all I've known are my father's and Ethan's and theirs are so overinflated they'd never admit anything like this.

To them, vulnerability is an emotion to be manipulated. Toyed with. Taken advantage of. And yet here's

Zander, freely telling me things—readily making himself vulnerable—when I get the impression it's not something he does often.

So sitting here looking at him—dark hair tousled by the wind, lips pursed as he contemplates the situation, dark sunglasses hanging in the neck of his shirt, allowing me to see his eyes, and strong hands linked with my slender ones—I go with my gut.

That's all I can do.

"No, Zander. I don't think you're being a wimp. At all. That's a lot for anyone to handle. I'm just trying to figure out how you're such a normal, functioning guy who hasn't lost it sooner."

His laugh rumbles through the car. It's long and deep and I can tell a little levity was what he needed from me right now. I'm glad I could give him that.

"I'm far from normal."

"Ah yes. Not normal at all. Just *pretty*."

*"Getty,"* he warns, but the laugh he follows it up with has more humor than cynicism this time. When our eyes meet, I can feel a part of me—the walls I've kept high to guard my past, my reasons, my motivations—start to crack.

And with that simple notion, I realize the spotlight has been turned toward me. Suddenly feeling trapped, I abruptly get out of the car. The breeze is chilly but feels good on my skin. I gulp in a deep breath and try to calm my nerves as I walk toward the front of the car.

The slam of a door tells me Zander's not going to let this go. Crossing my arms in a false pretense of toughness, I lean my hip onto the hood of the car. He follows suit.

"Are we really going to do this?" My question encompasses all aspects of our relationship: cross boundaries, tangle sheets, and hopefully not break my heart when he sorts himself out and returns to his old life.

"What *this* are we talking about?" he muses with a lift of his eyebrow while one side of his mouth curves up into a knowing smile. His eyes tell me *yes, to all of it,* and yet the tone of his question remains benign.

"Are you answering a question with a question, *Mander*?"

"Only if you're going to keep avoiding answering it."

Our eyes clash in a battle of wills as the smirk on his lips challenges me to talk.

I sigh in resignation. "What was the question again?" I ask, knowing damn well what it was.

He laughs when I ask another question and bumps his shoulder against mine. Reaching out, he links our fingers and narrows his eyes. "Yes, Getty. We're really doing this. Crossing boundaries." He twists his lips and just stares at me for a second. "You know . . . I had no intention of telling you any of that. Zero . . . but I want you to trust me. How can you trust me when I'm not being honest with you?"

And there he goes. Laying down the gauntlet to see if I'll pick it up and reciprocate. I tilt my face up to the sky and focus on the swaying pine trees above me to buy time as I gather my courage by the bootstraps.

"My father came to visit me today." My voice is steady, even, and yet all I hear in my own ears is the sound of my nerves. My anxiety over letting someone know about my old life. I hate the feeling that comes over me, anticipating the flush of shame when I confess who I used to be, what I used to let happen to me.

Then I try to pull my hands from his, create some space between us, anything so he can't feel my hands grow damp or the nerves tremor through them, but he squeezes them tighter. "No," he says resolutely, and brings the back of my hand to his lips and kisses it.

Tears burn in my eyes. At a kindness I don't deserve from this man who has withstood so much more than me and yet is standing here asking me to trust him. And in the safe moment he's created for me to purge my fears.

My gaze scans the horizon, the ocean and its continuous ripples, before I find my voice again. "My name is Gertrude Caster-Adams. Or rather Gertrude Caster, since I'm no longer married." I laugh nervously because the name that's been mine for almost twenty-six years sounds foreign to my own ears. And I'm not sure if I expect him to recognize the last name, but a part of me sighs in relief when he does nothing more than brush his thumb over the top of my hand in reassurance. "I grew up in Silicon Valley. Computer giants may have run the town, but my father built an empire selling real estate to these overnight millionaires."

Recognition flashes across his features and yet he remains quiet. Allows me to move at my own pace. And my mind's a scattered mess. Unsure how to start. Where to go. So I begin when it all changed.

"When I was eleven, my mother died of a pulmonary embolism. A freak thing after a routine knee surgery."

"Oh, Getty." The sound in his voice almost breaks the dam holding back the tears that I don't want to shed. He knows the pain of losing a mother. I take comfort in the thought and clear my throat to continue. "At a young age, I recognized my father as being a controlling elitist. Or as much as a child can understand that concept . . . but I never knew the full obsession of his need to maintain his societal status until after she died. It was crazy how much she'd sheltered me from it, but once she was gone, I was the only one left to bear the brunt of his wrath. A teenager who needed her mother more than anything, and his solution was etiquette classes and debutante balls. Education was imperative—the best private schools where who you were friends with was way more important than your grades." I shove away the memories of being told I couldn't play with kids who were just as miserable as I was in the prison of a school. How I was forced to go to social events and boring teas just because of who was hosting it or its attendees. Barbies were unacceptable child's play. Video games were akin to the devil. But hours spent with the women's Junior League was time well spent.

"I was miserable. All I wanted was to be a normal teenager who listened to music way too loud and talked back enough to get put on restriction so I could have time to myself." My laugh sounds miserable at best. "My junior year, I was introduced to Ethan Adams. I knew of him because his father ran a commercial development company that was growing by leaps and bounds as much as my father's was on the residential side of the business. Little did I know that chance meeting—or I guess I should say *orchestrated* meeting—would be the beginning of the end of me."

So many memories flash through my mind from that time.

"My father was this cold, harsh man. He demanded perfection. *A lady never makes mistakes or causes a scene, Gertrude.*" I sneer at the thought. "So when I met Ethan, he was like a source of the warmth I'd been missing in my life. He made me laugh. He focused on me, when for years I'd been focusing on how to make my father happy. He courted me properly. Stolen kisses here and there because sex was for marriage and he planned on marrying me. He made me feel loved when for so long after my mother's death, our house had been like a morgue. He made me feel hope . . . like if I just hung on through my father's demands long enough, then he'd marry me and whisk me away and it would all be better."

"Now I know how hard it was for you to sit here and listen to me without saying anything." The strained resignation in Zander's voice pulls my eyes toward him. I can sense his anger at where he thinks this story is going. There's concern, warmth, compassion there too. Three things I haven't felt in so very long and yet I now know why I'd been hesitant to believe they were genuine.

Because Ethan had made me feel that way and look how that turned out.

"I know." I smile, because it's so easy to do with him. I nod, ready to unload more of the weight from my chest. "What I didn't know until after the storybook wedding was that I was basically a dowry in a business merger. The tying bond between two families that allowed my father to take over the Adams empire when Ethan's father passed away and gain someone to take over all of his when he eventually retired."

"A pawn." Disgust laces his tone.

"Yep." A lone tear slides down my cheek. I rub it away instantly. I'll allow myself only one. *Retell this like the story it is, Getty. Like you're the narrator, and then you can break down in private later over the memories that still hold your*

*heart hostage.* My breath is audibly shaky when I draw it in.
"It was gradual at first, but it didn't take long for Ethan's
true colors to shine through: He was as cold and callous as
my father was. Maybe even more so, now that I've had time
to reflect on it. Our wedding night should have been my first
indication, but I was too nervous to really comprehend how
bad of a situation I'd gotten myself into." Silence falls as the
memory that stains my soul and stands out as the one that
hurt the most replays in my mind's eye. And I'm so glad that
Zander is polite enough not to ask more, because the wounds
are still raw all this time later.

The fairy-tale first time was anything but for me. There
were selfish demands and disregard of my pain instead of
soft words of encouragement and proclamations of love.
A few grunts, some criticism from Ethan, and then I was
left alone in a gigantic bed with tears drying on my cheeks
and blood on the sheets as he left the hotel room for a
while. Only to return later with the scent of perfume on
his collar and alcohol on his breath.

"Getty?" Zander's searching tone pulls me from the
black memory.

"Sorry. I was just . . . Never mind." I force a smile to my
lips to tell him I'm okay. "If I'd felt controlled under my
father's thumb, living with Ethan was more like a noose
around my neck. Perfection was expected and anything less
was punishable: organization, white-glove cleanliness, appearance, manners, meals, *everything.* His paranoia grew
over fears he was going to lose his position in the company
and lose everything. That fear was taken out on me. Ridiculous accusations, constant criticisms, complete control
over my life." My voice breaks on the last sentence, too
many memories haunting me to remain unaffected.

"So you left?" Zander prompts in a way that tells me I
don't have to explain about the reasons any more. That
he understands how personal they are and he doesn't
need to know the specifics because he can infer.

"Yes." I swallow over the lump in my throat. "I filed
for divorce in secret and then left in the middle of the
night, but somehow he was prepared for it, because he'd

already frozen all my accounts. My father did the same to my trust accounts, when it shouldn't be possible."

I can all but see the cogs of his mind clicking into place. How upset I became at his accusation of being a trust fund baby. Why I have expensive things but need my job desperately.

"And now they're here," he says in affirmation.

"Just my father—that I know of." And I hate that momentary panic of wondering whether Ethan is lurking nearby in town. I push it away. Focus on getting it all out. "I knew he'd find me eventually. The long-reaching arms of Damon Caster are inescapable. But I needed enough time to make sure I was strong enough to face him. That their hold over me had lessened. And those words, *hold over me* . . . I'm so embarrassed to even admit that I let someone have that."

Shame has me averting my eyes from his. I look out to the water, watch the ocean breeze create patterns in the water, and bite back the self-reprimands over the life I used to live.

"Getty, don't. Please don't." He tugs on my hand for me to look at him, and I can't just yet. "No one knows anything about being in your shoes unless they've walked in them. But I'm not thinking that. *Not at all.* I'm thinking how much courage you must have had to leave that life. One others thought was full of privilege and perfection, but instead it was like a prison."

"Not so courageous now, though, when I saw my father standing in the bar today and my first thought was to run again." I choke on the words. Another tear falls. The heat of the confessions feels like they've stained my cheeks red. "And then you brought the car and it was running and . . ." My words trail off and my train of thought gets momentarily lost in the emotion.

"What did he want, Getty?" There's concern in his voice. And maybe some anger.

"He wanted me to stop my charade, as he called it, and come back home. That as Ethan's wife, I need to uphold our family's social status," I mimic in my father's stiff baritone, and laugh listlessly. "I told him a word he's never heard from me before: *no*. That I was staying put."

Zander squeezes my hand and when I turn to look at him, his smile is wide and proud.

"Then he told me he's picking me up tomorrow night for dinner so he can talk some sense into me. Make a plan to mitigate the gossip when I return."

Zander must sense the resignation in my voice. "If you go, I'm going with you."

His words shock the hell out of me and are nothing close to what I'd expected to hear. Yet I've never heard anything sound better. "I couldn't ask you to do that."

*Please go with me.*

"You're not asking me. I'm offering." He nods his head resolutely as if the discussion is over.

"He's not going to respond well to your presence." And why am I apologizing for a man who obviously has no regard for me?

"Even better." Zander smacks his hands together and rubs them. "There's nothing I like more than to thumb my nose at authority."

We stare at each other with matching smiles, hips resting on this heap of a car amid the beauty of nature, and there is a sense that something has shifted between us. Trust has been exchanged. Boundaries have been crossed.

So many doors have been opened.

Even though all our questions haven't been answered or our fears completely confessed, we both seem okay with the secrets that still remain. This is a huge step forward for the both of us. A leap of faith.

We stand with my head resting on his shoulder and our fingers entwined—in the middle of an unexpected bright spot in my new life—and I feel utterly naked even though I'm completely clothed. It's unnerving. It's exhilarating.

It's empowering.

And it's about time.

# Chapter 18

Out of habit, my eyes scan the streets on the drive home through town as if we're going to accidentally run into my father. I hate that I'm back to this feeling after being on my own for over four months. It reminds me how I felt in those first days—like a fugitive on the lam about to get caught and dragged back to jail at any moment.

Zander pulls into the driveway and the minute we enter the house, I'm immediately restless. Maybe it's the *Now where do we go from here?* realization or just a sudden thrust back into my reality when the lookout point was more of a reprieve.

Keeping busy, I put dishes away, fold a load of laundry, change the sheets on my bed. Zander's on the couch when I enter the kitchen, legs stretched out, feet crossed at the ankles, his laptop on his thighs. He doesn't look up or bug me and I'm thankful for the space he's given me, because even though I'm relieved at having told someone, my mind is now working a million miles an hour. I grab a drink and then put it back down, my stomach suddenly in knots. Unsure what to do next, I walk into my bedroom, where a blank canvas looks tempting to me, but for the first time, I'm not sure what to paint.

Resigned to this unsettled feeling, I opt for a long, hot shower that does nothing to ease the discord. After I dry off, I slide on my robe and the smile is automatic when I see Zander's products on the counter tipped over, crooked, backward. The irony is it's so perfectly messed up that I know he did it on purpose.

His intent makes the act so much sweeter. And my next decision that much easier to make.

The house is quiet when I exit the bathroom and I catch myself moving toward the sliding glass doors leading to the outdoor deck. By the light of the moon I can make out the tools still strewn around the platform, the errant two-by-fours waiting to reinforce the existing structure, the patchwork quilt of wood still waiting to be sanded and painted.

But it's the lights on the water that hold my attention. The boats coming home to their families or ones leaving on a new journey. I watch them for what feels like forever, my legs chilled beneath the robe and my breath fogging the window in front of me. I stand motionless in the darkened hallway, because like at the restaurant, I lose myself in the story I create for each one of the glimmering lights.

Because sometimes thinking about others makes it so much easier to forget about yourself.

"Getty?" Zander's voice is soft as he steps up behind me. And I don't jump, because for some reason, I knew he'd find me. Bring me back when I'm trying to forget myself.

"Hmm?" I keep my eyes on the lights, their stories still loud in my head, but my body is most definitely shifting its attention toward his undeniable presence.

"You're quiet. Have been since we came home. You okay?"

Like that's not a loaded question when it comes to the two of us. I meet his eyes briefly in the reflection of the glass before looking back toward the lights. It takes me a moment to answer him. "Yes. No. I don't know."

He chuckles softly and I know he's thinking of the last time our conversation involved this phrasing. When he rests his hands upon my shoulders, it takes everything I have not to sag into him. His touch ignites something within me and it's like I can't think straight when he does it.

But I'm not sure if I want him to move his hands,

because I'm so sick of thinking and worrying that I welcome the lack of thought. And if his hands on my shoulders can mess up my head, I wonder what the weight of his body on mine could do.

It's a fleeting thought as his chuckle fades and the silence descends around us once again. The draw of his breath and a car driving by outside are the only sounds.

"It's okay to feel a little all over the place after baring your secrets to someone." I want to believe him that this is normal, but I'm so far from recognizing normal anymore I don't know what to think. When I don't respond, he continues. "I know I do."

"I'm sorry. I don't want you to feel—"

"I told you no more apologies, Getty." His voice is stern, implacable. "You didn't do anything wrong." He squeezes my shoulders gently and my eyes flash up to meet his in the reflection again. Our gazes hold through the darkness, a mixture of concern and understanding in his. "Talk to me. Turn around and tell me what's going on in that beautiful mind of yours."

Hesitation is my friend tonight. And so is the glass in front of me that allows me to look at Zander without really looking at him. Call it feeling exposed or vulnerable, but for some reason right now I can't look him directly in the eyes.

"I don't know." I pause, take a deep breath, and try to find the words to express how I'm feeling. "It's like I'm so sure that I did the right thing in leaving, so positive that I didn't make up how I was being treated in my head or overreact, like Ethan used to tell me I was doing. Regardless, I can't help the doubt from creeping in. And I hate it. Am so ashamed of it because I'm stronger than that now. A different person than that weak woman I used to be. But after all of those years being controlled and criticized and told I was wrong . . . I loathe that I feel so strong one minute and the next fall apart. It makes me question my sanity." My chest constricts as I lay the contradictions that rule my life out on the proverbial table and hope he understands what I'm trying to say. That he doesn't judge me as weak for the admission.

"That's okay. So very normal." The heat of his breath hits my neck as he leans his forehead against the crown of my head. Such an intimate action when all I want to do is pull away, because I don't deserve this from him. What I deserve is for him to give my shoulders a good hard shake to knock some sense in me and tell me I need to buck up. But he doesn't. He gives me patience, understanding, and compassion, when I least expect them. "You can't undo something in a few months when it's been hammered into your head year after year after year."

"I don't want to be that person anymore, Zander. I don't want to be Gertrude Caster-Adams." My voice is soft but conveys my inner turmoil.

His hands on my shoulders pressure me to turn around so that I come face-to-face with him, my back now to the sliding glass door. His blue eyes are full of determination when they meet mine. "You're not her anymore. You're Getty Caster, from PineRidge, who likes messy silverware drawers, thinks a mini-blind wand is a formidable weapon, and is the only woman I know who can rock a pair of mismatched knee-high socks and make them look sexy as hell."

"Whatever." I roll my eyes and try to step to the side. His words hit my ears but fail to sink in.

"No. Let me finish." He steps closer, and I can't deny the powerful feel of the heat of his body against mine. Next his hands are framing my jaw and directing my face up to his. "You're Getty Caster. A fighter in every sense of the word. A person who is ten times better than any man who puts her down. A woman who knows it's okay to be afraid sometimes so long as she also realizes it takes a helluva lot more bravery to be scared and succeed than to fear and give in."

Tears well in my eyes. Even with his hands on my cheeks, I subtly disagree with a shake of my head, because words aren't possible right now. What he's telling me is so much harder to accept than the lies and the doubt.

"You're Getty Caster," he continues, "first-time beer drinker and apprentice deck carpenter, who has a wicked imagination when it comes to making up other people's life stories like in the restaurant. Now you just need to finish figuring out what you want your story to be."

"No." It comes out without any conviction and with a sob lodged in my throat. Because his words are causing all my hopes and wants and desires to surface when they've been pushed down for so very long.

"Yes." His voice is soft yet definitive. When I lower my eyes, he just lifts my head higher so I have no choice other than to look at him. "You're Getty Caster. Artist extraordinaire, painter of sunsets instead of stormy seas."

"Or of white squalls." My words are barely audible. The moment feels at once too real, too raw, and yet poignantly perfect.

"Or of white squalls," he repeats just as quietly.

His smile is genuine. His gaze is steadfast on mine. And there's something in the way he says the words that tells me he really means them. He doesn't see that other woman I used to be when he looks at me. He sees the new me.

Getty Caster.

We stand in that suspended state of anticipation for what feels like forever. His hands are still on my face and his breath feathers over my lips as my heart pounds in a new rhythm. One filled with expectation, hope, and a fear so very different from what I'm used to. It's the kind that makes your palms sweat and stomach drop because the man standing before you is so incredible inside and out that you're afraid he isn't real.

"Zander." It's not a question—rather it's an admission of wanting and telling him *yes* and *I don't know* at the same time.

"Getty."

He closes the distance at such an achingly slow pace that by the time his lips brush ever so slightly against mine in a kiss that hints at things to come, I feel like I've waited years for it to happen.

Our lips meet, once, twice, a third time before he leans back, eyes searching, demanding, wanting, and yet we are completely motionless and utterly silent. Desire flows like a raging river through me while nerves, doubts, and insecurities fight their way upstream.

"I'm nervous."

"Of what?" And the curiosity laced with hope in his voice tells me he's asking me to verbalize my decision about wanting to be with him. My understanding there's only so much he can give me.

"I'm . . ." I clear my throat as my hands fidget where they rest on the bare skin of his waist. I avert my eyes before I speak so he can't see my embarrassment. "I'm not any good at this."

"What are you talking about?"

"This." My cheeks burn with mortification and I wish I'd just kept my mouth shut. I shrug, embarrassment stealing the words from my lips as I open and then close them again. "Sex." When I finally say the word, it's barely audible, my insecurities overruling the heat of his touch on my skin and the ache it makes me feel.

His answering chuckle is low and rich and all I hear is Ethan's mocking tone in the sound. Needing space, I try to shrug out of Zander's hold on my cheeks, to be alone, to lick my shameful wounds in private, but his hold remains steadfast. "Getty, look at me."

He waits until I comply. I can tell my jaw is set with the hurt I don't want to convey, but when my eyes find his, the mocking look I expect isn't there. In fact what I see is exactly the opposite: disbelief, understanding, compassion. A million questions and answers pass between us in a single moment of connection.

And then something shifts. Maybe it's the rub of his thumb over my parted lips. Or the way that soft smile lifts up one corner of his mouth and carries through to his eyes. I can't place it, but it's as if someone has vacuumed all the air from the room and replaced it with electricity. My skin burns with desire where he touches me, and a strange mix of anxious arousal surges through me.

"I don't believe you for a second. If the sex wasn't good, I assure you it *wasn't you*. There's no way you can kiss the way you kiss and not be any good at it. That's not possible," he murmurs as he leans forward and brushes his lips against mine again. "I have a feeling it was your partner who wasn't any good."

"Mmm," I murmur against his mouth, willing myself to believe him.

When he leans back, the lift of his eyebrows is a subtle warning not to doubt him. His eyes are begging me to trust him. I do, but I'm scared. I want him but don't even know where to start.

"Let me show you differently," he says before he takes my hand in his and leads me down the hallway toward his bedroom.

There is no turning back now. My heart beats faster with each step and my body becomes more attuned to every single thing about him. The bunch of the muscles in his back as he walks. The intricate splash of ink on his shoulder. His hair mussed. His unmistakable but subtle scent of cologne. The confidence in his stride.

When we enter his bedroom, I'm glad he's holding my hands so they can't tremble out of control. He stops in front of the bed and pulls me to him so we're face-to-face, eyes locked on each other's, our matching shaky breaths the only sound in the room around us, and the glow of the moon the only light in it.

With his eyes trained on mine and the rush of blood pounding in my ears, I feel his fingers fumble with the tie on my robe. The smooth silk rubs against my bare skin. Then the cool air of the room hits me as the sash falls to the ground and the fabric parts. We stare at each other for a beat before the heat of his hands slides over my waist.

I hold my breath in reaction to the unknown that's exhilarating and terrifying all at once. He doesn't break our visual connection as he slowly runs the palms of his hands up my rib cage and then back down to the curve of my hips. His touch crosses to the middle of my back and then moves up the length of my spine before his fingers knead into my shoulders. Then they retrace their path all over again.

He continues this slow, tantalizing seduction, but it's the look in his eyes that holds me rapt. He watches my reactions to every single brush of his hands over my skin. Every inhalation. Every flutter of my eyelashes. Every time my eyes widen from the temptation he offers.

My body aches in delicious ways that are brand-new to me. Each nerve at the delta of my thighs and along my nipples is left frenzied and standing at attention in the wake of his touch.

Foreplay was a waste of energy before. Seduction non-existent in my marriage. My pleasure, my needs, my wants, all of that forgotten in the face of Ethan's greed and disregard for me.

*But he's not Zander.*

Zander is hypnotizing me slowly. Pulling me under his spell by giving me time to settle my nerves. Showing me tenderness with his patience. And we haven't done anything more than kiss.

"Getty . . ." His voice sounds strained, rough with desire, as his hands run up my rib cage, this time rubbing his thumbs over the tips of my nipples. And I can't respond. Not with his touch owning my mind and body. My back arches, lips part in a gasp, and my head falls back as he takes a moment to appreciate my breasts. But this time, he pushes my robe off my shoulders so that it slides down my arms and pools at our feet.

He threads his fingers through my wet hair at the base of my neck and fists it while his other hand splays wide against my lower back. And there's something to be said about the fact that his eyes haven't left mine yet. They haven't wandered over my bared body like I'd expect from a man. It's like he knows I'm scared, partly self-conscious, and a whole lotta flustered, and is making sure I know he wants me for so much more than just what my body can give him.

The notion is heady as he steps against me.

The cool air of the room, the undeniable heat of his body, and the anticipation of what's to come all overshadow the nerves humming through me as I stand there naked and vulnerable.

He pulls gently on my hair to angle my head to the side and exposes the curve of my neck. His lips meet the top of my shoulder and he laces a row of openmouthed kisses up to that sensitive spot just below my ear.

"Let me worship you, Getty." The deep timbre of his

voice fills my ears, warms my soul, and erases any remaining doubt I have.

But there isn't much.

"Let me show you how sex is supposed to be. Supposed to make you feel. Let. Me. Worship. You."

I'm not sure who moves first, but within a beat our mouths
meet in a kiss to rival all kisses. It starts out slow and sweet—
parted lips, tentative tongues, contented moans—as his body
moves into mine. My breasts press against the firmness of his
chest and I lose myself to him. In him. The flex of his muscles
beneath my hand. How he moves my head to control the
angle of our kiss. The scrape of his five-o'clock shadow over
my chin. The vibration of his chest as he hums in strained
appreciation. The taste of him on my tongue. The strength
of his body when he pulls me tighter into him. The unmistakable thickness of his erection, hard and straining against
the inseam of his jeans.

And then our patience slowly evaporates. The tenderness of the kiss turns from want to need. From tentativeness
to greed. From wait-and-see to now-or-never.

There's a desperate hunger in his actions now. A nonverbal demand for more. While our teeth nip at each
other, soft sighs intersperse the definitive moans of desire. With one hand cradling the back of my head, his
other grabs my ass so he can grind himself against me.

The ache burns bright as we dance together and push
our willpower to the point of no return. And then it's
gone.

Lost to the seduction.

Forgotten in our mutual need.

It's like a switch is flipped in both of us simultaneously.
Our kiss turns more possessive. Our bodies fixated on
the next step, the next high, the next connection.

My hands are on the button of his jeans. His palms cup
my breasts. His tongue licks a line down the curve of my
shoulder before his teeth take a playful nip there. My hands
are covered by his so we can push his jeans down together.
And I know I've seen his dick before, but hell if the feel of
his erection rebounding up when it's released from the confines of the denim doesn't make my breath hitch.

I don't get much time to think about its hardness rest-ing against my lower belly because Zander pushes me backward so that the backs of my knees hit the mattress. With his mouth on mine, derailing all other thoughts, he directs me back onto the bed. We move in unison. Our bodies responding to each other's demands without any forethought about it.

I'm on my back across the bed, Zander's knees frame my hips, his hands braced on either side of my head, and he leans back to look in my eyes. With my mouth still vi-brating from his kisses, a slow, crooked smile lifts up the corner of his.

"Do you know how hard it is to do this and not take a step back to admire you naked and lying here in my bed? I know you're scared. Know you've been hurt. And I know you worry about what I'm going to think of you. That I might compare you to other women. Listen to me when I say this, Getty. *I'm. Not. Him.* There is no history in this room. No history between us. Just here. Just now. Just you and me. And fuck yes, I want you more than I've wanted anyone in as long as I can remember. God, you're sexy as sin. I'm kind of wishing you had those knee-high socks on right now."

The smile on my lips is instantaneous. His attempt to soothe my fears and then make me relax reminds me why I'm here with him, despite knowing this can go nowhere. I push the thought away. Focus on the here and now and how he's making me feel. Worthy, sexy, and wanted for the first time in forever.

How he's worshipping me with his slow, sweet seduction.

I let out a laugh as I think about his fixation on the socks. And then it turns into a desperate moan when one of his hands slides between my thighs as he shifts on his knees to push my legs apart.

With featherlight touches he runs his fingertips up one thigh, over my lower belly, and then down the other. Af-ter doing that a few times, he trails them up the insides of my parted thighs so just a whisper of a touch is felt along the outside of my sex. Each time he traces the same path, his touch becomes a little firmer, his fingers more intent.

He sits on his knees, face angled down, watching my body tense in anticipation of his touch. When he lifts his eyes, a shadow blankets one side of his face, but the intensity of his gaze blazes through the moonlit darkness.

"There are so many things I want to do to you, Getty. We'll get to all of them. I want to dip my mouth down and taste you. Spread your pussy, use my hands and my tongue to work you into a frenzy until you come. I want the lights on. So I can look into your eyes and see your face when you lose yourself to the things I do to you. So you can't hide from me. *Or from you.* I want to look down as you wrap your lips around my dick and look up with your mouth full of me. I want you on top. So I can have your tits in my mouth and my fingers on your clit while you move however you need to so you can come. I want you bent over on your knees so I can grab your ass as I work you from behind." His eyes burn bright as he leans forward to make sure I can see him.

And I can see him all right. Dark hair, clear eyes, and teeth biting into his bottom lip, he's a damn Adonis leaning over me, stealing my thoughts and awakening every part of me that has been dead for so very long.

"I want you on the kitchen counter, the patio, in your bed, in the woods. I'll take you anywhere you'll have me, Getty, because you make me want you that bad, and I'm not a man who wants much at all. So when you doubt whatever it is you'll doubt when we're finished here, I want you to remember this. All of it. Because I will deliver on that promise. I'm here to prove I'm a man of my word and with you is no different."

His words are as suggestive as his touch. I never knew you could be seduced by words alone and yet I'm seduced. Dragged under the spell of explicit promises that don't feel cheap or false. I'm ready. Willing. Desperate. For him to put any of those plans into action.

"But first this." He leans down and kisses me with reverence before pulling back. "First, we take it slow."

His hands run down my torso, thumbs brushing over the undersides of my breasts. His tongue traces a circle over my nipple. Then he closes his mouth over it and sucks. My hands grab at the sheets beneath me while I gasp.

"We take our time."

The tip of his tongue slides down the midline of my abdomen. An openmouthed kiss. Another tempting pass of his tongue as he licks a circle around my belly button. My shaky inhalation fills the room.

"I want to show you that sex isn't about being good or bad at it but about finding the right rhythm. The right pace."

He runs the tip of his nose back up my stomach between my breasts as his fingers find their way to my inner thighs and slide between the lips of my sex to the wetness at its core. Our sounds grow loud enough to fill the room—his guttural groan and my gasping moans—as a rush of warmth overwhelms every part of me from his lips teasing the underside of my jawline and his fingers gently adding friction over my clit.

"It's about having patience."

He murmurs against the sensitive skin of my neck as my hips shift and lift. And beg for more. My breath grows fainter. My concentration is on the sensations his fingers are evoking rather than remembering how to breathe. Because doing both is a struggle when he tucks his fingers into me and begins to move them in a slow rhythm that matches the kisses he laces over my skin.

"It's about being selfless. Wanting your partner to get off just as badly as you want to. Knowing satisfaction comes in more ways than just the endgame."

His warm mouth on my earlobe. His adept fingers inside me. The perfect amount of pressure and friction. My head falls back. My legs tense up. My lips part. My mind abandons any thought but him. Zander. And what he's doing to me. Indescribable.

Mind distracted from the doubt. Body brought to that brink of free fall from his erotic and intimate mix of words and actions.

"It's about letting yourself go because you trust the other person to take you there."

His breath begins to labor against my cheek as his

hand moves faster. The one rubbing against my clit. A pleasurable heat begins to burn hotter within me. Sears my core. Robs my inhibitions. Ignites my libido. Pushes me over the edge.

My hands hold on to his shoulders. Fingernails score into his flesh. My legs tense against his knees between my thighs. His name falls from my mouth. His teeth nip that sensitive curve between my neck and shoulder as my muscles pulse around his fingers.

"Let go, Getty," he encourages, voice thick with desire.

I struggle for coherency as that white-hot rush of heat flashes through me. The release is all I can focus on. I think he says my name. Encourages me as his fingers milk my orgasm without giving me any reprieve to gain some sense. And I think that's what he wants, because his soft chuckle vibrates against my chest, where his lips are still kissing softly.

With my body floating high on the orgasmic haze, he allows me only a second to catch my breath before he withdraws his fingers from within me. My soft moan of protest is smothered as his mouth meets mine again in a kiss chock-full of desperate desire. It's like I'm trying to come up for air and he's trying to pass me his.

"Goddamn," he murmurs against my lips. His hands roam and mouth claims. The urgency between us increases and I want the greediness I can sense in his touch. So I welcome the telltale rip of foil after I hear the nightstand open as his pushes himself back onto his knees and protects himself.

He takes my legs in his hands and pulls me closer to him so that the backs of my thighs rest over his hips. I don't know if I should hate or love the flutter in my belly at the feeling of the crest of his dick positioned at my entrance. If I should give in to the criticism embedded in my psyche over my lack of sexual prowess or let it go and just enjoy the man in front of me.

With his cock in his hand, he rubs up and down the line of my sex, and as much as the anticipation of him entering me makes me want to move things forward, I can't resist the urge to look up and meet his eyes. And with a slash of moonlight across his face highlighting the slow lick of his tongue over his bottom lip and the unfettered desire burning in his eyes, I know the fluttery feeling is one I'll hold on to.

"This is mine now, Getty," he murmurs into the silent room, eyes locked onto mine, and slowly pushes his way into me. Inch by achingly sweet inch. My body burns in the most pleasurable of burns as he fills me in every way possible.

When he's sheathed root to tip, the muscles in his neck and shoulders visibly demonstrating the restraint he's holding on to by a thin thread, he leans forward so there is no mistaking what he's about to say. *"Not his."* He grinds his hips in a slow circle that has us both moaning at the litany of sensations he's creating for both of us. *"Mine."* Hands keeping the insides of my thighs apart in a possessive hold, he slowly withdraws so that just the head of his dick is inside me. He wraps one of his hands around his shaft so that he can tease and taunt me before resuming the slow, all-consuming slide back in.

And when he bottoms out, the word he enunciates in a pained groan is the sexiest one I've heard from him yet. *"Yours."* A grind of hips. *"Mine."* Then a shift of my legs upward as he pushes into me as deep as possible. *"Ours."*

With our bodies connected, he leans forward on the last word and kisses me softly. And I love that although he's inside me, he still treats the kiss as if it's the most intimate of actions between us. When he pulls back, those blue eyes heavy with want meet mine. "Understood?"

"Yes."

Our lips meet once more before he shifts back up onto his knees and begins to take what I'm offering. My trust. My body. And I'd be lying to myself if I didn't say a little bit more of my heart.

His hips begin to move faster with each thrust. The crest of his dick keeps perfectly hitting on that hub of nerves within me that I never really knew existed before. It's a different kind of sensation from when his fingers worked my clit. A pressure that intensifies as he picks up the pace.

Time passes in pure sensations. The bite of his fingers into my thighs. The mist of sweat on my skin. The groan he emits as he slowly comes undone. The tingle of ecstasy throughout my body. Then all the pleasure surges and crashes after his cock slides expertly over the coveted spot within me. Incoherency reins as he swells bigger, harder, and he continues his unforgiving rhythm.

"Getty."

It's the broken groan of my name that drags me from the onslaught of sensations he's created. I focus on him just in time to see him in all his glory: head thrown back, muscles taut, hips thrusting relentlessly as his orgasm shudders through him. I stare at him with a mixture of awe and embarrassment: awe over how incredibly hot he looks and embarrassment that I don't want to be caught staring.

But I can't help it. The expression on his face as he lowers his head and looks down at me—satisfaction, desire, exhaustion—is so overwhelming to me because I put those there. *Me.* Getty Caster.

And I don't have much more time to think about it before a smug smile slowly curls his magnificent mouth as he leans forward to press a thorough and lingering kiss to my lips, which causes everything to stir once again in my lower belly.

Zander carefully pulls out of me and rises from the bed to clean up. The panicked feeling I expected of *What next?* doesn't come. Maybe it's because I'm almost twenty-six years old and for the first time ever I've been properly sexed.

And *properly* doesn't even begin to describe what Zander just did to me. I'm exhausted, and exhilarated, and can see why sexual intimacy is so important to a relationship. To cementing the connection between two people. Especially when that person has the skills of Zander Donavan.

Lost in my scattered thoughts, I emit a content sigh when Zander slides back into the bed and pulls my body against him, my back to his front. He presses a kiss to my shoulder and tears unexpectedly sting in my eyes, the emotion of the evening overwhelming me.

"You okay?" he asks, his mouth moving against my skin.

"Yeah." I nod and slide my hands over his arms, wrapped around my waist. "Yes. Thank you." Those words aren't even close to adequate to thank him for the tenderness and sense of security he just gave me. Or the little slice of confidence that Ethan just might be wrong about me.

"You don't have to thank me," he laughs. "It's not like you're the only one who benefited." The sleep-drugged sound of his voice tugs on my ego and I let the smile he can't see spread unabashedly over my lips. "And next time, it's okay for you to speak up and tell me what you want. What you need. I can handle being told what to do." He chuckles softly again, the reverberation rumbling against my back.

*Don't talk, Gertrude. Your voice distracts me. Reminds me that it's you I'm fucking. Next time you talk, you know what happens. . . .*

I shove the horrible memory from my thoughts. My ex-husband's decrees had previously ruled my sexual experience. But I don't want them to invade this moment with Zander. Ruin this taste of normalcy that I now know I'm entitled to. I will myself to hear the words Zander said instead—*next time*—and hold on to the knowledge that he wants there to be a next time. That he actually wants there to be more. *With me.*

"Okay?" he prompts when I don't respond.

"Okay."

"Uh-uh," he says as he pulls me tighter. "You don't get to fade away into your doubts again. I'm not going to let you. Today was . . ." He blows a breath. "A lot happened today, but I need you to hear me when I say *this* wasn't a mistake. Every time I touched you, everything we did, was because I wanted to. Not because I felt sorry for you or because of your past. But because *I. Wanted. To.*"

"You don't have to do . . ." *Inhale confidence, Getty. Exhale doubt.* I squeeze my eyes shut and repeat the mantra silently. Allow myself to really accept his words. Let them sink in. Tell myself that the feeling of his body warm and firm against mine isn't a fluke. Somehow its fate's fickle way of proving me wrong. That I'm capable of everything I was told I wasn't. I work a swallow over the lump in my throat and correct myself. "What were you saying?"

And of course it's made that much easier when I feel his mouth still pressed against my shoulder spread into a smile, because he understands me enough by now to know I'm trying to be the Getty Caster he's encouraging me to be.

"Confidence is sexy, Socks, so you better be careful with it or we might not ever leave this bedroom."

# Chapter 19

ZANDER

"Goddamnmotherfuckingshit!" I drop the hammer and suck on my thumb. It hurts like a bitch, but that's what I get for trying to replace roof shingles when my mind's elsewhere.

Like back in the damn bed, cozied up against Getty and her warm, tempting, sexy-as-fuck body.

I groan. And not because of the pain in my thumb. But rather because images of last night flicker through my mind. The same damn ones that distracted me and are most likely going to give me the purple badge of honor under my thumbnail.

But hell if that badge wasn't worth the pain.

I'm standing on the roof in the cool morning air, with the view of the harbor spread out in front of me, but all I see is her: lips swollen, thighs spread, pussy wet, nipples pink. *Down, boy.* And yet it's the look in her eyes that keeps coming back to me. A combination of wounded trust and hopeful desire. Plus shy vixen. The last one she doesn't quite see yet, but I sure as fuck can.

But it's her eyes that I woke up remembering. As I lay there with our bodies tangled together, I kept thinking about everything she'd told me about her past—the half of which I'm sure wasn't confessed. And what kept repeating over and over in my head was how much trust she gave me last night.

I grab the hammer and a nail. Pound it with vigor over the frustration I can't shake.

The frustration that made me shove out of bed. Away from her warm body and hot curves and pillow creases in her cheeks. Because I needed distance. Space. I got what I wanted—Getty naked and beneath me—but I think I also got a few things I didn't want. That I can't have. That I don't deserve.

Another nail. Another noncathartic pound of the hammer.

*She shouldn't trust me.* Shouldn't look at me with those chocolate eyes, a warring combination of damaged and innocent, as she puts her mistreated self in my hands, because I'm in no position to make her life better. In fact, I'm just as fucked-up as she is. Maybe even more so.

Slide a shingle over. Hold a nail. Grab the hammer.

It was just sex. Friends-with-benefits sex. Mind-blowing friends-with-benefits sex. Wake-up-and-want-to-do-it-all-over-again sex. And then possibly again. And not because we did some of the kinky shit that makes it interesting, but more so because *we didn't*. It was simply her and me; trust and give-and-take and everything I said to her during it when I should have kept my mouth shut.

Pound the hammer until there is a dent in the shingle because there's nothing left to nail in.

No one believes what anyone says during sex anyway. Just empty words to fill the quiet. To turn her on. To make her feel special. To set the mood. Words you don't remember later because you lose yourself in the endgame.

So why do I remember every single thing I said last night? Each and every promise? Every last word?

*Because I meant them.*

I miss the nail. The hammer thuds into the composite material.

"Fuck." I grit out the word. Scrunch my nose and squeeze my eyes shut while I blow out a breath.

I can't mean them. I have a life to live. A career to pick back up. Wrongs to make right.

I warned her. Told her I couldn't give her more than a few months of fun. Figured that would be enough, to lay it on the table before anything happened. You'd have thought I would've been smart enough to warn myself too.

Seems I forgot that part.

But it's not like I could have predicted yesterday. The ride to the lookout. The unexpected confessions. How she stood in the hallway stepping into me with the ocean at her back and desire palpable between us.

I'm not a *have sex, then get up and leave while the sheets are still warm* kind of guy. But I'm also not a *let's fall asleep, wake up, have sex again, and figure out how to spend the day together* type of guy either.

So why was I wanting to do just that?

Positioning the claw of the hammer under the shingle, I push down and shove it up. Remove it. Toss it off the roof with a thud.

*Damn complications.* I have an agenda. Face the cardboard box. Thank Smitty by finishing the repairs to the house. Figure out how to make things right with my family: Rylee, Colton, my brothers, the crew, my fans. Then actually do it.

I'm here to simplify shit. Not make it harder. And yet the minute I got exactly what I wanted—Getty spreading her thighs for me—I dove headfirst into complication.

And hell if I don't want to do just that again.

Hammer. Nail. Pound the shit out of it. The release I was looking for when I came up here is nonexistent. Frustrated, I sigh and roll my shoulders.

I need to clear my head. Gain some perspective. Get away from the house for a bit so I stop thinking about Getty's soft lips and enticing body. Take some time for myself.

It's not like I haven't done the friends-with-benefits thing before. But I've never done it when I'm living with the person. That causes some problems. Like when you want more benefits, all you have to do is walk ten feet to the next bedroom rather than step back, tell yourself to cool your jets, and either use your hand or wait until you can meet up again.

That's gotta be why I'm feeling like this. Because the

meet-up is right in front of my face, so keeping my distance is going to be harder.

*Shit. I'm out of nails.* I glance down to the box of them on the sawhorse bench I've set up on the ground.

Adrenaline. It's what I need. To remind me I have a career to return to. To reinforce that my time here is limited. That I need to finish these repairs sooner rather than later. That Getty's just a fling: some hot sex. A friend with benefits. To stop making promises I won't be around long enough to keep.

Adrenaline's the cure-all. I'm decided. It clears my head. Reminds me of the start of a race when I'm forced to focus on me and only me, which is exactly what I need.

Not on Getty.

I give up on fixing the roof. I'm gonna grab my keys and a jacket and head out exploring. *Alone.* Might as well see the island, since I won't be here for much longer. Find an empty stretch of road and break the speed limit just for a bit while I'm at it. Get the adrenaline. The clarity I need to put my head back where it needs to be.

I take the first step down the ladder.

*Keep lying to yourself, you pussy.*

Next step down.

*If you're not on the roof, you're not repairing it.*

Move down another rung.

*If you're not repairing it, you can't leave yet.*

Almost there.

*If you can't leave yet, you get more Getty.*

Last rung.

*Pretty convenient, if you ask me.*

My shoes hit solid ground.

*Shut the fuck up,* I tell the voice in my mind. The one mucking it up with lies. I'm still shaking my head, convincing myself I just need a little *me time*, when I open the door and walk in the kitchen. I'm irritated, frustrated, and annoyed.

And when I lift my head up, the one person who's making me feel that way is standing right in front of me. Her hair is piled on top of her head, cheeks are flushed, eyes wide, and mouth shocks open into an O shape.

*Damn gorgeous.*

I snarl and clench my jaw, because the last thing I need is her presence here to cloud my thoughts. Give me reasons to want to stay. Make me want to walk up to her, back her against the counter, and kiss her senseless.

Which is exactly why I'm leaving. Right now.

Distance. Space. Clarity.

And yet I don't move. Just stare. Both of my heads at war over what they want right now.

Keys. Jacket. Wallet. *That's what you want. Get your shit and go.*

"Let's go."

*What the fuck are you doing?*

"Go?" she asks, forehead furrowed in confusion.

I stride into the kitchen, grab her jacket off the back of the barstool next to mine, grasp her hand, and pull her forward. "Yeah. You're coming with me."

*So much for distance.*

# Chapter 20

We've been driving for thirty minutes or so, mostly in silence except for the low hum of the radio. The terrain around us rises up, becoming more mountainous, the patches of pine trees getting thicker.

Everything about this morning so far has been unexpected. Waking up alone in Zander's bed. The flash of hurt he wasn't there. The confusion as to why he was up on the roof.

And then the hit of reality. The realization that even though last night was incredible in so many ways for me—a selfless lover, achievement of an actual orgasm by someone else's hand, praise and not criticism—it was probably just run-of-the-mill for him. I'm just another friend among a list of friends with whom he most likely has enjoyed benefits.

It was a hard thing to accept as I was lying in his bed, the subtle scent of his cologne on his sheets, and the memory of his hands on my skin and words in my ears. He was everywhere around me and yet still not really there.

Hence his warning, his offer to find the damn lighthouse, made perfect sense then. He somehow knew ahead of time that it wouldn't be so simple. That I'd probably develop feelings despite knowing there wasn't a chance of more.

But could you blame me? My mind can't help but skim back over the events of yesterday. First the confessions and afterward feeling like I finally let someone in. Then last night— reverent touches and murmured promises and his all-consuming hands on my body. I'd enjoyed being with a man who pulled me close instead of spewing insults while pushing me away. Who made me feel beautiful and competent and sexy. The last thing I'd ever thought myself to be.

I'd woken up giddy and satisfied with those butterflies in your stomach you read about in romance novels and expected he was going to be on the pillow beside me when I rolled over. So what if I've misplaced my gratitude and possibly turned it into feelings for him? Isn't that natural?

Asking myself the question yet again, I stare at Zander, his eyes focused on the road ahead, who hasn't spoken since he told me to put a seat belt on when he started the car. And the difference is this time when I ask myself the question, my concern about how this is all going to play out isn't just in my head like it was when I was in his bed. Rather I'm looking right at him and seeing it for myself.

The man beside me is very different from the one I was with last night. He's pensive, quiet, irritated. I sense something is wrong and all I can figure is that he's had time to think about it all and now realizes we made a mistake.

So why am I here, then?

I'm startled from my thoughts when Zander makes an abrupt turn off the main road and pulls in front of a log cabin of sorts. It's rather large with green awnings over the windows and smoke trickling from two chimneys. The awnings have some kind of logo on them, but from where we're parked, I can't quite make them out.

"C'mon." It's all he says as he gets out of the car and walks toward the front door. I stare after him, hating that for the second time he's telling me what to do. I immediately want to follow after him, while at the same time I want to know where the hell we are and what his problem is.

Eventually I scramble out of the car and around a few of the others parked in the lot to catch up with him. He waits for me on the steps with the door held open. At least there's that.

When I enter, I'm surprised to find a hostess stand and a full-fledged restaurant inside. Ornately carved wood seems to be the theme and the intricate pieces that adorn the interior are quite incredible. A few patrons dot the place and yet they seem to be talking across the tables as if they know one another. I turn toward Zander just as his smile spreads wide on his face at the lady approaching us.

She's as wide as she is tall, with silver hair cut short, and a warm smile lights up her face when she recognizes Zander.

"Good morning, Zander. Good to see you brought her with you this time," she says with a slight accent I can't place, but I'm more flustered by the knowledge he's been here before and has obviously spoken of me.

"Hi, Lynn. You twisted my arm . . . and the patio, please." The warmth in his voice after the chill I got in the car surprises me. And I hate that I kind of resent it a little.

She furrows her brow for a moment and then nods. "Sure. Of course. Right this way."

I'm a tad dumbfounded as we follow her through the maze of tables, the customers nodding in greeting to us, before entering and ascending a short stairwell. All the while I catch partial snippets of conversation between Lynn and Zander that make no sense to me, but then again this random cabin in the woods being a restaurant isn't really normal either so . . .

"Any openings today?" Zander asks.

"Ah, so that's why you're up here, then." Lynn laughs with a shake of her head. "Just can't let go of that need, huh?"

"It's in my blood." His laugh is sincere and the expression on her face when she looks back is one of adoration. He's been here, what, a whole month and he already has women smitten with him.

Not like that's hard, though.

"Russell'll be here at eleven if you guys want first spots." She glances down to her watch as we clear the top of the stairs.

"We'll take it. And the usual for both of us, please."

My jaw drops, mouth easily wide open, when I step out into the room around us. It's not really a room, though. More like a covered patio open on all sides, the pine trees within arm's reach if you tried to touch them.

I find myself wandering around the space, utterly lost in its beauty. There are tables and chairs up here too, but they are more the comfortable, outdoorsy type of sets with big cushions that sit lower to the ground. I run my hand over the back of a chair and then step up to the railing, a varnished, twisted log. The forest is stretched out before me—pine trees growing out of jagged landscape, a canopy of green.

And then I look down. I gasp in surprise and my head grows dizzy. From the entrance, the cabin looks like it's on solid ground. From where I stand, it appears to be perched on the edge of a canyon, the hill dropping away, giving the feeling that you're more than two stories up.

"It's like an overgrown tree house." I turn around to catch Lynn watching me with anticipation in her expression.

She nods, her soft smile growing wide. "I knew you were a smart girl," she says with a wink as she glances over to where Zander is moving a set of chairs and tables closer toward one of the railings. "That's what this place is called. The Treehouse."

Something in the far-off distance rings a bell in my mind over the name, something from when I first arrived on the island and looked through all the tourist pamphlets on the ferry.

"Go, get comfortable," she says as she squeezes my arm. "I'll go get your coffee and breakfast."

"Don't we have—"

"Zander ordered for you."

"Oh." There's not much else to say as I watch her walk back toward the stairs, not sure if I'm miffed or okay with the fact that Zander took the liberty.

I try to tell myself that it's not a control thing on his part. He's not Ethan, who ordered my food whenever we went out under the guise of being a good husband but really wanted to make sure I didn't gain any more weight. Zander was just being nice.

There's a thought—*nice*—considering he hasn't said a single thing to me other than telling me to follow him. The nerves return now that Lynn is gone, and we're alone. He's sitting in the chair with his back to me, feet propped up on the railing, when I turn around.

I make my way to where he is, look out to the forest beyond a bit longer, and then slowly sink down into the chair he's moved for me. It's silent except for the birds chirping and the rustling of the trees around us.

We sit for some time, the chasm of uncertainty increasing with each passing second regardless of how peaceful the setting is. And just as I'm about to say something, Lynn comes back with a busboy carrying a tray.

"Here you go, you two! Coffee. Eggs and bacon. Sourdough toast." She sets plates onto the small table between us, pours us some coffee, pulls silverware, napkins, and condiments off the tray, and gets us settled.

"Thank you," we both say in unison, and when our eyes meet, I realize it's the first time since we've left the house. We hold each other's gaze, unspoken words flicker across his face, and yet I can't read a single one of them.

"Eat before it gets cold," he finally says, and when I break away from his stare, I realize that Lynn is long gone and I have no idea how long we've waged this visual standoff.

The deck fills with sounds—the scrape of a fork on a plate, the clatter of a knife, the hiss of too-hot coffee burning his tongue—but the one sound I want to hear the most doesn't happen. His voice. And even though the food is good, I don't taste it.

The silence eats at me until I can't stand it anymore. There's too much doubt. I'm feeling like we screwed things up by sleeping with each other last night. And yet I don't think I'd want to take it back if I could. The way he made me feel was too powerful to want to wish it away in lieu of how I feel today.

So I glare at him as he takes a bite of toast, a sip of coffee, then another bite of toast, and looks anywhere but at me.

"Is there a point you're trying to prove with the silent-treatment, moody thing you've got going here? Because if this is your way of trying to make me forget about my dinner with my father tonight, I assure you this isn't the way to do it. And if not . . . if there is something else you're trying to tell me, it'd be much easier if you just laid it all out on the table." I gesture to the table between us. I'm irritated, hurt, unsure, and all three come through loud and clear when all I wanted to do was sound aloof and confident.

Zander's eyes flash up to meet mine above the rim of his coffee cup, eyes guarded, face expressionless, and he holds my stare as he slowly lowers his cup and leans back.

And of course now that my initial surge of courage is gone, the words thrown out there without any precursor, the doubt laced with nerves takes over and I begin to second-guess whether I should have kept my mouth shut.

His unwavering stare and continued silence scream for me to explain myself. I hate that I want to, that I don't want to, but this morning-after business is all new to me and I don't know what to do or expect.

All I know is how I feel. It's a jumbled mess of want and need and fear of the unknown and insecurity and confusion. I already know I've stepped over the imaginary line he's set for whatever *to us* meant that night at the Italian restaurant and yet don't know how to pull myself back.

In a move I'm not sure is smart or stupid but is spurred on by his unyielding stare, I try again. "Look, if you think last night was a mistake . . . or you were faking how you . . . oh, just never mind." I shift my gaze to my own fingers fiddling with the handle of my fork, hating my sudden inability to string words together to make a coherent sentence and my lack of nerve to stand behind my opening question.

"If you're gonna open the door, Getty, you might as well walk on through it." There's a warning tone in his voice that makes me fidget in my seat and I wish I'd just let things play out however they were playing out.

But now I can't. Now I have to finish what I started and I'm not so sure I want to. My mouth suddenly becomes dry as uncertainty clouds every ounce of hope I woke up with this morning. "I just—I understand why . . . if I wasn't . . . if you regret last night . . . that's all." My eyes sting with the rejection ringing in my tone.

"What gives you the impression I regret *anything*?" His eyes search mine and his voice scolds me in a way that makes every part of my body stand at attention. And I'm not quite sure what it is about him that gives him such pull over me, but as much as I want to look away, I can't. "Well?" The quirk of an eyebrow. The dart of a tongue. A lazy but more-than-deliberate glance down my body and then back up to my eyes.

"It's not like you've been exactly pleasant this morning." When he just raises an eyebrow again, telling me to go on, I continue. "A few grunts here and there followed by one-word commands . . . the caveman thing doesn't do it for me."

"I'm pretty sure I know what does it for you," he says as a smile ghosts over his lips and travels up to his eyes, but then it's gone just as quick as it comes. The fleeting appearance of the man I slept with last night feels just as confusing to me as the verbally stunted jerk of a guy from this morning. "I warned you." He shrugs. "I'm moody."

"*Seriously?* The Mander excuse isn't going to fly with me right now. I mean . . ." I huff out a breath and roll my eyes, distracted momentarily by a loud clatter of sounds on the floor above us. "Was saying good morning or granting me more than two words on the ride here that difficult for you to do?"

We sit in silence, eyes locked. I'm not sure what happens to cause it, but all of a sudden his face softens subtly and he shakes his head before looking down at his fingers on his coffee cup. His voice is gruff when he finally speaks. "I'm pissed at you."

"*What?*" I laugh in disbelief, more confused than ever. "What the hell did I do?"

When he looks up, I'm staggered by the sudden empathy in his eyes and the shy smile on his lips. The hard edge from moments ago is gone. Stripped bare. This is the man who was with me last night. The one I'm still trying to figure out but, more important, want to know more about.

He licks his bottom lip and then bites it as he leans back into his chair and shakes his head. There's a knowing look in his eyes like he wants me to understand something that he doesn't understand himself. Confusion wars across his handsome features as I just sit and wait for him to work through whatever is weighing so heavily on his shoulders.

A loud sigh. A toss of his napkin on the table beside his plate. "We're venturing into uncharted territory for me, Socks."

I angle my head and blink a few times, trying to understand what he means. His toast flashes through my mind: . . . *because friends between the opposite sexes leads to friends with benefits and that always ends in disaster, and you know what, Getty? I don't want that with you, so let's just say "to us," whatever us may be. . . .*

"Like as in 'always ends in disaster' territory?"

"Something like that," he says with a nod, but his eyes tell a different story I can't quite read yet. He twists his lips, lowers his eyes for a fraction of a second before raising them back up to mine. This time there's a bit more resolve in them. "When I left home after everything with Colton, I promised myself from here on out I'd live my life without regrets. That every step I take, every decision I make, everything I do, will be with that as a constant in my mind. So, Getty . . ." He shifts forward in his seat, places his elbows on the table so that we are as close as we can be with a table between us. "Let me make myself clear when I say I have *zero* regrets about last night and you even thinking it pisses me off." And the way he speaks, voice deep but still quiet and intent, makes any response I have insignificant.

"Oh" is all I can muster, considering he deliberately holds my gaze hostage with that amused glint in his eyes as he sits back in his chair.

"Yeah. *Oh.*" He says both words in a way that has my body standing at attention and taking notice of everything about him like it's my first time really looking at him.

He's sitting across from me, angled in the chair so that one elbow lies on the armrest, arm bent with his finger running back and forth over his bottom lip. I take in his unshaven jawline, dark hair hidden beneath the lid of a Giants baseball hat, the broad set of his shoulders, and the flex of his bicep.

*Ungodly handsome. And so damn pretty.* The last thought makes me smile and earns me a raised eyebrow asking me what's so funny. But I don't answer, because I'm so captivated by his fingers running over his lip. My mind immediately recalling what those lips felt like when they moved against mine.

And over my skin.

"Getty?"

I lift my eyes to meet his again and instantly the air begins to shift. Electrify. It fills with an underlying tension that vibrates all around us. My pulse picks up, body becomes restless.

His eyes still hold that hint of irritation they've had since he stalked in the house, but there is no mistaking the desire now clouding them too. And even though I'm still confused as to why he's pissed at me for venturing into this uncharted territory, there is no way in hell I can deny my body's immediate response to him.

I never thought sexual desire could be tangible, but my God, in this small space of time it feels like I've just been sucker punched.

He continues to rub his finger back and forth, visual foreplay that I'm pretty sure is a deliberate taunt to my awakening libido. I'm irritated that he can affect me so quickly and at the same time I'm turned on so much that I have to press my thighs together to ease the ache burning there.

Determined to let him know that I can play whatever game he wants to play, I shift my gaze from his mouth back up to his eyes. And those eyes? *Whew.* The look they give me, like he wants to clear the table, lay me down, and devour me, right here, right now, causes my breath to stutter in my chest.

"This is all your fault, you know." The censure in his tone is laden with suggestion.

*"Mine?"* I lean back and mirror his posture, try to

appear as nonchalant as he is, when my insides feel like an exposed live wire. "How so? If you're gonna open the door, Zander, you might as well walk on through it." A lift of my eyebrows in challenge. A hint of a smile to reinforce it.

His laugh is long and low, yet has an edge to it that I don't quite understand. He leans forward, elbows on his knees, eyes focused on his fingers steepled together until they shift to meet mine.

"I meant what I said last night." His voice is heavy with a sincerity that makes my heart beat faster.

"Which thing?" I have to ask because there were so many things he said. So many promises he made.

*"All of them."*

Oh. I worry my bottom lip between my teeth as I try to make sense of this conversation and the events of the past twenty-four hours. "So then you're mad at me because—"

"Look. I think we need to lay some ground rules is all." He lifts his hat and runs a hand through his hair before slumping back in his seat, completely disregarding the previous train of conversation and shifting gears.

"Oh. Okay. Sure." I nod, willing to agree so maybe we can bypass the awkwardness the next time we have sex. And even that thought feels so foreign to me. "Ground rules? As in *boundaries*, right?" I ask, full well expecting the flash up of his eyes, since he's the one who overstepped the previous boundaries we'd set.

"Yes, as in those types of boundaries." He takes a sip of coffee. Takes his time swallowing. Surveys the open deck around us and then looks up to the ceiling when there's another loud clank, before looking back to me with curiosity reflected in his eyes. "Have you ever done the friends-with-benefits thing before?"

My laughter is tinged with disbelief. "Considering I've only been with you and Ethan, I don't think you need to ask that." The hitch in his movement is subtle but noticeable. Almost as if realization has hit him over my lack of experience. I speak quickly, not wanting him to think too much about it. "The question is, have you?"

"It doesn't matter if I have before."

"Seriously? You're going to say that and think I don't know the answer is a resounding yes?"

"Look, Getty." He blows out a breath in resignation. "We live together, so this could get tricky. I figured maybe if we set some type of rules, it would help some."

"Like no-spending-the-night type of boundaries?" I snicker at how ridiculous it sounds, since our living in the same house makes that impossible, and catch the irritation that plays over his features.

"Very funny, Getty." My name is a verbal reprimand that he's serious and while I get what he's saying, heed the warning, I can't help it. It's almost as if I feel relieved knowing that there is no regret, no doubt, on his part, just rather a need for him to prevent the *disaster* from happening.

And I've had enough disasters so far, so I'm all for it.

"So that's why you've been an asshole? Couldn't you have just said, 'Hey, we need to talk' when you walked into the kitchen this morning instead of giving me the silent treatment while you drove me all the way out here?"

"No."

"No?"

"I'm out here because I couldn't sit at the house." His eyes are focused on his hands and I wish he'd look at me so I could see what he's not saying.

"Why?"

"Because I can't get you out of my goddamn head." He grits it out like it's a curse and every part of me sags in relief at the roundabout compliment. At knowing the feeling is mutual because all I was doing standing in the kitchen was thinking about him.

"But what does that have to do with bringing me here?"

He lifts his face up and the intensity in his eyes when they meet mine is unwavering. "Because I don't want to want you as much as I do, but *I do* . . . and if we'd stayed at the house, then I'm pretty sure I would have done exactly what I wanted to do when I saw you standing there in the kitchen."

His tongue twister of a response doesn't answer anything and yet it causes my pulse to begin to race at its implication.

"What did you want to do?"

The hunger in his eyes practically answers the question for him. *"To fuck you, Getty."* Each word sounds like a thread of his self-control is snapping. His body is tense, hands fisted. "To bend you over the edge of the kitchen counter and fulfill one of those many promises I'd made to you last night."

"Oh." That ache is back, liquid heat spreading through my core at his explicit words, which turn me on in ways I never imagined they could.

"Yeah. *Oh*," he repeats as again I'm left wordless. "And we're here because we needed to talk and I couldn't talk there at the house where there were so many convenient places to lay you down."

My breath comes faster and my mouth is suddenly dry as he does just what I'd asked, lays it all out on the table. *I wish he'd lay me out on the table.* I fight the smile, the giddy feeling fluttering through me at being wanted and desired running right beside the lust that's slowly consuming my thoughts.

"And road trips cure that?" I ask coyly, my confidence resurfacing suddenly now that I feel like the power has shifted and it's a more even playing field.

"I thought it would," he says as he abruptly moves the table between us to the left and then reaches out to my chair, scooting it so that my knees fit between his. I let out a yelp of surprise at the unexpected action, but before I can catch my breath, his face is inches from mine, both hands on my thighs, and his eyes darkening with lust.

"And?" I whisper.

"I was wrong." His kiss is soft and gentle, but I can sense the violent edge of desire just beneath his quiet control. I close my eyes and allow myself to fall into the kiss—the taste of coffee on his lips, the scrape of stubble against my skin, the sounds of the forest all around us—and realize that he ran off this morning because he's fighting the pull that's already reeled me in and taken hold of me.

I may not have a lot of experience with men, but after watching Ethan constantly for so many years, I'm observant enough to see a man wading into waters he deems treacherous.

The damn white squall.

He breaks our kiss with a laugh, rests his forehead against mine, and just breathes me in.

"So, boundaries, huh?" I feel his mouth curve into a smile against mine. "How's that working for you?"

He throws his head back, his laugh deeper and richer this time, and I feel a tad more settled after this awkward dance of trying to downplay and yet own the attraction between us.

"You're a little—"

"We're ready for you," a voice booms from the doorway, shocking us apart and drawing my attention over to a burly-ish guy. I take in his plaid shirt, worn jeans, and full beard before it registers that he's speaking to Zander and me.

"Hey, Russ." Zander stands up with my hand in his, prompting me to rise too. "Perfect timing."

"Not from what I can tell," he says with a resonating chuckle before turning his back and disappearing into the stairwell.

"C'mon," Zander says with a secretive smirk and a spark in his eyes that leaves me more than curious about what he and this mysterious mountain man are talking about.

"What's going—"

Zander turns around and places a finger to my lips to quiet me. "No questions, Socks. You can thank me later." He continues up the flight of stairs with a visible bounce to his step.

When we clear the landing, "No way in hell" falls from my mouth, my legs already retreating the way we came as I take in what's before me. But Zander's prepared and grabs my hand to keep me on the platform of sorts.

And even though I'm physically struggling against him, my mind rejecting what the contraption and the gear around me are used for, it's his laugh that echoes the loudest in my mind. Carefree. Excited. Daring.

"You've taken scarier leaps before. This is a piece of cake." The words knock the fight out of me. His even, encouraging tone telling me he's referring to how I came to be in PineRidge.

With his hands firm on my arms, pinning them to my sides so I can't back away, I take in everything around me. The thick metal cables and pulley system disappearing into the distance. The two harnesses laid out on the wood planking of the patio. The helmets next to them. The gap in the railing with the plank that extends beyond it.

How in the hell did I not notice the zip line overhead when I was down below? I was obviously so mesmerized with the incredible view and the unsettled feeling between Zander and me that I overlooked it.

"Getty." Zander's voice pulls me back. "You've jumped before. This time, though, you'll have a rope and a harness." He nods his head, eyes steadfast on mine.

"But . . . I . . ." Thoughts. Fears. *Heights.* The last of which causes a bone-deep terror at the idea of jumping headfirst into midair attached only by a cable to prevent me from plummeting to my death. "I can't . . . I just." My eyes blink rapidly as I'm trying to process this, when his hands move from my arms to my cheeks.

*"You can."* He bends his knees so we are at eye level, *equals*, and continues. "I came here needing one of the constants in my life: adrenaline. Something to ground me and clear my head, because it's getting all muddled up. *And you?* You've left your old life behind, leapt without looking, and I think before you face your father tonight, you need something to ground you too. Something to remind you that you did this on your own, started a new life, *your way*, and that you're not the woman your father or Ethan thought you were. You're strong. And beautiful. And brave. Maybe doing this will help you see it."

Tears blur my vision. My lower lip quivers. His words take root in my soul and wrap around my healing heart. And as much as I want to reject what he says, *all of it*, I also hear every single word.

"No regrets," he whispers.

The nervous smile that slowly spreads on my lips is mirrored on his. I subtly nod my head, not wanting to agree with him but realizing I want to live this new life without regrets just like he does. I want to be spontaneous and push past my comfort level and own my fears. And he's completely right—what better time to prove it to myself than right here, right now, the day I have to face everything I never want to be again?

"Don't you think you should have sprung this on me before we ate breakfast?" I ask with a nervous laugh, eyes wide, and not ashamed to stall any way possible.

"I'll hold your hair for you if you puke." He winks, grin widening as he just shakes his head back and forth. "What do you say, Socks?"

And how can I resist that?

"Okay," I agree, followed by an unsteady breath. "No regrets."

"There's my girl," he says with a flash of grin that lights up his face, and while I should be knocked on my ass by his sheer handsomeness, it's the words he said that make my heart jump. *My girl.*

"All set?" Russell asks as he steps forward and breaks up the moment.

After we've been debriefed, signed our life away with waivers—which I'm not sure really matter because how can you sue when you're dead?—we are strapped into our harnesses and helmets. They've explained the five-tiered zip line course to me: You go from one platform to another, five times, until you reach the bottom of the canyon.

"So," Russell says as he slaps his hands together and rubs them back and forth, "Doug is on the other end waiting for you."

Maybe it hasn't all sunk in yet, but when he says those words, followed by his smug smirk, I can feel the bottom drop out of my stomach. I thought I was fine with it after the safety rundown. I really did. I listened to Zander laugh as he retold a few funny stories about some of his previous zip-lining experiences. They made me comfortable enough; I even opted to go first after much internal debate. I know myself well enough to know that if I was second, I probably wouldn't step off the platform without Zander standing behind me.

The nerves kick in. My hands tremble, and my legs test my weight against the thick cable I'm tethered to, as I question my sanity. I refuse to shift my gaze from Zander to look forward at the forest valley above which I'm standing about one foot from the edge of the deck.

"C'mon, Socks. You know the first step is the always the hardest."

My heartbeat is so loud in my ears. Goose bumps cover my skin, pinpricks of awareness that I'm alive. My knees feel like rubber. But it's Zander's reassuring smile and the belief in me that shines in his eyes that have me turning to face my fear.

The valley spreads out wide before me in a painted canvas of greens and browns. The cable runs from above my head all the way to a platform I can barely see in the distance. It's breathtaking. It's terrifying.

*Don't look directly down.*

My slow, deliberate exhalation, like audible courage, fills the space around us as I talk myself into this, and take the final step forward, toes perched on the edge. I hear the clank of Zander's harness a beat before his hands squeeze my shoulders.

"Let go, Getty. Just jump."

*Just jump.* The words replay in my mind, their meaning encompassing everything about my new life as Getty Caster.

And about how I want to continue to live it.

I close my eyes, inhale a calming—if there is such a thing—breath, take the first step into empty air . . . and *just jump*.

# Chapter 21

*Just jump.*

I'll never forget the sensations. The drop of my stomach. The wind on my face. The frozen silence when I tried to scream, followed by the exhilarated sound of my laughter. The feeling of flying. Then the obvious pride on Zander's face when he came zipping along minutes later to see me standing there, grinning ear to ear, and shouting to him that I couldn't wait to take the next line down.

My reflection in the mirror shows how alive I felt today. How after the incredible sex last night and the rocky start this morning, this day turned out to be one I'll never forget.

And I hate that now it might be marred by the dinner with my father.

I have almost two hours yet, but I attempt to lose myself in the preparations, trying to think of this more as getting ready for Zander than to see my father. It makes the whole thing a little more tolerable.

The knock on my bedroom door startles me. It seems so weird to have doors shut and privacy like we're roommates when we've already seen each other naked. But at the same time, we still need to figure out the whole context of whatever we are together and so the time to myself is appreciated.

"Come in."

Zander opens the door and walks into the room, eyes doing a lazy walk up my bare legs where my robe has fallen open before he meets my gaze. That half-cocked smile is on his lips and damn if parts of me don't react immediately.

He walks over to the vanity and sets his cell phone down. "You need to call your father and let him know his car won't need to pick us up. We'll meet him at Piedmont's instead." Our eyes meet and I question him silently. "You're not her anymore. Obedient. Compliant. You're Getty Caster. You set your own terms. Not your father."

Taking a deep breath, I find myself wondering if he has any idea that this is the first time anyone has ordered me to do something with my better good in mind. It seems so silly but means so very much.

"How did you—?"

"It's a small town, Getty. People talk. All it took was for me to make a call to my new friend Mable to get the town gossip about the obviously well-to-do man who stayed at the PineRidge Inn last night. How his driver asked the clerk at the gas station for directions to the restaurant. And how he complained about the low thread count of the sheets, among other things, and the lack of Nespresso machines in each room." He rolls his eyes. "Cars with drivers are rare here and they stick out like a sore thumb."

"Right. I'm still not used to the *everyone knows your business* aspect." I shake my head, more for my father's elitism than anything else.

"I know, but we'll use it to our advantage tonight. Everyone here assumes we're dating, so be prepared that your father thinks the same thing."

"Okay." I'm not sure why that phrasing bugs me, but I shrug it off, shift in my seat, and reach for my phone.

"No. Use mine. Unless you want him to have your phone number."

I freeze momentarily, understanding the implications of what he's saying—the possible tracking of my phone— before sitting slowly back down and picking up his phone.

\*    \*    \*

With a fortifying sigh and Zander's hand firmly wrapped around mine, we enter the restaurant. I focus on remembering Zander's reaction when I entered the family room earlier, instead of acknowledging the nerves humming through my system.

His quick inhalation. The widening of his eyes. The whistle he blew out. All three made for the confidence-building reaction I needed in order to do this.

It's unsettling for me to walk into the most expensive restaurant on the island looking like the woman I used to be—hair in a chignon, the Stepford makeup on, wearing a classically cut dress more expensive than most people's rent—when I'm nothing like her anymore.

I glance over to Zander for reassurance—strange to see his styled hair when I'm used to it messy, face smooth when sometimes he goes days between shaving, his button-down shirt and khaki trousers when he's typically in gym shorts or jeans and a T-shirt. And while I like this dressed-up version of him, I like the everyday look better.

"Here goes nothing," I murmur as the hostess leads us to a table on the far side of the crowded restaurant. It is by far the best seat in the room with the table perched against the wall of glass facing the ocean. My father sits with his head angled down, attention on his cell phone, a bottle of wine already open, and the tables immediately surrounding his are void of customers. I have no doubt he heavily greased some palms to make sure it remains that way during our dinner.

We're ten feet from the table when he lifts his silver head of hair and meets my eyes. And there's a moment—quite brief, but it's there—when he jolts in surprise and narrows his eyes in shock over the unexpected guest beside me. Between the dismissal of his driver earlier and now Zander's presence, I know he's already irritated with me. Displeasure owns his expression as he shifts his gaze back to me, that subtle sneer I know all too well gracing his mouth.

"Gertrude," he says after clearing his throat as he stands up, always the polite gentleman.

"Father." I nod and bite back the comment on my tongue, for him to call me Getty. Because as much as I want him to acknowledge the new me, I also don't want to have the memory of his voice saying my nickname in that tone of utter disdain like he does my birth name.

I hate that for a split second, I still want him to be the father I remember him being when I was a little girl. Smiling. Cuddly. Caring. But that was before my mother died and I think I'm remembering even those times through the eyes of a child wanting her father's unconditional love. Desperate for his affection.

When I really look closely at him, his hand motioning me to have a seat without any overtures to hug me after he hasn't seen me for months, a small part of me dies, one I hated anyway for wanting that gesture from him.

"You can go now," he says to Zander with an indifferent flick of his wrist and without so much as looking at him. "Please, Gertrude, take a seat."

My lips pull tight and before I can gather an acceptable response for the formidable Damon Caster, Zander responds for me. "Zander Donavan." He reaches his hand across the table in an open-ended offer of a shake. "And thank you, but I'll be staying for dinner."

My father looks down to Zander's hand and then back up to his eyes while they have a silent battle for control of the situation. As the seconds stretch out, my heart pounds like a freight train. My body is so riddled with adrenaline that I have to clasp my hands to prevent any trembling from showing.

Sitting down without shaking Zander's hand or saying another word, my father makes a show of sharply snapping his napkin and placing it in his lap. Zander turns and places his hand on my back—a simple gesture of warmth as he ushers me into the chair he's pulling out farthest from my father. As I step past him to sit down, we make brief but reassuring eye contact. His smile is encouraging as he mouths, *"Just jump."* And I welcome that subtle reminder that I can in fact face my fears.

When I look up to my father, he's directing his glare solely at me.

"Thank God you still know how to dress like a lady. I was afraid you'd lost all sense of class and your responsibility to uphold the Caster name when I saw you in that disgraceful outfit yesterday, Gertrude."

"Well, if someone hadn't manipulated my accounts, there wouldn't be the need for me to have a job that requires a uniform. . . ." I shrug, finding strength to stand up for myself with each word. Beneath the tablecloth, Zander's hand rests on my knee and squeezes ever so slightly in silent support.

"Hey, I kind of like the socks," Zander says with a smirk, eyes darting to my father with an unapologetic lift of his shoulders before he returns his look to mine. And then without preamble he leans in and unabashedly plants a kiss on my lips. It's a simple brush of lips, but the statement it makes packs quite a punch.

"Gertrude." My father's sharp warning resonates around the room. We've been here no more than five minutes and his temper has already surfaced—the hum of conversation in the restaurant stops, forks scraping against plates cease, and the uncomfortable air around us thickens with tension.

And while everyone else around can sense the underlying and unapologetic rage in my father, *including me*, Zander fights back the sarcastic smirk playing at the corners of his mouth.

"Is there a problem, sir?" Zander's voice sounds completely innocent, but the lift of his eyebrow and the tension in his jaw say, *Try me. I have no problem making a scene*.

My father refuses to acknowledge Zander or the words he's spoken. "How dare you let this grease monkey touch you when you're a married woman?"

At that, I'm quickly transported back to my teenage years. To the endless criticisms over whom I was and was not allowed to hang out with. To the genuine friends I lost, who were replaced with shells of parent-pleasing kids afraid to be themselves. Afraid to step out of their carefully constructed lines. And I'm so flustered and rattled that I don't have a clear enough head to wonder why he referred to Zander as a grease monkey, because the tears burn in the back of my throat, his words ring in my ears, and Zander's fingers tense on my leg.

But it's not until he gets that gloating hint of a smile on his lips . . . the one I've seen countless times as he prepared to screw over a competitor and seal the deal through some type of unscrupulous means . . . that I regain my courage. *Distance is the only reason I can recognize it now.* The only way I'm able to see once and for all that the man who was supposed to kiss my scrapes and hold my hand through the death of my mother was more interested in manipulation and his success.

It hurts like a bitch. The truth often does. And I've known this, but I think when I see the smirk that I've seen countless times from him, it really hits home.

So I grab on tight to the knowledge. Push down the hurt that resurfaces. And use both to my advantage.

"I'm not married, Father. I can do whatever I please with whomever I please." My voice is soft but sure despite what feels like a bowling ball pressing on my chest.

"Casters don't divorce, Gertrude."

I cringe at the mantra I've heard countless times. The obligation he threw in my face the one time I confronted him about Ethan's cruelty. "You're wrong. This Caster *did*."

"That's where you're wrong. Ethan still loves you—"

*"Love?"* By this point I'm practically shrieking. My mind scrambles, trying to recall any ounce of emotion during my marriage.

"Yes. He loves you and therefore will not sign the paperwork. Your marriage isn't over. He and I talked and came to an agreement. We let you have this respite before coming to collect you. But now your vacation is over. It's time to come home."

Heat rushes over me. His words feel like a knife scraping over my skin. The memories of all the ways my father would exert his stifling control had started to fade in the time I'd been away. Now I'm reminded how he must have control over everything in his life. People included. His daughter especially.

My hands fist into my napkin. *"An agreement?"* I grit

out as the anger makes it hard for me to concentrate on the topic at hand without throwing in every single wrong that has transpired. "My life is not an agreement. It's not something you and Ethan get to discuss and barter over while I stand by in silence. My marriage, on the other hand, was an agreement. One between Ethan and me, and frankly, it is *none* of your business. It is over—dead, done—whether you and Ethan like it or not. I filed a request to enter default over a month ago when he refused to accept the paperwork, as is my right. The divorce will finalize whether he signs it or not."

My father *tsk*s at my tone and gives me a dismissive roll of his eyes. I should be used to his blatant disregard, and maybe before I would have let it pass, but not now. Not the new Getty Caster.

"And there will be no collecting of me. I am not a stray dog or a helpless child. I am a grown woman who you've controlled for too long, and that stops now. I have a right to go or stay or do as I please. Neither you nor Ethan *owns* me."

He takes his time sipping his wine, rolling the liquid around on his tongue to mask his fury over my unexpected disobedience. "Haven't you disgraced this family enough?"

"Disgraced?" I whisper angrily. "Half of all marriages end in divorce. Caster or not." My shoulders hurt, the tension so tight in them my head aches.

"You've made your point, Gertrude." He huffs out a breath—the sound so full of disdain it feels like it's coating my skin.

"My point?" I scoff. "I know you chose to come to a public place to keep the dramatics to a minimum. To try to *control* the situation. Thinking I wouldn't dare attract attention by raising my voice, because *society ladies don't cause scenes, now, do they, Gertrude?*" I mock in his tone, mimic his expressions, the ones I've memorized over my lifetime.

"You're acting like a spoiled child. It's time you stop this charade of being Little Miss Independent and come back to your family."

"No."

"Do. Not. Test. Me. Gertrude."

Zander's fingers tense on my leg at the sound of my father's hinted threat. "Or what?" My voice is just as even and spiteful as his. I've shocked myself by now at the conviction with which I speak to my father.

With perfect timing, the waiter appears and sets salads down in front of us. "Thank you," my father says stiffly, although by the expression on his face and his rigid mannerisms, it's clear he thought I would acquiesce to his demands without much of a fight.

"Ah . . . let me guess? The gentleman ordered already for everyone?" Zander says sarcastically, noticing something my scattered mind has overlooked.

"Yes," the waiter says cautiously, his eyes looking to each of us in turn, noticing the obvious tension at our table.

"Control at its finest," Zander says with a laugh and a shake of his head, leveling a challenge at my father with his glare. I may be a ball of bundled nerves, but there is something comforting—a relief almost—in knowing that I'm not the only one going head-to-head with my father tonight. I'm not alone. And I can't remember the last time I didn't feel like I was alone.

*Maybe since my mother died.*

My shaky inhalation goes unnoticed because Zander, feeling like he's made his point, turns back to the waiter. "Thank you. We'll take the salads, but you can cancel the main courses. We've had something come up unexpectedly and won't be staying long enough to eat."

The waiter nods his head and shuffles away quickly as Zander returns his glare to my father.

"It must be devastating to not know your daughter anymore. But then again, I don't think you ever took the time to really see her. Rather you used her as a pawn to secure the future of your empire." My father turns his full attention toward Zander for the first time. The vein in his neck is bulging, his jaw set, and his eyes burn with a vitriol I can't remember ever seeing before. Zander chuckles long and low. *"Oh, yes.* I've done my research on you, Damon." He leans across the table and lowers his voice as if he's telling a secret.

My eyes must be as wide as my father's in reaction to seeing this new calculating side to Zander, as well as knowing that sometime between now and coming home from zip-lining, he researched my father. "Google's a wonderful thing, isn't it? I read all about the multimillion-dollar government contracts you were awarded once you merged with Ethan's company. You must be one helluva parent to trade your success for your daughter's happiness."

"You son of a bitch—"

"I saw the society pages, Damon. The pictures from their perfect, storybook wedding where all the captains of industry attended. How rumors flew that palms were greased and—"

"Young man, you don't know who you're messing with." My father spits out the threat, but Zander stares at him unfazed with a cocky smirk on his lips. My heart pounds and my head is spinning. When did Zander find all of this out and how did I not know about it?

*You were controlled, Getty.* That's how. When you live in a bubble, he who controls the amount of glycerin can also constrict the size of the bubble around you and what it contains.

I'm so grateful Zander is here and more than astounded at how hard he's fighting in a battle that's not even his to fight. I link my hand with his, fingers intertwining, as he continues.

"I know exactly who I'm dealing with. You think I'm scared? You think this *grease monkey* is scared of you? Yeah, I noticed you sitting across the street while I worked on the car the other day."

His words connect the dots for me. Yet I'm too mesmerized watching Zander stand up for me in a way no one has before to react to the revelations. In a way I've never seen anyone stand up to my father.

"How's it feel to have to sit behind the tinted windows of your town car parked on your daughter's street to find out about her life? But if you ask my opinion, I'm not really sure you care. You've washed your hands of her well-being for years, so why change now? Ahhh, but you were controlling her in those years, weren't you? And now *you're not.* So you sat there and took in the weathered house and the blue-collar guy under the hood of a car and made assumptions just so you could pass more judgment on her. You have no clue what she's been through. But I guess I shouldn't expect anything less from you, should I? She's just the collateral damage in your empire, and how dare she fight for herself for once, because she might leave a stain on your pristine reputation." Silence descends around the table. Tension so thick it could be cut with a knife. Both men are frozen in a silent standoff.

My father breaks it first, striving to get the upper hand in a situation he clearly has no control of. "I'm not going to sit here and listen to your immature and unfounded bullshit any longer." My father throws his napkin down, the picture of flustered fury. And I don't think I've ever seen anyone ever get to him like Zander has. "Stand up, Gertrude." He shoves his chair back, where it crashes into the wall behind him as he raises his hand to summon the waiter.

*"What?"* Reflex has me saying the word. Shock has me rising to my feet without me even realizing I'm following his orders. Rather I'm so stupefied over his audacity that he'd think I'd want to go with him even now.

"It's time to go pack your things and get you back home where you belong." He grits the words out, temper so close to snapping all I can do is stare at him wide-eyed.

Then Zander's laugh rings out in the restaurant. Mocking. Taunting. An audible *fuck you.* "She's not going anywhere." The words are delivered with a measured slowness. His tone ice-cold.

"You. Don't. Control. Her." The silverware on the table rattles as my father uses his finger to jab its top with each word he spits out. His shoulders are squared and body stretched to full height as he looks down at Zander, who is casually leaning back in his chair.

Zander flashes a smarmy smirk, but his eyes are dead serious when he stands up, now clearly at a height advantage. He leans forward, voice quiet but powerful. "Neither. Do. You."

My father glares, jaw ticking, before shifting his gaze

back to mine. "You have a soft heart, Gertrude, and in this cruel world, it's a major weakness. Falling for this man is proof of it. He'll take advantage of you and you'll come running home broken, with your tail between your legs. I have no doubt."

My eyes burn. My heart hurts. My head spins.

"Having a soft heart in this cruel world is brave. *Not weak*. But you wouldn't know the first thing about bravery, now, would you?" And without another word, Zander links his hand with mine and we walk out of the restaurant together.

"This isn't over," my father calls after us.

But all I can think is that it was over a long time ago.

# Chapter 22

The hammering begins before I take my makeup off. Loud, forceful blows echo through the house and feel resoundingly similar to the way my father's words felt when he spoke them. Impactful. Relentless. Damaging.

And as much as I want to go and ask Zander why, right now of all times, he's working on the deck, I don't. I need a moment to myself. Time to decompress.

Sitting in front of my vanity, I stare in the mirror and go over the events of the day. Waking sated and feeling incredible. The morning of discord. Zander's confessions at the Treehouse. The zip-lining. *Just jump.* His voice fills my memory and a trace of a smile turns up my lips. The dinner with my father. Zander's surprise offensive on my behalf. The absolute silence on the drive home, both of us lost in our thoughts.

I close my eyes momentarily and allow my composure to crack. Weeping for the loss of a father who was never really a father—but I'd always held out hope he would see his wrongs and right them some day. A little girl always wants her daddy to love her. Tonight proved to me that will never happen and that not everyone sees love the same.

But then again, I should have known that already, since

Ethan once professed his love for me and look how that turned out.

Outside the sounds of the hammer continue. Five sharp hits before a reprieve, during which I can assume he picks up another nail to start the process all over again.

With a sigh I lift the makeup-remover towelette and wipe it over one eye. And then the other. I rub and scrub and remove the mascara and eyeliner as best as I can. Try to rid myself of the face of the weak woman I no longer want to be.

Bang. Bang. Bang.

When I open my eyes to my reflection, my lids are clean, but traces of black shadow remain under my eyes. A smoky black stain telling me she will never leave me. That I'll always be that woman until I can erase the darkness that still lingers. The shame. The insecurity.

So I scrub harder. The pounding noise becomes a sound track to my burgeoning panic as I wipe and scrub to rid my face of every last reminder. Of the past I desperately wish I could forget.

Before I'm done, my movements have grown frantic and my emotions run haywire as the tears that I've held back all night slowly slide down my face. Some of the black makeup smears and makes trails down my cheeks. Visual reminders when all I want to do is get in the car and drive. To somewhere new. Away from the pain. Away from the hurt.

But I can't.

Zander proved that tonight with the truths he threw in my father's face. I showed it too. I stood up to him for the first time in my life. And God yes, it was hard and it hurt, but at the same time it felt so damn good. To finally have a voice, a way to assert myself, and prove not only to him but to myself that I am earning my new place in life. That the meek, scared Gertrude no longer exists. Sure, her memories remain, but I will try to use them as fuel to encourage me to succeed rather than as a fear preventing me from doing something.

Rising from the vanity, I pick up my discarded dress

on the bed. I rub my fingers over the expensive fabric and place it in the laundry with the knowledge that I'll never wear it again. To Mable's it will go.

A symbol of my past sold for pennies on the dollar. I wish my memories were as easy to get rid of.

With a grumbling stomach, I head toward the kitchen. I'm hungry but don't have any desire to eat. That sick-to-my-stomach feeling I had listening to my father's disdain still lingers.

When I glance out the kitchen window, I see that Zander didn't even bother to change. The first few buttons of his shirt are undone, cuffs rolled up at the sleeves. His shoes are off, bare feet sticking out beneath his trousers. But it's the etched look of concentration and anger that holds my gaze.

He moves to a rhythm only he knows and I can't help but watch and wonder why he's so upset. Because he is upset. On the way home, I thought his silence was just a courtesy so I could work through how I was feeling. But now as I watch him, shoulders squared, body tense, face reflecting the civil war of emotions going on inside him, I know his silence has nothing to do with being respectful and everything to do with him.

I just wish I knew what it was.

There's a precision to his actions that's mesmerizing and probably best explained as controlled fury. And I'm not sure how long I stand there and watch him, but the more time that passes, the need to do something for him after all he's done for me tonight develops to the point where I can't ignore it.

*Food.* Food helps and comforts. He skipped dinner like I did, so I'm sure he's hungry, but more than anything, it gives me something to do and will ease my restlessness. Normally I'd lock myself in my room and paint, but for the first time in what feels like forever, I don't feel inspired. I'm drained and not sure I can handle any more emotion being thrown into the mix.

So I'll attempt to cook.

The flashbacks come out of nowhere while I'm rum-

maging through the cupboards and the refrigerator to see
what ingredients we have on hand.

The beef bourguignon I had to prepare every Monday
and the herb-crusted chicken that was mandatory on
Wednesdays and all the other particular preparations
Ethan required when our house staff had the night off.
The plates upended in my lap because the beef was too
tough or the sauce wasn't thick enough. My answering
scramble to hopefully fix what I could so I didn't have to
give him the *proper apology* he'd deem fitting for the in-
fraction.

The sound of the hammer pulls me back to the present. *Never again, Getty. Never. Again.*

I look back to all the offerings in the kitchen and
struggle with what to make, slightly amused that while I
can cook four rather complicated meals to perfection, I
really have no idea how to cook anything else, since
Ethan never accepted any variation.

Settling on the one meal I can't screw up too horribly,
I opt for eggs, bacon, and toast. Simple. Almost error-
proof. And with the hopes that the same meal we had this
morning will bring us back to that feeling of contentment
we found at the Treehouse.

Soon I'm lost in the easy preparation, but when I reemerge, the hammering triggers thoughts I don't want to
acknowledge. How I want him to slow down, take a night
off . . . because the faster he finishes the repairs on the
house, the sooner he'll return to his everyday life.

*Away from here.*

Once the food is cooked, I load the plates and head
toward the sliding glass door just as Zander comes in.

"I figured you were hungry. . . . We skipped dinner. . . .
So I made you something." Suddenly I'm stumbling over
the words, feeling ridiculous that I'm nervous about it.
"It's nothing special."

His eyes widen at the sight of the food. "Yeah. Thanks.
I'm hungry." Somehow it seems the words are just as hard
for him to come by too. "Let me go wash up. Thank you."

When Zander returns to the kitchen, a strange look

flickers over his features as he sits down. "Breakfast for dinner, huh?"

I fight the inherent need to apologize. "Yes. Is that okay?"

A soft smile graces his lips as he shakes his head. "Just reminds me of my parents, Rylee and Colton. They used to do this thing when I was younger. They'd pick one day out of the month where we got to eat pancakes for dinner and ice cream for breakfast."

My laugh floats through the room as the warmth of his smile translates into his eyes. There's something about the quiet nod of his head that tells me this is a good memory. One he's fond of. After a night filled with tension, it's a welcome sight and I want to know more. "Why?"

"It had something to do with when they were dating. Holds some kind of special significance, but anytime I asked to know more, Rylee would shoo her hand at me and say that sometimes you need to live in the moment and enjoy the little things, because you never know what tomorrow brings."

"She sounds like a neat lady." My comment causes a shadow to fall across his face before he concentrates too hard on the food on his plate. "You must miss her." My voice is soft; I'm treading cautiously into unknown territory.

There's no response aside from silence. Then the scrape of the fork over the plate. The crinkle of the paper napkin. The clink of ice in his glass. So we sit and eat in the quiet of the house that only moments ago was filled with the angry noise of the hammer. Now we both seem loaded down by the weight of our own solemn thoughts.

"It's good. Thank you," he finally says with a nod of his head, but he still doesn't meet my gaze. And I'm left wondering what exactly he doesn't want me to see if I look too close.

"Mm-hmm." My vague response earns me a lift of his head so I can finally see his eyes.

"How are you doing . . . after earlier . . . tonight, I mean?" And I know he's serious, wants to know, but there's a sadness in his gaze that has me wanting to delve further into what's going on with him. I only wish I knew how to go about it without him feeling like I'm crossing those boundaries of his.

I shrug listlessly. Scoot my eggs around on my plate as I try to figure out the answer. "I'd be lying if I said I wasn't hurt. . . . Everyone wants their parents to love and approve and want the best for them." Something flashes in his eyes and disappears just as quickly. "But at the same time, what was shocking for you to hear was my everyday reality. I'd assumed some of those things were true for so long . . . and then hearing you say them out loud, throw them on the table, was a double whammy. Recognition and hurt all in one swoop. And his reaction . . . his lack of response told me it was all true."

"Shit, Getty." He blows out a sigh and runs his hand through his hair, sounds apologetic. "I'm sorry."

"For what?"

"Because it was your battle to fight and I couldn't help myself. I stepped in when I shouldn't have. Because sometimes there are truths you know deep down, and it's only when someone else says them aloud do you really hear them. Those are the ones that hurt the most." His voice is barely audible. I know he's not just talking about tonight but rather his own life too. "So, I'm sorry."

"No. Don't apologize. Don't you get it, Zander?" I hold his stare for a moment before I continue. "You're the only person who has ever stood up for me in as long as I can remember. And you're right. The truth stings when you hear it validated by someone else . . . when someone else who has known you for a whole five minutes sees it clear as day. But do you know what that meant to me, knowing that my feelings mattered to someone enough for them to stand up to one of the two people who have disregarded me for so long?" Tears well in my eyes. The ones I promised I'd never shed again when it came to my father.

He nods ever so slightly, lips twisting and eyes closing momentarily in thought. "You deserve to have someone fight for you, Getty."

My heart swells at his soft-spoken words. "We all do."

He opens his mouth several times to say something

before stopping himself. And even without words I can see his vulnerability. His need for more from me and yet what that *more* is I'm not sure.

Without warning, he shoves his chair back and averts his eyes as he grabs his plate and brings it to the sink. "It was good. Thank you," he repeats. "You cook a mean break-fast." His voice is gruff, the chuckle he emits strained.

He begins washing his plate and when I look down at mine, I realize that I barely touched it. Well, except for the bacon . . . because, *hello, it's bacon*, but the rest of my food just looks spread around. The food I fixed for comfort now seems to have done anything but that.

At a loss, I clear the table in silence and wipe down the counters I already cleaned before we ate. I keep busy while I try to put my finger on what has upset Zander. When I set my plate next to the sink, his wet hand reaches out and grabs onto mine. Startled, I look up to him. His eyes are intense. Angry. All-consuming.

The handsome, valiant, considerate, funny, drop-dead-sexy man in front of me after such an emotional day stops me in my tracks. There's an undeniable need within me to feel close to someone. Everything collides at a fierce pace. And from one beat to the next, throwing reason and boundaries and everything I'm supposed to think about but don't want to right now out the damn window, we meet in the middle.

Our lips crash together in a whirl of need and want. Passion ceding way to pure greed. Finesse disregarded by our hunger. We turn into a frenzy of motions. Hands groping. Mouths demanding. Bodies grinding closer.

His mouth closes over my nipple through the thin cotton of my cami-tank. My head goes dizzy. My hands un-buckle his trousers without any conscious thought. Goose bumps race over my skin. Hands finding his skin warm, cock hard and ready for me. My body begins to ache. His hands slide inside my waistband, and the cool air of the room strokes my skin as he pushes my pajamas down. The ache turns molten; liquid desire burns its way through every muscle. The clatter of dishes being swept into the sink startles me. Our smothered laughs as his lips find mine again. His hands on my waist, lifting me up, setting my butt on the counter. My legs part automatically. The tear of the condom wrapper from his wallet.

My desire is ravenous. Real. Unbridled. So very new to me.

Our movements slow. Our gazes focus downward where his dick is unhurriedly pushing its way into me. The torturous anticipation of watching me take him in—while the sweet burn of my muscles accommodating him inch by inch seeps through my entire body. Nerve by nerve, sensation by overwhelming sensation.

And then when he's fully sheathed—with his hands gripping my thighs and my fingers digging into his shoulders, a moan falling from both of our mouths—the urgency returns. The carnal need takes over as our bodies move in sync, trying to give and take and own and sate.

Murmured words fill the room, the running water of the sink the only other sound. *Now.* I want you. *Yes.* I need this. *Oh God.* Right there. *Fuck.* Harder.

He pulls me into him. His hands slide under my tank and brand themselves to my back as he picks me up a bit to adjust the angle. And just that tiny change—my weight the determining factor for the depths he can reach—catapults the sensations he's drawing out of me from borderline heaven to full-blown ecstasy.

His name on my lips. His dick swelling inside me. The need to lose myself in something other than what happened tonight. His hushed pants in my ear as he works our bodies into that point of no return.

When it hits—first me and then him shortly thereafter—there's no scream into the room, no harsh grunt to let the other person know one of us has come. Instead there is a tensing of bodies, an honest connection of our eyes, and the sound of Zander saying my name in the softest of groans. It's a quiet acknowledgment that the moment held as much for him as it did for me.

I can see the flash of panic in his eyes right afterward. Feel it in the sudden tensing of his hands.

And I'm not sure what prompts me, but right when he begins to pull out and break our connection, I wrap my arms around him, bury my face under the curve of his neck, and hold on. Understandably, his body jerks in response.

"Just . . . I just need a minute," I murmur against the warmth of his skin.

Being the great guy he is, he pulls me tighter against him and kisses the crown of my head without a single word.

And when I realize that I just crossed another probable boundary of some sort, a part of me is brutally embarrassed at my sudden neediness. So much that I don't want to let go so I have to actually meet his eyes. But the other part of me breathes him in and realizes it's his warmth I'm craving now. My life has been so filled with coldness and cruelty, Zander's basic show of warmth and compassion is something I cling to.

"Sorry," I sniff after a bit as I pull back from him, gaze angled down, and teeth biting my bottom lip as awkwardness sets in. "Just a lot to handle today. I needed a minute." I try to save face, not feeling very certain that I did.

"I understand," he says as he slips out of me, both of us unsure what to do.

Yes, our lust is undeniable, considering we just screwed like rabid rabbits against the kitchen counter, but it's that something else—that almost palpable shift between us—that's causing this sudden uneasiness.

"I'm . . . I'm gonna go clean up."

I nod my head, not trusting myself to speak, since the urge to cry returns, tears stinging like a bitch as I try to hold them back. The problem is I'm not sure why I feel like crying. Is it everything with my father? Is it the fact that Zander stood up for me? Or is it Zander in general? I know I can't have him and yet increasingly I want him in my life regardless.

I'm left sitting on the counter, pajama pants hanging off one foot, to ponder the answer as the pipes creak when Zander turns on the shower.

And I still haven't figured out the answer over an hour later as I lie in the darkness of my bedroom, surrounded solely by the warmth of my comforter. Too chickenshit to face Zander after his shower because I'm overwhelmed by this feeling that I need to explain myself, apologize—I don't know what—about my sudden moment where I needed more from him than just friends with benefits.

Maybe I just needed the friend part.

Ha. But the benefits part was pretty damn good too.

And therein lies the crux of the problem. I want more already when I know that's not an option with him.

His movements around the house carry through the two inches of space where my bedroom door is cracked open. I purposely left it ajar, not wanting to feel cut off from him after everything that happened between us today. My ears trace his footsteps down the hall and into his bedroom. More footsteps, then they hesitate this time, and I swear he stops right outside my bedroom door. But just as I convince myself I'm right, the steps retreat down the hall toward the kitchen. There's the rattle of the rest of the dishes being loaded into the dishwasher. The telltale sound of his MacBook turning on. His exhalation that's loud enough to travel into my bedroom.

There's a comfort to the sounds, to not being alone, and I hate that as much as I don't want to face him, I also want to go out into the family room, sink down on the couch, and just watch him do whatever he does on his laptop.

It's only ten o'clock. I'm tired but can't sleep. There's some laundry to fold. I'm still hungry. I run the list of reasons through my mind over any excuse why I should get up, but when I hear his voice, I freeze.

"Hey, man, I know. . . . I know. . . . I've missed you too." There's so much affection in his tone I can hear it all the way down the hall. There's a pause while the other person speaks. "I'm glad to hear that. I'm proud of you. Is Mom there?"

I sit up in bed in reflex. Surprised. Intrigued. Curious. He's calling home. To his mother. To his real life.

*The one without me in it.*

The notion stings, but I'm so transfixed by the fact that he's calling home for the first time that it overrides the hurt.

"Rylee." His voice is cautious and solemn. "It's good

to hear your voice too. . . . I just wanted to call to let you know that I'm all right. I'm doing well actually." He laughs in a way that sounds like it's hard for him to believe his own words. "I know you deserve answers, apologies, a whole shitload of things. . . . I'm still working through some stuff, trying to find my way, but I *am* finding it. . . ." He murmurs in agreement to something she says. "I called because—I know, I know." His voice is sympathetic and the simple mix of sounds proves to me that whatever happened, whatever crappy things he says he did, he at least feels sorry over his actions. And that says a lot to me about the measure of the man.

"I'm sorry I can't give you a time frame. . . . I know the season is almost— Yes, I know, but I screwed so much up that I—" His answering sigh is audible as she cuts him off. I hate that as much as I want him to go put things right with his family, I'm also selfishly happy that he didn't put a finite limit on his time left in PineRidge. "I know you're not pushing, Ry, I . . . yeah, I get it. . . . I wasn't going to call. Not until I had my head straight, but something happened tonight that put things in perspective. Made me realize how much you two have always stood behind me, and so I wanted you to hear my voice, because I know how much you worry." His laugh again. A little more relaxed this time.

And with the sound of it, a picture starts to emerge for me. The angry hammering. His need for the physical release—in the work on the deck and in the unapologetic, no-holds-barred sex in the kitchen.

I smile softly to myself, thinking about the differences between last night and tonight. How last night I was seduced, pleasured, placed on a pedestal that left me feeling swoony compared with tonight's bruising pace that left me feeling recklessly desired and utterly exhilarated.

The thoughts circle in my mind as I focus back on the silence in the kitchen, waiting for him to speak again.

"No. I can't." The distress is back in his voice. "I have . . . shit, I don't have a reason why, other than I made promises I need to keep before I talk to him. . . . Yep. Uh-huh. I've gotta go, but . . . I just needed to call." He says something else I can't hear, but it's obvious to me by his sudden backpedaling and defensive tone she asked if he wanted to speak with Colton. "I love you too. Bye."

Silence descends on the house once again until I hear the creak of the floor in a pattern that sounds like he's pacing.

As I sink back into my bed, guilt over eavesdropping on his private conversation ties my hands from comforting him. My mind replays his comments, homing in on the notion that his meeting with my father tonight triggered something in him. Did he see how callous and cruel my father was and realize that his family isn't half as bad as he thought when he left?

No, he already admitted he screwed up and hurt people. But maybe tonight just reinforced that for him.

The knock on my door startles me.

"You awake?"

"Hmm?" I murmur, trying not to sound obvious that I'm in here concerned for him.

The door creaks open farther, but the light from the hall is off and so I'm left with his shadowed figure in the darkened doorway. He stands there for a moment, and somehow I can sense his need to talk across the distance.

"Can I come in?" His voice is quiet but gruff.

"Yes."

He crosses the few feet in silence and the mattress dips as he sits on the edge. But he doesn't stop there. He surprises the hell out of me when, without another word, he pulls back the covers and slides into the bed beside me. Strong hands reach out and pull me firmly against him, my back to his front, before he wraps his arms tight around me.

I'm shocked, surprised, and every other adjective there is to describe being thrown for a loop from his actions—and yet I try not to let my body relay that to him.

"This okay?" he murmurs, his chin moving against my shoulder where it rests and the heat of his breath on my ears.

Coherent thoughts are hard to come by, so I do the best I can with a murmur of agreement.

"I just need a minute," he whispers my own words from earlier back to me.

"Okay." I sink against the firmness of his body, that warmth I craved earlier seeking me out this time. I can all but hear his mind turning next to me. His silence more powerful than a scream.

I know we both want to say more, but instead we let the magnitude of the moment—the unspoken admission that he needs me—eat us whole. Devour our insecurities. Gnaw at our doubt. Consume us with emotion. Relish in the connection. Create potential. For what? I can only hope we're moving toward something.

After a bit of time, my nerves feeling more alive than ever from the body-to-body connection and my mind overthinking the situation, I realize how much he is missing out in his life by being here: his family, his passion, his job. I hate the thought as soon as it fleets through my mind, but I still can't deny that the quicker he confronts his past, the sooner he can decide when he wants to return to that normalcy. And while that means I'll be here alone again, I can't hold him tight for my own selfish reasons.

*But oh, how I'd like to.*

I break the silence. "If you want me to help you go through the box, I will."

I can hear immediate rejection of the idea in the subtle hitch of his breath. But he doesn't speak, just pulls me in a little tighter, giving the idea time to settle.

"I think I'd like that. . . . Thank you," he murmurs to my surprise when I thought he wouldn't respond. "I can't promise you I'm not going to be a moody jerk over it, Getty, and I'd like to think I should do it myself . . . because, you know, boundaries." I feel his shoulders shrug and the reverberation of his soft chuckle against my back makes me smile.

"Boundaries, huh? How're they working out for you right now?"

His laugh grows louder and joins mine. It's a comforting sound in the quiet of the room, but he doesn't answer the question. I don't know what I expected, but this wasn't it: Zander curled up behind me, his breath evening out, and his muscles falling lax.

Seconds turn to minutes and minutes to an hour as we

lie in a tangled mass of arms and legs, him asleep and me awake, while I wonder what just happened. We've created a day-to-day routine, and after tonight, we've knowingly added our pasts to the equation.

Thoughts, hints of more, flicker and fade. My pulse accelerates. My mind tells me to shut down. To fall asleep. To stop thinking how nice this feels.

But it proves impossible. So the digital clock on my nightstand shows the passage of time, when I just want to stay right here in this moment.

# Chapter 23

With a flick of the power switch, the table saw falls silent. After I gather the freshly cut wood and shake the sawdust from my hair, I glance up and my eyes fall on the lone figure on the beach beyond.

*Getty.* Her brown hair is pulled up in a loose bun and her feet are bare. She's enjoying the warmth of the sun with her face angled up to the sky, and she's holding a bag of shells I've been watching her aimlessly collect in one hand.

And that's the problem—how much I've been watching her. How much I've been reliving that unexpected, purge-your-emotions, use-each-other sex we had in the kitchen. Then immediately thinking about the way she bounced back after the cruel shit her father said to her without shedding a tear. Who says that kind of unbelievable crap to their kid? I realize that I'm starting to care about her in other aspects beyond sex.

But fuck, how can I not? I'm not that much of a prick. To think she lived in that life for twenty-five years before finding the courage to escape. To make a life on her own terms.

To be messy and unorganized.

Talk about being brave. Strong. Tough. And yet I don't think anyone knows the half of it, including me.

And what kind of shitbag is this Ethan prick? To go right along with her father's plan? Treating her as less than worthy . . . although I have a feeling his treatment of her was a whole lot worse than I'm allowing myself to think about. My blood boils. Distant memories of my own mom and dad return and I wonder just how bad it was for Getty.

My eyes veer back to her. To where she's bent over petting a jogger's dog. I didn't know she liked dogs. In fact there's a lot I don't know about her and suddenly the idea of finding out more is very appealing.

*Jesus, Donavan. Quit thinking about her.* Or how good she smells. Or how goddamn warm her body was against mine all night. Or how fucking great the sex was last night when it was a little rougher. And oh, how I'd like to show her just how fun rough sex can be. Or that little sound she made when she grabbed me tight and didn't let go.

*Any more* or*s and you're gonna need a damn boat to use them.*

My laugh rings out. I'm fucking losing it. *In more ways than one.* I lift my hat and run my hand through my hair as she bends over to pick up something from the sand. And I hate that she offered to help me go through the box.

*Let someone in instead of shutting everyone out.*

Colton's words echo through my head. Cause pangs of guilt that I couldn't let it be him. Or Rylee. Or anyone else close to me for that matter.

But last night . . . fuck, last night watching Getty's piece-of-shit father treat her like she was his pawn—it not only pissed me off, but made me step back and realize how goddamn lucky I was. I was so angry at myself for not seeing it sooner, at Damon for not giving that to Getty, at the whole fucking world, that I just needed a minute. Some time on the deck with a hammer in my hand to work through my thoughts, my aggression, because I have a feeling Getty's had enough taken out on her over the years that she didn't need any more from me.

And what did I get in return? Her taking the initiative. Her reaching out to me when she probably felt so exposed after what I saw at the restaurant. How she needed me:

for sex. To work out the emotional overload. To just be held.

And of course, I'm the asshole. The one running away from his family because they care about me, when she'd probably give anything to have what I have. A loud, interfering, patient, meddling, intrusive, chaotic family that lays down the law only because they love me, not because they want something from me.

Talking to Rylee and my little brother Ace last night only solidified that for me. Reinforced that regardless of the bullshit I pulled and the hurt I caused, they still missed me and wanted me back home. Only wanted the best for me. Even after the stunts I pulled, acting like a goddamn prick so lost in myself that I couldn't see the forest for the trees. Couldn't ask for help, an ear to listen, an explanation to dispel my assumptions—anything— because it was so much easier to feel the rage than accept the vulnerability that came with it.

For a man, showing weakness, letting people see the one thing that will instantly knock him to his knees when he's supposed to be standing tall on his feet, isn't an easy thing for him to do voluntarily. Myself included.

And yet why the fuck am I willing to let Getty see what my past holds when I wouldn't let my own parents know about it?

The thought lingers, feeds my train of thought, creates ideas that I shouldn't even be entertaining. Like the type that made me slide into her bed last night and pull her against me simply because she understands without me having to say a single damn word.

The two-by-fours in my hand begin to get heavy. A reminder of what I should be doing—finishing the damn deck instead of thinking about *her*. Paring down the to-do list. *Not Getty*. Fulfilling my promise to Smitty, to Colton, to my fans, instead of sitting here with scattered thoughts. *Not knee-high socks*. Overthinking shit that should be simple. *Not a certain mini-blind-wand-wielding female*. I miss home but at the same time I have a perfectly good reason here as to why I'm not headed there just yet.

And all points lead to *Getty Caster*.
*The woman I can't get out of my damn head.*
Collector of seashells.
*A breaker of boundaries.*
Painter of stormy seas and broken sunsets.
*And one I sure as hell like having in my bed.*
Or hers.

# Chapter 24

**Repair List**

~~Replace Front Step—third one~~

~~Replace Missing Roof Shingles—Wet is only good in one place~~

Back Deck = Death Trap

Fix Lock on Patio Door—Sorry, Mr. Ax Murderer

~~Fix Bathroom Mirror~~

~~Clean Out & Fix Rain Gutter Spouts~~

~~Repair Shutters~~

Add Handrail to Front Steps & Paint

~~Connect Internet for God's Sake~~

Boat Shit I Don't Understand

Bulldoze House and Rebuild ☺

Electrician—Call one

Plumber—Creaky pipes

Kiss the Repair Guy

As my eyes skim the list, it's a visual reminder that Zander's time left here on the island—with me—is limited. And while the new addition at the bottom of the list makes me smile, I'm also preoccupied in adding up all he has left to do and calculating how much time that might mean.

*Push it away, Getty. Carpe diem.* My new motto.

It's one I decided I needed to adopt while I lay in bed with Zander the other morning. He was snoring quietly beside me—one of the rare times he wasn't up first—and I realized that every day that passed was one fewer I'd be able to spend with him.

So my decision? I was going to seize the day, enjoy each moment with him, and then worry about tomorrow when tomorrow happens. Heartbreak is okay. Because at least that means my heart was full enough to feel love—and I don't think I really ever knew what that felt like before.

*Get a grip. It's called lust, Getty. Hot sex with a hot guy. Let's not jump the gun here.*

"Easier said than done," I murmur to myself because I know full well the difference and I'm still trying to deny it. Setting the to-do list back down, I lift my head to peer out the window to the sunny beach outside. I can't help but smile. Things seem to keep getting better and better.

Sure, the disastrous dinner with my father from last week still lingers in my mind, but I'm dealing with it. I'm moving on. I didn't expect him to change with a miracle about-face, so I'm focusing on reveling in this new life I'm building. In the handsome man who has been ignoring his boundaries by sharing my bed with me most nights. In my creativity that's resurfaced and has me picking up my paints again. In the beautiful day outside that I plan to take advantage of while Zander is on the boat meeting a mechanic, since my shift doesn't start until tonight.

My good mood still has me smiling hours later when I'm running my fingers over items in Angelique's Antiques on Main Street. I've been in to see Mable to just chat, had a pedicure, sat on the boardwalk, watching the tourists fret over sunscreen and optimal sun-to-sand towel positioning, and even ventured to the craft store to look at replenishing my supply of paints.

Then just as I was about to head home, an idea came to mind. I wanted to buy something for Zander—a thank-you for fixing my car. It's the least I can do, since he refuses to let me pay him for his time or the expense of the repairs.

When I open the antique walnut humidor, I'm surprised and pleased to find it doesn't smell of cigar smoke. The rectangular box strikes me as dark and masculine. It's in perfect condition, fits into my price range, and is the perfect size for what I want to use it for.

Just as I meet the store clerk's eyes to tell her I'm going to take it, the bell on the door rings.

"I've been looking all over for you." Zander's voice fills the small shop.

The smile is automatic as I look over to him, immediately stepping away from the shelf with the humidor, hoping my eyes don't look as panicky as I feel in almost being caught.

"Hi." And I can't help that my heart stumbles in my chest when I see him standing in the doorway, wearing a T-shirt and board shorts, a Donavan Racing Team baseball hat low on his head, and a smile wide enough to light up a room on his lips.

"I ran into Mable. She said you were out and about on Main Street." He shrugs shamelessly over the fact he was asking about me. And that little flutter in my belly only strengthens with each step I take closer to him, which is silly considering that we share the same house and most nights we've been occupying the same bed.

"I've been running some errands."

He gives me an even bigger smile. "It's good to see you out and about. Can I take you to lunch?"

And now I'm doubly surprised at his presence with that unexpected offer. "Well, my list of possible lunch companions is long and distinguished, but I'll let you skip to the front."

"C'mon, you smart-ass."

"I'll probably be back later," I tell the clerk as we leave the shop, which earns me a sideways glance from Zander that I shrug off. "I've never been in there. It's fun to look around."

"I'll never understand women and their never-ending need to buy useless crap."

"Not useless," I correct. "Sometimes it's just fun to look. What did the mechanic say?"

"A lotta shit. He's running some diagnostic tests. I'm gonna head back in an hour or two and see what he finds. You like chips and guacamole?"

The change of subject paired with how he suddenly grabs my hand in his means it takes me a second to respond. "Yes. Um, I do."

"Good. I've got a table saved for us." He tugs on my hand to lead me toward the island's lone Mexican restaurant. And while it's more of a hole-in-the-wall with a palapa-style canopied patio overlooking the water, the place is a tourist favorite, where it's not uncommon to see a line of people waiting outside to eat.

As we make our way in that direction, I welcome the hustle and bustle of the crowded boardwalk around me. It's a new and surprising sensation, considering populated areas are the very thing I'm so accustomed to avoiding.

Maybe it's because I'm no longer looking over my shoulder expecting my father or Ethan to be hiding in the crowd. I know my father well enough to recognize he's not going to give up his quest to get me back so easily. But at the same time, he knows where I am, so the constant on-edge feeling I've lived with for four months is slowly fading.

Or maybe it's because I'm holding the hand of a handsome man who's taking me to lunch on a beautiful, sunny island day. The situation makes me feel like a normal twenty-six-year-old woman, carefree, enjoying life, having fun on my Saturday before I head to work.

My steps slow down as we hit the line twenty or so deep outside the door, but Zander just keeps my hand in his and passes by the crowd. When we enter, the hostess's eyes light up at the sight of him. She lifts her chin and signals for him to go on through. I can't say she gives me the same warm smile, but I guess with my hand in his, I also don't blame her.

Zander maneuvers us through the maze of tables until we reach the far corner of the crowded patio. Our table has a perfect view of the sparkling ocean.

In less than fifteen minutes, we're eating chips and guacamole under the shade of a huge umbrella that's angled perfectly to block out the stares from some of the patrons who have realized who Zander is. It's a weird feeling to be under the microscope in a completely different way from what I'm used to. The excited murmurs and the constant feeling of being watched. The camera phones being used on the sly. The constant flux of people slowing by our table building the courage to ask for an autograph.

"God, I could get used to this," he says with a tip of his bottle of Dos Equis toward the ocean view. "You sure you don't want a strawberry margarita or something?"

"Ewww. No thanks. Besides, I have to work later."

"Ewww to the margarita, says the bartender," he teases with a shake of his head and a sudden bumping of his foot against mine beneath the table.

"No. The margarita part is fine. It's the strawberry part that's ewww."

"Are you serious? How can you not like strawberries?" he asks like I've lost my mind, followed by a loud crunch of his chip. How could I ever resist him? He's like an animated little boy wrapped inside this irresistibly perfect grown-up package.

"The same way you don't like tomatoes." I purse my lips and raise my eyebrows as he looks at me in befuddled amusement.

"How did you know that?"

"That night at Mario's, you pushed all the big chunks of tomato in the sauce to the side of your plate like a little kid who doesn't like something."

"Huh." He leans back in his chair, his eyes narrowed at me. A few moments pass—the crash of the waves on the rocks below, an outburst of laughter a few tables behind us, a quick rush of breeze that makes the umbrella sway—before he speaks again. "I guess there's a lot we don't know about each other besides the fact that we both have unique names. Like what's your favorite color?"

I eye him cautiously, see the curiosity blazing in his blue eyes, and wonder where he's going with this. I'm so used to keeping everything about me under lock and key to prevent gossip that it takes me a moment to realize I don't need to be as guarded anymore. Or defensive. It seems Zander can do his own fair share of investigative googling and so it's not like telling him my favorite color is going to divulge any hidden secrets.

Besides, I can't be okay with sleeping with him and not be okay about letting him know my idiosyncrasies.

"Orange. Yours?"

"Black."

"Nope. That's no good. Black technically isn't a color—pick again." I know I'm being a smart-ass, but by the lift of his brow and the curl of his lip over the edge of his beer bottle as he nods, he's accepting my challenge.

"Blue, then." He raises both eyebrows as if to ask me if his answer is acceptable. "Dark chocolate or milk chocolate?"

The question makes me laugh at how silly this is. But the conversation feels good in the same way as walking through the crowded boardwalk and not feeling anxious. "Dark. Definitely dark. You?"

"I'd have to agree with you on that one. There's something about it drizzled over a ripe strawberry that makes it so appealing."

"Oh, please. We're back to the strawberry thing again?"

"I'm not sure I can trust a girl who doesn't like strawberries. I mean that's one of the best fruits there is."

"No. If you want to talk the best fruit out there, then let's discuss pineapple. That's by far the clear-cut winner here."

He rolls his eyes and laughs. "Never knew a woman to be so protective of her fruit before. Geesh!" My only response is to sigh in mock frustration, because he's truly adorable in so many ways. "Oh! I got one. Sock, sock, shoe, shoe, or sock, shoe, sock, shoe?"

I find myself bursting out laughing at the ridiculous question. "Seriously?" I ask as I dip a chip in the delicious guacamole.

"I was going to be happy with simple questions like favorite food, sunrise or sunset, Indy or NASCAR, movie theater or Netflix, comedy or drama, but then you went and got all technical on me, so I had to up my game."

The challenge to answer those questions is clear as day

in his eyes, but the boyish smirk that ventures into dimple territory wins every damn time. And the bad thing is, I know he knows it and I have a feeling he will use it to his advantage any time he needs to.

I pick up my lemonade and take a long, slow draw on the straw while keeping my eyes on his. "Well, Mr. Technical." He *hmphs* in response to my sarcasm. "Pancakes. Definitely sunrise. I've never watched a race in my life, so I'll have to say Indy because I think that may just work in my favor. I haven't been to the movie theater in years, so I'll say Netflix and anything but horror." I nod my head at him in triumph for answering but then realize there was one more. "And sock, sock, shoe, shoe, because that is the most logical, but I'd much rather just say flip-flops, because that's what I'd prefer to wear."

"Wow," he muses as he leans forward and puts his elbows on the table. "That was impressive . . . but you're wrong."

"I am not."

"Pancakes are definitely a favorite I can deal with, although apple pie à la mode is a far better choice. And it's a serious travesty about your lack of racing knowledge, but I do agree with your Indy pick. That answer definitely works in your favor." We've ventured into dimple territory again and I shift in my seat to prevent myself from staring too long, because that smile does funny things to my insides. "Netflix because less crowds. And horror because a scared woman will want you to protect her from the dark and that means you might just get laid." He winks on the last one and I can't help but laugh out loud.

"I should have guessed. And it's sad if a horror movie is your only game to try to get laid."

His laugh garners attention from nearby tables. "Hey, being a man can be rough. We need to take any advantage we can get."

I roll my eyes at him. "Oh you poor, deprived, sex-starved man. But you forgot one answer."

"Oh yes . . . while I disagree with your discrimination against strawberries, I do have to agree with you on sock, sock, shoe, shoe." He taps the neck of his beer against my glass and then takes a long pull on it.

"At least we can agree on that." The breeze blows off the ocean and the sparkle of the water distracts me for a minute.

"But I'd pick you in knee-high socks every damn day of the week if I had a choice." This time his wide smile carries through to his eyes. And I know he's just being nice, but every part of me perks up at the silly compliment. "So we've got some of the basics covered—what else don't we know about each other?"

"You know I'm messy," I say off the cuff, a shadow spreading across his face as he purses his lips.

"Nah. I don't think you're messy." His comment catches me off guard.

"Are you kidding me?" I laugh, suddenly nervous as my gaze fastens to his. Deep down this feels like so much more than a *tell me yours and I'll tell you mine* example.

"Nope. The first night we met, I thought you were messy, yes. What with your skirt trapped around my ankle, but now I know it's your way of making a point to yourself. A reminder that you can do whatever you want, even if it's leave a trail of clothes down the hallway." He offers me a slight smile, but it's the intensity in his eyes and the words he's spoken that really hold my attention.

He understands me. The why. The how. Even though I've never specifically told him about my time with Ethan, he still gets me. There's something extremely poignant about being heard and having your reasons validated by someone who matters to you.

Because no matter how hard I try to convince myself otherwise, Zander does matter to me. Way more than I want to admit to myself.

And just as I start to grow uncomfortable about him seeing me so candidly, faults and all, as if he's pulling my thoughts from the depths of my eyes, he leans even farther across the table and says ever so quietly, "You're forgetting the really important question, Getty."

"Like what?" *What am I missing?*

"Like . . . what is the point-of-no-return spot on your body?"

"Point-of-no-return spot?"

"Yeah, that one spot where once your lover touches you there, there's no turning back. The only thing ahead is sex and reaching an orgasm." His voice is barely audible and yet I hear every single word along with suggestion lacing each one.

The question throws me. We've gone from playful, to serious, and now to the kind of interrogation that makes me squirm in my seat because I'm not used to the flat-out directness of him asking about my erogenous zones.

"Why?"

"It's important for your lover to know these things, Getty."

I laugh nervously as the air between us shifts and twists into an unexpected undertow of desire. Unable to think with his salacious stare asking so much, I avert my eyes back to the ocean, thankful he's willing to give me a moment to collect myself before I respond.

*Oh my God.* How do I answer him? First of all, this isn't something Ethan ever cared to ask me, and second, I'm not very good at voicing something like this aloud. Maybe under the covers in a dark room . . . but not with piercing blue eyes holding steadfast to mine watching for my answer. Add on to that the fact that every part of my body—mind, nerves, pulse—is reacting in some way to the look he's giving me and the topic he just introduced.

"Don't be shy, Socks," he murmurs, and places his hand over mine on the table. My eyes flash back to his. Those parts of my body that were reacting a second ago now go into overdrive. "You don't get to be shy after last night."

That grin again. But this time it's one reflecting full-blown arrogant male smugness over yet another bout of incredible sex. And there's something about that look that restores my confidence. The part that realizes I'm the one who put it there.

So I take a fortifying breath before looking back at him. *"Everywhere."* It takes everything I have to maintain our eye contact. Every ounce of self-confidence I've found in myself to not look away and be ashamed for being honest. "In all the years we were together, Ethan never took the time to care . . . so I can't tell you for sure. My lips maybe? Because you kiss me like I matter. Like I'm innocent and a vixen all in one. You worship them. Demanding at the same time you're so patient with me. Or maybe my skin? Because I love the feel of your hands and how when you run them over me . . . their strength and noticeable restraint reflects your desire for me. Or the curve of my neck? Because when your lips are right there, I can hear that hitch in your breath when I put my hands on you. That sound tells me you want me to touch you. So I don't have an answer for you. I like when you touch me *everywhere*, Zander. . . ." I pointedly emphasize the last words. Draw them out, making sure my tone sounds like how his touch makes me feel. *Greedy. Desperate. Consumed.*

Before I can even take in his expression—wide eyes, tongue flicking out to wet his bottom lip, the bob of his Adam's apple—and gauge how he took my confession, I think about me. About my unexpected candor and the comfort level I have with him.

What a far cry this woman I am is from the shadow I was months ago.

Now that the words are out, I can't take them back. And if the look in Zander's eyes is any indication, I don't think he'd want me to if I could.

"If that's not a challenge to touch every erogenous zone on your body until you can pick just one as your favorite, I don't know what is. *Shit.*" He blows out a whistle and unsuccessfully fights to hide the surprised grin on his lips. "I think I need a cigarette after that."

It's my turn to laugh. Long and loud. And to wonder just what other parts of me he's going to awaken on his quest to make me pick a favorite.

No complaints here.

# Chapter 25

There's only one word to describe how I feel as I head home after wandering aimlessly around town for a bit. Content. I picked up the humidor, sat on the waterfront for a while eating an ice-cream cone, and then headed over to the farmers' market to pick up some peonies.

But the unyielding smile on my face is because of Zander. It hasn't left my lips since he unexpectedly kissed me good-bye on the boardwalk with the parting words, "I still can't believe you don't like strawberries." Then he flashed that disarming grin of his as he took a few steps backward before turning around to head home and grab some kind of something for the mechanic on the boat.

*Guess I can cross "kiss the repair guy" off the to-do list.*

I laugh at the thought as I unlock the front door, making a mental note to add an item of my own to the list for him. Aware of the waning time before my shift starts, I put the flowers in a vase and head straight to my bedroom, distracted with thoughts of where I can hide the humidor. I don't want Zander to see it until I can explain my intentions.

Within seconds of tossing my purse on the bed and setting the humidor down, I have my shirt over my head and am toeing my shoes off.

"Now that's the proper welcome I'd expect from my wife."

Every part of my body freezes—the toes on my right foot from pushing down against the heel of my shoe on my left foot, my fingers behind my back beginning to unfasten the clasp of my bra, my heart, my breath. The only things moving are the hairs that slowly stand to attention on the back of my neck and the dust dancing in the light of the room.

*I'm not your wife.* The thought echoes in my head but never makes it to my lips. Nothing does. Instead, I concentrate on the buoyant specks for a moment. It's the only thing I can focus on, because it takes everything I have to tell myself to breathe, to exhale evenly, and to rein in every ounce of emotion that I feel. To put up the mask. To disassociate. To make him believe when I turn around that I'm not scared of him.

But I am.

Every.

Single.

Part.

Of.

Me.

Because while I'm Getty Caster now—strong, independent, confident, *hopeful*—all it took was the sound of his voice to transport me back. That calm, even, arrogant, calculating tone that never rises in pitch and yet orders, criticizes, punishes, demeans me. Fear returns instantly as I'm reminded of the times he'd lose his temper or take a ruthless and often unfounded revenge on an adversary because he got off on being the judge, jury, and executioner. And his methodical ways of putting *me back in line*.

"Now, now, Gertrude." It's his warning tone. The condescending *Do as I say so you won't cause me to do something I'll regret* tone. The one that used to make me want to try to be as small as possible to avoid the dead zone from the fallout of his temper. "Did you miss me as much as I missed you?"

I swallow the bile that threatens to rise and take

another deep breath. "No, Ethan, I didn't miss you at all." My voice is quiet, but at least its even tone doesn't reflect the fear ricocheting within me.

"Amusing, Gertrude." Disdain. His voice drips with it. "As you were. Take your bra off and turn around. *Now.*"

My eyes flick around the room. To my purse on the bed with my cell inside. I wonder if Nick would be able to hear me scream next door through the closed bedroom windows.

The rush of blood is so loud in my ears I can't hear anything but its whoosh as I answer. "No."

His hand hits something—a loud crack of a noise—at the same time his voice thunders, "Turn. Around." I physically jump at the sound, and the dead calm in his voice is even more frightening.

And as scared as I am with him at my back—my mind trying to calculate how far away he is from me or where he is in the room—I also don't want him to think I'm obeying him. Or that I fear him. Because those two reactions will give him the one thing I refuse to give him ever again: power over me.

"Don't be scared, Gertrude. It's just me. *Your husband.*" His chuckle grates on my nerves.

*Just jump.*

The thought comes out of nowhere, but it is exactly what I needed to fortify everything I've learned about myself in the months since I left this asshole.

I bite back the bile threatening to rise again. Stiffen my spine. Lift my chin. And turn around to face Ethan. He's sitting at my vanity, leaned against the back of the chair, perfectly groomed as always, but it's the hatred in his eyes that reveals his state of mind.

"Get. Out." I grate the words out between gritted teeth, not wanting him to see my chin tremble.

The sound of his laughter fills my bedroom, but it's anything but humorous. It's empty, chilling. "I'm just here to take back what's mine." A lift of one eyebrow. A mocking curl of his lips. His unrelenting stare, which causes chills to race up and down my spine.

"Fuck. You."

He's on me in a flash. Closes the distance in a split second of time. I don't even have time to scream. Maybe I do. I don't know. There's a sound. A crash. A thump on the floor. His voice full of anger. Me trembling: my body, my mind, my heart.

But even through the haze of fear, I do something I never did before. *I fight back*. Using my hands and nails and legs and feet. Whatever it takes to stop him. I'm a ball of pent-up rage and hurt, even though I know I'm no match for his strength, honed by obsessive workouts and the most expensive supplements on the market. Yet, still, *I fight*.

I aim for connecting my knee to his crotch, to deliver the only kind of blow I know might incapacitate him, but he blocks it. I'm not sure how long we struggle. Seconds. Minutes. They feel like hours.

My lungs scream. My muscles burn. The sting of pain from his blows to subdue me doesn't register. Only my rage. Only my hate. Only my fear.

And in some move I can't even comprehend, he spins me so that I'm facedown on my bed, his knee pressed to my spine, my arms wrenched behind my back with one of his hands while the other fists in my hair.

My face is pressed into the mattress. The thick comforter smothers my mouth and nose. My lungs scream for air. I thrash my head from side to side, try to heave in a breath, try to think clearly, when all I can focus on is the comforter hot beneath my mouth as I suck in any air I can get through it. *Panic*. I'm no match for his strength.

And just as my mind starts to grow fuzzy and weird spots dance in the blackness of my closed eyes, I yelp out when he yanks my ponytail back sharply, lifting my face off the mattress.

There is no fear. There is no thought other than air. Gulp. Gasp. Suck it in as fast as I can.

I know this game. He's played it before. Deprive and demand.

Show who's in control.

Prove that I'm weaker.

But I don't care. Don't have the wherewithal to focus

on how to prevent the next push into the mattress, because when your body is starved for air, it's your only focus. How to get more. How to store it. How to inhale it. How much you're going to get before it's taken away again.

His breathing hitches from his exertion. The warm pant of it hits my ear as he leans down over me. "Are you this disobedient with your new boyfriend, *Getty*?" he sneers my new name. His fist twists in my hair, but I bite back the yelp of pain.

*Don't let him have the power.*

I close my eyes and wince at the pinpricks of pain all over my scalp. At the fire still burning in my lungs. At the ache where his knee digs relentlessly against my backbone, and the strain on my rotator cuffs as he pulls my arms up from my back.

"Does he know what a worthless whore you are? How your husband had to fuck other women because you couldn't satisfy him?" I draw in a ragged breath. The affirmation still hurts all this time later, although I always suspected it. The sudden meetings. The subtle scent of perfume on his clothes. And even in my oxygen-deprived state of mind, I know that my marriage wasn't a marriage by any real standards, and yet hearing the truth still stings. "Yeah." He laughs. Taunts me. "I'd leave you with your listless legs spread in our bed and go straight to another's. A real woman who could pleasure a man."

There's simply no comparison between him and Zander. Between selfish and selfless.

"I doubt you pleasured her." The comment surprises me, coming out of nowhere, and my own voice sounds unrecognizable. Calm. Mocking. *Confident.* Something I'm sure I've never sounded like when responding to one of Ethan's verbal blows.

My chuckle follows the remark and it's audibly laced with a taunting tone. And I swear I must be going mad, because when he orders me to shut up, I just laugh harder. Yes, he's in complete dominance over my body, but my mind remains crystal clear and I'm so fed up with everything about him and this absurd situation.

*Why come to take me back if you need others to get you off?*

But before I can voice it, my face meets the mattress again and what I thought humorous moments before now becomes a struggle to draw in air. To feed my body. And my mind.

I tell myself to calm down as the panic returns. Tell myself that if I struggle, I'll need more air, and I can't get more air, so I'll pass out sooner and he'll do who knows what with me.

Then as the seconds drag on . . .

. . . and on . . .

. . . and on . . .

My thoughts align one last time as the edges of my mind start to turn fuzzy.

With a clarity I've never known before, a new thought crosses my mind: He's going to kill me.

*My vision turns white. Head feels light.*

Before, I was *needed* in his life. I was Damon Caster's daughter. A symbol of their union. Of his future.

Did I fear him? *Absolutely.* Did I worry if he'd kill me? *Never.* He was too greedy to risk ruining that relationship with my father.

I was the glue in their business dealings. The flag raised in victory. The mascot for their world domination.

And now that I've walked away, I single-handedly proved to them that their relationship is solid without me. That I'm not needed.

*My limbs are heavy. My chest has a wildfire blazing inside it. My thoughts fade. . . .*

The sharp pull on my hair as he yanks my head up means oxygen. It means another chance. Tears sting my eyes as I gasp like a fish out of water. And when he hauls my body up to a standing position, the removal of his knee from my back opens up more space for my lungs to expand.

My legs are rubbery. My head still woozy. Was this his plan? Make me weak. Find the submission I refused to give him by starving my lungs and forcing me into our old roles.

When I open my eyes, he's face-to-face with me. His hazel eyes hold the fraudulent apology he's given me so many times over the years. The one I believed in at the beginning of our marriage. How I owned the guilt he placed on me when he said my disobedience made him do it. There was a cycle of my acceptance, his apology, then his promise never to do it again.

All the while there was also shame that would eat me whole, gnaw at and erode my self-esteem, because I knew I was never at fault. That he didn't really mean his apologies. That he was to blame. He was always to blame.

The apologetic look went hand in hand with his actions that broke me. As a human. As a woman. From feeling worthwhile. It was the catalyst that stole so much from me. The *me* that I'm trying to get back now.

So I find strength in the memory. Find myself clinging there, holding on tight to her, and meeting him stare for stare.

"Why, Ethan?" My voice is hoarse but steady. "If I'm such a horrible wife . . . then why do you want me back?"

His jaw pulses as he tries to wither my resolve with his stare. "Because image is *everything*, Gertrude," he says, running the back of his hand down my cheek. "And the Caster name is the ticket to getting it."

As prepared as I am for his kiss when he leans forward, I can't choke back the disgust. I thrash my head, but the unforgiving twist of my hair makes me freeze as his lips bruise mine. Revulsion ripples through me. The bile returns.

"Do you believe the lies he tells you?" he whispers against my ear.

He holds my hair hostage so I can't look to see what he's doing.

"Does he tell you you're beautiful? And smart? And funny?"

I close my eyes momentarily. Shutting out his words. Not wanting Zander anywhere near Ethan in my mind.

"*All lies*, Gertrude." He singsongs the words in a hauntingly childlike tone that creates goose bumps all over my skin.

His free hand haphazardly hits against my lower belly. Then I hear the telltale sound of a belt buckle jingling as the end goes through the loop, the metal clasp hitting against itself.

*No.*

"Does he promise you things only I can give you?"

The sound of a zipper being unzipped.

*My mind shutting down.*

I choke on the rising bile. Knowing what comes next. Panic returns. Hatred so strong the thought of having to touch him makes me physically ill.

"I deserve a proper apology, Gertrude."

*My mind disassociating from this reality.*

"No." I swallow over the lump in my throat. Fight back my fear. Prevent the tears from welling in my eyes. Try to hold on to Getty Caster as he attempts to strip her away, layer by layer, until she becomes Gertrude Caster-Adams again.

Weak. Compliant. Fearful.

"No. Is. Not. An. Option."

Our eyes war. His telling me *now*. Mine telling him to *fuck off*.

He yanks on my ponytail again. Trying to force me to drop to my knees like I would have done before. Take his punishment by giving him a *proper apology* without a fight, because a fight just made the repercussions that much worse. In my old life, giving in was the only way to survive.

But not now. Not here. Not the new me.

"Now!" His demand eats up the air in the room, but I remain standing tall, jaw clenched, hands fisted, resolve unwavering.

"No." It's the only thing I can say without betraying my courageous facade with the fear and panic and desperation overwhelming me internally.

Pain radiates as he tugs harder than before on my hair; I yelp automatically. But this time he steps up against me. "*Yes*. You remember how to do this. You'll get on your knees. You'll suck my dick. You'll take it all the way to the back of your throat. You will not gag. You will not move."

He uses my silence to his advantage. To emphasize what he expects. To draw out my fear. To unnerve me. To let me think long and hard about what I know from experience will happen next.

"It's not my problem if you can't breathe, Gertrude. You just proved to me you can hold your breath an awfully long time . . . so no excuses. But be warned." He chuckles maniacally, letting me know he's really getting off on this. "The next punishment hurts a helluva lot more than my dick blocking your thro—"

# Chapter 26

ZANDER

*Your head's in la-la land, Donavan.* Better get it the fuck outta there quick or you're gonna forget a helluva lot more than just your cell phone next time.

You ask a woman what her point-of-no-return spot is and the answer is supposed to be simple. *My neck. My ear. My nipples. My clit.* Hell, even her G-spot if she's blunt.

But then there's Getty. Answering me with a sweet expression and innocent body language casual as can be . . . but her words? Fuck, they were a seduction all their own. A verbal striptease. Giving me an answer but then telling me so much more than a simple location on her body. Instead she told me how it made her feel.

Fucking feelings, man. They'll get you into trouble every damn time.

No exceptions.

*Good thing I like a little trouble.*

My mood's pretty damn great with my mind full of ideas of exactly how I want to touch her when she gets off work. The exact spots where I'll tempt and test. The decision I'll force her to make after I tease her mercilessly. Maybe edge her out, withhold her climax until she decides on her point of no return.

Damn. The options are endless. Lucky fucking me.

I glance at my watch as I jog up the front steps. Eight

minutes. Not bad time. The mechanic can't be too pissed for the short delay. After all it's his fault he doesn't remember the replacement engine parts Smitty is already having delivered so he'd know which ones he needs to order. But I do. On an e-mail, on my phone.

The phone I left on the kitchen counter.

So he can bitch all he wants about the twenty-minute round-trip for me to go back and get it. It's a helluva lot more convenient to wait the twenty minutes rather than eat the cost of shipping for duplicate parts he's supposed to remember.

"Just where I left it," I murmur as I grab the phone and head back to the door, surprised Getty's not home getting ready for work. Maybe she's already come and gone. There are flowers on the counter, but there's no perfume. No barely there scent like after she usually sprays it. The thought lingers, bugs the shit out of me as I start to close the front door.

"It's not my problem if you can't breathe, Gertrude."

The words ring loud and clear right before the door shuts. Instinct takes over at the sound of the unfamiliar voice down the hall. I've never heard it before but know instantly whom it belongs to.

". . . hold your breath . . ."

I need to get to her. *Getty.*

". . . be warned . . ." His laughter.

". . . The next punishment . . ."

There's a split second after I come through her doorway to assess the situation. My brain takes snapshots of the scene. Getty: eyes wide, lip trembling, fear on her face. Fear. Fear. All I see is fear. Ethan: pants pushed down, muscles tense, his hands on Getty.

His. Hands. On. Getty.

My only coherent thought. Then rage. Bloodred.

"Let. Her. Go." My voice, but I don't recognize it. Don't care, because my only focus is getting him away from Getty. His hands off her.

All I feel is the sting in my knuckles as my fist connects with his cheek. His head snapping back. Getty cries out. The lamp crashes to the ground.

And all I can think is *more. Again.*

Avenge. Retaliate. Protect.

His grunt. My growl. A burst of pain on my cheek. The whoosh of air he exhales as I hit his abdomen. He stumbles. I follow. Another shot: him to my gut, me just grazing his cheek.

"Don't you ever touch her again." A threat. A warning. *Never again.*

I get ahold of his shirt. Twist my hand in the fabric. The scatter of buttons on the floor. Ram him hard against the wall.

His laugh. Arrogant. Uncaring. Unaffected. Like she's nothing. A pawn. "You can have the frigid bitch."

His words hit me, threaten to confuse me, but the rage is louder. Drowns out reason. Blinds me. Fuels me.

"Only a spineless son of a bitch sends his father-in-law to fight for the girl. But by the way you treat women, I guess *chickenshit* is pretty common in your world."

His grin. Maniacal. Taunting.

*Finish this, Zander.*

My fist flies forward. The click of his teeth. The crunch of his nose. The warm spray of blood on my arm as his head swivels. The thump as his body hits the floor.

"Touch her again, and I'll kill you myself." The words are out before I even think them. The threat is more real than anything I've ever said before in my life.

But he's knocked out. Will never hear it. Will never know how real it is.

Seconds tick by. My knuckles throb. My body vibrates from the adrenaline. My thoughts clear. *Getty.*

Desperate to see her. To feel her. To make sure she's okay. I turn around. And there she stands.

Time slows down. Seconds stretch out.

Hair a mess. In her bra and shorts. One shoe on. Her brown eyes are wide. Her lips parted. They quiver. But it's the look she gives me that steals every last part of me.

"Oh, Getty." It's all I can say, all I can think, as I cross the room.

"I'm okay," she says. And just as I reach her, she collapses in my arms, against me. Into me. So I do the only thing I can. Hold her. Breathe her in. Feel her heart pounding against mine. The warmth of her breath under my neck.

And I repeat her name again. Over and over. To tell her I'm here. That it's over. That she's okay.

"I'm okay," she repeats, but I know differently. Can feel her body trembling. Can hear the hitch of her breath. How her fingers dig into my biceps.

"Let me look at you," I murmur against the crown of her head as I breathe in the scent of her shampoo one more time before I take her shoulders and hold her away from me. "Getty. I— Did he hurt you?" My gaze roams over every single part of her. Checking. Looking. Making sure. "I forgot my phone. I didn't know—I would have—"

"No. No," she repeats again, shaking her head, trying to stop me from blaming myself, but good fucking luck with that. "I'm okay. It wasn't that bad—"

*"Wasn't that bad?"* Is she fucking serious? The fury returns again. The need to make him pay returns with a vengeance. But something flickers in her eyes.

And suddenly I'm struck with a memory of my mom with that same look. The same response.

It's hard to swallow after that. Hard to think. Hard to breathe as my worlds collide.

My hands are on her cheeks, eyes trained to hers. There are no tears. There is no show of emotion other than her fingers gripping my arms tight, telling me to not let go yet. I can't help myself, though. I need to touch her, feel that she's safe, to know she's really okay. I brush my thumbs over her cheeks.

"You could have told me, Getty." I have to say it. Have to let her know I understand. I already knew. And it's okay.

"About what?" The aversion of her eyes. Dodging the question. The shifting of her feet.

"I would have understood. About him, about the abuse." I realize I'm walking a thin line in this moment. One she can no longer deny after what just happened. One I've suspected all along.

"He's never hit me, Zander." Her words are rushed. Panicked. Denying the obvious.

But I also see the shame. The fear I'll see her differently after knowing the truth. And it kills me. Fucking wrecks me that she'd think I'd put the blame on her.

Gently, proceeding cautiously, I use my hands to direct her gaze back to mine. To make sure she sees my eyes when I tell her what she needs to hear. What she needs to know. What she needs to believe.

"You don't have to hit to leave bruises, Getty."

*Stubborn fucking woman.*

She ignores me like she's done since she got here, despite my constant glares from the far end of the bar. Just like she did when the cops left with Ethan in cuffs and I told her I'd already called Liam and she wasn't going in to work. Our conversation replays in my head.

"I'm going," she stated, voice defiant, while pulling one knee-high sock up.

"No, Getty. I explained to Liam that something came up. He understood." My frustration grew as she picked up her second sock. "What happened was serious. You need time."

And then she leveled me with a look. The same one she'd been giving me since we called the cops. The *I'm fine.* The *it's not a big deal.* I know that look hides all the emotion she's trying not to show. But it wasn't until she finally spoke up that her reaction knocked me flat on my ass.

"No. I don't need time. I need to get to work. I don't want to sit here and think about it right now. I want to be busy."

"But—"

"No, Zander. Don't you see? This was my life. For years this was all I knew how to do. How to cope. Tears weren't allowed. Something like this would happen and then I'd have to paint on a pretty mask, go to some event, and pretend I was okay." Her breathing sounded shaky. I had to fight every instinct I had not to pull her against me because that statement made me see the brutal truth of how she'd lived for so long. Not lived. *Survived.* "I'm putting on my mask, Zander. Let me do the only thing I know how to do so I don't fall apart. If I fall apart, he wins."

And goddamn if her words didn't break parts of me that I never even knew I had. They tamed my temper. Made the order to stay home I was going to say next die on my lips. I had to switch gears.

"You're not her anymore, Getty."

As I watch her move behind the bar, mask up, emotions under control, I'm not sure I'll ever forget how doubtful she looked when I told her she had nothing left to prove. Because with her strength, her resolve, and her tenacity, she'd already won against both Ethan and her father. And while she may be coping just fine, using the tourist-packed bar to keep her busy, *I'm not.* The longer I sit here, the more time I have to stew. *And the angrier I become.*

At myself: for not seeing that I'd left my phone at home sooner. At not getting there quicker.

At Damon: for sending his son-in-law after his daughter, because he won't take no for an answer.

At the sheriff: for telling me what I already know— that Ethan will be out on bail in a matter of hours. And I appreciate the fact that he's going to push the envelope, wait until the last minute to give the fucker his one phone call to his lawyer, so that hopefully his ass will have to stay in a cell overnight. But I know the truth without the sheriff ever saying it. Money means privilege. And privilege means high-priced lawyers and special treatment.

I have a sinking feeling Ethan will get nothing more than a slap on his wrist.

At Ethan: because he's a royal fucking prick who needs far more than that slap on the wrist. All I can hope for is that as he settles back into his posh mansion high in the hills somewhere with a fading shiner, every time he looks in the mirror and sees the bump in the ridge of his nose from where I broke it, he'll remember me. That he'll remember my threat and never touch Getty again.

At Getty: for being so goddamn strong. The woman needs to break. To cry. To rage and scream so she can leave it behind.

*She needs to need me.*

The last thought comes out of nowhere. Blindsides me. And I cope with it the only way I know how, by lifting my hand to get Liam's attention.

I had no choice but tell him the bare minimum about what happened with Ethan when I called Getty in sick to work. I know how important her job is to her. Besides, the small-town gossip mill was likely already in full swing and so I figured why not tell the one person who hears it all so he can set anyone straight.

I'm sure Getty might feel differently, but while she's busy tucking everything away, I wanted to make sure the town knows the truth so they can back her if it's ever needed.

"You need some ice for that?" Liam motions to my knuckles where they're red and swollen.

"Nah." I open my hand to stretch them and shake my head. "I'm good, thanks." Actually I wish they were worse. I'd like to have gotten one or two more good ones in. For me. For Getty. Because he deserved so much more than that.

"For your cheek, then?"

Did he hit my cheek? Shit. Never even thought about it. When I open my mouth and stretch my cheeks, sure as shit, there's a burn of pain, but I just shake my head again and sigh as I glance back over to check on Getty.

"She still ignoring you?" He laughs and lifts his chin toward Getty. There's concern in his eyes, very different from the surprise that was there when Getty waltzed in an hour after I called to tell him she wasn't coming, and took her place behind the bar.

When he went to tell her to leave, that he'd covered her shift, the look I leveled stopped him dead in his tracks. And thankfully when I explained she needed to be kept busy, that I'd pay the extra set of wages if he needed me to, all he did was nod his head, point to an open seat near the end of the bar, and ask me what my poison for the evening was.

Definitely a good guy.

"Yep," I sigh as my eyes find her again. "Stubborn damn woman."

Liam laughs again as he lines up two shot glasses and takes the top off the Jägermeister. "You know what they say. . . ."

"What's that?" I'm distracted, eyes staring at the door to the storage room Getty just disappeared into.

"Men wear the pants in the relationship, but it's the woman that controls the zipper."

I throw my head back and laugh. The rebuke on the tip of my tongue that we're not in a relationship remains unspoken because the stress relief is more important. "Very true." I tap the top of my glass against his and toss back the shot.

The burn is quick, but I welcome it. It's real. That and the laugh Liam offered by trying to lighten the mood.

This time when he goes to help another customer, he leaves the bottle for me. Smart man. I relax back in my chair as soon as I see Getty come back into the bar. She pulls a pint for two men in front of her. Chats them up. Laughs. Appears normal. But I can see the strain under the smile.

It wasn't that bad, *my ass*. Her words echo in my mind. Cause fury to beat through my veins. Make me think of my own mother again. Wonder how often she put that mask on to protect me, let me think everything was okay when she was bruised inside and out.

*Turn it off, Zander. Another day.*

But I can't push away the train of thought. I realize I haven't thought about the box or the bullshit it's caused in my life in days. All the noise that had been screaming in my head fell silent. Why is that?

Because of *her*. Beautiful. Brave. *Goddamn Getty*. For the first time in the three hours we've been here, her eyes meet mine and hold across the distance.

All she gives me is a soft smile and a subtle nod in acknowledgment. But it's the words she mouths that sucker punch me harder than anything: "Thank you."

Two words. So damn simple and yet they could be for so many things: for helping her. For being patient. For letting her put her mask on. For being here. For showing her not all guys bruise women.

I nod back, completely tongue-tied with a woman and I'm not even close enough to speak to her.

Her attention is pulled elsewhere, but I can't get the one thought out of my head that keeps circling. I threatened to kill a man tonight. *For her.* The woman with the knee-high socks, the soft brown eyes, and the laugh that you can't help but smile at. Funny thing is, I feel absolutely zero remorse for how much I meant my threat.

Does that make me more my father than I ever thought I was?

Another shot. To kill the thought. To drown out the comparison.

But then I look at Getty and I can't help but think back. To my mom. My dad. To what happened. And all I can think is that maybe somehow I righted a wrong tonight. Made some kind of amends in my fucked-up universe. I sure as hell don't know what Ethan's intentions were, but if Getty was somehow forced to go back with him, isn't that the same?

Her smile. Her laughter. Her confidence. Her spirit. Her sexuality. He'd take them all without thought and wouldn't that be just the same as killing her slowly?

Parallels. They're fucking everywhere all of a sudden. There's no escaping them. Me to my dad. Getty to my mom.

And yet I don't want any of that. I just want whatever this is here on a clean slate. Getty needs her new life. I need to get over my old life.

That makes what I came here to do all the more important.

For Getty to see why this isn't her fault.

And for me.

For me to realize it wasn't my fault.

Goddamn parallels.

# Chapter 27

The summer of storms—that's what Liam has deemed it. The continual onslaught of wintry-type weather hitting the island has taken a toll on the tourism-dependent economy. And by the looks of the sky, another one is about to rattle the island. Good thing my shift is over and I'm free to watch the storm snuggled on the couch looking out the windows of the family room.

After walking home from work, I pass my car parked in the driveway on the way up the front path and have to smile that the sight of it brings such a different response now. Before, the blue heap of metal represented the liberty to make my own choices, an escape, a chance at freedom. Now, a week after Ethan's appearance, all it signifies to me is a means of transportation. A way to get around the island if I want to explore.

And I also see Zander. Because this car is a reminder of the moment I started to fall in love with him. Running my hand over the fender, I'm tempted to try to deny it, but know it's no use. I knew what I was getting into when we started this "friends with benefits" thing more than a month ago. I just thought I'd be able to keep the emotions in check.

But in retrospect, it was this car that started it all. When I stepped out into the alley behind the bar to find this old car in front of me, and Zander, the handsome and unexpected stranger, beside me. *Who would have thought I'd remember that moment the most?* Yet every night when I lie in bed with the sound of the surf beyond the windows and his soft snores beside me, it's the one memory I keep coming back to. The one I can pinpoint as being the moment when I started to fall for him.

When he fixed my car, gave me the chance to run, and I chose to stay.

Because he gave me a choice without ever knowing it.

The thunder claps above. I jump at the sound, a part of me taking it as a warning that I'm only going to be hurt in the end. But at the same time, what I'm feeling is a first in my life. And you never forget your first, so I'm glad in a sense my first real love was Zander.

*Carpe diem, Getty. Carpe diem.*

I shake off the thought and enter the house, feeling tired and hungry. Once I shut the door, I listen to the silence for a minute, just to make sure. . . . It's been over a week and I know Ethan's not here, but I'm still a little freaked.

Blowing out a sigh, I toss my purse on the counter and purposely don't look at the to-do list slowly losing items on the counter next to it. My virtual hourglass telling me time is running out.

All I want is some food and a glass of wine while I watch the gray and black clouds cluttering the sky open up on the stormy seas. An uneventful evening after a long day.

Preoccupied with the thunder rumbling outside and wondering if Zander is back on the docks after his test run with the mechanic on the boat, I need a second to realize what I'm looking at in the refrigerator. All three shelves are piled high with crate after green plastic crate of dark red strawberries.

I can't help but laugh at Zander's display of strawberry love. And am instantly brought back to the afternoon *before* . . . to our flirtatious lunch and carefree afternoon. *Leave it to Zander to think of something like this.* To bring back that feeling that had been subdued and replaced with phone calls to lawyers and the formal filing of charges and restraining orders.

I reach out and touch a crate with a big smile. When I shut the fridge door, I have a strawberry in my hand, determined to try it one more time. For Zander.

The funny thing is, I seem to be trying all kinds of things because of him.

A hand brushing hair off my face startles me awake. I look up, eyes wide, heart racing, and meet Zander's amused blue gaze.

"You're safe." I immediately feel stupid for blurting that out. But it was a lone thought nagging at me as I slowly drifted off to sleep with the howl of the wind and the pelt of the rain in my ears. "Of course you're okay. You're here."

He laughs softly and shakes his head but never removes his hand from the curve of my neck. And normally I'd shove up to a seated position so I could face him where he's sitting on the edge of the coffee table in front of me, but I like the feel of his hand on me—the warmth of it—and don't want him to move just yet.

"I got you something." His eyes are mischievous, his smile sweet.

"I saw," I laugh out. "Strawberries and strawberries and more strawberries."

"Oh. You saw those, did you?" His smile widens, while his thumb rubs back and forth casually on my skin.

"Yes. And I even tried one just for you." The face of disgust I make must be funny because he belts out a laugh.

"Well, I guess all that matters is you tried . . . but I'm still determined to make you like them. Maybe I'll smother them in chocolate or something."

I shake my head. "I'd just lick the chocolate off."

"Mmm." And there's something about the way he responds, deep and guttural, that makes me think his mind has ventured way past licking chocolate off strawberries and on to licking it from somewhere else. When our eyes hold, mine must be telling him I know where his line of thinking has gone, because his lips quirk into a smile.

The silence holds. Tension builds. And I welcome it. The snap of desire between us. The welcome ache in my lower belly. It's been a week since he's looked at me this way. Or touched me other than pulling me against him at night to sleep, a sweet kiss pressed against the crown of my head.

The bruises on my arms, my back, my legs, were too much for him to bear. So I've allowed him to hold me at arm's length, with kid gloves, when all I've wanted was to lose myself in him again. And to let him make me feel.

Maybe the space has been for the best. In order not to taint the bed we've made together with the marks Ethan made on my skin. Not to have Zander reminded of it when he touches me. Those bruises are almost gone, though—the ones that can be seen anyway—and thank God for that, because it's torture sleeping beside a man you're craving to have again.

And as if our thoughts are in perfect sync, Zander breaks me from mine by leaning ever so slowly and brushing his lips to mine in the sweetest way.

With one hand on my cheek and the thumb and forefinger of his other hand holding my chin still, he deepens the kiss. A soft seduction ensues, of tongues and sighs and tenderness that steals my breath and sends chills racing over my skin strong enough to rival the ache deep in my lower belly of irrefutable desire.

As the kiss continues, the intimacy of the action is rivaled only by the first time Zander and I had sex. But maybe this feels even more powerful, because so much more has happened since then. Or maybe just for me, since I've confessed to myself the feelings I have for him.

Because a man doesn't kiss a woman like this if there isn't something there.

And just as I start to believe my own propaganda, he breaks the kiss and leans back. "I bought you something."

It takes me a minute to respond with my head feeling foggy from his intense kiss. "You didn't have to buy me anything." I shift on the couch and sit up, my mind flickering to the cigar box still in my room to give him.

"It's nothing major really," he says with a shrug as if he's suddenly turning shy, "but I saw it and . . . I don't know."

"What is it?" I ask with total curiosity as to what has him blushing.

He reaches down on the floor in front of the couch to a little white box with a blue ribbon around it. "Here." He hands it to me without meeting my eyes, so I make sure my fingertips graze over his hands during the exchange. A touch. A little something I can offer in return.

"Thank you." Noticing the small card taped to the top sans envelope, I set the box on my knees and lift open the flap of the card.

*Socks—*

*Just in case you ever want to be found . . .*

*—Zander*

My eyes flash up to his and all I see is complete kindness in his gaze—all I feel is the sincerity of his gesture—as my mind returns to that conversation we had weeks ago. Even before I untie the ribbon and open the box, I already know what's inside.

And when I do open it, the brand-new iPhone sits nestled in the packaging.

He's given me a way to ask directions if I should ever want to be found. The importance of this moment, his words, the gift he's offering—it's all so heavy it takes a minute for me to blink the tears from my eyes before I can look up to meet his.

"Zander." Hopefully the sound of my voice can convey what I can't quite put into words—appreciation, surprise, humility. "You shouldn't have. You didn't have to—it's—wow."

His face breaks into a dimple-territory smile. "There was this great promotion. Buy a phone and get two years prepaid for all services, so I couldn't resist."

"Zander . . ." And I know he's lying. Know he's trying to save my pride and my budget by prepaying for the service and the phone. "Thank you, but I can't accept this. It's too expensive."

He takes the box I hand to him and sets it down before grasping my hands in his. "This isn't about money or pride, Getty. This is about me being a man and"—he looks out to the storm outside—"and knowing that if you need help, if you're lost, or as the card says, if you want to be found, you can be."

*Only if you're the one finding me.*

I swallow over the lump in my throat, wondering in this world of friends without long-term possibilities if he gets how much his words mean to me. Like maybe he wants there to be a future for us. And then I realize I'm getting this *all wrong.*

The damn to-do list . . . the one I refused to look at earlier today. Well, now I desperately want to know how many tasks are left to complete. Because this gift suddenly seems like his way of telling me the end is near, that he's going home soon and he wants to make sure that I'm okay when he leaves.

I fight the immediate panic, the urge to reject the gift because if I don't take it, then he can't leave, and instead just meet his eyes, while he's completely oblivious to the silent war of emotions going on inside me. So I do the only thing I can, nod my head, try to take the gift for what it is, and not read too much into it.

"I just want you to be safe. Okay? So please accept it?"

"On one condition." I love the quirk of his lips and the lift of his eyebrows. "If you accept a gift I have for you."

He starts trying to refuse immediately as I rise from the couch. "I don't need any gifts."

"I got it last week," I tell him over my shoulder as I enter the kitchen, my eyes immediately glancing toward the list as I walk by the counter. But I mask the sigh of relief and scold myself at my ridiculous melodramatic panic when I see the list has only two more items crossed off than it did last week.

*He still has time.*

The thought runs over and over in my head with each footstep down the hallway.

"Getty . . ." The way he says my name is equivalent to an exasperated toddler throwing a tantrum. Defiant. Resolute. Wanting what he's not supposed to want.

"Hush." It's the last thing I say before I enter my bedroom and head for my closet, where I hid the humidor. Luckily its package went unnoticed on the bed in the melee with Ethan.

"Did you just tell me to hush?" His chuckle reaches my room, telling me he followed me.

"Hush," I repeat with a laugh. And of course I'm bent over, ass up in the air, so I'm sure he's taking his time enjoying the view.

"Nice socks, Socks." *Enjoying the view, indeed.*

But I love that just like that, he brings us back to that fun, flirty banter when moments ago I was silently freaking out over him leaving. It's like he somehow knows what I need to hear when I need to hear it, and you can't put a price on something like that when it comes to a relationship.

*A relationship? There you go again, Getty, with rainbows and pots of gold that don't really exist.*

When I stand up with the humidor in my hand, I turn around to find Zander leaning with his shoulder against the doorjamb, hands shoved in the pockets of his jeans, and this adorable little crease in his forehead as he tries to figure out what in the hell I have in my hands.

"Let's open it here," I suggest, lifting my chin toward the bed, as that crease grows deeper.

He steps forward, confusion still etched in his face contradicted by the little-boy smile on his lips. Within seconds we're seated on my bed: me cross-legged with my back to the headboard, and him a mirror image of me at the foot of the bed with the bag-covered box in between us.

He starts to open the bag and all of a sudden what seemed like an innocent purchase seems so very personal, which makes me hesitate in explaining my reasons behind selecting it. I thrust my hands out to his. "Wait. . . ." Everything I want to say dies on my lips.

He just looks at me and links his fingers with mine. "What's wrong? Are you finally sharing that huge box of sex toys you murmur about in your sleep?"

"What?" I sputter out, completely taken aback by his statement. From the heat flooding my cheeks, I'm sure they must be beet red. And all he does is sit in front of me, a stone-cold expression staring at me blankly. A nervous laugh falls from my lips as I shake my head in a rapid denial, immediately rejecting his comment. "Wh-what—I don't—are you—"

His face transforms instantly. Smile wide, head thrown back, hand to his stomach as he laughs so loudly it echoes around the room. He falls onto the bed, trying to stop laughing except he can't. "Your face. Oh, Getty. That look was priceless."

I reach for the pillow closest to me and hit him with it before he can duck out of the way. "That's not funny at all." Now *I* sound like the toddler having a tantrum. But my God, that was so not cool.

And I do the only thing I can after swatting the pillow at him one more time: I cross my arms over my chest. And pout. And glare at him. But hell if it's not the hardest thing in the world to be mad at a man whose face is half-covered by pillows, with a laugh so contagious I'm fighting back a smile, and who looks so damn cuddleable I just want to crawl over the bed and curl into him.

"I'm so sorry, but everything about that was classic." I can still hear the laughter in his words as he pushes himself back up to a sitting position, eyes now locked on mine.

"I'm pouting." *Just thought I'd make that statement since I don't know what else to say.*

"And you're adorable," he murmurs.

"That was mean."

"No, it wasn't. It was perfect timing because you were second-guessing buying whatever this is for me and so I distracted you." My attempt to level him with a glare serves only to widen his grin farther. "And it worked, because now you're more mad than worried. Secondly, you should know sex toys can be a whole helluva lot of fun, so never count them out, Socks."

"Your present . . ." I redirect the conversation with a lift of my eyebrows, because I'm not going there with him right now.

"Hmmm." He leans forward, giving a quiet chuckle as he reaches out and taps the tip of his finger to my nose. "Sex toys for your next present, then." And before I can even finish rolling my eyes, he continues with impatience. "But now, tell me about mine."

I can only stare at him with a wide smile and a shake of my head in exasperation, but my nerves are now non-existent. "I wanted to get you something to say thank you . . . to say I understand . . . to tell you to *just jump.*" My voice fades off as his eyes darken before he looks down to start unwrapping the gift.

He takes his time. Pulls the humidor from the bag. Runs his hands over the smooth surface. His eyes glance up to meet mine momentarily before shifting back down to where he's lifting the lid to look inside.

"Getty . . ." It's barely a whisper but once again, he knows how to tell me everything he's feeling in the simple utterance of my name. Surprised. Awed. Confused. Gracious.

"We both came here escaping from something. And you've spent so much time helping me . . ." I struggle with the right words to say but then realize he already said it for me. ". . . want to be found again that I wanted to get you something to do the same."

When his eyes find mine again, I can tell he understands this has something to do with his mother, his reasons for being here, but isn't quite sure how.

"This is to keep the good memories in." Something sparks in his eyes in acknowledgment, but I continue. "That box in your room might hold both good and bad. And when you choose to go through it, I wanted you to have somewhere to put the good. A safe place. A new home. That way when you leave here, you can leave the bad in the cardboard box behind you and bring the good home with you in something new." I struggle with getting all the words out. Too much emotion for him. Too much sadness thinking of him leaving me.

But when he reaches out over the box and cups a hand

to the side of my face without speaking—his eyes swimming with emotions I can only assume are similar to what I feel inside—I know I did the right thing.

"Thank you, Getty." He looks down to where his hands are on top of the box, his voice rough, his fingers fidgeting. "This is perfect and thoughtful and timely."

"Timely?"

His chuckle fills the room, but there is a tinge to it I don't recognize. "Yes. Come here. I want to show you something."

He gets off the bed, picks up the humidor, and reaches back to grab my hand to make sure I'm following him. I'm surprised when he turns abruptly into his room and then stops. But the confusion lasts only for a second because the cardboard box sits squarely on the center of his bed.

"I had planned on asking you to go through this with me tonight." He twists his lips, eyes focused on a seemingly innocent cardboard box. Except I know it's something that holds so much power over him. "I guess we were on the same page."

My smile is soft as I nod, but he doesn't see it. He lets go of my hand and sets the humidor down beside the box. Silence weighs us down. Zander's discomfort so palpable I can feel it.

"It's time."

# Chapter 28

GETTY

"What do you remember of your mother?" Zander asks me.

At his question, I glance over from where we both have our heads back on the pillows of his bed. The cardboard and walnut boxes sit between us, and I take in his profile as I consider the answer. His straight nose, his strong jaw, the fan of dark lashes against his tanned skin—he's biding time, taking a moment before delving into the unknown.

And I'm not sure why he fears it other than the fact that it is something unknown to him. But I can't imagine it will hold anything other than parts of his past that he can piece together and then put it all behind him.

Then again, I know better than anyone how your past can own you even in the present. Steal your hope. Taint your soul. Change your outlook, your expectations. And even after you break free from its clutches, it's still there. In the crevices of your mind. In your reactions to everyday things. In the smile you show to the world while you cry inside.

He turns his head to look at me, his blue eyes so solemn, prompting me for an answer I forgot to give.

"My mom?" My smile comes quickly; although some of the memories have faded, the feelings are still fresh. "Her name was Grace. She was beautiful. Full of life. She was everything." Quietly I sigh, hating that there's doubt now when I think of her because of what I've experienced.

"I bet you were her life." His voice is nothing more than a murmur, but I can tell he knows I'm struggling with the truths I've come to learn as an adult.

"I'd like to think that." I nod as Ethan's and my father's words come back to me. The ones that were thrown in my face. *Can't you be more like your mother? Your mother never disobeyed your father. Your mother would be so ashamed of your lack of class.* "But now . . . now I wonder if she really was as happy and perfect as I thought or if she was just putting on a show, hiding it all to—"

"To protect you?" he adds.

I nod, a lump lodging in my throat as distant memories hint of the truth. Of her taking me out for our special dates when my father would rage. Of impromptu sleepovers at the Four Seasons to pretend we were Eloise. Of carefully applied makeup or large-lensed sunglasses she'd even wear inside because she had migraines for a few days.

"Yes." My voice breaks and he reaches out and links pinkies with mine in the space between us. "I have a feeling, looking back with what I know now, that she played the part perfectly but hid so much, mostly from me."

*"You were her truth."*

The way he says the simple statement—quiet, matter-of-fact, like it's the most obvious thing in the world—nearly undoes the waning composure I have left. But at the same time, I think it's exactly what I needed to hear. It lights some of the darkest places within me to know that as much as I loved her, wanted to be just like her, I think she'd be proud that now I don't want to be anything like her.

*I was her truth.* My smile returns. I can handpick the memories to hold on to the best times with her. To shut out the bad. And a reminder for me to live a life, on my own, void of big sunglasses and sleepovers at the Four Seasons, because she couldn't. And because I want to make her proud that I did.

Nodding, my mind overloaded with emotion, I curl my pinkie a little tighter around his. He shifts some, the mattress moving as he reaches past us. The nightstand drawer opens. Closes. And then he's handing something to me.

I take a stack of about ten pictures from him. It's obviously they are old—the clothing and car dated—but it's the people on the paper that hold my attention. A brown-haired boy with skinned knees, a dusting of freckles across the bridge of his nose and the tops of his cheeks, and blue eyes that seem to express a mixture of happy and weary.

The eyes of a child who has seen way too much in his short life. He has a baseball glove in one picture, makes a funny face in another. Items that should denote a normal childhood, but the backgrounds of the pictures reflect something different.

A five- or six-year-old Zander stands on the grass in front of a run-down house, one window boarded up, the other with metal security bars over it. Zander with a stuffed dog clutched tight to his chest sitting on a stained couch in a darkened room. A small section of the coffee table is visible in the shot; it's littered with scraps of tinfoil, two bent spoons, a child's looped belt, and the discarded caps of syringes.

I stare until I can't stare anymore at the surroundings to try to understand as best I can the things he wants to shut out. It's not very hard to comprehend.

The one bright spot in the stack of pictures is the woman who accompanies him in some of them. She has long brown hair, an olive complexion, and blue eyes identical in shape and size to Zander's. And I notice the only pictures where she seems happy are the candid ones where she is paying attention to her son. Her smile is magnetic, expression one of complete adoration.

Then there's the man in the photos. Standoffish. Arms always crossed, a cigarette habitually dangling from the corner of his mouth. Maybe it's because I know the end of the story, but I dislike him instantly on sight.

I sift through the pictures several times, each time my eyes drawn to the little boy, making comparisons with the man I know now. And when I finish, I turn my head and meet the intensity in Zander's gaze.

"She was beautiful, Zander. You look so much like her."

He nods his head ever so slightly, one ear on the pillow, the white pillowcase in such a stark contrast to the dark shadows across his features.

"I'm sure you think I'm being a pussy about this."

His bluntness surprises me and leaves me clamoring for the correct response. "No! This is your past, Zander. Your history. There is no judgment on how you're handling it or the pace at which you're choosing to. Sometimes looking back is so much harder than looking forward. Just remember that while whatever is in that box may be part of your history, it doesn't define the man you've made yourself to be today . . . unless you want it to."

I hear his shaky inhalation as his eyes flicker to the pictures in my hand. One of him and his mother rests on top. His Adam's apple bobs and he exhales a sigh of exasperated confusion.

"Until this box arrived, I didn't have any pictures of my mother other than my memories." I shift some to sit up so I can face him, let him know that I'm listening and ready for whatever he needs from me. "I keep telling myself that no matter what else is in the box, this is enough for me. That this is more than I had before."

I angle my head to hold his gaze, my mind turning, transforming the thoughts I had previously. When he first told me about the box, I thought it was just the idea of it that freaked him out and reopened old wounds a little boy had managed to forget. But now, with the way he's so apprehensive, I'm realizing it's so much more than that. What does he think is in the box that has him so worried?

"I hope there are more good memories in there for you, Zander."

His chuckle is soft, exasperated, self-deprecating. "Well, considering the only other thing I pulled from the box and looked at says I was the one who killed my mom . . . let's hope you're right."

His words startle me. "Wait. *What?*" My hands are in midair between us. He's thrown me so thoroughly for a loop that it's like my gestures and my thoughts are in two different worlds.

Zander doesn't say anything; he just stares at me. And I'm not sure if he's waiting to watch my reaction or if he's testing me to see how I process the ridiculous comment he just made. But the longer he searches my eyes, the more I see that he really believes what he's just said. It's in the quiet intensity of his eyes, the gritted clench of his jaw, the unflinching tension in the muscles of his neck, and the overall deflated sadness that I'm watching slowly sap the vibrancy from his expression and posture.

Needing to make a physical connection with him, I carefully move the pictures out of the way with the mind to cross the small space separating us. But before I can finish, he shifts suddenly so that he lies sideways across the bed, head in my lap like a little child, face toward my stomach and one arm hooked around my back.

My heart breaks and swells all at the same time.

"Talk to me, Zander," I murmur softly. My fingers run through his hair on reflex. His breath is hot through the thin cotton of my shirt. His fingers cool beneath the hem of it at my back. Contradictions. Everything about him right now tells the same story: a grown man struggling with the memories of the little boy he can't quite remember being.

And so I do the only thing I can: I give him time to find the words to speak. He's been flying on broken wings for so long, I'm sure it's going to take him a minute to figure out how to land so we can repair them and make him whole again.

I thread my fingers through his hair. Over and over. Soothe. Comfort. Let him know I'm here.

"The first thing I pulled from the box," he begins, voice thick with emotion. And I just keep doing exactly what I'm doing: fingers through hair, body relaxed, thankful for the trust he's bestowing upon me. "It was her autopsy report. I don't know why I even looked at it. It's not like I didn't know how she died. I was there for fuck's sake. How could I ever forget that?" The break in his voice breaks me too.

"What was her name?" I speak softly, wanting to bring him back to the important thing. To her. Not the blood that I can imagine stains his memory of her. Because, yes, while we both know the pain of losing a mother isn't something that can be quantified or compared, Zander, by far, has had the tougher of our situations.

"Lola. Her name was Lola."

"Lola," I repeat. His fingers flexing against my back are the only sign he's heard me. "I think Lola would be proud of the man her son's become."

His ragged sob catches me off guard. All the emotion he's held in for what I can assume is so long manifests in that single, heart-wrenching sound. The storm rages outside the windows and I have a feeling it's similar to what's happening inside the man before me too.

All I can do is sit here, wait it out with him, and hope to be his lighthouse this time around.

"I remember her lying there, blood everywhere," he finally continues sometime later, a dreamlike quality to his voice. The emotion that was nonexistent the day he told me amid the pine trees comes back tenfold in his tone right now. "And there was the handle of the scissors against her neck. She couldn't . . . her breath . . . it was hard for her to breathe and I thought it was because of the scissors . . . so I pulled it out."

And that last statement tells me what the report says. What the adult in me can infer but what the scared little kid could never have known: that dislodging the scissors most likely opened up an artery. Caused her to bleed out. But she was bleeding out anyway from all of her other injuries. Zander did not kill his mother. A fact that he has to recognize on some level.

But I think the brutality of the report, the reopening of old wounds he couldn't remember himself, was a reality he wasn't ready to face.

His sudden spiral out of control. His continued avoidance of an innocent cardboard box. His lashing out at his family, his career—everything makes so much sense to me now. A man can't control the uncontrollable.

"Oh, Zander." I lean forward and press a kiss to his temple, leave my lips there, right above his ears, so he can hear what I need him to hear over the noise I'm sure is roaring in his head. "I don't care what that report says. You did not kill your mother. Your dad did. I know the report might state otherwise, but you know differently. You were there. You were with her. You were the last thing she saw, her son, her baby. *Her truth.*"

The two of us are huddled together, his mouth against my stomach, mine against his head, my hands still in his hair, and we just sit here for a moment. Thinking. Accepting. Dealing.

"I know." His breath is hot against my shirt. "I know," he repeats, sorrow morphing to anger in a matter of seconds as he sits up and stares at me, head shaking, fingers on one hand fidgeting with the fingers on another. "But that's the problem, Getty. I dealt with this shit years ago. Fucking therapists upon therapists upon therapists and then some more. I talked about feelings and drew pictures of my feelings, of what happened. Christ!" he barks out as he rises from the bed, paces back and forth, restless with anger, and scrubs his hands over his face. "I'm supposed to be over this shit. The memory of my mom shouldn't fuck me up and yet it did and I'm so goddamn angry that it did. All this time later and something I fucking lived, breathed, and dealt with did it again. Took ahold of me. At first I thought my anger was at not knowing this. At how it was kept from me by Colton and Rylee. So that's why I lashed out at them. But then when I came here, I had distance. Time. Space. I realized I was just angry because it shouldn't affect me AT ALL and it does. *And I can't stop it.*"

I get how a grown man can be so angry at being blindsided. At fate's way of proving he's weak when it's all he's bucked against his whole life. At feeling like you've overcome something only to have it resurface later and beat you back down, make you question what you always knew to be the truth.

"Zander," I say his name, watch his feet falter. His eyes full of duress and emotion lift to meet mine. "You want to be angry? I would be too. I'd be fucking furious. Shouting and screaming and hating the world. There is no shame in that. There is no brushing her under the rug. She was your mother. *Your everything.* If this didn't affect you, I'd be worried."

Silence. The thunder rattles the windows.

"The robe I wear? The ridiculously expensive one you noticed? That robe was my mother's. It's the little piece of her I get to touch every day. I slip it on and feel close to her. It's silly, Zander. It's a reminder of the pain and a memory of her all at the same time. But sometimes we have to take the little things we are given to help on those days when all you feel is the hurt." I look down to the box on the bed with me and then back up to him. "My robe is your box. It's brought you both so far, the good and the bad. . . ."

His brow furrows, lips twist as if he's having a hard time believing what I'm saying. "I don't know what to say."

The lost look in his eyes is so hard to handle and yet I can't look away. My love for him is so strong that I can't deny it anymore. The need to pull him into my arms and take all the pain away is so powerful, but he's the one who takes the step forward. He's the one who takes a deep breath, a forced swallow, and reaches out to slowly open the top of the cardboard box.

I watch him, methodical in his movements but his face a sea of emotion, and hope that my comments aren't pushing him to do something he's not ready for yet. And in the same breath I think he needs to face this, because until he does, the unknown will eat him whole.

He unfolds the flaps of the box, then moves the humidor beside it and opens the top. He picks up the stack of pictures he let me see earlier and places them gently in the humidor. The sight is bittersweet. A first step toward closure.

When he lifts his eyes, they are the brightest of blue and hold so much turmoil, but it's the words he says that tell me he's ready to do this.

*"Just jump."*

# Chapter 29

Hurt Till It Hurts No More.

Twenty years is a long time to suffer. Getty's right. It's always going to be there, even if just a whisper of the pain. How come she can simply tell me it's okay to be angry and I already feel better? How is it she can break through the bullshit clouding my head and make me really hear her? Validate my feelings with a simple statement?

*Let someone in instead of shutting everyone out. . . . Sometimes it takes a new ear, a fresh voice, to put things in perspective for you. . . .*

Colton's words come back to me. *Son of a bitch.* How'd he know? I glance up to Getty, the faintest of memories coming back to me. Of after my mom . . . being at the House, the boys' home where I was Rylee's charge. And I'm not sure if it's from hearing them tell my little brother Ace the story of how they met that's created the memory, but it's there: Rylee helping Colton overcome the trauma of his past. How she broke through and he actually heard her.

How in the end she helped him be the man he is today. The man who stepped up to the plate to adopt me, save me, set an example for the kind of man I want to be.

"Because he knew," I murmur to myself as I stare out the window, my mind fucked, my emotions disjointed.

"Who knew?" Getty asks from behind me where she sits on the bed sorting through the papers.

"Nothing." I give myself a mental swift kick in my ass for how I treated him. The things I said. The shit I did. The disrespect I showed to him. I sigh and run another hand through my hair. "Just something I should have known."

I glance over to where Getty is stacking the unimpressive contents from the box on the bed. After we spent an hour going through it, I realized it looks like nothing more than the contents of a desk drawer upended and dumped into a cardboard box.

Maybe it was my dad's desk. Maybe my mom's junk drawer in the kitchen. I don't know, but the inflammatory things I expected to find on the heels of her autopsy report just aren't there.

And I'm not sure if I'm more upset or relieved that it doesn't contain more about my past. More pieces of my mom to hold on to. A bigger insight into the life I lived and the man who stole it from me.

"Fuck." I blow out a sigh and turn around to face the bed where Getty's sitting, categorizing the items in piles. Old bills, maxed-out credit card statements, unpaid parking tickets, handwritten grocery lists, a warrant for my father for drug possession, an eviction notice. Nothing I can really draw conclusions from other than knowing what my mom's penmanship looked like—she was still so young she signed our last name with a heart for the dot over the *i*—and that my parents were late on a lot of payments and about to lose the house.

I lift up the first thing on the stack closest to me, a folder from Child Protective Services. The letter inside turns out to be a warning addressed to my parents that the county had received a phone call from a concerned citizen about my well-being. CPS would be visiting unannounced to do well-checks on me.

I toss it back in the pile, then consider the humidor filled with the few things I wanted to keep. A picture I drew on a scrap of paper of two stick figures, both with belly buttons, one labeled *Zee* and the other *Mom*. The stack of pictures, a credit card slip with my mom's signature on it, my original birth certificate, a cheap bookmark with a rainbow tassel that I remember used to hang out of the top of her paperback books, a red paper clip she had bent into the shape of a heart and had given me one night when we sat in my room and waited for all my dad's friends to leave.

There's one last item—a Matchbox Indy car. The tires barely roll and the paint is almost completely worn off from where I carried it with me everywhere, but I still see the shiny red paint. I still remember the elaborate tracks I'd make in my mind. And how I'd clutch it in my hand while I sat riveted to the television next to my dad for the one thing he'd make time to do with me, watch Indy racing.

Tears unexpectedly burn my eyes as I stare at this little piece of my past that somehow became such a huge part of my future. For the first time in forever, I wonder what my dad would say if he knew what I did for a living. Shouldn't even think about that piece of shit, but at the same time, I wonder.

And that makes my mind shift to Colton. To the man who stepped up to the plate and took me as his own when no one else would. To the father I let down because I was too goddamn chickenshit to talk to him.

I set the old car back down beside my other mementos in despair at the depressing amount of things I have to represent the first seven years of my life.

"You okay?" Her voice is soft and her brown eyes are compassionate when I look up to meet them.

"Yeah. I'm just . . . I don't know. I'm disappointed there's not more and at the same time relieved there's not the ticking time bomb I expected in there . . . if that makes any sense at all."

"It does. It makes perfect sense."

I exhale loudly and sit down on the bed beside her. The mattress dips, the old cardboard box falls onto the floor, and I grab her hand to stop her from getting up to retrieve it. "Yes. No. I don't know." She laughs softly at the phrasing and links her fingers with mine.

"What's bugging you?"

"I'm pissed at myself." I rifle through the perfect stacks she just spent time organizing and I love how she doesn't rush me to finish the thought. There's something about her silence that is comforting and encouraging. "I mean, *why*? I did all this, caused all of this bullshit for this box? And this is all there is? I hurt my family, fucked over the trust people had put in me, possibly screwed up my career, and for what? For a report I knew deep down wasn't true and for some small trinkets of a life I'm probably glad I didn't have to live?" My voice rises as I throw my hands up and walk back to look out the window, where the sky is darkening.

"Zan—"

"Shouldn't I at least get some kind of closure? Some kind of valid explanation so I don't look like the asshole I was when I have to go back and apologize to my family?"

God. Even that makes me sound like a prick. Like I'm not man enough to admit I overreacted and lashed out for no reason. *Fuck, this is fucked.*

"Zander."

"What?" I hear myself snap at her and the minute I do, I cringe in regret. "I'm sorry, Getty, it's just—" My words are cut off when I look to where she's pulling something out of the box as she picks it up from the floor. "What's that?"

Her eyes lift to meet mine. "The bottom flap was stuck. We didn't see it. When the box fell off the bed, it jostled it loose."

She hands me the white envelope, and I see that my name is scribbled on the front, with two hearts scrawled on either side of it that match the one my mom put above the *i* in her signature. My eyes flash up to Getty's in shock and then back down.

Moving closer to the lamp, I perch on the edge of the bed and slide my finger under the lip of the sealed letter. It gives instantly, time lessening the adhesive's effectiveness. When I look up, Getty is softly shutting the door behind her to give me privacy.

As if she already knows whatever is in this envelope is going to knock me on my ass.

With a lump in my throat and unsteady fingers, I carefully pull the paper from the envelope and unfold it.

*Dear Zander—*

*If you're getting this letter, something has happened to me. He's finally followed through on his threats. I know you're scared and you're sad, but don't be. I will always be with you. The greatest gift I've ever received was getting to be your mommy, so please, always remember how much I love you. You are my heart, my moon, my sun, and my stars. Please never doubt or forget that.*

*I'm sure you have so many questions and all I can hope is that maybe when you are older, this can help you make sense of everything that has happened.*

*Love can be pure. Love can be fierce. It can be volatile. It can turn black. But even when it does, you can't always stop loving. The way I love you is pure. Nothing can ever take that away from us. The way I love your dad is all four of those things, even the black. It's the kind of love that's almost as bad as the drugs he loves.*

*I've tried to leave. We've stayed in a shelter. We've stayed with friends. But I'm weak. I can't turn the love off. Even now when it's black. Even knowing that if I walked away, I could protect you better. But I couldn't. I've placed calls anonymously to CPS, telling them to check on the little boy in our house, in hopes that they'd see your dad's addiction and make him get help. Then we'd be safe. Then we could start over.*

*I've failed you, Zee.*

*If you're reading this, I've failed the only thing I've ever done in my life that is perfect—YOU.*

*I'm so sorry.*

*But I need you to do something for me. I need you to remember this advice I have for you. Because while we might not have much, while I might be a weak woman who stayed when she should have left, while I have done so many things wrong, you are the*

*one thing I did right. So please, Zander . . . if you can
live your life with this in mind, then you will keep me
alive in your heart.*

*Love. Love fiercely. Love purely. Love blindly if
you want, but never let love turn black. If it turns
black, walk away and never look back. For me,
because I couldn't. Your heart only sees the good in
everyone right now. I know that won't last forever.
Love is incredibly powerful when it's right.*

*Live wildly. Not recklessly. Follow paths that
wander. Take roads that are fast. Chase your dreams.
Race into your future and forget about your past.*

*When you are older, find a woman who makes
you laugh. One who is strong and who can fight her
own battles because when you have to fight one
together, you'll be stronger knowing she can hold her
own. Treat her well. It's the little things that get lost in
the big picture. Don't forget this, Zee. Women like
grand gestures just to know that you didn't forget the
little things. And love her with all your heart. We only
accept the love we think we deserve, and you . . . you
deserve the universe.*

*Make mistakes. It's allowed. Don't get upset over
the little ones. Learn from the big ones. And whatever the mistake, right the wrong as soon as you can.
If you don't and you grow up to be anything like me,
you'll want to bury your head in the sand and put off
fixing it, refuse to admit you were wrong—but don't.
You might never get the chance to fix it. I didn't. If I
had, you wouldn't be reading this.*

*Have patience. But not too much. When there's
something you want, go after it. But if there's
something worth your while you want bad enough,
be patient.*

*I hope you never have to read this. That I'm
writing it as a reminder to myself why I need to leave
and get help. A wake-up call.*

*There's one more thing. You have something you
love almost as much as me. It goes everywhere with
you—even to bed. I left something for you inside it.*

*Remember when I told your dad I lost it? I fibbed
because I wanted to put it aside for you—just in case.
I hope this makes sense. You're such a smart boy,
you've probably already figured it out. I hope that
when you find it, it will bring you comfort.*

    *I love you, my Zander, my Zee-man, my Zee-bug.
I always will. Every time you feel the sun shine on
your face, that's me wrapping you in my arms and
hugging you from Heaven.*

                                      *Remember me always.*
                                            *Mommy*

I can barely breathe. I look again at the letter, ink splattered with my mom's tears. My thoughts are all over the place. Salt on my lips. Tears, when I don't cry. I wipe them off my cheeks. The letter trembles in my hand.

Then I read it again.

The numbness that burned within me for so long aches like a bitch, but I swear to God it's because I've finally found some peace.

*She knew.* That's all I can think over and over. She knew he would kill her and loved me as much as I remember she did and needed me to be okay.

*She really loved me.* What a stupid thought, a bittersweet emotion that threatens to overwhelm me.

"Getty."

I don't even know if I say it out loud or if I'm just thinking it, but when she pushes open the door, I get my answer. One look at me, and she's across the room with her arms around my waist in an instant.

I can't speak. Don't know what to say, how to explain, so I shove the letter at her so she can understand.

Still lost in my own storm of emotion, I watch her read it. Her bottom lip trembling. Her other hand flying up to cover her mouth. Something clicks in my mind. A moment of clarity amid the haze. And I scramble for my suitcase shoved in the bottom of the closet.

I'm a madman. Throwing shit out of the way, unzipping it, flinging it open to find the one thing I grabbed at the last second on the way out the door before I left home. The errant thought to grab the only thing I had from my childhood, the ever-constant security blanket of sorts to maybe help with the sting of the goddamn box that had shown up in my life.

And of course after the fact I felt like such a pussy for grabbing it that I left the damn thing in my suitcase. Made it easier so I wouldn't have to explain to Getty why a grown man toted around a ragged, lumpy, threadbare stuffed dog.

In haste I grab the dog, my childhood lifeline after my mother died, and fall back to my ass on the floor.

"Do you think . . . ?"

Getty's voice startles me. I almost forgot she was there. But when I look up to meet her tearstained face, I know she's thinking the same thing I am. She's off the bed as my hands press and push at the lumpy stuffing inside the damn dog.

They are the same lumps that have always been there. The ones I've worried through the outside cover when I rocked myself to bed as a little kid, scared and mute from the fear. Lost in my own mind from the sadness.

Getty runs out of the room and returns in seconds with scissors, her eyes alive with encouragement as she hands them to me. "On the seam in the belly," she says as she shows me. "I can sew that back together like new."

Excitement and emotion and every other fucking thing I can't even name courses through me as I try to steady the blade and snip a small opening in the seam. Carefully I make a two-inch-size hole, drop the scissors, and use my fingers to dig around inside. I can't feel shit other than stuffing clumped together and turned stiff from age. The high hopes I had of finding this one last thing from my mother slowly crashing.

And then I hit something hard with my fingertip. My breath hitches. My heart races. The little circle inside the doggy that I used to rub my fingers around and always thought was just a part sewn inside.

"What is it?" Getty's voice is loaded with the same emotion that I feel.

I know before I pull it from the hole. Know that it's my mother's way of letting me keep a piece of her with me forever.

I put the small gold band between my thumb and forefinger and hold it up so Getty can see. "It's her wedding ring."

She gasps.

I'm paralyzed. Swamped with memories.

Her arms go around me.

I break.

Every fucking thing I've been holding in since I was seven years old comes out.

The anger. The hate. The loneliness. The relentless questions. The need to feel my mother's love again. The guilt.

Every single piece.

Except her love for me.

Because I know that was true.

# Chapter 30

**Repair List**

~~Replace Front Step—third one~~

~~Replace Missing Roof Shingles—Wet is only good in one place~~

Back Deck = Death Trap

~~Fix Lock on Patio Door—Sorry, Mr. Ax Murderer~~

~~Fix Bathroom Mirror~~

~~Clean Out & Fix Rain Gutter Spouts~~

~~Repair Shutters~~

Add Handrail to Front Steps & Paint

~~Connect Internet for God's Sake~~

~~Boat Shit I Don't Understand~~

Bulldoze House and Rebuild ☺

~~Electrician—Call one~~

~~Plumber—Creaky pipes~~

Have sex with ~~Kiss~~ the Repair Guy

The sun is shining and the ferry's horn sounds off a warning that a new wave of tourists is heading ashore, but as we walk through town, my mind's focused on the man beside me, holding my hand.

And on the dwindling repair list on the counter I've set to memory. Each item that gets crossed off means one fewer day with him.

I have to try not to be sad; this was how our story was scripted to play out. I've come to terms with it more in the last few days after seeing a more lighthearted Zander. I knew him only with the weight of the unknown resting on his shoulders. And now that it's been lifted, he's still the same guy he was before, but there's a significant change. He's more carefree. His smile is broader. He's not so moody.

That alone, watching the man I love live a happier life, will make saying good-bye to him a bit easier. Knowing I helped him get what he came here for and he in turn helped me overcome my past when it caught up with me.

*Who the hell am I kidding?* I'm going to bawl like a freaking baby, eat tons of ice cream, and paint dark stormy seas and skies again when he's gone . . . but at least it was by my own choice. I chose to walk into this relationship with Zander when I knew the end before it began. Such a weird, liberating thing to have for myself after being controlled for so many years.

*Carpe diem, Getty.*

The thought really strikes me for some reason. Like if I really mean the saying, then I'd better do something about it. And so without preamble I tug on Zander's hand. He stops to look at me, but I only catch a millisecond of the confusion on his face before I slant my lips over his.

I love the sudden movement of his body, the hitch in his breath. Even better, I love how, within a second, his hand slides against my lower back and pulls me into him so he can deepen the kiss.

He tastes like desire and the chocolate ice cream we shared moments ago. I think I'll always equate him with that newly awakened sensation he's brought out in me.

Our tongues meet, hands press our bodies closer, and our lips express our need. The tourists littering the sidewalk have to walk around us, and for once, I really don't care who is watching. Because it feels like it's just him. And me. And he's not going to leave and I'm not going to cry and all will be well.

The warmth of his kiss allows me to believe the fantasy for a few seconds before Mable's loud, identifiable laugh sounds off to the right of us. "Well, thank God. It's about time you kissed her senseless, Zander."

Zander breaks the kiss but not before I can feel his lips curve into a smile. "You keep denying me, Mable, so I had no choice but to move on. A man has needs after all."

She throws her head back and laughs, bosom jiggling and cheeks turning red from the attention. "Young man," she says with a shake of her head and a point of her finger, "I think that lass right there is taking care of your needs just fine by the looks of that kiss."

"No complaints here, ma'am," he says with a lift of his eyebrows and a smile well into dimple territory.

"Such a gentleman." Mable pats her chest in mock swoon. "Oh, Getty! We got a great bid on that sequined cocktail number today. It's going to bring in some good—"

"Excuse me a second," Zander says unexpectedly as he sees someone over my shoulder. I watch him jog over to where Liam stands out in front of the bar. Zander calls his name to get his attention as I turn back to Mable. She continues on about some of my dresses up for sale, but my attention remains focused on Zander and Liam, whose eyes keep glancing back at me.

We meet up a few minutes later. "What was that all about?" I ask, hating that I suddenly sound nosy.

"Nothing really. Just wanted to ask Liam a few things." He falls silent, which means my curiosity is piqued.

"What were—?"

"He wanted to give me this," he says with a laugh as he holds out a white Lazy Dog Bar T-shirt like the staff has to wear, with the logo prominently displayed across the chest of it.

"Always the opportunist. He's probably hoping you'll be photographed with it when you head to the race or something and give the bar some notoriety."

"I'll wear it." He shrugs. "Although I like how you wear yours much better," he says with a wink, referring to how all the servers tie the back of their shirts to make them a bit tighter for the male patrons' benefit.

"I'm sure you do." I laugh and smile at him.

"It's even better when you're not wearing it, though." I go to playfully hit him in the arm, but he catches my arm before I connect and presses an unexpected kiss to the top of my hand. While I'm startled, he acts casual when he links his fingers with mine and starts walking.

"You going to be okay while I'm gone?"

"Yes." *No.*

The question stops my heart, but I try not to show it. I know he's referring to his flight the day after next. And of course I feel ridiculously stupid that I'm panicking over how this will be the first time we're going to be apart in almost three months.

But I know my feelings are haywire over more than that. Once he goes back to his real life, the anchor holding him here on the island will slowly lose its hold.

He's addressed the reason he ran in the first place. Going home means he's going to try to right the wrongs with his family. If he's successful, he'll have no reason to stay here anymore.

"I feel like after everything that happened the other night, I should be the one asking you that question. How are you doing?"

He blows out a breath as we take the turn off the main street to start back home. The weight of his thoughts fills the silence. "I'm good," he finally says. "A part of me wants to be angry at her for not getting out when she clearly knew what was going to happen, but I'm just so tired of being angry, Getty. It's all I've known for what feels like so long. And being pissed isn't going to change anything."

He sounds very different from the man I met a few months ago. His state of mind, his openness to introspection, and what he's going to take away from the heart-wrenching letter his mother left for him.

"I agree," I murmur, knowing these are the conclusions he needs to come to on his own, and so the less I say, the better.

"I think what I feel is closure more than anything. A small sense of peace that I've never been able to have. I mean, I may not like her answers about why she stayed with him, but at least I have them and at least they were in her voice, not something I conjured up to make her the martyr and him the monster. And stupidly enough, hearing her tell me she loved me in her own words . . . that made all the difference."

"It's not stupid at all." I lean my head against his shoulder, a smile on my lips, my heart swelling with pride for him. "It's validation for your feelings. Hearing the person you love tell you they love you back is something every person wants to hear."

# Chapter 31

I forgot how much I missed this. How much I needed this. And it's crazy to me that I've had no desire to paint over the past few weeks—even after the dinner with my father and the chaos with Ethan—until now, on the eve of Zander's leaving.

Maybe that says a lot about where I stand now in my life. My father and Ethan can no longer affect me. But Zander . . . by the flurry and fervor in which I've lost myself to the bold colors on canvas, he most definitely makes me feel.

I'm just not sure if that's a good thing or a bad thing.

By the looks of what's taking shape before me, it's an all-new thing. Instead of blended soft colors of a sunset over turbulent water, the painting depicts sleek lines and defined edges. It might be called abstract at best and crappy at worst, but my first attempt at a moving object is much harder than the fluidity of nature.

"Wow." Zander's voice startles me. The absence of the hammer noise outside had gone unnoticed, my earbuds falling out overlooked, while my work once again consumed me.

"You think?" I set the brush down and look over my shoulder at him where he stands.

"Yeah. It's actually incredible."

He leans in closer while I scoot my chair back to get a different perspective. I angle my head and stare at it through judgmental eyes. The outline is just enough to make out the image of an Indy car flying across the canvas. It's blurry on purpose, but I'm still not happy with it.

"It needs work yet," I muse as I shade and frame the image more in my mind. "It's only half-done and I've never really painted anything so technical like this before, so who knows how it will—"

"Shush." He places his hands on my shoulders and begins to rub at the knots from my sitting hunched over a canvas for however long I've been here. "Quit being so critical of your talent. I can't wait to see the finished product."

"Well, I'm glad, because I was painting it for you." *And I've never felt the need to paint anything for anyone.* The thought ghosts through my mind. And all I can think is that I need to give him something to remember me by.

"Thank you. I love it already." He presses an absent kiss to the top of my head, which causes tears I refuse to acknowledge to burn in my throat. Such a casual gesture from him but so very telling of how far we've come since that first night when we made a toast to *us*.

"What are you up to?" I let my head fall back some, his fingers magic on my sore muscles.

"I finished up a few things on the deck and just wanted to see what the world-famous painter was up to."

My smile is automatic. How ironic that he brought up a memory from that night out when I was thinking about it too.

"Oh, and here I thought you were finally coming to have me paint that nude of you."

His laugh is sharp and fills the room with the suggestion lacing its edges. "You were, were you?"

"Yeah, but I'm not sure I have the right paint to give you the look you were going for."

"What look is that?" he murmurs.

*"Pretty."*

I yelp out a laugh as he spins my chair around without warning to face him. He braces his hands over my forearms on the armrests and looks at me, eyebrows raised, a lopsided smirk on his face, and eyes darkened with desire. Our laughter ceases instantly. The air of the room quickly heats from the chemistry sparking between us.

My breath catches in my chest. My hands tense on the arms of the chair. His look alone is causing my synapses to misfire. But this time, I'm much the wiser.

I want to use the match to light the fire. I know how good his burn is.

"Say it again, Socks. *Pretty* please," he murmurs against my mouth before dipping his tongue between my parted lips and giving me a quick taste of the hunger inside him before pulling away—leaving me wanting so very much more. "Give me a reason."

My lips curl as he leans back. My nipples harden against the cotton of my shirt from his proximity. The heat of his hands on my arms burns in the best way possible.

"A reason for what?" I'm breathless. Needy. Desperate for him.

"To make you beg." His smile taunts. The look in his eyes tempts me. The lick of his tongue between his lips does all kinds of funny things to my insides. The intent in his words has me pressing my thighs together.

*And oh, how I want him to make me beg.*

I feign nonchalance. Try to act unaffected, but it's impossible when he's standing over me and every part of my body is aching for his touch.

But I try.

"How would you make me beg?"

His laugh sounds deep and rich. "You think you can bat those gorgeous eyes at me, act like you're all sweet and innocent, when I know exactly what you want and just how to give it to you?"

"How do you know what I want?" My voice is coy, lips pursed, as I look up and play this game with him.

He laughs again, but this time it sounds like his hands feel when they run over my skin: smooth with a hint of roughness and a whole lot of desire. "I was born to give you what you want, Socks."

It's my turn to laugh. My body hums with anticipation.

There's a hint of edge to the gleam in his eye and the sexual side of me he's awakened really wants to test it.

*"So. Damn. Pretty . . ."*

His lips quirk. His eyebrows lift. His breath catches. He stands up ever so slowly, mouth sliding into a smile that's part victorious, part devious. I wonder what I just awakened in him at the same time as I can't wait to find out.

"Stand up," he demands, eyes daring, fingers twitching as they hang by his side.

I rise slowly. My heart pounds as anticipation becomes adrenaline. He steps forward and doesn't touch a single part of my body aside from the hem of my shirt as he pulls it up. "Lift," he orders, and I comply without question.

The only break in eye contact we have is when the shirt passes over my face, but we instantly find each other the minute it passes. His breath feathers over my cheeks as he lifts his shirt over his head to match my state of undress.

"This isn't about me trying to control you, Getty." He leans forward and brushes a kiss to my lips, his voice a soothing timbre now. Hands behind his back, our bodies are only inches apart. "This isn't about me getting off on ordering you around." An openmouthed kiss on the side of my neck, the scrape of his stubble as he rubs his chin over it. "This is you handing over the control of your sexual pleasure right now." The other side of my neck this time, no urgency in his voice, but rather he sounds like he has all the time in the world. "This is you trusting me, Getty." He leans back from me and I swear the hair on my body stands on end just to try to reach out so I can touch him in some way. "This is you, giving me your body." His fingers slide inside the waistband of my yoga pants. "Your mind." Strong hands continue their slide down the outsides of my thighs until my pants and panties fall to the floor. "Your consent."

I inhale a shaky breath. His words entice. Intrigue. Inflame. He wants me to let him have control when he knows I have issues, but he's created a situation where my body is aching to give control up to him. And I know there's no way in hell I'm going to say no.

Desire's thick in my throat as he stands to full height and steps toward me. I hear the wheels of my chair as he kicks it to the side so he can stand behind me. One finger slides down the line of my spine. My back arches at his touch. My mouth gasps. My eyes fall closed.

The heat of his breath hits right at my ear. His voice feels like aural foreplay. "I was outside working on the deck and all I could think about was how bad I wanted to taste you. Dip my head between those tan thighs of yours and flick my tongue over your clit, work you up nice and good. Your-hands-pulling-at-my-hair kind of good. Then I'd slide down to your pussy so I can taste how goddamn sweet you are when you come."

Dear. God.

"But a *pretty* boy wouldn't do that. No," he murmurs, teeth nipping at the lobe of my ear. He nudges my head to the side so he can run his tongue along the curve of my neck, then back. He then places openmouthed kisses from the nape of my neck to the other ear. "A *pretty* boy would lay you down, go through the motions to get you off, but he'd be too afraid to get *dirty*." He draws the last word out, his voice low, raspy. And yet he still denies my body the touch of his hands. "And I like dirty, Getty. I like hands-on." He purrs the promise despite removing his lips from my skin.

My body feels electric. Needing the connection with him. Desperate for him to make this current between us spark.

"I like my fingers slowly working in and out of your pussy, my mouth sucking on your nipples or kissing behind your knees, my dick rock-hard with wanting you, and my control holding on by a thread, begging it to break *kind of dirty*."

My mouth goes dry. Between my thighs goes wet. This gentle, considerate lover of mine has all of a sudden turned into a man on a mission to seduce.

The old me, the one in designer clothes and perfect makeup, would have blushed at his words while secretly getting hot and bothered and would have mentally filed them away to think about later when she was alone. But the new me, the one he's sexually awakened with his considerate touch and evident attraction to me, stands up and takes notice. She waves her hand frantically in the air and says, *Pick me. Choose me. Do those things to me.*

"Do you still want me *pretty*, Socks . . . or would you rather I be *dirty*?" I can feel the warmth of his breath on my neck.

"Zander?" His name comes out part plea, part question.

"Begging already?" A soft taunt of a chuckle. "And I haven't even started yet."

He steps back behind me. Fingers undoing the clasp of my bra. The scrape of the straps down my arms.

"So damn beautiful . . . Come, sit down."

I turn to meet his eyes, the steamy look in them seduction all in itself, before I move to where he's pointing: an ottoman that runs along the foot of the bed. I sit dead center against a pillow he's placed there, our gazes still locked as he kneels before me. When his hands finally reach out, they touch my ankles. The spark ignites at the apex of my thighs as he slowly pulls my ankles as far apart as possible, my knees falling against the seat.

My arms are next. He directs them to the top of the bed's footboard, then curls my fingers in position around its edges.

"Keep them like that," he warns as he stands, my body screaming in protest when he steps away from me. "While tying them there might be fun, I don't think you're ready to give me that much control yet."

My body trembles at the thought. An excited fear I can't describe but think I could handle if he was at the helm.

"Another time. That I can promise you." He stands before me, eyes scraping over every single inch of me. Such a different type of scrutiny from what I'm used to. One that says *I want to touch every single part of you. Take and taste and sate and claim until you can't handle any more.*

And while he's looking at me, I definitely get my fill of him: his tanned chest, the happy trail that leads below where his jeans hang low on his hips, the bulge straining against the seam of the denim, his bare feet. When I look back up to meet his eyes, there's a lift of his brow, a kind of *you like what you see?* smirk on his lips, and before I can find an adequate nonverbal response, my eyes are drawn back down to his hands.

With a methodical slowness, they start undoing his jeans, shoving them down, and he steps out of them. All six-foot-plus of him stands back up to full height, giving me more than an eyeful of every firm, rippling, desirable inch of him. My nipples harden. My breath grows shallow.

"I have half a mind to paint you like that. Just how you are. So you can see what I see when I look at you. Sexy." He takes a step toward me. "Confident." A step. "Beautiful." Another step. "Innocent." He's between my thighs again. My face angles up to his. "But I'm not a painter, Getty." He drops to his knees. "So I'll have to show you in a different way."

With eyes still on mine and his hands on his own thighs, Zander leans forward and slides his tongue between the seam of my sex. I can't hold back a moan or the unabashed writhe of my hips. The eroticism of him watching me react to the devastation of that single swipe of a tongue is more powerful than anything I've ever experienced with a man.

Even better, he doesn't stop. Yet he takes his time. With tongue and lips and stubble all affecting me in different ways. His attentions make my muscles tense and every nerve ache and want and need, before he backs off and looks up at me with my arousal on his lips and a gleam in his eye. Just as fast, he's diving back in to start the buildup all over again.

On the third time I'm so pent up with need that as he begins to pull his mouth away, my hands grip what I can of his short hair and hold his head against me. It's his chuckle that reverberates against my sex, though, not his tongue like I wanted.

"Did you just beg, Getty?"

"Yes. No. I don't know!" I'm breathless. Worked up. Desperate. And his laugh is not what I need right now.

"Do you want to know what happens when you beg?" My eyes flash back to his and the mewl falls from my mouth as his fingers find me, part me, and begin to work in and out of me. He watches my reaction for a few seconds until my head falls back as the sensations he's evoking prove to be too much.

And then when he adds his tongue to the mix, it's me bucking my hips into his hand and my voice begging for more, because if this is his type of punishment, then I'll take it.

"Zander." His name on my lips as my body climbs higher and higher. His fingers stroke. My nerves react. His tongue is godlike. "Oh God." My hands tense in his hair. "Yes."

And then nothing.

My head whips up as he leans back, uses his fingers to coat his cock in my wetness, and begins to stroke himself. Slowly. Adeptly. Thoroughly. Thumb sliding over the precum on his head before the palm of his hand slides all the way down until it hits the base. And then repeats the process all over.

*This.* This is the repercussion of my begging. He's withholding my orgasm while making me watch him chase his.

And holy hell, I'm not sure if it's much of a punishment, because I am so turned on by the sight of him, by what I do to him, by seeing my arousal on him, that I'm afraid to look away for a single second.

But when I force myself to take my eyes from his hand as it begins to pick up the pace on his cock, his eyes burn into mine. And that single look alone is almost as arousing as watching him jack himself off. *Almost.*

Especially as our gazes hold and the unmistakable sound of him working himself harder begins to fill the room. His teeth dig into his lower lip. His breathing speeds up. His head falls back and a guttural groan overshadows all other sound.

And I can't help myself. I've never seen something so damn sexy or been so aroused in my life as I am from watching him. My hand goes between my thighs without thought. My fingers slip into my wetness before sliding back up and circling over my clit, already swollen and sensitized from his touch.

I fight my own need to close my eyes and fall under the haze of pleasure, because I know watching Zander is enough to help me get there. The sense of voyeurism has brought me to new heights of arousal.

The thought of getting off watching your lover get off does something incredible to me.

The visual before me and the emotions within me create a potent combination that has my breath growing shallow, my body aching, as I watch the strain of Zander's forearm, the swell of his dick, his crest disappear between his thumb and forefinger before coming back out to his visceral groans. I falter momentarily and close my eyes under the ecstasy of the moment.

And when I open my eyes, Zander's blue gaze looks back at me with absolutely no barriers between us. In an instant, every single boundary between us is erased.

Because letting someone see you pleasure yourself is almost more intimate than pleasuring each other. The veil is dropped. You're completely exposed in a primal intimacy.

The moment he shoves up, I scoot my ass off the edge of the bench. The jingle of his belt as he picks his jeans up off the floor and digs in the pocket. My hand still circling my clit gently. The rip of foil.

"Getty . . ." The groan of my name is part *Are you ready?* and part warning he's not going to last long. And it's okay, because I'm so primed, neither will I.

"God, yes . . ."

I catch the quick flash of his grin, followed by a moaned, "Fuck," as he parts my folds and slides into me without stopping, from root to tip. His fingers dig into the sides of my hips as he tries to hold on to some restraint.

But I can't. Mine's gone. I rub my finger over my clit, my hips lifting out of necessity to drag the crest of his cock over the sensitive bundle of nerves that are burning for him. And once he hits where I need him to, I begin to buck my hips against his to urge him on, to tell him what I need.

Restraint has snapped. Control lost. In an instant we're a mass of hips thrusting and voices crying out and hands grasping and fingers digging. The room fills with a symphony of noises but ends with our both calling each other's name moments apart as we succumb to the moment, to the challenge, and to each other.

# Chapter 32

"Getty."

The room is still dark, the clock on the nightstand reading three fifty-five a.m. My mind tries to clear away the haze of sleep as Zander's hand runs up and down the length of my back.

"Mmm?"

"I've gotta go, sleepyhead."

Now, those words get my attention. My mind startles awake and I shove up to a seated position.

"No. Don't get up. Go back to sleep."

"No. I'll get up."

"Please, go back to bed. I just wanted to say good-bye before I left." He leans forward and presses a kiss on the top of my head, his lips lingering there long enough that I wrap my arms around his hips and just hold tight.

"I programmed Rylee's phone number in your phone. Just in case you can't get ahold of me and need me. You can call her. She'll know how to find me."

"'Kay. Thank you." My face presses harder against him and I draw in his scent. The leather of his belt feels cool on my cheek.

Another kiss on my head. "See you in a few days."

He steps back. Our fingers link out of habit. As always, the need to connect seems instinctive on both our parts.

"Fly safe. Have fun. Good luck."

"I'm gonna need it." I appreciate his chuckle and return it with a smile he can't see in the dark. Then sleep calls me back as my eyelids start feeling heavy.

"Bye, Socks."

Our hands release.

"Bye," I murmur.

His footsteps down the hall.

The sound of the front door.

The click of the dead bolt.

"I love you, Zander."

I fall back on the pillow. Close my eyes. And don't even bother to wipe the lone tear that escapes and slides down my cheek.

Friends with benefits don't kiss you on the head good-bye in the dark of the morning.

They leave a note on the counter.

They text from the airport.

They don't kiss you good-bye.

# Chapter 33

ZANDER

The infield is abuzz. The vibration of a car testing on the track rumbles in my chest. The rev of a motor elsewhere adds to the sound. The sensations are like a second skin.

I feel at home. And strangely I feel out of place.

My hat lies low over my eyes, my bag slung on my shoulder, as I search for the coach and hope that the man I flashed my credentials to minutes ago doesn't put two and two together. It didn't seem like he knew who I was, so hopefully my appearance will stay under the radar—this is something I need to do on my own time frame.

Because fuck if I'm not going to need time and courage to go with it when I face Colton.

I hit the row where all of the racers' coaches sit, massive motor homes that serve as a refuge for the racers while we're at the track, and instantly spot the one I've sat in for countless hours over the years. The trepidation I'd felt increasing with each footstep into the raceway dissipates instantly at the knowledge Rylee's in there.

Crossing the distance, I climb up the steps, peek my head inside the unlocked door, and knock, calling out her name. "Ry?"

The look on her face . . . her yelp in surprise . . . Then she rushes the few feet to me and almost knocks me over with the force of her hug. And I just hold on tight, emotion taking over as so many things hit me.

How strong her love is for me. How she picked up the broken pieces of a seven-year-old me and helped put me back together. How she didn't give up on me when so many others would have discarded me as damaged goods.

The things you forget when you're in your day-to-day life. The things you appreciate when you step back into it with an all-new perspective.

What kind of person gets the chance to have two mothers love him as fiercely as I have?

*A damn lucky one.*

And it's the expression in her tear-filled eyes and the smile wide on her lips when she pulls back that reinforces this fact and guts me all at the same time, knowing what I put her through.

"You're here!" she finally sputters out before pulling me against her once more like I'm going to disappear again. And I do the only thing I can, laugh out loud and hug her tighter. The subtle scent of vanilla she's worn for as long as I can remember fills my nose and makes me really feel at home.

Once her surprise is out of the way and she's calmed down, then asked a million trivial questions, made a hundred observations—I look tan; I look good; where was I?—we sit down together on the couch. Silence descends as she gives me the time I need to say what I want to say.

Just like Getty does.

The thought flickers and makes me smile as I take a deep breath and lean forward with my elbows on my knees.

"I'm sorry," I finally tell her with a nod of my head. Her violet eyes search mine when I look up and meet them. Voicing my feelings has never been an easy thing for me, even with her. Add to it the situation I've put myself in, and I don't know where to begin. So I start with the truth. "A few months ago something was delivered to my house. . . ."

I proceed to tell her everything. The uncertainty I felt about the box. The shock over the autopsy report. The hurt that I hadn't known. The betrayal I felt because they had to have known. The rash of emotions I went through. My fight with Colton. The hurtful things I said to him. My trip to the island. Helping to repair Smitty's house. How it felt good to use my hands. And my unexpected roommate. Fighting with her. How by watching her go through her battles, I realized I held on to my anger like a shield. Wore it like a grudge. Used it to punish myself.

And then I tell her about finally opening the box. The unexpected letter. My mom's wishes for me. Her wedding ring sewn in the dog.

Tears fill her eyes. Her hand covers her mouth. She nods while tears slide down her cheeks. Her expression tells me she hurts for me. That she's proud of me. That she loves me.

But she doesn't utter a single word before I blow out a breath and say the words that began the conversation. "I'm so sorry. All I can tell you is that Colton was right. I needed to step away from everything, to take a long look at myself and deal with my own shit. I'm sorry I didn't let you in, Ry. But I was hurt. Thought you'd lied to me. Kept something so important from me, when now I know it doesn't matter. Whether you knew or didn't know, you were being a parent. You were protecting me from the bad things, just like my mom tried to protect me from the stuff in my house. That's your job." While I'm talking, Rylee reaches out and covers my hands with hers. A mother's touch. A way to tell me she understands. "I told myself I couldn't come back until I faced whatever the box held and finished the repairs for Smitty. I wanted to prove I'm a man of my word again. That I'm different from the man who hurt his family, his team, himself . . . and I did face it. It gave me the closure I never really knew I needed but now understand was what I was always seeking. I still have to finish a few minor things on Smitty's house, but I had to come back and face Colton. There's nothing I can say to you other than thank you for giving me time, for letting me figure it out on my own, and . . . I'm sorry."

Her lips spread in that soft smile that has been there encouraging me, comforting me, laughing with me for most of my life, and I immediately know it's going to be okay. "You don't need to apologize to me, Zander. A parent loves their child no matter what they do. That's just how it is. While I wished you would have talked to me so that maybe I could have explained to you and forgone all of this, I'm glad now that you didn't." My heard jerks over to her, surprised by her words. "I think figuring the answers for yourself was ten times more powerful. It will mean more to you. You'll trust yourself now."

I nod my head. Clear the emotion clogging in my throat by taking in a deep breath.

"I knew, Zander," she confesses softly. "But you are right. It was my job as your guardian and then your parent to protect you. Did it really matter for me to tell you about the autopsy findings? Your mother wasn't going to survive whether you touched the scissors or not. So why add that burden to your already aching soul? I made the choice. I'm sorry it caused you pain, because that's exactly what I didn't want to happen, but I did what I thought and still think was the best for you." She wipes a tear away and I hate the sight of it, that I've made her cry, but can't do anything about it.

"I've missed you. I've worried about you. You were out of control when you left and I feared the worst, because I know pain like that can cause you not to care about yourself. I can't tell you how happy I am to see you whole and healthy . . . and changed."

"I didn't bring it with me, but I'll show you the letter—"

"No." Her smile is kind, eyes compassionate.

"No?"

"That letter is something you've waited over twenty years to find, Zander. It's her gift to you. I don't need to see it. The man before me who's all grown up is all I need to see to know how powerful her words were. Okay?"

"Okay."

She stares at me, eyes narrowing, and a knowing smile plays at the corner of her mouth. "I'm glad you met whoever this Getty woman is, because it means you didn't go through it all by yourself, and as your mother, I'm so glad you weren't alone."

"I'm glad I met her too." My mind drifts back to that first night we met and I can't help but smile.

We talk a bit more about the island, about my brothers, catching up, and I promise her I'm here for a few days before I leave, but we completely avoid talking about the one person that I still need to speak to.

"Is he in the pits?"

Her smile is automatic. The love in her eyes genuine. "Yes. He already tested. He's with Becks making adjustments or bullshitting. One or the other."

My mood doesn't lighten at her teasing comment, because this is the tough part. "I need to go talk to him. Make things right." I rise from the couch and kiss the top of her head.

"Zander."

I turn back at the sound of her voice just as I'm about to step out the door. "Just so you know, Smitty never told us where you were. And Colton never told me what happened in that hotel room. He's kept that between the two of you, even though whatever happened has been eating at him. He's spent a lot of time sitting in your trailer with your car. Not sure what he's thinking about when he's there . . . but I just thought you should know that."

Fuck.

I nod my head in acknowledgment. My chest hurts.

Time to make amends.

To just jump.

# Chapter 34

ZANDER

"Look what the cat dragged in!" Garret shouts across pit alley.

"Motherfucker. He's alive! Alive!" Brad mocks me as he rolls out from his creeper at the nose of the car.

"The love. I feel it!" I shout back to them, grinning as I walk into the garage—my second home. Some crew members pat my back in greeting as I walk by. Loud welcomes surround me.

There are a few of the guys who peer at me from beneath the bills of baseball hats. Leery of my return. The ones I pissed off or let down. Or they know Colton's bite and aren't sure how he'll react to my being here.

I meet Smitty's surprised eyes over the lid of a Snap-on tool chest, but he doesn't say a word. Instead the questions are written all over his face. I lift my chin toward the stairs, asking him for a single answer, and when he nods again, I know where I'll find Colton.

Heart in my throat, I take a deep breath as I start the short climb. Uncertainty about how he'll react makes my gut churn.

I hear their voices before I reach the top—Colton and his best friend and crew chief and my pseudo-uncle, Beckett Daniels. They're talking about a competitor, trying to figure the adjustments his team made that resulted in his trimming two-tenths off his lap time.

When I clear the landing, Becks is facing me, leaning against the counter behind him, and Colton is sitting with his back to me, feet propped up on the counter. Becks sees me first, his head startling, his conversation momentarily stopping midstream as his eyes lock with mine—a warning fired off to tread carefully—before he finishes his comment.

"You've got company," Becks says casually as he stands and cuffs him on the shoulder. "We'll finish this later."

"Get it ready, Becks." Becks's feet falter at Colton's words as he walks toward me. He stops, looks toward my dad, who simply nods in response, before he continues to the stairs where I stand, and gives me a quick hug, then heads down the stairs without another word.

The hum of a far-off engine is the only sound in the booth as I stand there and stare at Colton sitting just as he was, back to me, head faced toward the track. "You just gonna stand there all day, Zander?" His voice is quiet, devoid of emotion, and I shouldn't be surprised he knows it's me. He points to the chair a few feet away from him without looking back. "Take a seat."

But I hesitate, don't move. A part of me feels like I'm a completely different man from the last time we talked, almost four months ago, and if I do as he says, then I'm not projecting that. I wipe my hands on my jeans and set my shoulders as I prepare to say the things I need to say.

"Now's not the time to fuck with me. I'm not telling you to sit down as some sort of power play. I'm telling you to sit down because we're going to talk man-to-man. If you choose not to sit, you can turn your ass around and walk back out. Your choice."

I clear my throat. And I move my feet until I'm seated in the chair beside him. When I finally risk a glance over to him, his eyes are still focused on the track below, but he nods his head ever so slowly to acknowledge my presence.

We have a battle of wills against each other through the silence. He had the final word last time we spoke, his reprimand still sharp in my mind, and so I struggle with how to begin this when I know a simple "I'm sorry" isn't nearly enough.

"Did you see your mother?" he asks after a moment, eyes still pointed straight ahead.

"Yes."

"Good. She's missed you."

A part of me immediately starts wondering if he missed me too. My tongue is thick in my mouth. My heart pounds. And yet it feels so damn good to be here beside him. In that dominating presence of my teenage years where you're scared of the tongue-lashing you're about to get and yet revel in knowing he cares enough about you to give you one. His testosterone-laced version of love.

"I fucked up." Those definitely weren't the words I had planned to start this conversation with and yet they perfectly sum up the truth.

He nods slowly. Purses his lips. "Yes. Sure as shit you did."

"You were right," I begin.

"Remember that." He lifts a lone eyebrow but says nothing more.

"Something had happened and I didn't know how to cope. . . ." I carry on with my explanations for the second time in less than an hour. The difference is this time around it's much harder to explain.

I could read Rylee's body language, knew she understood, but he just sits face forward, expression stone cold, breathing completely even the entire time.

The silence stretches when I finish. My muscles are clenched so taut they ache. My knee jogs up and down.

"You came to me that morning . . . ," I continue, knowing I need to address the things I said to him now that I've explained the background behind it. "and there's no excuse for—"

"You're goddamn right there's no excuse," he shouts, his sudden reaction shocking me after his total silence. He turns to face me for the first time since I've been here. His green eyes burn with emotion. Fury. Disappointment. Hurt. Sadness. The same damn things that ran through his expression the last time I saw him.

I shove up out of the chair, the anger I thought I'd gotten rid of now back front and center and fueled with the bitter taste of rejection. My intention to come back here, explain what happened, and fix things without any more fallout suddenly feels way off base.

When I move across the small space, I can feel his eyes boring holes in my back the whole time. Taunting me. Daring me. Questioning. The stairs call out to me. I told myself that I was done with anger. I was over the pain. Why did I think it would be this easy to come back and apologize and step back into my place in his life?

My hands are on my neck. My head hung forward. Tension smothering the open air of the booth.

"Colton." My voice breaks, tone solemn. His name is the olive branch I extend. Whatever I need it to be to try to make this right, because I can't do this anymore. I can't be at odds with him. And it hits me. Of all the words I need to say, I know the ones that will matter the most.

"Speak."

"Thank you for coming to the hotel that day. For forcing me to hear truths I refused to listen to. *For firing me*." I shake my head, drop my hands, and turn to face him. I need him to see my face when I say this. To see that I've become the man he showed me how to be. The one I want to be. Our eyes lock again, but there's hope now as he waits for me to continue. "I can give you every bullshit excuse in the world as to why I did what I did, why I was hurting how I was, but in the end, it doesn't matter. None of it does. They'd only be words. We all have bullshit we have to deal with. I left pissed, refusing to acknowledge you were right, and wanting to prove the point that I needed no one. That I could handle everything on my own. And I did. But I also learned that anger gets me nowhere. That the truth is harder to face on your own. And yeah, I can do it on my own, but I don't want to. That's what family is for. To lean on when life gets tough."

"Are you fixed, then? Your shit all worked out?" His questions sound casual but have so much weight to them as we hold each other's glare.

"Yes, sir." I nod to reinforce my answer.

"Good, because it's my turn." A lift of his eyebrows in a nonverbal warning to see if I'm going to challenge him. "Number one: Family comes first. Always. We don't have to share the same blood, Zander, for me to care about you. You ever insult me again by telling me you're not my son, then there's going to be a whole helluva lot bigger problem than this. And then I'm going to be even more pissed because the fallout will break Rylee's heart, and that's something neither of us wants, so I suggest you watch your tongue next time you want to be an asshole to me. You can figure out something more creative to say." His voice is a quiet steel that's barely audible and yet I hear every single word and the implication behind it.

He rises to his feet, shoulders square to me, eyes boring into mine. "Number two: You've got a problem? You need to talk? Fucking talk. You're pissed at me? Think I'm lying to you because I say the goddamn sky is green? Confront me. Yell at me. Tell me it's blue. I don't give a flying fuck so long as you don't turn your back from your family and you don't disrespect me. But if for one second I think the sky being green is going to prevent you from being hurt, then I'll fight you on it till the goddamn cows come home. Lie to you if I have to. And I'll never apologize for it. Not once. Because you being okay is part of my job and the only thing that matters. And speaking of that, you need to blow off steam? Get on the track. Race the fucking wind and outrun your demons there. Nothing good's ever come from throwing them onto someone else. Understood?"

To an outsider his words might seem harsh, but to someone who knows him, they sound like love. I nod my head.

"Third, you ever insinuate again that racing is more important to me than you, you'll never touch the track again—I don't care how good you are." He stares at me, warning loud and clear, and waits till I nod in understanding before he continues. "A long time ago racing was all I had. It mattered more than anything to me. Then Rylee happened. And she changed everything. A man can love more than one thing, Zander. You need to remember that."

"Yes, sir."

"Lastly—your past? *You're. Not. Him.* A coward. A man who runs from his mistakes. I've spent too many nights in my life worried about the same fucking thing, so it's something you need to hear. You coming back here, having the courage to fix your mistakes, proves that point." His voice lightens some and he takes a step closer to me as his words dig deep within me, a salve to help heal the cracks still on my soul. He reaches out and puts his hand on my shoulder. "Leaving that hotel room was the hardest thing I've ever had to do. It killed me to walk away from you when I knew you were hurting . . . but it was worth every day I worried about you, because I couldn't be more proud of the man who just walked in here. I'm sorry you went through losing your mom all over again on your own. But I'm glad you got the closure you needed."

There's a moment that passes where I just shake my head disbelieving the last thing he said to me. But there's pride in his eyes now. Love. Acceptance.

He pulls me into a hug. And I feel like I can breathe for the first time since I stepped foot back on the track. I've righted a wrong and hopefully made my mom proud.

And him. And Rylee.

And Getty.

When he releases me, he hooks an arm around my neck and keeps me near him. "I missed you, Zee." His voice sounds gruff, emotion clouding it, as he tugs a little tighter on my neck.

For months I let the fear and the worry and the angst over what was going to happen when I returned wiggle doubt into my mind over the connection we shared. I let the concern that I had ruined this relationship keep me up many nights I was away.

Who knew watching Getty's father's warped sense of family obligation and getting the nerve to come back and apologize with this new view of what family means were all it would take to get this feeling of *rightness* back between us?

"I missed you too," I murmur with a huge, silent sigh of relief, a purge of the discord in my soul.

We stand together, father and son reunited—and better

for the time apart—taking in the one thing that flows through our blood just as strongly as our love for each other, the passion for the track. The adrenaline. The rush of speed.

So we stand in silence for a few moments, the sound track of our lives in a buzz all around us. It's comforting. In the same sense as the rustling of the trees on the island.

"So tell me about this girl," he says unexpectedly.

"Getty?"

"Cool name. Yeah. Her."

"There's not much to say really. There was a mix-up about the place and she was staying there. That's all."

"Uh-huh." It's all he says, followed by a nod of his head, before he steps away and takes a seat in his chair, eyes narrowed, lips pursed.

"What?"

"She the one you talked to?"

"Your point is what?" And we're right back to where we were *before*, him egging me on, fucking with me when I don't know what those amused green eyes of his are saying.

"She okay being there? That prick going to come back?"

I do a double take until I realize that in my explanation and apology I gave him way more than I realized I had. I told him about Getty and her father and Ethan. Dumbfounded, I look back toward the track for a moment. When did I start thinking of my time on the island as pertaining to both of us? As ours?

"Zander?"

"Sorry. Yeah," I stutter out an answer, try to clear my head. "I think he's gone for good. Besides, I had words with her boss, the bar owner; he's looking out for her while I'm gone."

"You're going back, then?" I can't gauge the tone of his voice. Don't know if it's surprise, acceptance, or dislike, but the fact that I don't even hesitate when I respond has him raising his eyebrows.

"Yes. I still have a few things to finish on the house."

"Just the house?"

I meet his eyes—goading green—which ask me so much

more than his question, but there's no easy smile in response, because fuck if I don't already miss Getty. Her long legs in those damn socks. Her soft hum as she paints. The scent of her perfume lingering in the hallway after she leaves for work. The feel of her body against mine at night. And that last little tidbit is something he definitely doesn't need to know.

"Yep." I nod, look back out toward the track. "Just the house."

"Uh-huh." He chuckles. "You just keep telling yourself that and I'll pretend like the sky is in fact green."

# Chapter 35

GETTY

To avoid the emotional sting of Zander's departure, to stifle the hurt, I've thrown myself into work and have found myself stepping out from behind the bar more than usual. Helped some of the servers carry drinks to the tables. Wiped down the tables on the patio out front. Anything to tell me I'm going to be okay when all is said and done. Luckily business has been bustling. Last-minute vacations taking place in the late-August heat before the unofficial end of summer with Labor Day fast approaching.

I lose myself in the noise of the next wave of customers off the ferry. I pour their drinks. Make small talk. Ask where they're from. Anything to keep my mind off how lonely the bed felt last night. How empty the house seemed this morning.

Yes, we were able to speak for five minutes last night when I ran back into the storage room to take his call, completely disregarding the long line of orders to fill, but it still wasn't enough. With the change in time zones, by the time I got off work, it was almost four in the morning his time. And as much as I still wanted to call him, to get the details of how it went talking to his dad other than "Things are good. I'll tell you all about it later," I also knew I couldn't let him think I was a crazy stalker either.

And I'm not.

I just miss him. *Ridiculously.*

For that reason alone, even though I've picked up my cell and pulled up his phone number ten (or twenty) times this morning before my shift started, I never actually hit send. I wasted time trying to justify it all to myself: why he hadn't called me this morning. *Was it because of the time difference? Maybe he was being courteous by letting me sleep after having a closing shift so he didn't want to call and wake me? Or maybe because it's race day? And race day means he's spending time with his family, helping his team somehow, and fulfilling numerous media requests?* Regardless of which way I try to justify things, a large part of me recognizes that he's back where he belongs. The newness of being with me will have faded. The benefits in our *friends with benefits* will be gone.

He'll be moving on.

At the same time, I know I'm being ridiculous. It's been less than forty-eight hours, which means I'm definitely bordering on stalkerish behavior. He's coming back. He said he was. And I'll get to tell him how I feel then. I can carpe the hell out of the diem when he returns.

Because I made a promise not to live life with regrets—and I already regret not telling him.

"Hey, Getty, Liam's looking for you."

"Thanks, Tracey," I say with a smile and a sigh at my constant mental games.

Within seconds, I'm back at the counter, hands full of empty glasses and bottles I've cleared along the way. Liam's face is alive with excitement when he looks up from the phone at his ear to meet mine.

"Phone's for you," he shouts above the clamor of the bar, holding the phone up so I can see what he means in case I can't hear him.

And of course my heart drops. Why would someone call me at the bar? I move behind the counter and realize he wouldn't be smiling if it weren't good. "Who is it?"

"Take five and head to the back so you can hear," he says, shoving the phone at me. "I've got to go change all the TV channels."

The minute I clear the back room and shut the door, I put the phone to my ear. "Lazy Dog, this is Getty."

"You're very sexy when you sound all official. You wearing your socks, Socks?" His voice is like liquid sex coming through the phone: low, suggestive, and one hundred percent attractive male.

"Zander! Why are you—?"

"If you'd answer your cell, I wouldn't have to call the bar," he says with a laugh that has me digging into the back pocket of my shorts to see several missed calls from him on the screen.

"What the hell?" I comment more to myself than to him as I check my phone. "Sorry. I think I hit my Do Not Disturb button when I put it in my pocket. I'm such a dumbass."

His laugh coming through the line makes him feel close, like he's right behind me. The damn doubt I've been trying to ignore for the past two days disappears at the sound of his voice. "Today's been ridiculously crazy, so I don't have much time and I know you're probably swamped with orders, but I wanted to call to say hi and tell you to make sure you watch the race today."

"Okay. Sure. I'll get Liam to tune one of the screens near the bar to it. Why, what's up?"

"Because I'm in it."

*"You're what?"* I don't know why all of a sudden my stomach drops at the same time my eyes widen and heart races with excitement. "How is that even—"

"It's a long story, but you were right, Getty. About all of it. All my dad wanted was the best for me. I was blinded by the pain I was in." Tears burn in my eyes. His voice sounds so surprised. So untroubled. And the sound of it truly makes me happy. "He'll never admit it, but I found out he's been hauling my car to every race. Paying my crew to show up, just in case I did."

The awe in his tone makes me smile to myself. Even if a part of me is sad that I'll never have that kind of love, it makes me so happy that he does. After everything he's been through, he deserves to realize its presence in his life.

And while to others that may sound like some weird show of affection between a father and a son, I understand how important this is to Zander. He accused his dad of loving racing more than him. And yet his dad took that love, hauled it from city to city around the country. And waited for him. He had faith in the son that he'd raised into a man to know he'd figure his problems out and come back around.

He believed him to be the man he knew he could be.

"Oh, Zander." My eyes well with tears over what I'll never have and for what he always will.

"I know," he says with that tone of his that allows me to see him nod. I can picture the soft smile on his lips and the appreciative look in his eyes.

There's a blast of noise in the background. A voice on a PA system. The roar of a crowd in response. And it shocks me back to the here and now and the excitement he must be feeling and the sense of rightness with the world he's gotten back.

"So, oh my God, you're racing! Does it feel good to be back in your car?"

"No. Not my car." He laughs. "When I get back, we're going to sit down and I'm going to teach you all about what I do."

I hear nothing else except for *when I get back*—the words I didn't even realize I was waiting to hear—and it takes me a minute to wrap my head around them while he's talking.

". . . so it's too late for me to race my car. I didn't qualify, so she's out. But unlucky for him and lucky for me, Alan came down with the stomach flu early this morning. They've been pumping him with IVs to try to hydrate him, but he's still sick as a dog . . . so I'm going to drive his car. I'll have to start in the back since I'm a different driver than the one who qualified for the race, but I'm confident I'll be able to move up the pack pretty quickly."

My head is spinning and my cheeks hurt from grinning. "I'm nervous."

His laugh fills the line again and calms my anxiety. "Me

too, Socks. But nerves are a good thing. They keep you on your game. Make you focus."

"Then stay super nervous so you stay safe for me."

The line falls silent for a moment. There's so much commotion in the background I wonder if he even heard me. And a part of me hopes he didn't, because I just possibly went into boundary territory, implied too much between us. I close my eyes and mentally chastise myself.

"Sorry, but I've got to go to the drivers' meeting in a sec."

"Okay." *Don't go yet.* "Well, be safe and good luck. I'll be watching."

"Bye."

I'm useless behind the bar.

Every rise in the pitch of the announcer's voice has me leaning over the counter to look closer at the screen, in order to find the distinct lime green color of the car Zander's driving.

And despite an already-packed house of tourists, word got around the island and all the locals have joined us here too. Wanting to cheer on the man they've adopted as their own. Zander has definitely won over this tough crowd.

Either way, every face in the bar is riveted to one of the multiple television screens. Even the tourists have gotten caught up in the *atta-boy*s shouted in support as Zander methodically passes car after car, working his way up the field, during the first hundred laps of the race.

The *atta-boys* slowly morphed into sighs of frustration and groans of disappointment and gasps when he steered clear of a car touching the wall and careening out of control.

And now with fifteen laps—thirty-seven and a half miles—left in the race, the crowd is on edge. The announcers' continual reference to the track's Tricky Triangle hasn't helped my heart rate slow down any either.

With a scattered mind and restless fidgeting, I make myself focus back on my work. On the next order. Not the next lap. At least I try to. I know Liam's just as excited as

I am about Zander's unexpected entrance in the race—and not just because this has given the bar a little celebrity status in this typically uneventful town. But because he really likes him.

I grab a bottle of vodka. Pour a drink. A female tourist looks bored to tears as her husband watches with the rest of the crowd, and I silently thank her for being patient while I watch too.

Suddenly the bar gasps collectively and I'm around the counter in an instant with my eyes pinned to the television. Heart in my throat and afraid to look at the smoke and debris ricocheting off the track's concrete barrier. My hands clutch the edge of the bar as I search for the unmistakable lime green car.

"Donavan's through," the announcer says, and while I breathe a sigh of relief, the car that flies out of the tunnel of smoke is red. It's Colton. Chills rack my body as I walk closer to the television, twisting at the bar towel in my hands as the seconds tick by. "Mason, Jameson, Dallas, Dane, are all through. Zander, Green . . ." I don't hear the rest because the crowd erupts in a communal sigh of relief.

Mine included.

A caution flag is waved and I step back behind the bar, my eyes trained on Zander as he pulls into the pits, and within the span of time from when I look down and back up—ten seconds max—he's already driving again. The announcers shout in excitement as he gains two spots on cars with longer pit stops.

"Son of a gun," one of them laughs out. "The Golden Boy's here for one race and already Lady Luck is back on his side."

The nickname makes me smile wider because I know how much he loathes it. Plays it up. Makes fun of it himself.

I try to fill as many orders as I can while the yellow flag is out so I can get caught up and watch the rest of the race without getting in too much trouble. But when the green flag waves again with only nine laps left, I don't think Liam cares about the pace at which we're filling orders, because he and everyone else in the bar are glued to the action.

They fly around the track. The mass of cars on the restart sit so close together that I worry about another wreck. About two tires touching and Zander going head-first into the wall or even worse.

My heart beats in my throat and I'm gripping the towel so hard my knuckles are white. Adrenaline runs through my system like a drug. I can't stand still. And yet I don't want to move in case it blocks my view of the television.

Six laps left.

The announcers are talking fast with excitement, but I can't pay attention to them because my eyes are locked on the lime green car pushing boundaries like I've never seen before. And I know I'm not savvy about racing, know nothing about it, and yet Zander's talent on how to read an opponent, when to push the car that much more to get an edge on the car beside him, is uncanny. He's aggressive and arrogant with his attempts, but at the same time even a novice like me can see his knowledge and precision about when to take the risks.

He's mesmerizing to watch. I'm sure the facts that my nerves are skittering out of control and that I have an emotional investment skew my opinion, but there's something extremely sexy about watching him in his element. Doing his thing and taking charge. Especially when I know this domineering, skillful man also has a sense of humor ... and calls himself *Mander* to ease an anxious woman's nerves.

He passes two cars in front of him within a one-lap period, and with each one the bar becomes more and more frenzied. "C'mon, Zander" and "Just four more" sound out repeatedly until it's practically a chant.

Four laps left.

"It's like Zander Donavan returned on a mission to make the other drivers remember this young man's incredible talent. And look at that! He's making another move on the twelve car. There is no limit he's not willing to push today. I'm sure his crew chief is having a heart attack, but man oh man ... this is some spectacular racing, folks."

"And he did it!" the second announcer yells in surprise

as Zander skirts the high side of the track and just ekes by the twelve car.

The noise level of the cheers in the bar has me wincing, drowning out all sound from the television. But it's got nothing on when the second-place car right in front of him moves down on the low side of the track with a trail of smoke billowing out of the back of the car.

Three laps to go.

Strangers exchange high fives. Testosterone rages. The air grows thick with excitement and energy and I can only imagine what it would be like to be in the grandstands at the race right now, let alone in Zander's shoes.

But once the camera pans to the stretch of track where they're racing, I realize the only person left for Zander to pass to take first place is his dad, Colton. My eyes flicker back and forth between the red lead car and Zander's second-place green car, and I wonder if he even thinks about the thirteen car being his dad or if he's so focused on winning it doesn't even faze him.

"And the twelve car is trying to reclaim the second spot," the announcer says as the camera cuts back to where Dane's car is edging its nose up alongside Zander.

My hand flies to my mouth. I stretch up on the tip of my toes and lean forward toward the television as if my silent pleas for him to go faster will make it happen. Will help him stay in second place.

"And Donavan pushes the car. How much more can his engine take?"

The network posts graphics on the bottom of the screen. The cars' RPMs sit side by side. Zander's shoots up as he pulls ahead and cuts back in front of the twelve car. Barely. While the customers hoot and holler, I close my eyes momentarily to rid my mind of the vision that had flashed through my imagination of his car smashed into bits.

Two laps left.

The cars catch up to traffic that's a lap down. And when the drivers come out the other side of it, they sit one, two, three—Colton, Zander, and Dane—like a train of race cars. They are so close. All I keep thinking is it takes only one mistake. One blown tire. One rub. And then devastation.

One lap left.

I don't know what to watch. The cars in the center of the track. The RPMs on the bottom of the screen. Or the floor so I don't have a heart attack from the stress of it all.

The twelve car zags out behind Zander. And Zander reacts just as quickly, zagging out right in front of him with a perfect block. The cat-and-mouse game happens a few more times. Colton's red car pulls away some. Gets a car length ahead as Zander continues to hold steady and fend off the twelve car.

And the customers cheer in a flurry of noise and high fives and clinked glasses as Colton crosses the finish line in first and Zander a moment later in second place. Liam grabs me in a quick hug in his excitement before he realizes what he's just done and then immediately lets me go and clears his throat.

We both return to our opposite ends of the bar to fill the orders flying in from the servers now that the race is over.

But the TVs remain tuned to the race.

On Colton driving his car into victory lane. Getting out and pumping his fists. On the crew around him that high-five and pat him on the back, and the stunning woman with her hair pulled back into a baseball cap whom he pulls into a heartfelt embrace before kissing her soundly on the mouth.

I watch it all unfold when I should be pulling pints. There's no way I can resist taking in these important pieces of Zander's life with such a different perspective from that of everyone else in the bar.

And then the camera pans away. To a figure fighting his way through the crowd. In a dark blue ball cap and with a sense of urgency in his movements. Body language I know by heart. The crowd parts at its epicenter, where Colton stands, and Zander and his dad embrace in a long hug. The picture they portray conveys a message so much stronger than the words any announcer could ever say.

The rest of the world must see a son congratulating a father, but I know the backstory. I know the history. And so when I drop my eyes to hide the tears welling there, all I can think about is how happy I am that they worked it out. How lucky Zander is to have supportive parents who only want the best for him.

My muscles are sore from tensing them so much, my voice sounds hoarse, and the stupidly silly grin I can feel on my face isn't going anywhere. It's exhilarating. This feeling. Watching him race. And being comfortable enough to readily admit I'm in love with him.

How could I not be?

Colton's interview airs while I fill orders as fast as I can, trying to keep up with the demand, but when I hear Zander's voice fill the bar, I forget the pulled tap or the beer slowly sliding over the edge of the frosted glass.

He looks tired and sweaty but exhilarated and so damn handsome.

"So, not a bad finish when you've been off the circuit, wouldn't you say?" the announcer asks, sticking a microphone in Zander's face just as he lowers his bottle of Gatorade.

"Not at all. I would have loved the win today as a great way to make a statement for my team and all of the sponsors, but I can't complain with the Donavan Racing Team taking a one-two finish here in Pocono."

"Some people are saying you could have taken the lead with how you were burning up the track."

Zander nods and shrugs. "Perhaps. From where I was sitting, Colton had the one spot nailed."

"So you weren't giving up the chance at claiming a victory today to block for the thirteen car?" he persists.

Zander flashes his grin. The dimple-territory grin, and I immediately understand the reporter is right. "You only get one family," he says before the camera pans away, leaving me with the image of those dimples front and center in my mind.

# Chapter 36

"You should have seen the place. It was packed. Even the tourists were rooting for you, Zander! It's like you're the hometown hero, even though this isn't your hometown."

The pang I feel as Getty's laugh fills the line is undeniable. I write it off, though. Deny it. I'm exhausted. I'm antsy. I'm high on the rush of the race. And I smile at the thought of the Lazy Dog, picturing the packed bar like she's described.

"How's your cereal?"

Again she laughs. And the pang deepens. "How do you know I'm eating cereal?"

"Because you always eat cereal when you come home from work."

"Huh," she says more to herself, apparently surprised that I know her that well, and even with the simple sound I can hear her smile clear as day through the line.

I can envision the red bowl on the coffee table, where it will sit with the last bit of milk in it until she finally gets up to take a shower. And then that leads me to another train of thought. Of her naked. Of how she feels when my soaped-up hands slide over her wet skin under the stream of hot water. And the heat of her body, the press of her curves against my dick, while we fall asleep.

*Just the house, my ass.*

Colton's words come back to me. My refusal to admit the reason I need to head back to the island. It's so much more than just keeping my word to Smitty and finishing the last of the to-do list. And that *more* is currently sitting on the couch, legs most likely still in those damn knee-high socks curled up beneath her on the couch, after a long day on her feet behind the bar.

The knock on the open door to my room pulls me from the enticing visual. "You coming, Zee?"

"I'll be there in a minute," I tell Jon. I know the rest of the crew is ready to go out and party it up. Our typical MO after a good race. Bottle service in the VIP section. Rowdy and loud.

"You gotta go?"

*Is that disappointment in her voice? Does she want to talk more?* The guys can wait for all I care.

"In a minute. All the hotels are full with the race in town. Some of the guys on the crew had a suite here at the Four Seasons, so I'm commandeering one of the rooms in it."

"Pulling rank, are you, *Golden Boy*?" I roll my eyes and snort at the damn nickname but can hear the exhaustion in her voice. Those brown eyes of hers are probably closing slowly too.

"Something like that."

"You guys going out to celebrate?"

Why do I hesitate to respond? I'm tempted to stay here with a few beers in the cooler and sit and talk to her.

"Yeah. Just going to go out and have a few drinks. I need to spend some time with my guys—my crew—make some apologies and mend some fences after what I did. Everything's been such a whirlwind, I haven't had a chance to address them, and nothing quite says *I'm sorry* like when another man buys you beer."

"I work in a bar. I can understand that."

"Oh, and tell Liam I'm representing."

Her strong laugh belies how tired she must be. "You're really wearing the Lazy Dog shirt?"

"Yep. I told you I would."

"Hmm." Her response comes out so soft I can barely

hear it. Almost as if she's listening to me but thinking of something else. She clears her throat. "I'm really happy for you. I mean . . . it sounds like your mom and dad understood where you were coming from and you're on the way to fixing that. You had a great race today. I'm just . . ." Her voice fades off and I sit up immediately. Something's wrong.

"Hey, Socks? Everything okay?" My gut twists at the sudden suspicion that maybe that prick Ethan came back for her—snuck past the sheriff's watchful eye—and she's not telling me. And I'm not there to help her.

I sit forward on the couch, elbows on my knees, and wait for her answer, but she's stayed quiet. I hate that I want to be here at the race, back in my regular life, but I also want to be there on the island. No, not just on the island. *There with her.*

The realization hits me harder than it should, considering she's constantly been on my mind since the moment I kissed her on the head and left for the airport.

So much for boundaries.

"I'm fine," she finally says. "Just tired. Figuring a few things out."

A thought ghosts through my mind. I shove it away.

It's just not possible.

Not feasible.

Could never work.

"Get your ass out here, Donavan! We need to drink!" I rise from my seat and hold my hand up in a *one minute* gesture to where the guys stand at the door of the suite. Some of them flip me off, some raise up a bottle of beer to entice me, and some make the universal motion that I'm jacking off.

I raise my middle finger and turn my back to them.

"I take it the natives are getting restless." She laughs. It sounds forced. Or am I just reading into it? I can hear the bowl clatter in the sink. Know she's about to head toward the shower. "I'll let you go. It's kind of quiet here without the constant pounding of the hammer, so thanks for calling. I mis—and congratulations again on such an exciting race."

"Getty, wait."

*Why can't it be possible?*

"Yeah?" Is that hope in her voice? Want? I wish I could see her eyes, her face, the fidgeting of her hands, to know for sure what she's thinking.

I can't pin down the whirlwind of thoughts going through my head, but use the gist of them to stick myself out there and do something that never in a million years would I expect to be doing.

"What if I was wrong?"

"Wrong about what?" Her voice slows down, while my heart speeds up.

"What if I made a mistake when I made that toast?"

Silence again. Her mind trying to follow me. "You mean the *to us* part?"

When I pull the curtains aside and look down on a city darkened by the night, I know that I'd love for her to be going out with us tonight. Or just with me. It doesn't matter. I want her to be here to experience this. Meet my parents. My crew. To see what I do. To have her come give me a kiss on victory lane so everyone could see this incredible woman is with me.

And only me.

Holy shit. The world must be ending.

Because I've never wanted that before.

"No." I struggle with what to say next. How to say it. "Yes." She laughs in a way that makes me smile and relax a bit. "I mean about the ending-in-disaster part. What if I was wrong about that?" *You're not making sense, Donavan.* Stop. Think clearly. Try again. "What if I were to tell you that I really like the benefits part but not the friendship part?"

"Zander?" She's cautious. Fearful. Feeling me out here, since I'm fucking this up royally. "Can you just say what you're trying to say?" That laugh again. It's nerves mixed with hope. Exactly how I feel.

Am I really doing this?

How can I not?

"I'm saying that I miss you, Socks. More than I thought I would. Like I'd rather sit on the phone and talk about nothing right now with you instead of go drink with the guys." The admission comes out in a rush, but the simple "Oh" that falls from her mouth keeps me going. "So what if there wasn't going to be a disaster? What if we tried the friends thing and the disaster we expected never happened? Would you want to try more than that?" I pace the length of the room. Run a hand through my hair. Sigh as she once again gives me the patience I need to find the right words. And at the same time her silence is fucking killing me. "I mean, I'm here and you're there, and what if I said I wanted you here with me too? What if we figured a way to make this work somehow?"

She inhales a ragged breath and I cringe. The silence, her lack of response—absolute torture.

Dammit. What the fuck did I go and say that for? Why the hell did I just ruin whatever this was between us by creating a man-made disaster myself?

"Getty?" It's as close as I get to begging. I'm more nervous in this conversation than I was at the start of the race today.

A woman is not supposed to fuck me up this bad.

And then she laughs.

Giggles.

Music to my ears. I can breathe again.

"I miss you too." There's softness in her voice. The same tone she uses when we lie in bed and talk, her hair tickling my chest, her fingers tracing imaginary lines over my skin.

I heard her answer in her tone, but need to hear it from her lips as well. "So?"

"For you, I could get used to there being strawberries in the fridge."

My body, sore from fighting the wheel all day and the g-force of the turns after I've been out of it for a few months, finally relaxes from it all. The shots at the club help. The celebratory toasts with the beer. Funny thing is, as much as that was my scene, tonight I'm just not in the mood for it. It feels different. Too many people. Too much noise.

The young, dumb, and full-of-cum vibe just doesn't fly with me tonight.

Huh. Maybe I got too used to island life. The quiet nights. How we'd sit on the deck listening to the waves crashing in. The way I could tip my longneck at the girl who sent a drink over and not have her think I wanted to get in her panties, because she knew I was with the bartender.

The sound of Getty humming down the hall as she painted with her earbuds in.

*Getty.* It all goes back to her, doesn't it?

Maybe I'm just getting old. Burned-out on the party scene. Then again I wouldn't mind sitting in the club with Getty on my lap, having a few drinks, laughing with the guys.

I'd also like to have her sitting on my lap for other reasons when my flight gets home tomorrow.

"Hey you."

I glance over to the blonde snuggling in beside me on the couch, low neckline, a nice rack pushed up, and big blue eyes wide with expectation. I don't say a word. Just rest my head back, take a minute to let the room stop spinning before I look around the suite where the boys have decided to bring the after-party.

The room's large by any standards, but there are way too many people in here, pit crew and race bunnies alike. All wanting something from one another—and, by the looks of a few of the people hooking up, already getting it.

From the number of times I've been propositioned tonight—batted eyelashes, downright offers, tight little bodies accidentally rubbing against me—I could be right there with them. Hand up a skirt. Tongue down a throat. No one has sparked an iota of interest. It's gotta be that I'm exhausted. Drunk off my ass. Between the time change, the race, the stress over what I had to face in coming back here . . . But that's not it. And I know it.

Long nails scratch up my thigh over my jeans. I glance at the hot blonde over the bottle of beer I have at my lips and just raise my eyebrows, silently asking *What in the fuck do you think you're doing?*

"I could help you relax after a long, *hard* day on the

track," she purrs in my ear while her hand slowly slides toward my groin.

My hand's on hers in a flash—locked tight onto her wrist as I lift her hand off my cock. "Watch it, sweetheart. Not all packages want to be opened."

Her tongue runs over her top lip. She shifts so she's even closer. "I think your dick begs to differ."

All I give her is a shake of my head. A fucking warm breeze gets a man hard, let alone a set of nails scratching over the denim covering it. "Yeah, well, my dick's not the one making decisions for me."

"Maybe it should." A single finger runs down my bicep. "I could show you a great time."

I sigh. "While I appreciate your subtlety, I've got an early flight. Thanks but, uh, no thanks." After that, I rise from the couch on wobbly legs, and I have to stand there for a second as the room spins like a crash that never stops.

"Get a man drunk enough and he never says no," she murmurs behind me.

When I think I can walk without falling, I slowly make my stumbling way to the bedroom I'm sleeping in. Suddenly thankful I can shut the door on all this shit.

I brace my arm on the jamb for a minute before entering and locking the door behind me. I may be drunk as fuck, but I'm more tired than anything. I don't remember making it from the doorway to the bed, much less how I got my clothes off and left them strewn Getty-style across the floor.

But somehow I did, because when someone pounds on the door what feels like seconds later, I trip on my clothes as my bleary-eyed, drunk-as-fuck self heads to open it.

"What?" I shout as I struggle with unlocking the door in the dark and flinging it open.

"Dude, someone's hooking up in the other bathroom. I'm gonna hurl." Stevie hiccups as he pushes past me and runs to the en suite bathroom. I shut my door, blocking out the noise of the party still in full swing on the other side of it. Within seconds, Stevie's gagging sounds filter through the closed bathroom door and into my room, making me want to puke myself.

But I'm too goddamn tired to have the energy to throw up.

"Shut my door when you're done," I shout to him as I stumble back to the bed.

Fall on it. Head to the pillow. Eyelids heavy.

"And lock it."

The exhaustion captures me whole.

# Chapter 37

Since things are slower at the bar, I use the extra time to scrape the paint off my hands that didn't come off in the shower. I keep discovering it in new spots and yet I don't care, because my mood is through the roof. Not even the annoying guys at table eight, who keep complaining that their beer has too much foam, can dampen my mood. Impossible when the man I've unknowingly fallen madly in love with wants to try to turn this friends-with-benefits thing we have going into something more.

To say sleeping was difficult is an understatement. And I'm definitely feeling it now, four hours into my shift, with weary eyes and an achy back. But after his phone call my mind kept wandering to all the possibilities life holds for us. Fate just might be on my side this time around. I spent hours on his painting of the Indy car. Wanting it perfect. No, needing it to be perfect, because it's sitting adorned with a bow on his dresser for when he comes home. A "Congrats on the great race." An "I've never painted anything for anyone and yet I feel so strongly for you that I had to create this for you." A "Welcome home, I missed you, and I can't wait for this next step with you."

Excitement fuels me through the day. Plus the knowledge that he's high in the sky somewhere right now flying home to me. Bringing his sweet kisses closer. His infectious laugh. The sense of calm and safety he carries with him.

My good mood has probably grown annoying to bystanders. And yet after so many years of my having to fake every emotion, it's kind of cool to just feel everything and not hide anything.

When I return from the storage room, Liam and a few customers are crowded over something at the other end of the bar. The minute they see me, the huddle breaks up. So I stand there observing their suspicious activity for a moment. And I don't know how I never realized it before, but when men don't want you to know something, they're not exactly subtle in trying to act like nothing is going on.

At a loss, I pull the bar towel from my apron and wipe my hands, eyes still scanning the group, trying to figure out what's going on. It's only when I walk their way that Liam lifts his eyes again and meets mine. The look on his face is all it takes for me to know I'm not going to like whatever it is.

"Liam? What's going on? What are you hiding?" *Tell me.*

"Need something, Getty?"

My eyes narrow. The hair on the back of my neck stands on end. I don't like the sudden twisting in my stomach. I glance around the bar. Looking for my father. For Ethan. I don't see them. But one of them usually accompanies the uneasy feeling that's swamped me.

"What's going on, Liam?"

"Nothing," Liam says the same time another patron says, "Hella free publicity."

A guy I rarely see in here gets elbowed by Jim, sitting next to him, and leveled with a glare from Liam. It takes me a minute to place who he is. Jerk of a guy. Rumors of a controlling wife who doesn't let him out much. Likes his whiskey cheap and tips even cheaper.

But right now I don't care shit about who he is, because I want to know what he means..

"Free publicity? What do you mean?" I take another step closer as buttons on cell phones are pushed so that apps close out. Wide eyes greet me. Mouths remain silent.

"Just tell me, Liam." I know he's my boss, but something is wrong. And I don't know what he's protecting me from, but his sigh when he reaches for his phone causes goose bumps on my arms. He shoos the guys around the counter away, an extra glare given to Jim before he slinks away to another table.

"There was a picture posted on Instagram this morning. They tagged the bar, so some of the guys who follow my account saw it."

"Okay . . ." I'm not seeing why this is such a big deal or what it has to do with me in any way, shape, or form. And then I get it. It's probably a scantily clad chick and he's embarrassed and doesn't want to show me.

Now I feel like an ass for pressuring him. And overreacting to boot.

"I can handle it, Liam. I'm a big girl."

He blows out a breath as I reach for his phone so I can see the picture. But when the screen flickers to life, it takes a minute for my mind to accept what I'm seeing. Or to process anything beyond the *holy shit* that keeps running on repeat through my shocked mind.

The selfie was taken askew. Zander's head on a pillow, face angled to the camera, eyes closed. Sound asleep. The tattoos on his back are visible, sheet pulled down low so the top of his ass can be seen.

The problem isn't him. Well, more so, the problem is the person taking the selfie that included Zander. Her blond head of hair looks mussed, painted blue eyes are smudged, and pulled tightly around her braless breasts is a white T-shirt with the distinctive Lazy Dog Bar logo. The one that Liam gave Zander before he left.

I swear I must blink my eyes a hundred times while I try to process how the image could be misleading. But when I scroll down to the caption, my heart and stomach drop.

@ZanderDonavan definitely not a lazy dog in the sack. This girl wore his ass out. Thanks for the shirt @ LazyDogBar. It looks better on me than him. He looks better on me too. #RacerDown #VictoryLane #SexyZexy #MisterOrgasm #MansGotGoodHands #SexGod #NailedHim #SorryLadies #TeamDonavan

I lick my lips and strive for some kind of composure. The noise of the bar sounds like a jet engine roaring in my ears and I'm having trouble fighting the tears that burn at the backs of my eyes. I open my mouth to say something, anything, but nothing comes out. Every single emotion I've reveled in over the past twenty-four hours has just come crashing down around me.

I'd love to refute it. To say the picture is fake. That it can't be real. And yet I know it's him. Those tattoos. Plus the fact that's his preferred position to sleep. And I recognize the thumbnail turned blue from where he hit it with the hammer a few weeks ago. Know the shirt is real because it's the same one I have on.

It's a struggle to breathe. To comprehend. To function. And yet I feel *so damn much*. More than anything I've ever felt in my life and in a way I never want to feel again.

Liam tries to take the phone from my hand, but I hold tight to it, not wanting to let go just yet and wanting to stomp my heel into the screen at the same time. I take one last look at the picture, at her Instagram account name, @RaceBunnyBabe, and give it to Liam without a fight.

"Can I . . . I need to take a break?" I ask him as I walk to the back room without waiting for an answer, feeling the weight of all the stares from the patrons on my back.

"Getty," Liam calls after me, but I really don't want to talk to anyone. "Getty." Again. All I want to do is cover my ears and close him out. "The bar's slow today. Why don't you head home?"

My eyes flash up to his. His face expresses complete concern and apology, and I look away as quickly as I can while I untie my apron strings. "Yeah. Okay. Thanks."

Anger hits me on the brisk walk home. And not just anger, but a rage I've never known before. Not even toward Ethan. Like the air you inhale feels like fire and your chest hurts and your eyes burn and your whole body trembles, but you can't stop any of it from happening.

How could he? That's all that repeats in my head over and over and over. Am I really that gullible? Am I really naive to think this famous race car driver and desirable man could want to stay with me of all people? A shell-shocked woman recovering from her abusive past in this small island town? That he'd want to give up his lifestyle of fast cars and obviously faster women for this?

He played me for a fool. Took the small comfort zone I'd made in this little town where gossip thrives and made me a mockery to everyone. Paraded me around to just make fun of me in the end.

The ache in my chest increases tenfold as the questions run rampant in my head. How could I be so wrong? Why did he call me and say he wanted more? Was that his way of trying to make me feel better? But even that makes no sense.

Flinging open the door to the house, I finally allow the angry tears to run down my cheeks. I'm restless despite the crying jag. Antsy. Want to lie down and cry from the hurt that won't stop, and at the same time can't sit still.

Maybe I'm wrong. Maybe there's an explanation.

*How?*

So I run back into the kitchen and grab my phone out of my purse. With trembling fingers and blurry eyes I pull up the Instagram app. Have to wait for it to download onto my phone. I search for the name @RaceBunnyBabe. I don't understand the screens or the pages but see that there is only one picture under her account. The one of her and Zander this morning. I'd had a small ounce of hope this was wrong, but it's shattered by this.

Then I notice the comments below the pictures this time. The jealous women wishing they were her. The crass comments about if he's really *golden* in bed. The *Where was this taken?*

And it's that comment that draws my attention. Because there was a response. I don't want to click the button to find out the answer, but I have to. *The Four Seasons.*

All my hope leaves with the next sob that falls from my mouth. My fingers switch over to the Messenger app. I don't care if he's in the air right now. I text him: Don't bother coming home. I don't want to see you. You made your point. Have a nice life.

Pacing the house, I check my phone constantly. Know he'll have landed and will be heading this way soon—through the traffic, on the ferry, to the house. I can't focus on anything else. Can't concentrate. I know he will text me back. Not what he will say. It's not like there's a suitable explanation anyway.

It's on what feels like the five hundredth pass through the kitchen that I see his damn to-do list. The *Miss the handyman while he's gone* item he added onto it. And a fresh set of anger erupts within me. What a joke he played on the naive roommate. The fun he must have been having, calling to sweet-talk me while she was probably sitting in the hotel room beside him!

I don't know what provokes me but I see *paint front handrail* and since he's basically finished with the back deck, I know that's the one major thing he has left to do. Well, screw him. I'll do it for him so he has no excuse or need to be here at all.

None.

Suddenly I'm a woman on a mission. A mission fueled with spite and anger. I head to the shed for the paint-brushes and scan the cans for the wood stain. When my eyes hit a can with a tester drop of Pepto-Bismol pink on the lid, I grab it without any thought of right or wrong. Morality is out the window by the amount of pain he's caused me with his betrayal.

All I can think of is *I'll show him.* Focus on how his stupid list will be complete, so he can keep his word to everyone else but me, and then he'll be done here.

I'll never have to see him again.

I stroke the brush over the sanded wood. The settled paint doesn't spread well and I have to close it back up and shake it the best I can. Get my aggression out on a can that's years old from the previous owners. But I don't care. Because I'm doing something. Anything. To try to stanch the hurt. Dull the pain. Stop my feelings of stupidity.

And so I paint through the tears. Big gulping sobs that splash off my face and onto the railing, where I have to repaint what it washes away. It's sloppy and messy and as much as I'm going to hate myself in the morning for this, right now it's what I need to do.

When I cover it all and then some—with huge drip marks included—I collapse on the steps, drop the paint-brush, and just cry: elbows on my knees, head in my hands, feel-sorry-for-myself, want-to-kick-him-in-the-balls tears.

The headlights startle me. I'm not sure how much time I've spent staring into space. How many times have the tears started and stopped? Probably just as many times I've cursed him out for being cruel and chastised myself for being just what my father said I was, *gullible*. But when the headlights pull down the street and the car door slams shut, I don't think I have the effort to fight him.

Until I hear him call my name.

"Getty!" Full of worry. Fear. Confusion.

"No!" I'm on my feet in an instant, back to the wall, heart on lockdown. "You don't get to come here anymore. LEAVE!"

"What the fuck is going on, Getty? Why the hell did you paint that pink? Why is Liam calling me chewing me out? Why aren't you answering your goddamn phone? What the hell is he talking about a picture for?" His voice echoes around the empty street as it escalates in pitch with each and every word. His face is the perfect picture of panic in the waning daylight and I have to begrudg-ingly admire what a great actor he is. How he made me feel and believe when he had no intention of following through on anything he ever said to me.

"Go away, Zander. Go away and don't ever come back." This time when I speak, my voice is quiet but livid. "You said friends with benefits would end in disaster; well, thanks to you, it did."

"Will you please tell me what in the fuck is going on here?" He goes to grab my arms and I jerk back as fast as I can. So much so, his eyes grow wide, my response telling him I'm dead serious.

"Was it funny to you to call me, tell me you want to try at something more between you and me, *us*, and then turn around and fuck the girl in your bed?"

"Getty. What? What are you— Talk to me. *Please*."
He runs his hand through his hair. It stands atop his head
as his eyes beg me for answers that he already damn well
knows from firsthand knowledge.

I stomp in the house and pick up my phone on the
counter. It's easier to show him than meet his eyes and
hear his pleading. The screen is covered in notifications
from him, but I don't even read them. Don't have the time
to care. As the wood floor creaks to tell me he's followed
me inside, I open the Instagram app and shove the screen
out to his face.

His eyes widen farther. Lips pull tight. Panic passes
over his features as his eyes flicker from the picture back
to mine several times as he figures out what to say. How
to get out of being caught.

"You want to know what the fuck's going on?" I scream.
"That's what's going on. You. Screwing. Her."

He stumbles back and sits on the arm of the couch.
"No, Getty. No. That's not me."

"Not YOU?" My voice cracks from the emotion, from
the tears, from the hurt that's eating my soul alive right
now. "Yes, Zander, yes. It is you. How can you say otherwise? The bruised thumbnail. The goddamn shirt from
the bar. She. Has it. On! You're naked. At the Four Seasons. It all looks pretty fricking obvious to me."

"No. It's—"

"Thanks for proving me right. That all men *are* exactly
like Ethan. Even when I believed you weren't. The difference is what you did was ten times more cruel." My sob
hitches and I reach my hands out to keep him away from
me. "Don't touch me."

"Fucking Christ, Getty."

I scamper back against the counter as he paces the
room. Even lost in my own emotion, I can sense the turmoil
that radiates off him and fills the kitchen. "She was there
last night. At the club. At the fucking suite when the guys
brought the party back."

I jump as his fist tears through the drywall. His own
yelp of pain echoing right after it. Looks like despite the
pain, he's going to do it again. But all I can focus on is

that he knows who this woman was. He's admitting that she was there with him.

"She tried to hook up with me. I remember that. She tried and I told her no thanks. And then I went to bed. God, I was so fucking drunk that I don't remember anything much after that. The door to my room opening. The noise and light of the party in the suite. Then closing. I don't know." When he looks up to me, if I had thought my heart was broken before, I might have been mistaken, because it's definitely broken now. Zander's face is wrought with apology. His body tense but defeated. Everything about him screams *guilty* right now when all I want him to do is give me a definitive answer.

And he doesn't. Seems he can't.

He just stands there with puppy dog eyes in a conflicted blue and mouth lax as he tries to remember the one thing he can to right our world.

"Please tell me you'd know whether you slept with her or not." Tears slowly slide down my face because for some reason this seems so much harder to comprehend. Blatantly doing it is one thing. Knowing it ahead of time. Purposefully disregarding me.

But to sleep with someone, ruin what I thought we had, and it was so nonmonumental that he doesn't remember it at all? That his disrespect of me was so great that he'd ruin us for nothing?

I can't breathe. I can't think. I can't stand still. And I can't move. So I just stare at him with wide eyes and a heart that hurts so damn bad because I'm so in love with him right now and hate him all at the same time.

How did I let this happen? Again?

I've been cheated on. My husband had slept with countless women while telling me that I wasn't good enough. And now I'm looking at a man who was telling me I was good enough and he's gone and done the same thing? What does that say about me? That he was just telling me these things but that I wasn't satisfying him regardless?

I can't think straight. Not with him looking at me with those eyes and the unknown stretched in between us. Not with my past a constant fog in my mind telling me I deserve exactly this.

I refuse to accept that this is my lot in life: for men to think I'm disposable and only good enough until they want someone better.

Like a hot blonde with a great rack who services racers in hotel suites.

My sobs are the only sound in the hollowness of the house. Both hands cover my mouth as I try to fight it off and not completely break down in front of him, but the force racks my body.

"Getty. Please. There's an explanation."

My laugh hitched with my sobs is all I can emit. All I can give him when I've already given him so much of myself. More than I should have. More than I ever intended to: my trust, my history, my heart, my desire. *My truth.*

"We need to—"

"I need you to leave, Zander." My voice is serious. Quiet. Barely audible. And yet the jerk of his body, the flash of his eyes up to mine, tell me he can't believe what I've just said. "Please. You can't be here tonight."

And I know I'm lying. Know I'm weak and can't tell him that we're over. That I need him to leave because I can't breathe when he's so close. And I need to breathe. To be able to think. To have more resolve in my voice when I tell him we're over for good. That it's perfect timing for him to head back to his old life.

The one without me. The one where he meets women like her.

Because I can't stay with a man who doesn't remember if he slept with someone. Every trip, every race, the worry will always be there. The doubt will always linger. And I can't live like that again.

So I lie. I ask him to leave for the night, stay at the hotel, so we can clear our minds and talk when we are calmer. Tell him I need time. That I need to think.

I stay where I am as he walks down the hall and gathers some of his things. I don't move when he stands inches in front of me with my welcome-home painting tucked under his arm and his eyes pleading for me to give him the benefit of the doubt. I refuse to cry when he presses a soft kiss to my head before resting his forehead against mine in silence.

And I hold back the confession I was going to make tonight as I watch him close the front door, climb in his car, and drive away.

*I love you, Zander.*

*I was going to lay my heart on the line and give you the only thing of myself I had left to give you.*

And as I slide to the kitchen floor, tears on my cheeks and disbelieving hurt in my heart, I wonder *if* I had told him last night, whether it would have changed anything.

Or if it would just mean I'd hurt that much more right now.

That's the problem with *if*s. Of living with regrets.

You always wonder.

Even when the lies were exactly what you wanted to hear.

# Chapter 38

Days mix with nights.

I keep to myself these days. Lost in my paints. Consumed with the sadness. Burying the hurt the only ways I know how.

Stormy seas and rumbling clouds line my canvases stacked against the walls. Dark grays and blacks and blues. Endless turmoil in a sea that can only create more of it.

His knocks on the front door go unanswered. His words through the slab of wood tear me apart as I sit on the other side, heart numb, and mind in self-preservation mode.

And he waits. And he persists. Staying ten paces behind me as I walk to work. Sitting at table thirteen through my shifts. His way of reinforcing to me what his constant texts tell me:

> I'm trying to be patient, Getty. I'm trying to let you know I'm right here whenever you're ready to talk.

Or

> I'll get to the bottom of this, Getty. I'll find this woman and prove to you, I didn't sleep with her.

And

Don't you see I want this to work? You're not
getting rid of me yet, Socks.

All of them sit on my phone just as his presence is
constantly in my periphery. And I don't know if it would
even matter if he found this woman to prove otherwise.
The trust between us has been broken. The seed of doubt
planted.

The notion that I need to rely on myself and no one
else reaffirmed.

But damn it to hell, the hurt persists. In his presence.
In his absence. In the desperation in the tone of his texts.
In the temerity with which he's there day in, day out, so
that I can't run away and hide from him. Hiding seems
the best option, because the feelings are still there. The
want is still real. The desire is still ravenous.

And yet I've felt so much over the past few days that I've
started to feel nothing. I'm afraid. I'm doubting everything
about myself: my decisions, my choices, my own needs.

Liam eyes me across the bar when I walk in. Asks without words if he needs to suggest that Zander leave. And I
can't respond. I simply do my job. I collect my tips. All
under the curious gazes of the locals, whose eyes are like a
visual Ping-Pong ball between Zander and me, while the
tourists are oblivious to the town gossip unfolding beneath
their noses.

Then I walk home. Him behind me. Enter the house.
He stands on the sidewalk, hands in his pockets, eyes be-
seeching, and waits for me to tell him to come in. But I
shut the front door. I cry in the shower. I don't eat. I've
lost my appetite. My stomach churns.

So I paint.

All night.

Because sleep is impossible. Without his warmth to cud-
dle against. Without the heat of his breath against my hair.

Without the comfort I've gotten used to of him just
being there.

Of not being alone.

*    *    *

"I have to leave tonight, Getty. I was hoping you'd talk to me before I had to head out." His voice behind me is like an invisible magnet pulling me toward him.

With my hand on the front door and a bone-deep exhaustion running through me after my shift, I hang my head and close my eyes. I will myself to have the strength to talk to him without breaking down and letting him see how much this is killing me. While still wanting him, still loving him, I just can't be with him right now.

Not until I chase away my own demons, which make me question myself too easily. And him. And any possibility we might ever have at a future.

"What race are you headed to?" I ask the question although I already know the answer. Boston. A road race. A two-and-a-quarter-mile loop.

"Boston," he says quietly. "Qualifying first part of the week. Then the race on Sunday. But I'll be back."

I don't say anything. I'm too busy fighting the emotion in my voice to speak.

"Turn around. Please, Getty. Let me see your face."

My chest constricts. It's hard to pull in air. But I turn around and face him; his hand rests on the god-awful pink handrail and his eyes lock immediately on mine. They search, they beg, they question, and I just hope mine don't give away any answers.

"Don't cry." He steps forward and wipes an errant tear I couldn't hold back from sliding down my cheek. "It's killing me that you won't listen to me, Getty. You won't let me apologize, let alone even talk to you."

"There's nothing to talk about," I whisper.

"Bullshit. You know that's a lie. We're good together, Getty. *Goddamn incredible.* I've had nothing but time the last few days to think about this. To think about us. I can see that what I want has been right in fucking front of me, but I was so fixated on not letting it turn into a disaster that I made one of it myself."

His words are too much. They cause me to feel again. And I don't want to feel. I shake my head, try to refute him, and he reaches out and grabs my hands from where I've brought them to the side of my head to shut him out.

"No. You need to hear me. I'm not going until you hear me."

"Zander, I can't." I look up at him with tearstained cheeks and a trembling lip and meet his eyes.

"Yes. *You can.*" He cups the side of my neck, directing my gaze to remain on his. His voice comes out thick with reassurance, resolve, determination. "Think about us. Think about the past few months. We've laughed till it hurts. Made love till it feels so good it burns. We fight. We make up. We know each other's pasts. We accept them."

"But that doesn't fix—"

"You're right. But you're talking from fear. You're so fucking scared right now, Getty. You're so worried that *I'm him*, you're not looking and seeing me. The man you know. Well, guess what? I'm scared shitless too. I'm afraid of taking a step when I'm typically the king of *just jump.* I'm scared of hurting you. I'm petrified of loving you. But fuck, Getty, more than anything, I'm terrified of not taking the chance and knowing if any of that fear is worth it."

His words are undeniably powerful. They strike chords I don't want to vibrate with the impact they have on me. The look in his eyes—complete conviction in what he's saying—makes it so hard to think otherwise. My heart and head are in conflict. My sense of right and wrong on a demolition derby to see who survives with the least amount of damage.

"Do you hear me? Do you understand what I'm saying?" He steps back and turns around, walking the length of the porch, hands behind his head, body energized with determination but tense because of my lack of response.

"Yes." I finally speak. Petrified to say yes and terrified to say no. "I . . . I can't take any more hurt, Zander."

He turns around at my words. Walks back toward me. Smile slight, but there's hope in his eyes. Relief that I actually responded in his posture. "Then it's a good thing I'm here for the long haul." He pauses. Takes a breath. "I don't want an answer before I leave, Getty. All I want is for you to think about it while I'm gone. One week. I'll leave you alone so you can think through everything I just said. Because I can see it in your eyes. I can feel it in your sadness. I miss it from your touch. We deserve this chance. *No regrets, Socks.* Let us have a shot. Will you at least tell me you'll think about it?"

"Yes." I nod my head.

"Thank you." His hands are back on my cheeks, his lips pressing a kiss teeming with desperation against my forehead. We stand like this for a moment. And his lips move against my skin when he speaks in a hushed whisper. "Even if you gave me a hundred reasons why we shouldn't be together, Getty, I'd still look for the one reason to fight like hell for you. Remember that."

And with that comment he presses another chaste kiss to my forehead before turning and walking away without another word. I stand on the porch watching his car long after the lights have disappeared down the road, his last statement repeating over and over in my mind.

I'm breathing normally for the first time in what feels like days. And the funny thing is, I thought it was Zander's presence that was making it hard to draw in air.

Now I wonder if it was the fear of him not being there that was causing the burn in my lungs.

# Chapter 39

*Have patience. But not too much. When there's some-thing you want, go after it. But if there's something worth your while that you want bad enough, be patient.*

The words from my mom's letter repeat in my mind. But there's no indication of how much time is too much damn time.

*Fuck.*

That's the only way I can describe my state of mind. Or the paper cut left by Getty on my heart. She was like that swift quick slice you never saw coming but that stings like a bitch when it happens. *And aches even more with each passing day.*

Small but mighty. Goddamn knock-me-on-my-ass is what she is.

Especially since I want to call her. Hear her voice. See if she's made any kind of decision yet.

But I don't. I promised her I wouldn't. That I'd give her time. And fuck if that's not brutally hard to do. Lost time is something you can never get back.

So I've tried to focus on the race at hand. Using my frustration to own the damn track instead of tear myself apart. Well, that and try to get answers to the one thing that will fix this entire situation.

Identifying the woman in the picture.

I lift my face to the sky and close my eyes for a second, let the sun's warmth hit my skin while I take a deep breath. I stand like that for a moment, Boston Harbor spread out below me from the balcony of my parents' suite. I soak up the view, am reminded of the deck back on the island, and hate and love that I miss it all at the same time. The island had offered me quiet solitude. The feeling of being so small against nature's wrath. The scent of Getty's nail polish as she painted her nails when sitting beside me. That little "Good night" she murmurs before she falls asleep.

That's why the text on my phone pisses me off even more, because it's telling me I might still lose everything. The investigator I hired to look into the Instagram account hit a dead wall today. His text says the only info he could find is the account and the Gmail it's associated with were created in the last month, and all are linked to false background information.

A race bunny out for a good time hiding it from her husband or boyfriend. Great. Just what I need is another asshole to deal with if he eventually finds the picture.

"That bad, huh?" Rylee pats my shoulder as she and Colton join me out on the balcony. She sets a bowl of chips and salsa out and my first thought is of Getty sitting across from me at the restaurant, seducing me with her words.

She's fucking everywhere I look and nowhere I want her.

I roll my shoulders, try to focus on the positive in that she said she'd think about us. Hopefully the time apart will make her miss me as much as it's making me miss her.

"So how are you going to fix this, Zander?" It's Colton who speaks, but my gaze flicks over to Rylee. The one person I've confided in, and I know she's spilled the details of our heart-to-heart to Colton. Didn't expect any less but at the same time, *fuck*.

I want to roll my eyes. I want to cover my ears and pretend I didn't hear him. But more than anything, I want advice. Assistance. Anything to get Getty back.

"Fuck if I know." My laughter sounds hollow. I tip the beer back up to my lips and think of what to say next. "I know there's something there. She feels it too. I just can't figure a way to make her really listen to me."

"Tell her you love her."

Colton's comment has me sputtering out a response. Choking over the words. "C'mon, now. Those are seriously strong words."

"You don't love her, then?" Eyebrows raised. Lips pursed. Green eyes challenging.

"I didn't say that."

"Well, do you or don't you, Zee? Shit or get off the pot here. If you can't admit it to yourself, you sure as hell aren't going to convince her."

It occurs to me that he's absolutely right with his blunt truth. How can I ask her to overcome her fears if I can't even admit the one thing that scares me to voice out loud?

"I doubt saying 'I love you' at this point is going to make her listen. She's going to think I'm just saying it because I'm desperate. She's afraid—will find any reason not to believe me. *Fuck*." Panic settles in. I look at him, asking for help with my direct gaze. "How do I make her believe me?"

"Convince her she's *your water*."

"*What?*" I pinch the bridge of my nose. Look at him like he's losing his mind.

"What's the one thing you can't live without?"

"Water?" My voice hesitant. Answer hopeful.

He nods his head. "How does water taste?"

"Like nothing." I shrug, then glance over to Rylee, who is sitting there with a knowing smile on her face like she knows where he's going with this. She just nods her head in encouragement. I look back at Colton as thoughts align. "Like nothing, but it's really everything. You can't live without it."

"Exactly." A lazy smile spreads on his lips. "She's your water. Convince her you can't live without her, son. That's half the battle."

It might be that easy, but still my mind is spinning on how exactly to do that when I thought that's what I was trying to tell her before I left the house for Boston.

But I never told her I loved her.

Would that have mattered?

"What your dad's saying, Zander, is that she's been through a lot. You need to do something to prove to her you really mean it. Women love knowing you didn't miss the little things. They love grand gestures that say you pay attention to all the reasons you love them."

My heart stops. There are those two words again. *Grand gestures.* The same ones my mom used in her letter to me. The letter Rylee hasn't read yet.

I've never believed it when people say they received a sign to do or not to do something. It's all bullshit, if you ask me.

And yet how can it be a coincidence that both mothers in my life have said the same thing? Both used it to explain what I need to do to get the girl.

Now the question is, how grand is grand?

# Chapter 40

"This has got to stop." There's an exasperated smile on my lips as the delivery guy walks into the Lazy Dog with a fresh set of flowers. The fourth one in as many days. And even though I know who sent them and what the message says, I open the card anyway: *Anticipation. XO Zander.*

"Tell him if he keeps this up, I'm going to start a funeral parlor in the back as a side business," Liam teases as he walks past and smells them out of reflex. The look he gives me means he's secretly happy that Zander is proving to be the good guy he thought he was.

The problem is he's winning me over too. And it's not just the gifts that have been arriving to the house and the bar since Tuesday. No. I've lived a lifestyle where I could have anything materialistic without a second thought about expense. It's more the thought that has gone into the gifts. The smiles they've brought to my lips. The happiness they evoked about that moment in time I shared with Zander.

The little things he's trying to remind me of so I don't forget how good we are together.

Like the four dozen pairs of knee-high socks in all different patterns and colors he had delivered. The card attached mentioned how much he enjoyed those socks wrapped around his hips.

Or the two cases of fresh golden pineapples followed by the empty green crates void of strawberries. The note that mentioned he'd asked the strawberry council to go on strike because pineapples are the decidedly best of all fruits.

Next was the case of new paints and brushes and canvases in all shapes and sizes that now clutter my little alcove in my bedroom. The card still makes me smile. The dedication "to the world-renowned artist" from her model who still needs his six-pack and other delicate places painted and committed to canvas.

Then there was the hammer with the flowery handle. So I had something to use when I needed to get out aggression or emotion. An *outside use only* sticker attached to it.

The bubble mailer delivered to the house with the kid's jump rope nestled inside. A note along with it that said *Will you?* followed by the few minutes it took me to figure out what Zander was asking. But once I did—his gift a reminder of his *just jump* encouragement—I lost the battle against holding back a smile.

All the items tugged on my heartstrings. Reminded me of his generosity. His kindness. His thoughtfulness. They all made me want to pick up the phone and call him. Hear his voice. Close my eyes and sink into the warmth of his presence.

But none of them were the one thing I so desperately needed. Him to tell me he didn't sleep with someone else.

Am I being stubborn? Yes. Unreasonable? Maybe. Will my anger and hurt fade with time, and will all these small gestures that tell me he realizes what's so very important win out in the end?

God, how I want to be able to say yes. I want to let love prevail. Win. Sweep me off my feet and carry me off into the island sunset.

But I also know love doesn't fix everything. Trust and honesty are huge factors too. And I've lived without all three of those for so long. Is it really so bad to require them the next go-round?

*Time.* That's what I keep telling myself. I have three

more days to convince myself one way or another. To just jump or to say good-bye and go our own separate ways.

Even the thought of it gets me teary-eyed. And makes me question why I'm fighting this so hard. Shouldn't the fact I'm resistant to walking away be enough of an answer?

"I placed some calls to some friends. We'll find something for you. You're a local now—you get the inside track," Liam says with a wink, pulling me from my thoughts of Zander and placing them where they should be. On finding a place to live. Because as if I needed more shit to deal with right now, Darcy called this morning to tell me the house has been bought. Word of mouth around the island about the house being fixed up, in a market where real estate goes fast, had brought in an irresistible offer.

So not only do I have to deal with a broken heart and whether I want to mend it or just cut my losses and accept the hurt, but I now need to find a new place to live.

Maybe this is a sign. A clean break could be just what I need. A new place to live means no more memories of Zander everywhere I look. No more reminders when the pipes creak or when I pass the mini-blind wand still sitting on my bedroom dresser.

The one absolute is that I'm staying here on the island. The easiest thing would be to pack up the car and run again. Set down roots somewhere else. But I don't want to take the easy route. I like it here. I've made friends. I feel at home. Accepted. And that's not something I ever expected to find, so leaving the island is not an option.

"Thanks. It's all so sudden. I just . . ." I fight the tears that well in my eyes.

Liam pats my shoulder in support. My tears instantly making him uncomfortable. "It's all going to work itself out for the best. We'll all make sure of it."

"Thanks. I appreciate it. Everything with Zander and now this . . . I don't know what I'd do without—"

My voice stops midsentence, my breath hitching, when I see who's walked into the bar.

My heart clenches when I meet eyes that match mine.

I just can't take anymore right now.

I just can't.

Let alone him.

"What does he want?" Liam mutters beside me. His words surprise me. His rigid posture even more.

My body tenses with each step closer my father takes to the bar. I know I'm strong, can hold my own against him, and yet exactly what he predicted would happen with Zander happened, and I really don't want to go toe-to-toe with him right now on it.

"Good afternoon, Gertrude. You're looking well." Sharp eyes. Stiff demeanor. Zero emotion.

"Father." I nod. My head is so cluttered with everything that I can't think straight.

We stare at each other. The patrons around us take notice. Liam stays put by my side.

"Can I help you?"

He angles his head. "I'd heard you'd had a falling-out with that guy. I came to make sure you were okay. Heard your house had sold. I thought you might need help. Figured you were ready to come back home."

I stare at him wide-eyed as everything starts to make sense. "You bought the house, didn't you? You bought it so I wouldn't have a place to live." My blood boils. His pulling strings in my life is no longer acceptable.

"No. Never. Do you really think I'd buy property in this town of all places?" The disgust-laced defiance that tinges his denial has a few more heads turning in our direction in the bar. Backs and pride standing at attention.

Liam's feet shuffle beside me. A warning growl sounds off deep in his throat that's for my ears only.

How could I not have put two and two together? The real estate mogul would have known somehow it was up for sale. Used his insider knowledge to his advantage. Tried to run me back home by getting rid of the place where I live, in a town where room vacancies are few and far between.

I stare at this man whose blood I share and feel absolutely zero connection besides sadness. And missed moments that, no matter how hard I long for them, he'll never be able to give me.

My resolve is stronger than ever when I speak again.

"Insulting the town you're standing in isn't going to win you any favors in this bar. Thank you for your concern, but it's no longer needed. I think it's best if you leave." My voice wavers on the last word even though I stand tall. My anger fueling my tone rather than my fear.

His jaw pulses. The dislike of being dismissed by me of all people is the only transparent emotion he shows. I can pick up on his anger, though. Disappointment. Frustration. And I'm perfectly okay with it.

"You're making yet another mistake, Gertrude. It's a pity you can't seem to make a man happy enough to keep him loyal."

Fury heats my blood. My face turns beet red with embarrassment as he insults me in a bar full of my neighbors. I try to save face despite the rush of emotions vibrating through my body. "Zander was only here for the summer, Father. It was time for him to go back to his life." My voice is loud enough so the customers can hear me. So I can hopefully make them believe what I've said and restore some of my dignity that has been run through the public wringer over the past few weeks.

He tucks his tongue in his cheek, eyes unyielding. "Oh. My apologies. I assumed the picture circling the Internet of him screwing RaceBunnyBabe Katy to be the reason you weren't together. Guess I figured that would be more damaging to your relationship than anything. But then again, seems you like to make a habit of playing the martyr in relationships. . . ."

His words paralyze me. The insinuation that I brought this on myself—with Ethan and with Zander—causes such a strong wave of diverse emotions that I don't know which one to focus on. Humiliation. Anger. Surprise that he went there.

I stand looking at him with a slack jaw and a litany of words I want to say but can't process quickly enough to combat the damage he just caused.

"I think it's time you leave my bar." It's Liam who speaks. My father's eyes move with methodical slowness over to his. They challenge. And mock. It's only when chairs scrape across the floor as other locals stand up, cross their arms, and stare down my father that he takes a step back.

"Good-bye, Gertrude." He nods his head and turns on his heel.

Then I finally sag against the counter. Breathe for the first time in what feels like hours. Try to comprehend everything that just happened. Try to overcome the disbelief that he's going to buy the house just to force my hand to return home.

Liam runs his hand over my back. A small show of support on top of his strong stance in asking my father to leave.

And in a split second of time, it clicks. What he said.

I tear from behind the counter and out the front door like a madwoman. My mind stumbles over the idea. The why. The how. He was behind it all. The *holy shit*.

When I fling the door open, I look left, then right. Eyes searching for the gray jacket and the silver head of hair.

"Father!" I shout down the street, not caring who stops and pays attention to the crazy lady with wild eyes and a desperate voice.

He stops in his tracks. There's a smug smile on his face when he turns around and walks back toward me. All my mind can process is that he thinks I want to go with him. That his ridicule has done what he wanted and worn me down so I'd realize I need him and Ethan to survive.

His arrogance knows no bounds.

"I knew you'd see things my way, Gertrude. Come." He motions for me to follow him with visible impatience.

But I stand my ground. Hands on my hips as the door of the bar opens and closes behind me. The locals most likely all standing there to make sure I'm okay.

"How'd you know her name was Katy?" My words ring out across the distance, but from his reaction it's like they slap him in the face. His accidental slip in the heat of the moment. It's a split second of shock that flickers before it's gone, and I know his every nuance, his different combative faces, yet never have I seen him surprised like this.

My heart pounds in my chest. My blood rushes in my ears. And hope . . . it surges and swells like a tidal wave threatening to pull me under its welcome haze, because I realized somehow my father knew the name of the mysterious woman when no one else does. Not even Zander himself.

With his reaction giving me a stronger foundation beneath my feet, I take a step toward him and ask again. "No one else knew her name. How did you know her name was Katy, Father?" I shout the words, tears of anger thick in my voice, such a different kind of hurt in my heart from what's been plaguing me the last several days.

And with his sputtered lack of coherent response, my mind starts to pull together hints and connect them. "It was his phone, wasn't it?" I shake my head. It's spinning and yet I can see things very clearly now. "When Ethan broke in the house. Zander's phone was on the counter. He tracked it somehow, didn't he? While Ethan waited for me to come home, he found the phone on the counter and uploaded the app to it just like he did to mine before. Must have been a big surprise for him to come home after you bailed him out, go to snoop on my whereabouts, and find out the phone wasn't even mine. I bet that pissed both of you off until you figured Zander's phone worked just as well. It allowed you to know where Zander was going to be. Where he was going to stay. What was going on between us. You tracked him, his travel plans, outgoing texts, and made sure Katy was right there. Paid her to set up the photo opportunity worthy enough of making me think he cheated on me. The shirt. The tag to the Lazy Dog account."

Oh my God. How could I have been so stupid? How could I not have seen this from a mile away? Control. It was always the name of their game, and they did just that, even when I wasn't anywhere near them.

"Gertrude." All he can say as he tries to stop me from putting all the pieces together. From realizing the extremes to which he and Ethan would go to deflate my confidence, to ruin my self-worth, in the hopes that I'd come running back home.

"You wanted me to believe he'd slept with her, didn't

you?" I scream. Emotion overflows out of me at this point, heart torn in so many pieces and yet being put back together on a whole different level. "You wanted me to see the photo and run back home with my tail between my legs." He steps toward me and I step back. "How could you?" Tears stream down my face. They won't stop. "How could you take the only happiness I've had since Mother died and try to ruin it for your benefit?"

Emotion finally flickers through the ice of his stern expression. Regret. Apology. Embarrassment. But I don't believe them for a single second.

"I don't ever want to see you again. You are dead to me."

I turn my back and walk between the twenty or so customers standing out in front of the Lazy Dog. They part as I stride through, murmurs of support surrounding me and buoying me forward.

# Chapter 41

From the scramble to make travel arrangements to throwing clothes in a suitcase to running between connecting flights, I feel as if I haven't had a minute's time to catch my breath.

And yet I wouldn't have it any other way because I know the truth now. I know Zander was right. That I should have listened to him. That what we have is real and worth the chance.

Now I just can't wait to get there and tell him face-to-face. Kiss his lips. Wrap my arms around him. I'm just hoping I can do it before the race starts, because I don't think I can wait four or five hours. I've waited long enough as it is.

The cabbie honks his horn. My knee jogs up and down from my seat as I bite a desperate shout for the other cars to get out of the way. I have a man to make mine.

I extract my phone from my backpack to text Rylee that I've landed. And I silently thank Zander for programming her number in my phone. It feels like days ago, but I don't think I'll ever forget her response when she answered my call. After a rambling explanation about how I needed to get to Zander and see him and talk to him—and she could direct me how to get to the track once

I landed, because it was dire that I see him—she told me, "You *are* his water."

Too focused on the details of how soon I could get to Boston, I had no idea what she meant; now I'm trying to figure it out.

By the time the taxi gets me to the location Rylee had indicated, my body is riding high on adrenaline. I'm so close.

"Okay. I see the taxi," Rylee says through the phone as I collect my bag and backpack and stand there amid a massive amount of people milling around in the prerace excitement as the cab pulls away.

"Getty!" Her voice is in my ear and behind me simultaneously.

As soon as I turn around, I'm engulfed in her arms. She pulls back and stunning violet eyes meet mine with a smile lighting up her face. We just stare at each other for a moment. It's like I don't have to say a word for her to understand how much I love her son. I can see it in her eyes. She already knows.

And the nerves I thought I'd feel disappear as she laughs out loud and pulls me against her again. "I'm so glad you're here, Getty." Her voice holds so much warmth, so much welcome, that I'm not sure how to respond, because I'm not used to it. "I'm Rylee. So nice to meet you."

"Hi. Thank you for helping me get here." Tears well in her eyes and she just shakes her head as if she's really trying to believe I'm here.

"Anything for one of my boys." She looks away from me and around at the crowd. "We'll talk properly during the race, but right now I want to get you to Zander. Here. Put this on." She loops a lanyard around my neck with all kinds of official-looking information on it that matches the one she's wearing. "Let's go!" She grabs my hand and begins to lead me through the crowd.

We move through security, around barricades, and weave in and out of the crowd of people that line the street. Their excitement is contagious. The exhilaration of being so close to Zander and the chance to right my wrongs is like nothing I've ever felt before. And strangely enough, the woman whose hand is holding mine is also providing me with a sense of acceptance that I never expected.

We can't really talk, given the noise of the crowd and how fast we're moving as we skirt through openings in the mass of people.

The crowd begins to thin some. The security becomes tighter, its presence more visible. We have to show our badges at a gate before we're allowed through. Men in fire suits of different colors stand all around us now. Some say hi to Rylee as we pass by. Some just nod in greeting. The clatter of tools as they're dropped on concrete can be heard here and there.

My nerves jitter with anticipation. With uncertainty. With hope. But we keep walking at our brisk pace. And while the crowd may have thinned, Rylee keeps my hand in hers. I have a feeling she can sense how freaked out I am.

And just like that, in the middle of a makeshift alley where concrete barriers divide the track from the pits, she stops abruptly. I look at her, startled, my heart pounding. "Just remember, more hearts break from words left unspoken than from saying too much." I nod my head as the tears well up at her absolute compassion. The kind she's taught her son. Her eyes hold mine, encourage me, ground me. I take a deep breath and squeeze her hands in mine before she helps to take my bags from me. "Welcome to the family, Getty. Zander's right over there." She lifts her chin over my shoulder.

I turn around slowly, breath held, and heart close to bursting as I look through a sea of royal blue fire suits to find the one I want the most.

And there he is—I can barely see him. He's surrounded by a pack of fans, all reaching out something for him to scribble his autograph on. His smile is electric. His laugh genuine as it floats over the chaos and hits my ears. He focuses his attention completely on the person he's speaking to, giving a full moment to each one. And the sight of him so utterly in his element, undeniably in love with what he does, surrounded by those who support him, makes me fall in love with him all over again.

Now that he's in my sights, I realize I should have thought this out better. That I should have planned a way to make this reunion special and memorable. But I didn't. I was so focused on being in his arms, telling him yes, we deserve another chance, that it never crossed my mind. How was I to know that he'd be so swamped by people, I'd have to compete to get his attention?

I look toward the rev of an engine to the left of us and when I look back toward the crowd, Zander's eyes meet mine. Time stands still as we take each other in. And there's not a word I can use to describe how I feel as I watch the emotion play over his features when he realizes that I came here for him. If I had any doubts about my decision, his expression alone would have erased them completely.

All I see is love. All I want is him. All I feel is complete after being broken in pieces for so very long.

With the events of the past week, I often wondered if our love was worth fighting for. But in this moment, when I look at him, I know I'd wage a war and more to keep him.

The look on his face holds everything I imagined it would and then some: shock, relief, excitement, love. Urgency. I'm unable to do anything beyond stand there on the outside of the circle with tears in my eyes and a heart bursting with love.

He tries to move, attempts to head my way, and it looks like he's wading upstream. As he moves a foot forward, the mob moves with him. His laugh rings out again. His eyes hold steadfast on mine at the irony of the situation: how he's been trying to get to me for a week and now that I want to get to him, I can't.

And the one thing that has always been a part of who we are is being able to laugh regardless of the situation. Right now is no exception.

He trudges toward me making steady progress. A sea of fans in his team color of royal blue soon swallows me up in the throng. I'm bumped and jostled and I lose sight of Zander through the activity of the crowd.

A hand finds my arm. And before I can turn, I'm being pulled against the tide until I come face-to-face with the one person I'm searching for.

Flashes on cameras ignite. Voices shout his name. The crowd continues to want something from him. But when my eyes meet Zander's, all of it—the noise, the chaos, the hands that continue to touch him—fades to gray, because the only thing in living color is him.

The man I want. The man I'm fighting for. The man who tells me to *just jump* and I do because I trust him.

At least now I do. Lesson learned. Go with your gut. Listen to his words. Believe his actions.

"Getty." My name is on his lips. The only thing I want to hear. That smile I love of his going into mega dimple territory.

"Hi, Golden Boy."

His laugh vibrates from his chest into mine.

And then I forget everything once his lips are on mine. Of all the kisses we've ever shared, this one by far is the sweetest. It's an *I don't care who is watching—I'm going to take my sweet time with you* type of kiss. His hands are possessive on my cheeks and our tongues dance together like we have all the time in the world.

And when we break apart moments later, he pulls back a few inches, the smile I can't completely make out lighting up his eyes. "You're here." Awe. His voice warms me from inside out.

I nod my head. "You sent me socks. Thank you." I lean in to kiss him. "And pineapples." Another kiss. "And paints." And again. "And a hammer." I let this one last a little longer, the crowd slowly stepping back now that they know his attention is one hundred percent focused on the girl in his arms. This time I break the kiss and angle my head back so I can look him in the eyes. "Thank you for my gifts. But I don't have anything to give you."

It's his turn to kiss me. A chuckle murmured against my lips. "There's one thing I want from you, Socks."

His eyes are crystal clear. His palms are pressed against my back. My heart in his hands. My nerves skitter out of control. "Whatever you want, it's yours."

I love the lightning-fast grin. The flash of desire in his eyes. The suggestion in his laughter as he throws his head back and laughs while cameras continue to click and people continue to watch us. All I can do is lift my eyebrows and smile.

His hands come back up to frame my face as his eyes darken with intensity. "You, Getty. *I want you*. All of you. With your quirks and flaws and smiles and laughs and pigheadedness and sexiness and temper and every other thing I can't think of right now but know that I want."

My heart swells. . . . His words echo within me in time with the beats and breathe life, possibility, into me. Into us.

"I just remembered that I do have one thing I can give you." I move in closer, my lips up to his ear so he can hear me loud and clear. "I love you, Zander Donavan. Thank you for making me want to be found again."

His breath hitches while his fingers tense on my skin. His smile widens as he leans back so I can see his eyes when he says it back to me. "I love you too, Socks."

His lips meet mine as the crowd around us erupts in a roar of cheers and catcalls. But we sink into the kiss. Into the moment. Into each other.

And as real as the moment is, I love that the first time we confessed our love for each other was in the middle of a group of people. At the chaos of a track. In an unscripted moment. When he should be getting ready to race.

Because he just proved to me that no matter what the circumstances, he only has eyes for me.

# Epilogue

## GETTY

"It feels like forever," I murmur as I take in the view of PineRidge from the passenger-side window.

"Four months is a long time," he muses as he slowly eases his SUV off the ferry and onto the island. My eyes dart left and right trying to take in every little thing that has changed since I've been gone. The trees have grown bigger. The air seems cleaner. The town itself feels more like home.

It's not until we arrived here that I realized how much I missed this little slice of Heaven. Yes, the complete lack of availability of rental properties on the island (besides renting a room in someone's house) worked out to my benefit, since the only solution was to spend the last four months staying with Zander in Los Angeles. Lucky for me, that was during the tourism off-season, so Liam agreed to the time off with the promise that I'd return for high season again.

And there's no way in hell I'd complain that the months I stayed with Zander during his off-season weren't worth every single second together. We've laughed. We've loved. We've grown so much stronger together as a couple.

It still feels weird using that term.

Even weirder is how his family has welcomed me with the same open arms Rylee did that first day in Boston. I feel like I belong. And they want nothing from me other than to make their son happy.

And that is the easiest thing anyone has ever asked of me. To love Zander.

I glance over to him from behind my sunglasses. Take in his dark hair in need of a trim, the day-old stubble he's sporting on his jaw, and the smirk on his lips because he knows I'm taking my time checking him out.

"I think we should skip looking at the places Liam sent you and you should just agree to live with me full-time." I groan for effect. This conversation has taken place over and over the last few weeks as Liam and I made calls back and forth about places that were finally becoming available to rent. "C'mon, Socks. There's no better place to have your first showing than in Los Angeles."

"Don't remind me." I press a hand to my stomach, where nerves flutter at the very thought. My mind purposely repressing the fact that I actually let him and his parents and crazy cast of brothers talk me into finally taking the leap and organizing a show of my paintings.

"Are you telling me that after being together for basically nine months straight that we're going to be able to handle this distance thing?"

I hate his words as much as I hate the inevitable separation that will happen in the coming months with the racing season starting again. God yes, I'll miss him. But how do I explain that this place, this island, represents so much for me? That as great as we are together, as perfect as life has been for us, my past still clouds my thoughts occasionally?

What if I give this all up and things turn bad for us? Then once again I'll have nothing. I'll be in his house with his possessions and will be the one scrambling to survive again.

There's no way I can tell him that. Can't explain it properly. He'll think I'm comparing him to Ethan when he's nothing of the sort. It's me. My mental block. My need to have a fallback plan. Just in case.

"C'mon, Socks. Think about it." His soft smile tugs on my resolve.

"I promise you, you'll be sick of me. It just that . . . I need this place, Zander. It settles me. Reminds me of who I was and who I want to be. *It makes me happy.*"

He reaches out and links his fingers with mine. "It makes me happy too. But you make me happier. You make me *me*." The simplicity of his statement and the honesty in his words touch me. "Just don't rule it out, okay?"

"I won't. I haven't." I sigh. Maybe I just needed to come back here, be reminded that this will always be here, and that will be enough. "Can we stop by the bar before we start, to say hi to Liam? I told him we would."

"Sure," he says, distracted as he takes a turn the opposite way. "I want to stop by the old house first. I heard the new owners completely redid it. Inside and outside. The whole nine yards. I kind of want to see what it looks like."

"Okay. Sure." A part of me feels very hesitant about that idea, because I still think somehow my father had a hand in buying the place to push me out and back to him. And on the other hand, a big part of me fears the nostalgia of seeing it again. The place where we met. I'm not sure if it's going to make me want to stay here more or hold tighter to Zander.

"Wow. It's beautiful." All concerns flee my mind as we turn the corner and the house comes into view. I take it all in: the new clapboard siding, the relandscaped front yard, the windows replaced with shutters added. Even the front steps and the deck have been rebuilt.

Now I definitely know my father had nothing to do with it, because he'd never take the time to make this place pretty. He'd buy and sell without a second thought and out of spite.

"C'mon, let's go take a peek. No one lives in it yet."

I hesitate. Of course we don't belong here any longer and yet I can't deny how much I want to see what the house looks like now that she's been brought to her full potential.

So I climb out of the car and follow Zander up the walk, my eyes darting to take in everything that's new and shiny, but remembering the old. How I first saw Zander in workout gear repairing the step. Or the oil-stained concrete of the driveway where I watched him fix my car in the pouring rain.

"What in the hell? Why did they . . . ?" The laugh falls from my mouth as I take in the ugly pink handrail I painted that night in anger and haste. Why would someone replace all the old stuff and leave this hideous reminder of the former tenants?

"That is pretty ugly." He shakes his head. "Maybe they think it's art or something and didn't want to get rid of it."

I snort in disbelief. "Seriously?"

"Maybe they left it as a reminder that when your wife gets pissed, hide the hammers and paintbrushes."

"Ha. Ha. Very funny."

"Or maybe they left it so that every time one of them comes home pissed or they have a fight, it'll remind them that they always need to stop, listen to what the other person is saying, have some patience . . . because life's never going to be perfect, but in the end it's going to be okay." He's got his head angled to the side, and I have to wonder how he made all of that up on the fly.

"Perhaps." Something feels off here. I narrow my eyes at him as I try to figure what exactly it is.

"What do you think their story is, Getty?"

My smile is automatic at the memory of the night so long ago that started things for us. "Hmm. Newlyweds perhaps. He can't wait to bring her home, carry her over the threshold, and make love to her on the deck with the moonlight above and the sound of the ocean around them."

Zander's smile seems sentimental when he meets my eyes. "My, how much you've improved at this game since that first time at Mario's."

I shrug. It's easier to believe in the idea of happily-ever-after now that I have Zander in my life. "Then again, she could be a madam and is going to open the first brothel here on PineRidge."

Zander's laugh is sharp as he takes the two steps to the front door. When he presses the handle on the new front door, it swings open.

"Holy shit. It's open. Let's look," he whispers, and steps inside without hesitating.

"Zander," I half whisper, half shout, my head swiveling left and right to see if anyone's watching or calling the cops. "Zander!"

When he doesn't answer, I step hesitantly just inside the door. It's the new tiled floor beneath my feet that catches my eyes first. The fresh paint on the walls in browns and tans next. And I'm so taken with how this house could be the same as the one I lived in before, my feet take a few steps farther inside.

The kitchen's been redone with granite slab and glossy white cabinets. The sliding glass doors to the deck replaced with French doors. The mini-blinds switched out for shutters.

Forgetting that I don't belong here, I keep looking at the beauty that has been restored in this old house. The bathroom gutted and replaced. New fixtures. Crown molding added.

"Zander?" I realize I haven't seen him. Panic. Then I feel ridiculous.

"In here."

I venture into his old bedroom and my eyes widen. Not only at the striking image of him standing in the empty room with the sun behind his back. A halo of light around his head. But also because the entire room has been transformed. Bigger windows facing the ocean. Built-ins installed. Shelves and cubbies. Overhead lighting taken down and adjustable lighting put in.

"Zander?" Questioning. Asking. Wondering.

"*Yes.*" Coy. Smug. Implying.

*This can't be right. You're crazy, Getty.*

But when I turn around to face the wall where Zander's old bed used to be, the one where we spent our first time together, the hints and inklings I've been feeling walking through the house finally come together. There is a huge sign on the wall with three easels set up below it.

And the sign reads GETTY'S STUDIO.

I spin back around, hand to my mouth, heart beating

out of my chest. "Zander?" His name again, but this time it's fueled with even more emotion. Hope. Want. Awe. "Is this really . . . ?"

He takes a step toward me, jaw clenching, eyes so serious. "It's yours, Getty. One hundred percent yours. I know how much it makes you happy."

"No. Yes. Oh my God. What did you do?" I reach out to him, needing to touch him to make sure I'm awake, that this is real, so I can process this. And he is real all right, because he takes both of my hands in his and lifts his eyes to mine.

"It all came down to two words. *Grand. Gestures.* My mom mentioned them in her letter to me. Rylee mentioned them when I was trying to figure out how to get you to believe me. It was my sign. My moment of clarity. About what you need to feel safe. What I can provide for you." He shakes his head and smiles softly. "What I can do to show you I know what matters most to you."

He draws in a deep breath and all I can do is give him the time he needs, because he's effectively stealing the words from my mouth right now.

"It's not the house that matters to you. It's what it represents to you. It was your sanctuary when you first ran. Then it was your proof that you were making it on your own. And for me . . . for me it's my very first memory of you in that hall back there, naked except for those socks, and wielding that mini-blind wand," he says with a smile as he points to where the wand sits as a memento on one of the new shelves.

"I know the next step for us is hard for you. You may not say it, Getty, but you're afraid still. Fearful that if you move in with me, you're giving away everything you've gained back. You said it yourself in the car—this is who you are. The island. The sea. The town. And so I wanted to give you this. This place is your security. A promise that you'll always have this home you created for yourself no matter what happens between us."

His hands reach up to frame my face in that way of his that's strong but tender and tells anyone watching that I'm his and he's going to kiss me soon.

"This is incredible, Zander, but it's just too much. It's not a cell phone this time.... It's a house." I'm dumbfounded. My mind is skipping over every other thought, because I'm so overwhelmed by his love and that he'd do something so meaningful. "A gorgeous house, but a house nonetheless."

"You're right." His chuckle rings around the room but warms my soul, my heart, and any part of me left untouched by the beauty of this man in front of me. "She is beautiful. She was broken and bruised at first, but with a lot of patience and some hands-on attention, I think I was able to bring out the beauty that was hiding beneath it all. The real her."

My eyes swim with tears. He's talking about so much more than just the house.

"And since she's your house now, I think it's fitting you complete the final item on her to-do list."

I stare at him in wonder, heart swelling, as he pulls out a pad of paper from the drawer behind him and hands it to me.

**Repair List**
~~Gut House and Rebuild~~ ☺
~~Build Getty a Studio~~
~~Keep the Ugly Pink Handrail~~
*Have Sex with* ~~Kiss~~ *the Repair Guy*
MARRY the REPAIR GUY

My breath hitches when I read the last item on the list. My eyes flash up to meet Zander's. And every single thing I want to say fades at the look of absolute love on the face of the man in front of me.

"You don't have to run anymore, Getty. Not from me. Not from your past. But I understand you need to have a place of your own. A safe haven you can run to if needed. And like you, I know what I need. And I need you with me. Not just to move in. Not on a part-time basis. But in my life permanently. I want to make a life with you. Not because I want to control you or have you decorate my arm, but because you brought me back to life, Getty. You make me live. You make me feel. You make me laugh. You make me want tomorrows and sunsets and forevers when I never even thought twice about any of them before. And I only want them with you. I want to come back here often. In the off-season. On vacations. Bring our kids here someday—show them that god-awful pink railing and tell them about how sometimes you need to give someone a second chance because they are worth it. I want to sit on that deck and listen to the ocean while telling them the PG story of how you and I met. And someday I want to grow old here with you."

The sob catches in my throat. How can it not when he's creating memories so real I can feel them? So clear I can *see* them.

"You see, for so long I've feared the damn white squall. Being pulled under by its water . . . and then I realized how stupid I was, because *you're my water*. The one thing I can't live without. I want to marry you, Getty. I want years filled with kisses and memories and laughter and love and patience like only you can give me. And I want to give the same to you. You are my truth now. So *just jump* with me, Socks. Leap without looking, because I promise I'll be there to catch you no matter how far the fall."

I look at him—this incredible man, inside and out—and am reminded of my motto from what feels like forever ago: *Carpe diem*. Hell yes, I'm seizing the moment, so long as I can seize the man.

I laugh out loud. Grab his neck and pull him toward me so I can pour everything I feel and can't express into the kiss. Show him with actions.

"Is that a yes?" he asks, eyes hopeful as he pulls out a box from his back pocket and opens it. Inside rests a diamond infinity band. It's simple and subtle and exactly what I'd pick for myself.

And the sight of the ring makes this real. Makes his words and his intent and everything he just said hit home in an even bigger way.

"Yes. No. I don't know."

His eyes widen in shock. Just for a moment. But my

smile tells him the real answer. "Cute. Very cute, but this time you only get to pick one answer."

"Only one?"

"And here starts the questions to the questions," he says, laughing and shaking his head.

My heart bursts with love for this man standing before me. With belonging, with everything I've never had, and I wonder how all this happened. How this scared, gun-shy woman fell in love with this incredible, generous man.

And the answer's simple.

His love roared loader than my demons.

And he made me want to be found again.

I lean in and press a kiss to his lips.

And whisper.

"Yes."

Don't miss K. Bromberg's

## *HARD BEAT*

Available now from Signet Select.
Keep reading for a preview.

The door is stuck.

A part of me likes that fact because it means that possibly no one has been up here, and another part of me appreciates the physicality it takes to get it open when I put my shoulder into it.

The metal door slams back and clanks against the concrete wall behind it. The sound cuts into the silence of the night as I stand there, momentarily cautious for some reason, even though in this place I've found more peace than anywhere else in the strife-torn country.

I was worried how I'd feel coming up here—wasn't sure I'd be able to face this the first night back—but standing here, I know it's for the best to face the memories head-on. To fight the ghost of her that's been haunting my dreams with reliving the memory of her in "our" place.

The noise from the city streets below is faint and comforting, but I don't notice much beyond the dust particles floating in the stream of light from the open door. I have to talk myself into stepping over the threshold. After making sure the door is secured so I don't get locked out, I make my way across the rooftop to a little section on the far end. I walk around the stem walls erected in the shape of a plus sign that protect some air-conditioning units on three of the four sections to see if it's still here after almost five months.

When I turn the corner to see the tarp folded beside the covered mattress and the sign—a piece of paper taped to the wall bordering it that says WELCOME BACK, TANNER— I laugh aloud. At first the sound is one of amusement, and then it slowly fades off in relief when it hits me that the guys downstairs still drinking kept this up here for me. They preserved my little place of solitude in this crazy-ass world because they knew how much I needed it. And how much it meant to me.

Dropping to my knees on the mattress, I sit with my back against the wall so that the sign is beside my head. Once I've gotten comfortable, I look out at the lights of the city beyond, which calls to me like a curse and a blessing. A necessity to make my blood hum with that adrenaline I thrive on and a damnation for the dreams it suppresses for so many others. Lights twinkle in the distance, beacons of life in a minefield of hopelessness and destitution.

When I bring the bottle of Fireball up to my lips, the burn feels good, reminds me that I'm still here, still alive. And that Stella isn't.

"Oh, Stell," I say into the night with a shake of my head. "This feels so weird sitting up here without you."

The bittersweet memory of the last time I sat here comes back with a vengeance, and it blazes ten times stronger than the sting of the whiskey.

*"Do you ever wonder if you've missed that once-in-a-lifetime, Tan?" Stella looks over to me, the smear of dirt from the day riding with the embed like a badge of honor across her cheek. She has that look in her eye, the one that makes every guy in existence roll his eyes because it means his woman is going to talk about shit he doesn't want to address. But first off, she's not my girl, and second, I kind of want to know what she's talking about.*

*"You're not going to get all sappy on me now, are you?" I pass the Styrofoam cup filled with Kahlúa and coffee her way. She rolls her eyes and takes a sip, hissing when it scalds her tongue.*

*"Zip it, Thomas. You're stuck with me."*

*"Explain, then." I shake my head when she tries to pass back the coffee to me. It's been a rough day; I need*

something stronger than a keoke coffee, but I'll meet up with Pauly later for that. Right now I just need our routine, our wind down after a fucked-up day out beyond the city's walls of misconceived protection.

Stella's sigh pulls me from the images of blood-soaked camouflage and the sound of gunfire. I know she hates when I get all lawyer-ish on her, as she calls it, and so that's why I phrased my comment that way, needing to get us back to what has been our norm over the past decade.

"Never mind. You, Mr. I-fall-in-love-with-everyone, would not understand what I'm talking about," she says with a roll of her eyes, but I can tell something's bothering her.

"I don't fall in love with everyone. I prefer to call it infatuation." I try to lighten the mood by bringing up one of our long-standing conversations.

"Ah." She laughs aloud. "But it's such a short, slippery slope for you . . . one that lasts a whole two dates before you hit the barrel of love."

"Barrel of love?" I can't help but laugh at that, even though I don't appreciate the comment. "Fuck. Am I really that pathetic of a sap?"

Stella stares through the darkness before turning her face to the city beyond us. "No. You're not a sap.... You just have a good heart."

"That's what it's called nowadays? I guess I'd better work on changing that."

"No, it's endearing. This big alpha male with a soft heart. You'd never guess it was there beneath all of that testosterone." She falls quiet again, and I know whatever is bugging her is just beneath the surface, and yet here we are speaking about me. She reaches out and grabs my hand. "Don't ever change that, Tanner. Someday someone is going to appreciate that in you. Your quick love and big heart."

My mind immediately thinks to crack a joke about something else that I have that's big, but when I recognize the conflicted sorrow in her eyes, it dies on my lips. "What's going on with you, Stell? Talk to me."

"It's nothing."

Fuck. The most dreaded words in all of existence for a

*man to hear other than "I'm fine." "I'm not buying it. What did you mean about a once-in-a-lifetime?"*

*She refuses to look my way, so I poke her side until she starts talking. "I meant that one person that you're supposed to be with forever. The person that you're fated to love." She falls silent as she peers over the steam of the coffee cup to the city down below. "What if you've met that person already and screwed it up somehow? Or even worse, what if you met that one person but just at the wrong time in your life?"*

*I stare at her profile for a bit while I ponder what she's saying, taking in the slight upturn of her nose, and find comfort in the familiarity of her beside me. Is she right? It's not like I'm old, but I'm not getting any younger either. My life is transient at best and a mind fuck at its worst . . . but is there really such a thing as a once-in-a-lifetime? "There has to be more than one person in the universe you're fated to be with. That's just cruel if the powers that be only give you one shot, you know?"*

*"Yeah. I guess." She sounds less than convinced.*

*When I see the glimmer of tears welling in her eyes, I reach over and squeeze her hand. Who knows what's going on in that mind of hers? After all this time, if I can't figure it out, I know to stop trying. Her stubborn ass will tell me in her own time, when she wants to.*

*But when she doesn't squeeze my hand back, I scoot next to her and put my arm around her, pulling her in tight to my side. "Well, we both know that I'm not your once-in-a-liftetime," I tease with a laugh and press a soft kiss into the top of her head, but for some damn reason I question my own statement.*

*"We were a hot mess, weren't we?" She laughs softly as my mind flickers to the year we dated only to find out we were miserable as a couple. Explosive tempers leading to hot sex may be memorable but definitely not sustainable. How we broke it off but then were forced together because of our careers and in the end found out we could be incredible friends to each other.*

*"The Dynamic Duo." I reiterate Rafe's nickname for us,*

*photographer and reporter, best friends and confidants. She looks up to me and holds my gaze through the night's darkness.* "What?" *I ask, trying to figure out what her expression is saying.*

"I don't know. Sometimes I wonder if my being here, living this life we lead . . . if I've ruined my chances for it, that's all."

"Stell." *I grab at straws to comfort her about a topic that makes me feel completely awkward. And even more disconcerting are the thoughts her damn question has stirred in my mind. She's my best friend. After a decade she knows all of my quirks, my pet peeves, everything.... What would happen if we tried a relationship now?*

*I bite back the laugh at the thought. Stella is like my sister, Rylee, to me. Well, all except that Stella and I had sex way back when we were actually dating.*

*But the thought lingers in the back of my mind:* What if we are right for each other but met at the wrong time? *A backfire on the street down below has the both of us flinching, our instinctive training to duck at the sound of gunfire taking over.*

*We laugh at how ridiculous we look and how only here, only with us, would this be normal.* "Look," *I tell her,* "if in ten years we are still nomads, still single, then we'll revisit this conversation."

"What about it?" *she asks, her eyebrows narrowing as she tries to figure out what I'm saying.*

"If we are each other's once-in-a-lifetime."

*Her sharp inhale makes me realize what I just said, the stupid inferences she could make from it. But at the same time, when she laughs, I hear her nervousness, and the look in her eyes is so real, so vulnerable, that when I glance down to her lips, I'm forced to swallow over the lump in my throat.*

*It has to be the moment, a simple slice of time when two friends who have lived a lifetime together as a result of their volatile careers fall into that trap of need mixed with comfort and a splash of loneliness. The minute I lean forward and brush my lips to hers, I hate myself for it, and yet at the same time, the immediate recoil I thought would happen on my part doesn't happen. It's just a whisper of a kiss, but my lack of reaction scares the fuck out of me.*

*I rest my forehead against hers. "Sorry," I murmur, my hands threading through her hair.*

*"Well, that wasn't exactly the birthday present I was planning for you tomorrow, but ..." Her voice fades into a laugh.*

*"I told you I don't want anything," I say to squash that argument again, but then feel the need to repeat it. "I'm sorry."*

*"Don't be. After ten years, that's the only time we've ever crossed that line." The heat of her breath hits my lips and tempts me when I'm never tempted by her.*

*"I guess we have ten more years to see if it happens again." I can hear the smile on my lips in my tone, and even though we both are in agreement that what just happened shouldn't have, we sit in the darkness for a minute—foreheads touching, lips so close—almost as if the both of us knew what was going to happen the next night.*

*How this moment was going to be the lasting memory I would use to get me through the darkness her death would bring.*

"Here's to you, Stell," I say as I lift the bottle of whiskey up to the sky and take a long pull on it.

The circuit of thoughts that has etched a goddamn groove in my mind starts again. Hell yes, I loved her . . . in my own way. I just wonder if her absence has made me read more into that emotion than it really was. People place those who die on pedestals, forget their misgivings with a bat of an eyelash, and become more connected to them since they can no longer tell them what they feel. Is this what I've done to Stella and our friendship? Is this why I've held tight to this last kiss we shared even though it was a stupid move?

I've been through the seven stages of grief. You name each one of them, and I've fucking done them more times than I care to count. But when all is said and done, I'm here and she's not. Guilt is a goddamn vise squeezing out of me every ounce of emotion I never wanted to feel.

Plain and simple, I miss her. The easy banter, how we could sit comfortably in silence, that I could predict her remarks before she made them. We were a team and now I feel lost, wondering why I pushed so hard to get back here. So focused on getting out of my house, I didn't think about how many damn memories were here waiting to haunt me.

I just need to get back in the game. Meet my photographer tomorrow and get back in the swing of things, use the hunger I feel deep down to propel me through the flashes of sadness that still come. Then I'll be better. Besides, it's not like I have any other option.

Plug and chug.

The memories continue to come, the good, bad, and horrific, and who knows how long it's been when I lift the bottle to find it empty? *Suck it up, Thomas. This will be the only fucking rooftop pity party you're allowed to have. You wanted back; now you're here.*

"Fuck," I say into the emptiness around me as I rise on unsteady feet and let my buzz filter through my limbs. Once the mattress is covered up by the tarp to protect it from the dust that blankets everything like an irrevocable stain, I make my way back downstairs.

I smell her before I see her. That subtle scent of hers, which seems so out of place in the air heavy with spices, fills the stairwell when I hit the eighth floor. She's coming up as I'm coming down. Our eyes meet and hold across the dimly lit concrete landing.

Anger fires within me. She's stupid for being here alone. Does she know how much fucking danger there is in this country? The disrespect that's shown to women simply because of their gender? Add to that, she's American. I think of how many times Stella and I went round and round on this topic before she just gave in and allowed me to be at her side most of the time.

And I don't want to care about this loose cannon of a woman, but my feet are glued to the floor as an indescribable current shoots through the empty space between us. I try to deny it, want to deflect it somehow, but we stand there, gazes held, and remain silent.

"Did you want something?" I ask, eyebrows raised, impatient.

"Hmm," she murmurs. "No. I thought I did . . . but now? Not hardly."

She starts to brush past me. Something about that haughty tone of hers with a subtle accent I can't place pushes buttons I don't want pushed, and I reach out and grab her upper arm. The force of my hold pulls her body into mine so that our chests touch, and the sharp inhale of her breath is unmistakable since it presses her breasts further against me.

Our eyes lock, breaths mingling over each other's lips, and that straight shot of lust spears to my lower gut and takes hold. We stand in a silent battle of wills. The same woman I was irritated at for wanting me earlier, I'm now pissed at for wanting to walk away.

Talk about a confirmation that my head is a cluster fuck of emotions. *Jesus Christ. Let her walk the hell away, Tanner. Bygones.*

But my fingers don't relax. They hold tight just like the invisible grip she seems to have over me.

The air thickens, and the sexual chemistry that I felt earlier at the bar—the zing I tried to avoid by leaving the festivities—sparks and lights up the space around us like an exposed live wire. The sad fact is I know I'm about to get burned but don't let go.

"Just for the record, Loose Cannon, I would have bought you a drink." I grit the words out, angry at myself for even saying them.

She eyes me with caution, trying to figure out what the hell I mean by Loose Cannon. "It's BJ, and I prefer to stay off the record," she says with that little fuck-you lift of her chin as she asserts her obstinacy despite her quickened pulse beneath my fingertips.

And fuck . . . I have to bite back the laugh on my lips because isn't that a fitting name for a woman with lips like hers? Images of what she'd look like staring up at me while her mouth is wrapped around my dick flash through my mind.

She pulls me from my lewd but damn fine thoughts

when she tries to jerk her arm from my hold. My spine stiffens some because hell if I'm up for resistance right now. I'm emotionally drained, exhausted, and as much as I don't want to feel that grenade of desire sitting low in my belly, I still want to pull its pin so I can lose myself for a bit in the soft curves and sweet taste of a gorgeous woman no matter how fucking insolent she is.

I clench my jaw. A fleeting show of resistance before I give in to my need and the sexual tension. She gasps when I release her arm only to bring it up to her neck at the same time I crash my lips to hers.

And fuck yes, I'm a dick for not letting her push me away, for letting my own need for this woman who will most likely move on by the week's end control my actions, for taking without asking, but goddamn her small display of independence turns me on something fierce.

I brand my mouth to hers, press my tongue between her lips as she parts them. Her hands push me away, but the movement of her tongue tells me she wants more. She's a clear contradiction in all meanings of the word. Soft and supple body, but I can feel the toned muscle beneath. Between kisses she tries to pull back, but a soft moan in the back of her throat when my free hand cups her ass tells me how much she wants this.

Her hands fist in my shirt at the same time my hand takes hold of the loose bun at the nape of her neck to tilt her head back and look into her eyes. But her mouth stays right where I want it because I'm nowhere near done with her yet.

"I don't like you," she claims through gritted teeth. Our hands run possessively over each other, but derision laced with defiance glimmers in her eyes.

"I beg to differ." I laugh at the ludicrousness of her statement, considering the predicament we're in. She tries to step back, but when she doesn't release my shirt, I know she still wants more.

And fuck, I'm definitely all in. I need this outlet more than I ever realized until I was in the thick of it. I've kept to myself at home, fought with my sister when she attempted to fix me up with one of her friends, punished myself, and now with the heat of a woman's body pressed up against me and the taste of her kiss seared in my goddamn brain, there is no way in hell I'm walking away now.

"I don't like you," she reiterates.

"Too bad," I tell her as I go in for the next kiss. One that's full of angry desperation and irresistible need with teeth nipping and tongues meeting and that ache deep in my balls taking hold of me. My hips pin her against the cold cinder-block wall behind her.

Her fingers dig into my shoulders as she tears her mouth from mine, our chests heaving. And then just when her protests stop and her tongue starts to dance with mine again, I pull back.

"You're arrogant and—"

"You don't have to like me to fuck me," I say, cutting her off. "You just have to want me."

She protests, and I cut her words off with my mouth on hers at the same time my hands grab her wrists. Even as I gain the advantage, I feel like she's pulling out the ground from beneath my feet. "Fuck you!" She manages to get the words out between fervent kisses.

I chuckle against her lips before pulling back and looking straight into her desire-laden eyes. "That's the plan."